P9-DYY-632

Tortall and Other Lands

A Collection of Tales

Tortall Books
by Tamora Pierce

Beka Cooper
Terrier
Bloodhound

Trickster's Choice
Trickster's Queen

Protector of the Small Quartet
First Test
Page
Squire
Lady Knight

The Immortals Quartet
Wild Magic
Wolf-Speaker
Emperor Mage
The Realms of the Gods

The Song of the Lioness Quartet
Alanna: The First Adventure
In the Hand of the Goddess
The Woman Who Rides Like a Man
Lioness Rampant

Tortall and Other Lands

A Collection of Tales

Tamora Pierce

Random House New York

 Published in the United States by Random House Children's Books, a division of Random House, Inc., New York.

Random House and the colophon are registered trademarks of Random House, Inc.

Some stories in this collection were previously published in the following:

"Student of Ostriches" copyright © 2005 by Tamora Pierce, from *Young Warriors,* published by Random House Children's Books, a division of Random House, Inc., New York, in 2005.

"Elder Brother" copyright © 2001 by Tamora Pierce, from *Half-Human,* published by Scholastic Press, a division of Scholastic, Inc., New York, in 2001.

"The Hidden Girl" copyright © 2006 by Tamora Pierce, from *Dreams and Visions: Fourteen Flights of Fantasy,* published by Starscape Books, Tom Doherty Associates LLC, New York, in 2006.

"The Dragon's Tale" copyright © 2009 by Tamora Pierce, from *The Dragon Book: Magical Tales from the Masters of Modern Fantasy,* published by Ace Books, an imprint of Penguin Group (USA), Inc., a division of the Penguin Group, New York, in 2009.

"Time of Proving" copyright © 2006 by Tamora Pierce, in *Cricket* magazine, in September 2006.

"Plain Magic" copyright © 1986 by Tamora Pierce, from *Planetfall,* published by Oxford University Press, London, in 1986, and revised for *Flights of Fantasy,* published by Perfection Learning, Logan, Iowa, in 1999.

"Huntress" copyright © 2006 by Tamora Pierce, from *Firebirds Rising,* published by Firebird, an imprint of Penguin Group (USA), Inc., a division of the Penguin Group, New York, in 2006.

"Testing" (and comments) copyright © 2000 by Tamora Pierce, from *Lost & Found: Award-Winning Authors Sharing Real-Life Experiences Through Fiction,* published by Forge Books, Tom Doherty Associates LLC, New York, in 2000.

Visit us on the Web!
www.randomhouse.com/teens
tamora-pierce.com

Educators and librarians, for a variety of teaching tools, visit us at
www.randomhouse.com/teachers

Library of Congress Cataloging-in-Publication Data is available upon request.
ISBN 978-0-375-86676-0 (trade) — ISBN 978-0-375-96676-7 (lib. bdg.) —
ISBN 978-0-375-89689-7 (ebook)

Printed in the United States of America

10 9 8 7 6 5 4 3 2 1

First Edition

Random House Children's Books supports the First Amendment and celebrates the right to read.

To my editors for these stories—
Bruce Coville, Jack Dann, Gardner Dozois,
David Fickling, Douglas Hill, R. Schuyler Hooke,
Mallory Loehr, Ron McCutchan, Sharyn November,
Terry Ofner, M. Jerry Weiss, and Helen S. Weiss—
with my deepest thanks for these chances to expand
and my apologies for the many bad words I said
while trying to do so

Contents

Student of Ostriches	1
Elder Brother	26
The Hidden Girl	51
Nawat	75
The Dragon's Tale	146
Lost	208
Time of Proving	249
Plain Magic	258
Mimic	276
Huntress	318
Comments on the Short Story "Testing"	344
Testing	346

Student of Ostriches

My story began as my mother carried me in her belly to the great Nawolu trade fair. Because she was pregnant, our tribe let Mama ride high on the back of our finest camel, which meant she was also lookout for our caravan. It was she who spotted the lion and gave the warning. Our warriors closed in tight around our people to keep them safe, but they were in no danger from the lion.

He was a young male, with no lionesses to guard him as he stalked a young ostrich who strayed from its parents. He drew closer to his intended prey. Its mama and papa raced toward the lion, faster than horses, their large eyes fixed on the threat. The lion was young and ignorant. He snarled as one ostrich kicked him. Then the other did the same. On and on the ostriches kicked the lion until he was a fur sack of bones.

As the ostriches led their children away, my mama said, she felt me kick in her belly for the first time.

If the kicking ostriches were a good omen for our family, they were not for my papa. Two months later he was wounded in the leg in a battle with an enemy tribe. It never healed completely, forcing him to leave the ranks of the warriors and join the ranks of the wood-carvers, though he never complained. Not long after my papa began to walk with a cane, I was born. Papa was sad for a little while, because I was a girl. He would have liked a son to take his place as a warrior, but he always said that when I first smiled at him, he could not be sad anymore.

When I was six years old, I asked my parents if I could learn to go outside the village wall with the animal herds. Who could be happy inside the walls when the world lay outside? My parents spoke to our chief, who agreed that I could learn to watch goats on the rocky edges of the great plains on which the world was born.

Of course, I did not begin alone. My ten-year-old cousin Ogin was appointed to teach me. On that first morning I followed him and his dogs to a grazing place. Once the goats were settled, I asked him, "What must I learn?"

"First, you learn to use the herder's weapon, the sling," Ogin said. He was very tall and lean, like a stick with muscles. "You must be able to help the dogs drive off enemies." He held up a strip of leather.

I practiced the twirl and the release of the stone in the sling until my shoulders were sore. For a change of pace, Ogin taught me the words to name the goats' marks and parts until I knew them by heart. Once my muscles were relaxed again, I would take up the sling once more.

When it was time to eat our noon food, my cousin took the goats, the dogs, and me up onto a rock outcropping. From there we could see the plain stretch out before us under its veil of dusty air. This was my reward, this long view of the first step to the world. I almost forgot how to eat.

Lonely trees fanned their branches out in flat-topped sprays. Vultures roosted in their branches. Veils of tall grass separated the herds of zebra, wildebeest, and gazelle in the distance. Lions waited near a watering hole close to our rocks as giraffes nibbled the leaves of thorny trees on the other side.

Watching it all, I saw movement. I gasped. "Ogin—there! Are those—are they ostriches?"

"You think, because your mama saw them, they are cousins to you?" he teased me. "What is it, Kylaia? Will you grow tail feathers and race them?"

The ostriches *were* running. They had long, powerful legs. When they ran, they opened their legs up and stretched. They were not delicate like the gazelle, like my older sisters. They ran in long, loping strides. Watching them, I thought, *I want to run like that.*

For a year I was Ogin's apprentice. He taught me to keep the goats moving in the lands around the stone lookout place, so there would be grass throughout the year. He was patient and he did not laugh at me as I struggled to learn to be a dead shot with a sling, a careful tracker, and one who understood the ways of the dogs, the goats, and the wild creatures of the plains.

Ogin taught me to run, too, as he and my sisters did, like gazelles, on the balls of their feet. After our noon meals, as Ogin napped, I would practice my ostrich running. I opened up my strides, dug in my feet, and thrust out my chest, imagining myself to be a great bird, eating the ground with my big feet. Each day I ran a little farther and a little faster as Ogin and the dogs slept, and the goats and the birds looked on.

When I had followed Ogin for a year, my uncle the herd

chief came out with us. Ogin made me show off my skills with the goats and the dogs.

"Tomorrow morning, come to me," said my uncle. "You shall have a herd and dogs of your own."

It was my seventh birthday. I was so proud! I was now a true member of the village with proper work to do. Papa gave me a wooden ball painted with colored stripes. Mama and my sisters had woven me new clothes and a cape for the cold. I ran through the village to show off my ball and to tell my friends that I was now a true worker.

Five older boys caught me on my way home. They knocked me down and they took my ball.

When I came home, my family noticed my bruises. Papa limped through the village until he found my ball and brought it back to me.

My pride lay in the dust. I pretended to ignore my family's conversation, as my sisters demanded that the boys be punished and my father said he would appeal to our chief. Whatever punishment the boys got would have nothing to do with me, only the peace of the tribe. Their penalty would not make me taller or less ashamed.

In the morning, I alone took my new herd out to graze in the rocks of the seeing place. While the goats found grasses tucked into stone hollows, I stared at the plain. The village would deal with the boys. Later, they would take their vengeance on me. What would I do then?

I don't know why a wild dog decided to be a fool that morning, or why he left the protection of his pack. I only know that he was alone when he found the old ostrich nesting ground. It was not breeding season. There were no eggs or young to protect. The king ostrich, his queen, and his other wives were nibbling grass seed as a shift of wind brought them the scent of wild dog. My thigh muscles twitched as the pair ran to catch the intruder, their great legs eating up the yards between them. The dog fled too late. The ostriches were on him. The queen's first kick sent the wild dog flying into the air. He lurched to his feet, but the ostriches had already caught up. A few more kicks finished the dog.

He must have taken their ball, I thought, impressed with ostrich vengeance. If I had been an ostrich, those boys would have returned my ball to *me.*

The idea flowered in my mind. It was said the Shang warriors, masters of unarmed combat, could kill by kicking alone, but I had never seen a Shang. Our young men wrestled for the honor of our tribe. The only time they used their feet, it was to hook a foot behind an opponent's leg, to yank him off balance. But surely a person with strong legs could fight by kicking, as ostriches did, I told myself. One kick would knock an opponent—an enemy—onto his back. Onto his thieving, mocking back . . .

So I tried to kick like an ostrich, and fell on my behind.

I was a stubborn girl. As the dogs and goats watched, I kicked. And kicked. I learned that I had to stand a certain way in order not to fall. Then I learned to stand in a better way, so I would not fall or wobble as I kicked. My legs cramped, so I ran like an ostrich to stretch them. But I could not let go of ostrich-kick fighting. I chased the idea through my days as I took out my goats, found grazing, practiced my sling, practiced kicking with attention for both legs, practiced ostrich running, ate my lunch, and watched the thousand stories of the plain. After lunch, though it made me sweat and sometimes made me sick in the dry season's heat, I continued my many practices. At day's end, I went home too weary to do more than play catch with my little cousins.

Three months before my eighth birthday I was on my way home from an errand when the boys caught me again. "We could be playing kick-the-ball and building the muscles of our legs, while you only play with children," their leader told me. "The ball is wasted with you. You will give it to us and tell your papa that you are tired of it. If you do, maybe we will leave you teeth to chew with."

His friends laughed. The boy behind me wrapped his arms around me, pinning my arms. He was going to help me, though he did not mean to, by keeping me balanced and free to use both legs. I watched their leader come closer to take the ball from my hands.

They were wild dogs. I was an ostrich. I kicked their leader in the belly so hard that he bent over and vomited. One of the others tried to punch me. I kicked to the side and rammed his upper thigh. He fell. Another boy rushed me. Twisting in my captor's hold, I drove my heels into the side of his leg, knocking him down. Then I used my elbows to make the boy who held me let go.

I learned many things from this, like what will make a boy yell and what will leave him unable to chase me. And I kept my ball. They did not dare complain of me to the chief, either. They were older than I. Everyone would laugh to know they feared a girl.

The next morning I scrambled up onto the rocks to watch for my next lesson. The zebra, who are mean and tricky, had come to the watering hole after a family of giraffes. Giraffes take time to drink, spreading their legs to lower their bodies, then their heads on their very long necks. They took up half the water hole. I suppose some zebras got impatient waiting for their leaders to drink. You could see it in their wicked black eyes. If the zebras made the giraffes go, then all of the zebras would have room to drink.

One of the young zebras pretended to do something else as he circled the giraffe family. It was a male giraffe who saw him. He watched the zebra draw near. Then the giraffe did a strange thing. He drew back his head. The zebra took two more steps toward the giraffes.

The male giraffe swung his head like a mallet and clubbed the zebra with his heavy skull. The zebra went tumbling in the dust. With a snort, as if to say he had only been playing, the zebra struggled to his feet and went back to his herd to wait.

I soon learned the best way to imitate the giraffe was to make a giant fist of both clasped hands, fingers locked together. The flesh of my hands, though, was tender. A few blows against the nearby rocks and trees soon taught me that. I ground my teeth and began to toughen them as the warriors did, a little at a time, striking bark and stone, day after day. Young antelope toughened their horns, after all. I had toughened my feet on the rock-and-briar-strewn ground outside the village wall. I could toughen my hands to hit like a giraffe.

Two years passed as I studied my new work, out there with the goats and the dogs. I built calluses on my hands, feet, and elbows. I ran; I hit and I kicked. I drove off wild dogs with my sling. I began to hunt, bringing extra meat to my family at the day's end. When I was ten, I was eligible for the harvest games we held with neighboring villages. I entered in the girls' races. I was too slow to win short races. My gazelle sisters overtook me there. Then came the long race, three times around a neighboring village's wall. My gazelle sisters limped in after I ran across the finish line. I ran greater distances than that every day with the goats.

Five months after, before the spring planting celebration, Ogin and my sisters took me aside. "We want you to do something that will put coins in our purses," Ogin said. "We want you to run in the boys' races. We will bet on you and everyone will think we have run mad."

"Or let our pride in our village fool us," said Iyaka. "They will bet against you and we will win."

My sisters' eyes were bright and shining. Ogin—now fourteen and chief herd boy—grinned broadly with wickedness. I turned to my sisters, who were runners. "You think I can beat them?" I asked.

They giggled. "We know you can," said Iyaka.

And so I lingered on the sidelines of the boys' first short race until Ogin, according to our plan, dragged me over to the starting line. Everyone hurried to bet against me as the boys who were to race protested. The judge said that there was no rule against girls, only custom. The boys had to give in.

I was third in the first short race of sixty yards, second in the second short race of seventy-five yards, and first in the ninety-yard race, as my sisters had planned. I won the boys' long race, too. That night there were honey cakes with supper and coins in the family purse.

Our lives marched on through festivals and races. My sisters grew older and more beautiful. I simply grew. "She is turning into a giraffe!" the boys would tease me. I ignored them. Thanks to my height and strength, my boyless family had meat in the pot and coins for my sisters' dowries.

Besides, I liked giraffes. They looked silly, but wise creatures let them be, and they feasted among thorns.

My goats were exchanged for Ogin's old cattle herd when I turned eleven, while Ogin was made a hunter. As I learned the ways of cows, I studied the plains and the rocks. In the tall grasses and wiry trees of the plains I was free to join nature in its blood and power. There I practiced running, hitting, and kicking, using the blows to break fallen branches for firewood or to give a wounded animal a quick death. I learned more kicks from zebras, a double hand strike from lions, and a back-of-the-fist blow from elephants.

Sometimes I dreamed about the world beyond the plains, trying to imagine its shape. My first taste of it would come when I was thirteen, when I would be allowed to attend the Nawolu trade fair for the first time. It was a week's journey from our village, a gathering where tribes came from hundreds of miles to sell and to buy, to marry off daughters and sons, and to hold games of strength and speed.

Daughters were presented when they were thirteen, though they were not actually married until they were sixteen or seventeen. During my twelfth year, my next-oldest sister went with the others to the fair. She came back talking of nothing but boys.

Iyaka, who was seventeen, returned quietly. Mama told us the good news. A chief's son, a young, wealthy man named Awochu, had seen Iyaka race. He had fallen in love with her. It was odd for young people to choose their own mates, but Awochu's father could not deny his only son. It did not matter that Iyaka's dowry was tiny. For a bride price Awochu would give us thirty cattle and accept Papa's blessing in return. Awochu would marry Iyaka at the next trade fair.

"What can I say? I am so honored by my family-to-be," Iyaka said when we begged for details. "Thirty cattle will make Papa rich and respected. I could not have refused even if I had wanted to."

When she put it that way, she made me ask myself what I would say when a man's family offered for me. I thought about it as I watched over my cows the next day. Did I want to be married? I would have to leave my days on my beloved plains and never see the world beyond. I would retire behind a wall like the one around our village to weave, cook, sew, and bear children. No more watches for game at the watering hole. No more entertainment from zebras and giraffes. No more gazelle and cheetah races.

I could wait to marry.

Still, every girl must turn thirteen, and so did I. The time of the trade fair came around. Our whole family went to

Nawolu for Iyaka's wedding and my first fair. Nawolu was a walled city on a deep river, beyond anything I had seen on the plains. In the distance towered a lone mountain dusted with a white powder on the top. Everywhere there were travelers, animals, bright cloth, and flawless animal skins. I thought my eyes would burst from all the new sights.

Our village had its place on the fairgrounds outside the walls. Before we had even pitched our tents, friends from other tribes came to visit and stayed for supper. Our chief finally sent them away so we could sleep. In the morning we would wash and dress in our finest to meet Chief Rusom, who governed Nawolu and the lands around it.

I was close to sleep when Mama whispered, "I did not see Awochu."

After a very long silence Iyaka said, "He did not come."

In the morning we girls fixed our hair, put on our best dresses, and decked ourselves in our few pieces of jewelry. Then, with our mothers to guard us, we went to the fair. There was so much that was new. I saw the wonders from the world beyond my plains and felt a tug on my heart, a call to see where it had all come from. What exotic creatures wove the wispy cloth called "silk"? Who made fine jewelry from countless tiny gold beads, and small stone pots of cosmetics? What ingredients went into the strange new perfumes? I wanted to know these things. The people who sold the goods would only point and name a country, or a city, and speak in strange languages.

Our companions drifted away until it was only Mama, Iyaka, and me going from booth to booth. We were having a good time on our own when Iyaka suddenly fell silent. Mama and I looked up. Here came a handsome young man, well muscled, with the scars of a warrior on his cheeks and chest. A girl clung to his arm like a vine. She wore a blue silk dress and so much gold jewelry that it was impossible to tell if she was truly beautiful or simply dressed in money.

The young man, who also wore gold, halted. She had to halt with him, and to stare as he did, at Iyaka. The blue silk girl looked at Iyaka, who had gone pale, and she *smirked.* At *my* sister, who was more beautiful than she without jewelry or silk!

"Awochu," Iyaka whispered. The young man in gold licked his lips as if they were dry.

Mama stood in front of Iyaka. "Is this how you act before the family of the girl you are to marry in a week?" she asked sharply. "You parade this fair with a strumpet on your arm, mocking my daughter's good name?"

The girl with gold scowled. She will have wrinkles before she is thirty, I thought as I put an arm around my sister.

"She is no strumpet!" said my sister's betrothed. "*She* is my bride-to-be. I will not honor a contract with a witch and the family of a witch."

Mama put her hands on her hips. "My daughter is no witch, you pompous hyena! You slander her name and ours to speak so!"

"She put a spell on me last year," said Awochu. "My father's shaman cured me of her spell. Now I will have nothing to do with a witch!"

A crowd was gathering. People are jackals, always willing to feed off someone else's kill.

"You signed a marriage contract in blood," Mama said. "You did it with your eyes open and your mama bleating like a sheep, saying there were girls 'more worthy of you.' More worthy, with Iyaka and her family and chief standing right there! The only witchcraft was in you knowing she wouldn't lay down for you without marriage, and you being like a spoiled baby who won't hear no!"

"She put a spell on me!" Awochu cried. "She put it in the stain she used on her lips, so I was half-mad."

"Witch," someone whispered behind me. I whirled to glare and saw people crowded all around us.

"Unlawful to spell a man into marriage," a woman said.

"Oh, no," Iyaka said. She shook out of my hold and walked up to Awochu, her muscles tight with anger. "You courted me with flowers and sweets and promises until I barely knew my name. You pursued me because I said no that first day, when you kissed me like a barbarian. And now you sully my name and the name of my family?" She spat in the dust at his feet and looked at the blue silk girl. "You want to be watching now," Iyaka told the other girl. "This is what you want to marry. He will blame *you* when things go wrong between you." Iyaka turned her attention back to Awochu. "You want your freedom? You may have it—*after* you pay half my bride price for breaking the contract and lying about me."

He had looked arrogant, then petty, then furious. Now he looked smug. "I pay you *nothing,*" he told Iyaka. "Not to one who uses magic for love. Nawolu chief Rusom judges all trade fair disagreements. *He* will know what to do."

He marched off to the chief's pavilion. We had no

choice but to follow, to stop him from lying to Chief Rusom. The witnesses followed, eager for the sight of someone else's quarrel and judgment.

Luckily, friends heard Awochu's claim and ran to fetch our tribe. By the time we could see the chief's bright red pavilion, Papa, our shaman, and our own chief had come, with my kinfolk. My heart swelled with pride. All of our village had come to stand with my sister. Surely Chief Rusom would see that she was a girl of good family, the kind who would never use magic in a foul way. He would order Awochu to admit to his lie before everyone, so my sister's name would go untainted.

In order to hear the many people who came to speak with him during the day, the chief had the pavilion floor raised up a foot from the ground. He and his companions could then sit under the shelter of the canopy and talk with those who stood on the beaten dirt before them. We moved to the front, passed along by the people who knew why we were there. Iyaka clutched my hand and Mama's and would not let go. I had to move into line behind her as she stood with Mama, Papa, and our chief.

Awochu bowed to the man who had to be Chief Rusom. I glanced at the man on the chief's right and almost gasped like an ignorant country girl. I had never seen a man so pale-skinned. Everyone in my life was brown or black. Some of the fair's visitors were a lighter brown than I had ever seen before, but it was still brown. This man—this man was *white.*

He had brown-black hair, straighter than the hair of

anyone I knew. His eyes were brown-black, *close* to the color of normal eyes. He didn't dress like a normal man, though. He wore a loose cloth jacket and a garment made of two cloth tubes that covered each of his legs, instead of a long skirt. Instead of sandals he wore soft leather shoes that covered his feet and legs all the way to his knees. Only his hands looked right. They were hard, muscled, and scarred, the hands of a warrior. His neck was muscled like a bull's.

"Do you know who that is?" Ogin had worked his way up behind me. I looked at him. His eyes gleamed as he looked on the white man. He shifted his weight from foot to foot, unable to stand still.

"No, but he looks very sick," I whispered.

"Pf," Ogin said, pushing me a little. "You know the stories of the Shang warriors, who fight and kill with bare hands? That man is Vah-lah-nee, the Shang Falcon. He is a great warrior!"

He looked like a man, not a legend, to me. "He is a horse who will burn and bloat and explode in the sun," I replied. "Put him back in the oven and let him cook until he is done." I looked at the platform and got a very bad feeling. Awochu had left his blue silk girl beside the platform and climbed on it to go to the man who sat at Chief Rusom's left. He kissed this man on both scarred cheeks. This man wore gold on his arms and fingers. He also looked enough like Awochu to be his father.

Worse, there was a hospitality table placed between his seat and Rusom's. He and the chief shared food and drink, like allies or friends.

"Awochu, why have you brought these people?" asked the man Awochu had kissed, his voice filling the air. "Why do you disturb Chief Rusom?"

Awochu bowed to Chief Rusom. "Great Chief," he said with respect, "I come to you as a wronged man. Last year at this fair I was overtaken by a madness that made me want that girl as my bride." He pointed at Iyaka. "After I stole a kiss from her, I could not sleep or eat unless I was with her. I offered her my name and the wealth of my family. I begged my father and mother to accept the match with an ordinary plains girl." He shook his head in sorrow. "When we returned to our own great village, our shaman saw the traces of magic on me. He kept me in his hut for nine days and nine nights to cleanse me of the evil spell. He told me—he will tell you, if you ask it—that the girl had painted charm color on her lips. When I stole that kiss, magic made me hers. It made me desire her to the point that I had signed a marriage contract with her family.

"Great Chief Rusom, is it not the law that no contract entered into while under the influence of magic is binding? For so my honored father explained the law to me. I owe this girl nothing. She cannot have me, so she accuses me of a false claim, in order to steal my father's cattle."

"I do not steal!" cried Iyaka. "I happily release him from the contract. I do not want a man who is so fickle or so easily swayed." She glared at Awochu's father and the elegant woman who stood at his back, who had to be Awochu's mother. "But he has sullied my name and the name of my family with his accusation of love magic. He must pay half the bride price for his lies. He should be grateful I do not ask for it all. You see?" She took the delicate skin on which the contract was written from her sash, unfolded it, and offered it to Chief Rusom. "It is written there. If I release him, he must pay half the bride price to me. If he lies about me, he must pay it all and apologize for his evil, and admit he lied."

"It is she who lies!" cried Awochu. "It is also written that if I am forced to this or lied to about her honor or her maiden nature, I am free of the contract!"

Chief Rusom read the document carefully, his eyes flicking to Awochu, to Iyaka, to my parents, to our shaman, and to our chief. He did not look at Awochu's father. Instead, when he reached down to that hospitality table for his teacup, Awochu's father picked it up and filled it, then gave it to Rusom. It was as plain as a baboon's red behind: Awochu's father would find a way to fill Rusom's cup if the chief could help his son.

Rusom let the contract fall. "When there is such disagreement, and good names at stake, there are several ways to resolve the matter," he said in a voice like oil. "But involving magic . . ." He stroked his chin. "No, I think it must be trial by combat. The gods will allow the innocent side to win. Awochu?"

"I fight my own battles," Awochu said, thrusting his chest out. His eyes held the same gleam as those of the chief and his father. He knew the way was prepared.

"Me," Ogin said, thrusting his way past Papa and me. The Falcon, Vah-lah-nee, was also getting to his feet, as if a white man knew anything of us.

The chief was already shaking his head. "It must be a member of the girl's direct family," he said, proving he knew quite well who we were.

Papa took a limping step forward. The gleam in Awochu's eyes brightened.

I thrust ahead, noticing only then that I was as tall as my papa. "I will fight," I said, though my voice cracked when I said "fight." I ignored the laughter of everyone and made myself say, "She is my sister. It is my name, too."

"No!" cried Mama. "I forbid it! She is a girl! She is no warrior!"

But Rusom already was shaking his head. "Do you believe the gods will help you, girl? This is no time to thrust yourself into serious business if *you* are not serious."

I trembled and sweated as I made myself say, "I believe in the gods." What I believed in was the ostrich gods, the giraffe gods, the lion gods. This dishonorable chief knew nothing of them.

"If the gods decide, then surely it only matters that she is of the girl's blood," said Chief Rusom. "I call for the combat when the sun leaves us no shadow."

All was noise then. Mama and Papa scolded me. Iyaka hit me with her fists. My chief told me I was a fool and had cost my sister *and* my papa their honor. The gleeful crowd followed us to the enclosure set aside for trial by combat. Servants came to take away Awochu's golden ornaments as his girl poured a cup of wine for him. His mama set a stool in the shade for him to rest upon while he waited for the proper time.

Ogin and the white man brought a stool for me. They

made me sit and drink some water. Gently the white man, the Falcon, placed hands like iron on the muscles between my neck and shoulders. I felt him hesitate. Then he raised my hands, examining my callused knuckles. He probed my back muscles with those hard fingers, then bent down to look at my legs and feet.

"Well," he said. His voice was deep and smooth, like dark honey. "Perhaps this is not the folly it looks to be." His Dikurri accent was thick, but I could understand him.

Of course, peahen, I told myself. He sat with the chief. They must be able to talk.

He was asking me something. I turned to look up at him. "What?" I asked. My lips felt stiff.

"What do you wear under your dress?" he asked slowly, as if he knew I could only truly understand slow speech just then.

"How dare you!" cried Mama.

He put a hand on her shoulder. "Your daughter cannot fight in a dress," he said kindly. "The women warriors of the Chelogu tribes fight entirely naked, in tribute to the Great Mother Goddess. I think your daughter may wear a *little* more than that, but a skirt will hobble her like a donkey."

"She *is* a donkey," my mother whispered, her lips trembling. "A stupid donkey who does not understand what she has done here."

"She wears a breast band and a loincloth," Iyaka said.

"If they are snug, that is enough," said the Falcon. He told me, "Can you remove the dress on your own?"

I plucked at my sash until it came apart. Someone pulled it away, then Iyaka took the dress. I do not know why Mama was so upset. I raced in no more than this at every festival.

The Falcon crouched behind me and began to work the muscles around my collarbone with those iron fingers. They spread warmth and relaxation down into my arms. "What is your name, girl?" he asked me, his voice coming from behind me like a ghost's.

Ogin answered for me. "Kylaia," he said, his eyes as over-bright as Mama's. "She is Kylaia al Jmaa."

The Falcon picked up one of my hands and began to work on it. Across the arena, servants rubbed oil into Awochu's shoulders. "Kylaia," the Falcon said for my ears only, "who taught you to fight?"

I blinked at him like a simpleton. "The ostriches," I said. "The killers of the plain."

"She is mad," Papa said abruptly. "I will make them stop it. I will fight him."

The Falcon said, "It is in the gods' hands now, sir. I do not think they have chosen badly."

By the time the sun left us no shadow, the Falcon had loosened the muscles in my arms, back, legs, and feet. I was as relaxed as if I had just finished a quick sprint to get my blood warm.

Someone struck a gong to signal it was time. I walked out to the center of the arena, ignoring the comments of the crowd. If they were properly bred, like the people in our village, they would no more laugh at a maiden dressed to show her body's skills than they would laugh at a woman giving birth.

Awochu met me at the center. Rusom's shaman droned a prayer. I ignored him. My eyes watched Awochu. He would want to hit me hard and fast, to get it over with, so he could enjoy my sister's shame. I had said my prayers. Now it was time for me to take down this hunter who had come into my territory in search of meat. He was stronger on his right side, the muscles of that arm clearer than the muscles of his left. He would try to grapple with me, as the young men did in unarmed combat. If he actually took hold of me, I would be in trouble. He was taller, stronger, heavier. He had fought in battle to earn his scars. He had fought with his hands.

Now Rusom had something to say. He spoke, then stopped.

Awochu shifted his feet for his balance.

Someone struck a gong. Awochu lunged for me, his hands reaching. I pivoted to one side and ostrich-kicked him. The ball of my foot slammed just under his ribs with all the speed and strength I had built up. He gasped and turned to grab my kicking leg, but I was already behind him. He was so *slow,* or so I thought then. I did not understand that all those years of repetition had not just made me a fast runner. All that practice on wood and trees and stone, pretending they were living lions and leopards and wild dogs, had made me a fast kicker, a fast mover, a fast hitter. With my speed I also gained power behind each blow and kick.

I drove the ball of my other foot into his right kidney. He staggered away from me and fell to his knees. I lunged forward and hammered my linked fists giraffe-style into the place where his neck met his collarbone. He grabbed my hands as he wheezed from pain. I bounced up and came down with my knee in the middle of his spine. He straightened up with a strangled cry, letting me go. Then I wrapped my arm around his neck from behind, gripping that fist with my free one. I pulled back, resting my knee against his spine for leverage. He clawed at my arm, ripping my flesh with his nails.

"Confess," I told him. "Tell the truth. Swear it on your mother's name, or I will cripple you." I did not think I could do it, but it sounded like the right thing to say to a bully who shamed my family before all the trade fair.

He tried to speak and could not. I eased my grip just a little.

"The gods have humbled me!" he shrieked. "They sent a demon into this girl child to shame me! Iyaka al Jmaa is an honorable girl!"

"Mention the magic," I whispered. If he wanted to believe a demon had beaten him, I did not care. I only wanted my sister to get what was owed.

"I won't," he began. I tightened my hold, briefly. When he could breathe again, he confessed to everything and begged his father for the fifteen cattle for my sister. We did not trust them to arrange things honorably. Instead my chief made Awochu and his father sign new words on the old marriage contract, saying that it was ended and the right price paid for the slight to my sister. Then the men of my village went with Awochu and his father to collect the cattle.

This I was told of later. As soon as I let Awochu up, my

sisters swept me up, wrapped me in my dress, and took me back to our tents so I could vomit, clean up, and sleep.

When I woke, only a small lamp burned in our tent. From the light that flickered through the cracks around the door flap, I knew it was night, and the campfires were lit. I could hear the low murmur of voices outside.

I could also smell food. I got up, every muscle of my body aching. In my rage I had done even more than I was used to, and my body was unhappy. Slowly, like an old woman, I walked outside.

Val-lah-nee, the Falcon, sat at our fire with my parents, Iyaka, and Ogin, eating from the pot with one hand as if he had eaten that way all of his life. He nodded to me and said, "I have been talking with your parents about your future," as if he continued a conversation we had already begun.

"I have no future," I told him as I accepted a round of bread from Iyaka. I scooped food onto it and crouched between my parents. "Boys won't want a girl who gets possessed by demons."

"You were no more possessed than I am," said the Falcon. "Ogin told us about the way you watched animals and the way you tried to fight as they did."

I glared at Ogin, who grinned and shrugged. "I am a hunter as well as a herder," he said cheerfully. "If I cannot be quiet, I catch only grubs."

The Falcon grinned. I could hardly see his teeth in the shadows, his skin was so pale. "And so I was saying to your parents, while the Shang school for warriors normally does not take a new student of your age—"

"My age!" I protested.

"Their students begin between their fourth and sixth year," Papa said. "Let the man say what he must. Stop interrupting."

"I believe they will take an old woman with your unusual skills," the Falcon said to me. "In fact, I am so sure of it that I am willing to pay a proper bride price for you to your parents. But you would not be my bride on our journey to Shang; you would be my student. You would be as safe with me as you would with your father."

I scowled at him. "Are you buying me? I am no slave."

He chuckled. "No," he said, laughter still in his eyes. "This is an offering of thanks I give to your family, for the honor of being allowed to teach so inventive a young lady."

"We believe him," Mama said quietly. "We trust him. But you must choose."

"He says you may visit, when you have finished the studies." Iyaka smiled at me, but tears rolled down her cheeks.

Papa took up my hand and kissed it. "I think you saved our family's honor today at high cost to your future," he said, his voice as soft as Mama's. "Even less than a bride possessed by a demon will a young man like a wife who can kick his ribs in."

I looked at the Falcon. "Why should I want to study the ways of warriors out of grandmother tales?" I asked him, feeling my heart beat a little faster.

He got to his knees and pulled a stone half the size of my head over in front of him. His eyes half-closed, he seemed to go away a little, for a moment. I did not even see him cock his fist and punch the stone.

The stone broke in half.

For the first time since we had met Awochu in the street, I felt like myself again. "How did you do that?" I asked. "Will you teach me that? And what is your idea of a fair bride price? If I am to be a Shang warrior, I must not dishonor my family with a few coppers."

Elder Brother

Shriveling. He shrank. Leaves, twigs, branches, roots, all curled in on him. His trunk went limp. His apples dropped to the earth in a green rainfall. He mourned them with tears of sap. These apples were his last crop, his children-to-be. His chance to spread his family with his seeds now lay on the ground, doomed to rot.

Even his tears dried until he had no more. He was dying. He had to be dying, but this was no death he knew. Without lightning or axes no tree ended so fast, in one night. At sunset he'd been vigorous, alive. The rising sun touched him as he fell, dying, from his earth.

Wasn't death a hard dark? He was soft. Sharp and slick things pricked newly tender bark. Lumps under him were his apples, his unborn children. Would he feel such things if he were dead? Even his heartwood, where his thoughts were paced like the seasons, was different. Now his thoughts tumbled like hailstones in a high wind. They were not made by normal scents and vibrations but by things he could not even name.

Within his heartwood, among these new and frightening thoughts, a shape formed. It was the image of a big rootless one, like those who picked his fruit. This rootless made signs in the air with his twigs. The sign-shapes blazed, then vanished.

Suddenly the tree knew big rootlesses were *humans.* This one, his thoughts whispered, was a man, a *mage,* who had just used magic on him.

"I beg you, forgive me," the mage-human said. "I've done a dreadful thing to you, and I can't undo it. I turned an enemy into an apple tree. Half a world away an apple tree—you—became a man."

When the tree said nothing, the stranger went on. "I am needed here—I can't come help you. What I *have* done is place a spell so you can understand what your senses tell you. My spell also gives you the ability to speak. You won't be helpless, this first day of your new life." He cocked his head. "I'm being called. Listen—you need a name. It'll be easier to find you, if I have your name. Can you think of one?"

The tree was about to say that trees had no names, but a strange thing happened. Memory whispered that a human female had once spoken to him. A visitor, she had silently touched every tree there. Only when she came to him, the last, did she speak as she took her hand from his bark: "Qiom."

"Qiom," he said now, tasting the name with a human tongue. "I am Qiom."

"Qiom," the man repeated. "Thank you. Each night, when you sleep, I'll enter your dreams and answer questions. I'll do my best to help, I swear it."

The human faded in Qiom's heartwood—his *mind,* whispered new, magical knowledge. As he faded, the human said, "Some of your old self stayed with this body. You will know more about plants than most humans; you'll be strong. You can use those things to feed and protect yourself." He was only a shimmer of light among shadows. "*My* name is Numair. Again, forgive me." He was gone.

Qiom sat up and looked himself over with human eyes. He was rootless, his trunk changed beyond belief. His skin was a darker brown than Numair's had been; his shaggy crown hair was black. He looked down at human legs, wiggled stunted, ugly toes, and wept.

As the sun rose, his middle clenched. He felt empty; his head spun. New thinking said this was human hunger. If he wasn't dead, he wanted to live. Living meant food.

He struggled to stand, falling twice, and stretched out his senses. He knew the plants around him in the same way he had known them before this change, but now he also knew how to use them for food.

The apricot and almond trees that shared his grove would give food in some weeks, but not today. Their fruits would make him sick if he ate them right away. The grasses under his feet would not feed a human body at all.

Fumbling and tripping, he left the grove of his old life. He turned his nose into the wind as he had once turned his leaves to it, sorting the fragrances of plants. There, on his west side: food he could eat right now. He shambled into the next grove, where a bounty of ripe cherries waited to be picked. As he gorged himself on them, he pitched their seeds outside the orchard. They would get a chance to take root and grow.

Once he had fed, weariness struck. He folded his new

legs and sat under a cherry tree. Closing the flaps over his eyes, he fell into soft shadows.

He woke to the screams of humans and a feeling of pressure in his belly. Squatting, he passed dung and urine, like the wastes that dogs and other animals dumped on his roots. Human females covered from top to toe in leaves of cloth fled the cherry orchard, screaming, when he did this. As Qiom stood, swaying on his ugly stick legs, the females returned with male humans. These wore cloth leaves that fit their arms and legs closely and left their faces bare, unlike the females. The males carried wooden things—*hoes,* said his magical knowledge, and *staffs.* They hit Qiom with them, shouting, cursing him.

Qiom yelped—the blows hurt. He ran away from the men. They gave chase, still battering him, still cursing him. Qiom ran faster. Once he was a safe distance away, he turned to ask them why.

The first rock struck his belly, slicing tender skin, causing sap—blood—to well out. Qiom clapped his hands over the cut, wailing in fright and pain. The humans threw more rocks at him. One clipped his shoulder. Another struck his head, drawing more blood. Now Qiom ran in earnest.

He kept running until he saw not another human being. He lay down in a stream until his wounds, until all of him but his chattering new knowledge, went numb in the cold water. Free of pain, he rose and trudged on down a strip of beaten earth called a road.

At sunset he entered the woods. He needed to find shelter before the night turned cold. A fallen tree, massive and hollow, offered him a place to rest. He made himself a bed of leaves and curled up inside the log, shivering as the day's heat faded. He mourned his last apples again. Would they feel as he did, green and unready for this angry new life?

He drifted in the warmth of sleep for a time. Then light bloomed in the dark, showing him the human male Numair. "What happened?" asked Numair, reaching out as if he could touch Qiom. "You're hurt. And you're cold."

"Humans happened to me," Qiom said, his voice as sharp as new sap. "I rid myself of urine and dung and they attacked me."

Numair's shoulders slumped. "Oh. You see, they expect humans to hide when they, um, release urine and dung. We also bury wastes, and we clean ourselves afterward with leaves and water. Not cleaning makes us sick."

"The females screamed at me even before I did it," Qiom told Numair. "Why? I was not hurting them."

Numair looked Qiom over. "I think it was because you are naked," he said quietly. "You need clothes."

Clothes, his new knowledge whispered. The cloth leaves that covered the human form were clothes.

"With no money, you'll have to steal some," Numair said. "It's a bad idea, but you have no choice." Carefully, he explained what he meant. For every new word he used, knowledge tumbled into Qiom's head, showering him with images and explanations. At last Numair faded from Qiom's sleep, promising to return.

In the morning Qiom found a road. Numair had said it would take him to other humans, who would have things Qiom needed to survive.

In a small village Qiom found drying-lines, each of them heavy with wet cloth fruits. Making sure he was not seen, he plucked breeches from one line, a loincloth from another, and a shirt from a third. He might have escaped the village unnoticed but for the beautiful smell that reached his nose. Warm and heady, it combined wheat, chickens, and a touch of mother cow. *Bread,* magical knowledge told him. *Food.*

Qiom tracked the scent to a plump brown circle in the window of a human dwelling. When he seized the loaf of bread, he scorched his fingers. He dropped it, sucked on his fingertips to cool them, then grabbed it again. Inside the house, a child began to scream.

Again males came, waving their weapons. Qiom ran, bread and wet clothes hugged tight to his chest. He was not quick enough: a rock struck his spine, making him gasp with pain. On he ran.

"You have to be *careful,*" Numair told him that night as Qiom slept. "Stay out of sight, watch what they do."

Qiom tried. He did, but still he lurched from disaster to disaster. He was not good at sneaking. Someone nearly always saw him—when they did, the screaming, the hitting, the pain, and the running all began afresh.

One night, tired of the cold, Qiom took shelter in a barn. In its haymow he had the best sleep of his rootless life, warmed by the body heat of the cows on the floor below. It was not yet dawn when men woke him. Qiom blinked at them as they dragged him to his feet. Somehow they had brought daylight into the barn in the hours before dawn, light captured on the ends of sticks.

The sticks were burning. These men had made a servant

of fire, the great killer! He shrank from the flames, too frightened to struggle as the men forced him out of the barn. If he disobeyed them, would they burn him, too? It was hard to be calm and think, as Numair was forever telling him to do. Qiom was sure that no one had ever threatened Numair with fire.

The men dragged him to a building where a huge fire burned at its center. Qiom curled himself into a ball, terrified that the flames would jump to him. His captors forced him to look at a man in an orange turban and sash. This man, a priest, babbled of Oracles and gods, saying, "The mad carry the god's blessing." He talked and talked. When he finished, the men took Qiom out of the village, away from that great fire. They set him free and told him never to return.

Qiom fled, sure they would send the fire leaping after him. He ran through what remained of the night. At last he fell and slept.

Numair immediately came into Qiom's dreams, but the tree-man turned away. Where had Numair's help gotten him? When the sun rose, Qiom woke to bleeding feet, bruises, and a throbbing head. He was tired of human anything. He would finish the dying that began when he shriveled and return to the Great Pine and the Flowering Apple, the parents of all trees. Maybe they would give him a fresh start as a seed.

He sought a place in the open, where he would be sheltered from nothing. At last he found the perfect spot: a hill beside a road into a town. The boulders that formed the hill were capped by a lone, broad, flat stone. He could not ask for better. Qiom sat cross-legged on the rock and waited.

People on the road stared at him. Wagons slowed as they passed. Fearing him, thinking him mad, no one spoke to him. He ignored the humans, just as he ignored Numair when the mage entered his sleep that night.

It was the world apart from people that nearly changed his mind. How could humans rush through a day without looking at the blueness of the sky or the colors of butterflies? How could they ignore the miracles of growing wheat and flying birds? Qiom had to struggle to harden his heart against the beauties visible to human eyes, beauties that tempted him to live. He succeeded. If he needed reminders of why he wished to die, all he had to do was remember fire, and rocks, and screams.

In the afternoon of his second day on the hill, a boy walking toward the town stopped to gaze at him. Even Qiom knew his dark hair was badly cut. No two clumps were the same length. He dressed as all males did—trousers, sash, shirt—and carried a cloth pack on his shoulders.

Qiom saw the boy again that evening: he was working just outside the town walls. Often the boy stopped to stare at him. In the morning, he waved to Qiom as he walked into the town.

Two more days passed. A thunderstorm broke. Qiom begged for lightning to strike him, but it did not. He was hungry, thirsty, and dizzy from lack of food and water. He tried to ignore those feelings, but it was harder than he had expected. Dust blew into his eyes, making them water. He shivered in the chilly nights. Bugs that ate humans feasted on him.

Then he saw the boy leave the town with a fat and heavy pack and a dirtless face. When the boy reached the rocky hill, he climbed it until he scrambled onto Qiom's stone.

Qiom waited for an order or a demand for information. Instead the boy sat on his heels and opened his pack. He took out a pear. Slowly he set the fruit on the rock between them. "Good day, Elder Brother," he said. "My pack is heavy. Would you accept a pear, and lighten it?"

Other humans had given Qiom screams, threats, and blows. None had spoken gently. None had offered food. He could smell the pear. His mouth flooded with saliva; his belly, quiet for a whole day, snarled.

Elder Brother? "We are not family," he croaked. "I am no one's brother."

The boy's skin was paler than Qiom's, his nose a strong arch on a stubborn face. There was light in his eyes and kindness in his mouth. "'Elder Brother' is a courtesy title, to show respect. Please accept the pear and my respect."

Qiom felt things suddenly, not just hunger. The warmth in the boy's voice made his heart ache. "If I eat, it will take me longer to die," he said at last.

The boy sat back, surprised. "Die?" he repeated. "It is a beautiful day—bright with sun, cool with breezes. Surely it's a day for beginnings, not endings."

"I have begun. I don't like it," Qiom replied wearily. "I am useless. I am a tree who cannot be a tree. I know nothing of being a man."

The boy rubbed his chin. Qiom waited. He didn't expect the lad to believe him.

At last the boy said, "Trees don't want to die. They want to sink their roots deep, and open their leaves for sunlight."

A human who made sense. "I have no roots," Qiom replied, sorrowful. "And these branches don't work." He inspected his hands. "The one who changed me tries to explain human things, but he only comes at night. It is in the sun that I fail. I never know enough. People hate me. I will sit here until I die."

The boy frowned. "Aren't you hungry?" He rolled the pear closer.

Qiom swallowed a mouthful of saliva. "If I ignore it, I will die," he answered.

The boy wrapped his arms around his knees. Finally he asked, "If I teach you how to be a man, will you eat?"

A feeling struck Qiom like a stone thumping his chest. The feeling was shock. He stared at the boy. "Why? What good am I like this?"

"Everyone has some good," the boy said earnestly. "You can work. The Oracle says work is a blessing in the eyes of the god. And if there are two of us, we'll be safer from people who pick on strangers."

"Safer." The word had a good sound. "You can teach me to be a man?" If Numair, who had made him, couldn't do it, could this boy?

The boy smiled crookedly. "I'm good at teaching. My cousin is slow, but I taught him how to tie his sandals. No one else could."

Slowly Qiom wrapped his hand around the pear. It felt just right in his palm. "Why do you do this?" he asked. "Why do you help me?"

The boy looked down. "I know how it is to be without hope," he said at last. "I do this because I can." He put his palms together and bowed slightly. "I am called Fadal."

* * *

Qiom lightened Fadal's pack by eating four more pears and the flatbread the boy had tucked in his sash. "We'll get more," Fadal assured him. "There is little work to be had for money, but people will trade things for chores. First, we need better clothes for you. And aren't you cold at night?"

Qiom nodded.

"You can have one of my blankets. If you're as strong as you look and ready to work, we can trade labor for what we'll need."

When the western sun grazed the treetops, they camped beside a deep, clear pool. Qiom went in search of mushrooms. He wanted to add something of his own to their food. He also wanted to stay away from the fire that Fadal had started. Humans were so casual with the stuff, as if they believed it would never burn them. Qiom thought he would never be comfortable with fire.

Once he'd washed his mushrooms and given them to Fadal, Qiom retreated to the base of a chestnut tree to watch. Fadal put the sausage and mushrooms on a piece of metal over the fire to work the magic humans named cooking. The food hissed and spat, releasing a smell that made Qiom's belly talk. Finally the boy put most of the meal on a piece of bark for Qiom.

He scooped up a fistful, the way he had eaten his first meal of cherries, and thrust it into his mouth. Heat seared his hand and mouth. He gasped and nearly choked, burning his throat, before he spat out the food.

"It's too hot," Fadal said. "Put cold water on your hand." Qiom went to the pond and put first his burned hand, then his entire head, into it. The pain went away.

When he pulled out of the water, Fadal washed the dropped sausage and heated it again.

Once it was ready, he crouched before Qiom, holding the piece of bark loaded with steaming food. "You blow on hot food to cool it, like this." He blew on a mushroom, then gave it to Qiom to eat.

After that, Qiom fed himself. The sausage in particular was very good. "It is the best meal I have had," he said as Fadal put more wood on the fire.

"Did your mother never cook?" Fadal asked. "What was she like?"

"I don't know," Qiom replied. "When I was a seed, I was carried until I was planted. I never saw the tree from which I fell."

Fadal made a face. "Who named you Qiom, then?"

He told him about the woman, about "qiom." "I like the sound."

"How could you know what she said?" asked Fadal craftily. "Trees don't speak or hear."

"We hear," Qiom replied. "We hear with the mouths in our leaves, and we speak in their sound. But human talking . . ." He was quiet for a while, sorting out ideas he had never put to words before. "I was old even then. Changing, becoming different. The little ghost people—elementals—who live in stones and streams, they said I would soon give birth to myself, to my own elemental." He felt his lips stretch and turn up, as Fadal's had. He was smiling. It felt good. "Elementals are such liars. I did not walk out of my tree body. I am a tree that walks and talks."

"So you learned enough speech from just listening to

the visitors to your grove to talk now." Fadal sounded as if he did not believe Qiom.

Qiom shrugged. It was comforting in a way: at last Fadal acted like every other human he had met. Until this moment he had been so different that Qiom had started to think this friendly boy was a daylight dream born of an empty belly.

"Oh, no," he said. "Numair put magic on me, so I could speak. All these words . . . How do humans manage? I get confused. It hurts my heart."

Fadal sighed and doused the fire. He took blankets from his pack and gave one to Qiom. Then he wrapped himself in his own blanket and lay on a patch of thick grass.

Qiom thought Fadal was asleep, until a new question came from the dark. "Elder Brother, who is Numair?"

"He comes in dreams," replied Qiom. "He turned a bad man into a tree. The price of that great magic was that I turned into a man, half a world away."

"And you believe this," Fadal remarked. The boy sounded amused.

"I must," Qiom said. He closed his eyes and slept.

The next day they got work repairing stone fences around an olive grove. Resting at midmorning, they drank water and ate figs brought to them by the young son of the grove's owners. Qiom was ready to get back to work when the same boy ran by, chased by a crying little girl.

The boy halted beside the well, holding a soft, floppy thing over his head, out of the girl's reach. Magical knowledge told Qiom this was a *doll,* a girl's toy.

"I'll tell Mama!" the girl cried. She jumped frantically, trying to get the doll.

"So?" retorted the boy. "Nobody cares what girls say."

Fadal stirred. "Elder Brother, will you stop this?" he asked Qiom. "As the oldest man present, you should correct the boy."

"Why?" Qiom wanted to know. "This is not important. It is nothing to do with trees." Fadal glared at him. "Why are you angry?" Qiom asked, confused. "You said we must finish this work today."

Fadal marched over to the boy and took the doll. He gave the toy to the girl, who clutched it and ran. "Don't you know your sacred writings?" Fadal asked the boy. "The Oracle wrote, 'Women hold our future. Therefore, honor all women as you do your soul.' Honor does *not* meant torment! Go, and think on what I have said!" He pointed to the house. The boy ran inside.

Fadal returned to Qiom, his cheeks still red with anger. "He shouldn't have tormented his sister," he told Qiom. "If men aren't fair to women, women have no protection at all."

Qiom didn't know why Fadal was angry. "If you say so," he replied, lifting a big stone. "Where shall I set this?"

They finished the repairs and slept in the grove that night. In the morning they left, richer by a shirt that was patched, but warm, for Qiom, as well as by a pouch of dried fruit.

They walked into the hills, working when they could. They spent two days helping a man to slaughter sheep, an afternoon picking olives, a morning dipping candles. Fadal made sure that on each job they got something useful for Qiom: a knife, a sash, a blanket.

They had finished their noon meal after candle dipping and had gone some miles down the road when Fadal grabbed his shirtfront and sighed. "Wait here," he ordered Qiom, and strode into the woods just off the road.

Qiom waited, but Fadal took a long time. What if something was wrong? Was he sick, as Qiom had been when he ate a bad piece of meat? Then Fadal had given him herbs to stop his insides from their painful squeezing. Now Qiom found the herb pouch and went to find the boy.

Fadal was not squatting: he was shaking out a long band of cloth. His shirt was pulled up around his shoulders, revealing a body unlike Qiom's. Fadal's chest was not flat but carried two small rounds. Now Fadal held one end of the cloth to his ribs and passed the long end around them, as if he bandaged a large scratch. A third wrapping pressed the rounded parts of his chest flat.

"Are you hurt?" Qiom asked. He saw no blood; Fadal had said nothing of being in pain.

Fadal whirled, his face dead white. He covered his chest with his hands. "Go away!" he cried. "I wanted to be alone!"

The cloth fell. He bent to grab it, still trying to hide his chest with one hand. He was breathing in gasps.

Qiom returned to the road, as confused as he had ever been in his short life. His human knowledge said that what he had seen were *breasts,* that Fadal was a female. Why did she pretend to be male? Why use cloth to hide her breasts? Why did she not wear the shell of cloth leaves like other females?

When Fadal returned, she opened her pack. "I'll make

a bargain with you," she said. "We'll split the food and the things we've gotten working together, and take opposite paths. All right?"

Fadal wanted to leave? "I don't understand," Qiom replied. He did not like this. The thought of going on without Fadal was frightening.

"Oh, please!" Fadal exclaimed, dashing away raindrops that fell from her eyes. "You'll denounce me at the next temple—"

"Why?" Qiom asked, scared. What would become of him without her? "Temples have fire in them. I hate temples. You said you would explain things. You promised to teach me to be a man, but now you mean to leave. You make no sense, Fadal."

She stepped back and stared up into Qiom's face, her eyes searching for something. Her terror was still there, but it began to fade, to be replaced with bewilderment.

"You—" Her voice squeaked. She cleared her throat, then asked, "Why do women cover all but their eyes in veils?"

For perhaps the first time Qiom felt irritation. "I have no idea. Why do you ask me about clothes?"

Fadal sat in the road, plop, like a frog. Her eyes were huge. "You really *were* a tree."

Qiom blinked. "I said I was. What has my tree-ness to do with cloth leaves—with veils?" Fadal was quite pale. Qiom knelt and offered her the herb pouch. "Are you sure you don't need medicine?"

Fadal took the pouch but did not open it. Instead she asked, "What do you know of our religion?"

"There is a god who is in fires," Qiom told Fadal. "I am afraid of fire, so I know nothing of its god."

Fadal's mouth quivered like an aspen leaf. "Three hundred years ago, the Oracle came to this part of the world," she said carefully. "He spoke for the God in the Flame, our oldest god. He spoke clearly, when all others who heard the god's voice went mad, and he wrote down the god's commands. We follow what he wrote. He told us that women of an age to bear children are a temptation to men. They are disorderly and selfish. If they are not to distract men from the god, they must live apart from men, except for marriage visits. Outside women's quarters they must veil themselves until only their eyes, hands, and feet show. Old-fashioned women even wear a sheer veil over their eyes.

"My father wasn't from here. In his land, the God in the Flame is still one of many gods. Father taught me to hunt and fish and handle tools because he had no son. He died a year ago, and my mother remarried this spring. Her new husband is devout. The day he wed my mother, I was ordered to put on the body veil and move into women's quarters. He was planning my marriage." Fadal shook her head. "I couldn't bear it. I cut off my hair, bound my chest flat, and ran away. If I were caught—an unveiled woman . . ."

Her voice died away. Qiom, sitting on his heels beside her, nudged her shoulder. "What would happen?" he asked.

"Men would say I was a prostitute or a demon. They would stone me to death." She looked at him. "But you saw. You are a man of this country; you look it and your accent is ours. But you don't care that I'm female, do you? If you didn't mind for my sake, you would for your own—the man who travels with an unveiled woman is thought to be infected with vice. He too must die because he would spread that infection. Only one explanation fits why you don't care."

"Why would I lie about being a tree?" asked Qiom. "You must admit it is a silly lie."

Fadal laughed and laughed. When water streamed from her eyes, she went alone into the trees. By the time she returned, it was too late to travel. They made camp instead. After supper, Qiom asked Fadal to tell him more of her religion. He wanted to get it all exactly right when he described it to Numair.

A man offered cloth shoes for Qiom and a cheese if they would do his farm's work for a day as he cared for his sick wife. Fadal did chores inside the house; Qiom tended the animals. As Fadal set about killing and plucking a chicken, a process Qiom didn't want to learn, he went to chop up rounds cut from a dead hornbeam tree for firewood. The chore didn't bother him—the hornbeam would feel nothing that was done to it. Qiom envied it as he picked up the ax and began to chop.

He had only learned to use an ax recently. Soon his hands blistered. Qiom put the tool down and considered the heavy circles of wood. They were very dry; a split ran a third of the way across the topmost piece. Did he really need the ax?

He picked up the top circle of wood, set his fingers in the crack in its side, and tightened his muscles. It split in two. Qiom then broke each half over his knee. This was far easier than chopping, he thought as he worked his way through the pile.

He was nearly done when he heard steps in dirt. Fadal stopped nearby, silent. Was he doing something wrong? "It's easier if the wood is quite dry," he explained, facing her. "The ax hurts my hands. Am I forbidden to do it this way?"

There was an odd look in Fadal's eyes. Qiom had to search his knowledge to find the right word for it: *awe.* "You're very strong," Fadal said at last. "No, you aren't forbidden." She went back to her work. Was it important that he was strong? Qiom wondered as he finished the wood.

The next day they walked on. The road, nearly empty for so long, filled with human traffic. It streamed through gates in a log wall. "It's this town's market day. Towns are risky," Fadal explained as they approached the gates. "It's easier to be private in the woods or on a farm. Still, towns have plenty of work, and people will pay in coin. Fall is coming, and you need a coat."

On they trudged, part of the market-day throngs. Just outside the gates, Qiom saw a tall mound topped with strange wooden structures. Curious, he left the road to investigate. Fadal argued, saying they had to be inside before the gates closed for the night. Then, grumbling, she followed Qiom up the mound.

Qiom frowned. Why nail lengths of wood together to

hang four dead humans in the air? Buzzards, feasting on the dead, hissed at him, then left.

A board with marks on it stood halfway up the mound. "These were bandits, hanged yesterday," Fadal said, reading the marks. "Murderers, too. I suppose they deserved hanging, but they look so sad."

Qiom shook his head over the idea of dead men, hung like fruit on dead trees. "Twice a waste," he told Fadal as they returned to the road. "A waste of living trees for the wood, and a waste of fertilizer."

Fadal looked up at him. Her eyes were sad. "Lives are more than fertilizer, Qiom," she said. "Sometimes I don't think you even want to be human."

"I don't," he replied.

They found work just inside the gates. In exchange for cleaning his stable top to bottom, an innkeeper fed them and let them sleep in his loft. Qiom woke before dawn the next day. Normally he would have roused Fadal, but not now. She had slept badly. Her nights were never as quiet as Qiom's, who only dreamed his talks with Numair.

She always finds work, thought Qiom. Today I will find it and wake her when I do.

The town was stirring as he left the inn yard. Wagons lined up at the gates, waiting for them to open. Qiom drew a bucket of water from the well in the square between the gates and the temple, rinsing his face and cleaning his mouth. As he finger-combed straw from his hair, he looked around. He wouldn't try the temple. Even if the priest had work,

Qiom disliked the places, with those huge fires at their hearts. Fadal had said marketplaces usually had more workers than they needed. Qiom would have to look farther from the gates.

A smith offered him coins to fetch baskets of charcoal from storage; the smith's wife said they could spare another coin to have their garden weeded. Qiom was on his way to wake Fadal when he heard shouts. Two boys ran toward him, one bleeding from a cut eyebrow.

"We found a woman dressed as a man!" the injured boy told Qiom. "There was a fight; Jubrahal tore her shirt off, that's how we knew. They're taking her to the temple for correction." He scampered down a side street, yelling, "Men of the town, come to the temple!"

Qiom frowned. A woman dressed as a man—Fadal said it was rare and forbidden. Who had been caught?

Fadal.

Qiom raced for the temple. Running, he passed the well. Fadal's open pack sat there, unattended. Here was proof that their woman was Fadal, if he'd needed it. Fadal would never have left the pack here—it carried their money, their fishing hooks, their food, and their clothes. He stopped for a moment, breathless. The sight of that abandoned pack reminded him of the human dead, hung on dead trees.

"The temple is closed to ordinary matters!" a priest cried from the temple steps as men raced inside past him. "We must cleanse our town of this demon woman!" He entered the temple, closing the doors firmly.

Pain roared through Qiom like fire. They would throw stones at Fadal's human flesh. They would break her kindness, her patience, her stories, and her willingness to work hard.

Part of him cried: Fadal is no tree. You are no man. Escape! They will chop you down because you walk with her.

The heat in Qiom's heart burned that part of him to ashes. He ran up to the closed temple doors and laid his hands on them. They were tall, carved oak. When he tried to open them, he found they were locked.

Hurry, he must hurry, before they hurt Fadal beyond repair. Qiom set his right hand on one door, his left on the other, and pushed up from his roots. The doors creaked. He pushed again, opening his mouth to let the fire out of his heart in a vast, wordless howl.

The doors exploded off their hinges, smashing the closest benches, knocking down two fistfuls of men and boys. Qiom strode in, still howling, and seized a bench in each hand.

Men charged him. He smacked them with his benches until they fell and did not rise. Once he had made sure none of them got up, Qiom looked around the chamber. A huge fire burned at its heart, its roar mingling with the moans of those he had knocked aside. There was no one left on this side of the chamber, no sign of his friend.

Qiom moved until he could look around the central fire. On its far side, opposite the door, men held on to the shirtless Fadal. Qiom would have to go close to the fire to get her.

For a moment his courage wavered. The fire would reach out to devour him.

His mind showed him a picture as Qiom hesitated. It

was a pear, on a piece of flat rock—a kind offering to a man all other humans had attacked and frightened.

Qiom stalked forward, circling the fire. Its heat pressed his skin as he walked up to Fadal's captors. He knocked three of them into the wall, then flung the bench on top of them. He dropped his other bench, grabbed the orange-sashed priest, and tossed him into the wall. One man remained, clutching Fadal as he kept a knife to her throat. Fadal's face was bruised; her shirt, breast band, and shoes were gone. Even her trousers were ripped.

"Cut Fadal and I will tear you to pieces." Qiom hardly recognized the voice that growled from his throat.

The man was already white and trembling. He threw down his knife, shoved Fadal at Qiom, and ran.

Qiom slung his friend over his shoulder. It was time to go. He raced through the opening where the temple doors had been, into the square. Ahead lay the gates to the open road. Once away from the town—

The pack. Qiom swerved to seize Fadal's pack from the lip of the well. Awkwardly he passed the bundle to Fadal. She tucked it between her chest and his back to cushion her jolting body.

Now Qiom opened his stride, his eyes on the town gates. A guard was trying to close them. More heat soared through Qiom's heart. Stooping, he grabbed a rock as he ran; straightening, he threw it hard and fast. It missed the guard's head by an inch. The man fled.

Qiom ran through the gates and down the road, past travelers and fields, into the shelter of the forest. Only when they neither saw nor heard more humans did he look for a place to stop. He followed a game trail through dense brush for over a mile, until he found open space on the bank of a stream. Gently he lowered Fadal to the ground. He undid his sash, dipped it in the cold water, and carefully placed it against the worst bruises on her face.

Fadal said nothing as he cleaned blood and dirt away, but her eyes moved over his face. At last she stood and waded into the cold water, wincing. The center of the stream was deep enough that she could sit and be covered to her chin. She even ducked her head a number of times, her teeth chattering as she rinsed.

Qiom opened the pack. She had extra clothes. He shook them out: trousers, breechclout, kaftan, and another long band of linen for her breasts. She would need that until they were free of the fire god and his Oracle.

As she dressed, Qiom rolled up his trousers, removed his shoes, and put his feet in the stream. If she had nothing to say, he did. The night he'd learned Fadal's secret, he'd told Numair about her. The mage had made an offer for them both, one that Qiom had not cared about before. The morning's events had changed his mind about that.

"Numair says, if we go east to the sea and take a ship, we will come to his land. There many women are unveiled; they have respect and rights. He says, if we come, he will help us, because it is his fault I am a man."

Fadal was shivering still, despite her dry clothes. She crouched beside Qiom. "I thought you only cared for other trees," she commented, hoarse voiced.

"So did I," Qiom said, looking at his rootless feet in the water. "But you are my friend. I care for you, Fadal." He sighed. "I suppose I am human now." He pulled his feet from the stream and rose. "It is a long walk to the sea. We should go."

Fadal stood and held out her hand. "I have only lied to you once," she said quietly. "My name is Fadala, Elder Brother." She grinned. "The next thing you know, you'll learn to start fires."

Qiom shuddered and began to pack their things.

The Hidden Girl

It was late in the summer when my father brought me to the house of my aunt and uncle in the town of Hartunjur. I was relieved to be with them, because my aunt was my father's older sister. The moment she heard his deep, racking cough, she summoned a healer and ordered my father to submit to his care. I had begged him to do so for weeks, but a daughter's word did not have the weight of an older sister's, even if that daughter did his reading to make up for his fading vision.

That evening, as the healer examined my father, the innkeeper next door gave two strangers permission to sleep in his loft. Helping my aunt and cousins to prepare our supper, I learned the young man, Fadal, was handsome, if beardless, and quite funny. His companion, Qiom, was very tall and dark, with an odd, slow way of speaking.

"As if," said my aunt, "he had only recently learned to talk."

I told this to my father as I brought his supper to him. Father shook his head. "Have you women nothing more to do than gossip about men?" he asked.

He looked weary and sad. I answered in the voice I had

perfected for his amusement, that of my grandmother, Omi Heza. "Why should we not, whippersnapper?" I asked, surprising a smile from him. "In the Book of the Distaff it says that a woman's greatest weapon is her reason, and her greatest shield is her knowledge. . . ."

Father shook his head. "The temple priests are in the right of it after all, and the first error lies in teaching women to read," he said, his eyes twinkling. "And your mother and I made our second error when we let you stay with my mother when you were young! If I did not look at you, I would swear she was alive again, and scolding me."

I grinned at him. He did so like it when I made Omi Heza live again, even briefly.

That night I had the strangest dream. A voice that was two voices, a man's and a woman's, speaking as one, called to me. "Look. What lies before you?"

Before me stood veiled women, dressed in strict black from head to feet, some even covered in black to the roots of their fingers and toes. Their eyes watched me from the windows of their veils, brown, gray-green, blue-gray, all the colors of my people, set in every shade of brown and bronze skin, firmly young to dry with age.

"I see women and girls," I replied at last. Somehow I knew the voice was that of the God in the Flame, the god who spoke to my own Oracle. "I see watchfulness and waiting. I see silence."

"What else do you see?" asked the god's intertwined voices.

"I see veils."

"Then you do not see everything."

With that I woke. Since it was dawn, I chose to prepare myself for the day. Once I wore my veils, I picked up the yoke with the buckets and went to fetch water for my aunt. I passed few other people. Most women preferred to wait until later in the day to fill the water jars for their houses. On my fourth trip, one other person was at the well filling buckets, the young man Fadal my cousins had talked about.

I did nothing so improper as acknowledge him. One of my cousins might have smoothed a sleeve or looked at him sidelong. They were more daring than I. They also had prettier eyes and longer lashes. I bent to my work.

"How do you stand it?" To my shock, the voice was Fadal's. "Doing all that draped in veils? A slave in chains has more freedom to move."

Without moving my head, I looked around. We were quite alone. People were inside, eating breakfast. Worse—or better, I wasn't sure which—this Fadal spoke with the barest movement of his mouth in a soft, carrying tone. Girls learned it young. Had he imitated his mother and aunts, before they told him men never had to talk that way?

"Don't you want to throw the whole bundle in the priests' faces? Tell *them* to wear veils, if they like them so much?"

Some of the things he said were complaints I had made, it's true. Every girl has. Every girl who is not a twittering pushover for the nearest creature to grow a mustache. But still . . .

"Said like a man," I replied in the same way, only better,

because I was more practiced. "You see only the outsides of things, when it is we women who see the heart of it all." I checked our surroundings a second time before I went on. "These veils are freedom, beardless *boy.* Before I put them on, I was a sheep on the market. My nose was longer than my cousin's, my skin not so fine as my mother's, my hair not so curly as my aunt's. My teeth, my weight, my length of bone—pick, pick, pick. Then I put on the veil. Poof! The gossips have my eyes, my hands, my voice, my feet. They must judge me on my value to my family, and my family values me for who I am and what I can do."

"You *like* the veil?" He seemed so shocked! "You like being hidden away?"

"I *like* keeping myself to myself. My heart is hidden. It is mine," I told him. "And . . ." Suddenly I remembered the dream, the many women in black. "If you wished to have me beaten for speaking to a man, how would you find me? I could vanish among a crowd of women, and you would never even know which of us you spoke to."

"But you have no power," he protested. Now he sounded weak, or thoughtful, perhaps both.

"Again, said like a man who wears his thoughts on his face." Really, I was getting tired of this pup. "No power? Who cooks for you, when you have a home? Who weaves and sews the clothes you wear, the sheets and blankets you sleep in? Who is awake while you sleep? No power? Ask yourself how much power a woman has the next time she hands you a bowl of food. And taste it carefully."

My buckets were full. I shouldered my yoke, silently cursing as my veil twisted and caught under it, and walked away, careful not to spill any water. I was almost to my aunt's house when I heard shouting. I looked back. Some of the village boys had come to pick a fight with Fadal; who knew over what. Boys were always fighting, particularly with strangers. I went into my aunt's house and closed the door behind me.

I had just finished topping off the water jars when the innkeeper's wife came and pulled my aunt out into the courtyard. They whispered together urgently for a moment. Then my aunt ordered us girls to get into the kitchen and stay there. Swiftly she closed the kitchen doors and shutters before she went back to the courtyard and her friend. My cousins and I listened at the cracks in the shutters and doors, hearing distant male shouts. The noise faded, leaving us no wiser than before.

I finally gave up. My father needed his breakfast. We would hear the news soon enough. "What is going on?" he asked as I brought his simple meal. He was dressed already. From the smell of medicinal herbs, the healer had visited him while I was away.

"They did not tell us. We are only silly young girls," I grumbled.

"And how do they expect you to learn wisdom?" my father asked me as I guided his hand to his plate and cup. "Read to me, my treasure? From the Book of the Distaff, the third chapter, the fifth lesson."

I had reached the verse on balance in the land and water when my uncle and aunt interrupted us. "Quickly, quickly," my uncle said. "Teky, girl, come with us. The girls must go into the hidden room. The temple priests have found a woman dressed as a man—that boy Fadal, who stayed at the inn last night. They are taking her to the temple for burning. They will come for the girls next, to see if they were contaminated by the nearness of this Fadal."

I stayed where I was. I knew my father. He turned his fading eyes on his brother-in-law. "Is the faith of your girls so weak, that your temple priest will break it?" he asked gently. "Or is your priest so stupid, that he will find failure where there is none?"

My aunt folded her hands and unpinned her face veil. "That is what I told you," she said to her husband. "We have raised our girls to follow the Oracle's laws. They are no shame to us, that we may hide them."

"We could be accused of impurity!" whispered my uncle. His face was covered in greasy sweat. "We live next door to the inn; they may think we are tainted!"

My father shook his head. "Purity of faith is yours alone, brother. Only you can speak for it, and the only one to whom you should ever speak of it is the god. Not to a priest who teaches you only from half of the Oracle's books."

"And *that* is the kind of talk that will get my daughters burned if they repeat it!" my uncle cried. "We are sheltering heretics!"

My father looked down. "If you are no longer happy to house my daughter and me, then we shall find another roof, or the god's own stars," he said. "We will not disturb the peace of this house, brother. But do you really wish to live in fear of those who claim to speak for the god who cooks our food, heats our homes, lights our lamps? The God in the

Flame shines in the eyes of your wife and daughters, and in the sky by day and night. That god speaks with two voices, male and female, has two faces, the sun and the moon, and spoke through an Oracle who wrote two books, not one. Nothing changes that."

My uncle turned on his heel and walked out. My aunt followed him. Once they were gone, my cousins crept in, their eyes wide in fear. To soothe them, my father had me continue to read from the forbidden half of the Oracle's texts, the Book of the Distaff. I stopped reading on my aunt's return.

"He went to the temple, to witness Fadal's burning. He fears what they would say if he was not there, but he did not say to send the girls to the hidden room," she said, sinking down onto a pillow. "He hears what you say, brother, but he has lived in this town all his life. The temple priesthood is strong here. Until you came, the wandering priesthood was represented only by your letters and our own readings of the forbidden texts."

"Should we go to the hidden room now?" asked my oldest cousin, her voice trembling. "I hate it, but if they come testing . . ."

"They would not dare, my treasure," my aunt said. "They must not dare. Surely even they know that to burn the children of respectable citizens . . . There are reasons it has not been done for so long."

"A girl," my youngest cousin said, amazed. "A girl, dressing as a man. Why would anyone want to do that?"

"What of his companion?" asked my father. "The

strange fellow, Qiom, did I hear his name was? Has anyone told him?"

"If he is wise, he has fled. Otherwise they will burn him," said my aunt.

Since it was time to cook lunch, my father went to sit in the kitchen with us. My uncle found us there. He was ashen, as if he had seen his world unmade.

"It was the other one, the stranger Qiom," my uncle said as he sat at the kitchen table. "He ripped the doors from the temple. He beat every man who tried to lay hands on him. He killed the priest by throwing him into the wall. Then he took Fadal, and he ran from the town before they could close the gates." He mopped his face with the wet cloth my aunt brought for him. "No man can run so fast! No man could have ripped the temple doors from their hinges! It is a sign from the God in the Flame! A sign, that he sent this creature to save this woman!"

"But the god has never spoken in such a fashion before," said my father gently. "Brother, compose yourself. Breathe with the quiet strength of your wife and daughters. See how they wait? They do not spend themselves in panic."

My cousins and I rolled our eyes and my aunt smiled. My father's idea of womanhood was idealized. He always forgot my mother was not above screaming if she saw a furred spider or panicking if a temple priest looked at her the wrong way.

Sometime after lunch the greatest piece of news came, brought by other men who shared readings in the forbidden texts with my uncle and aunt. The temple had burned down. Somehow wood had fallen into its great fire as Qiom rescued

Fadal, setting the place ablaze. Now many of the people of Hartunjur asked each other if the god whose sole text was the Book of the Sword would have let his temple be destroyed by a creature who came to save a woman who had dressed as a man. Hearing that a wandering priest who taught the forbidden texts was in the town, they came to hear what the temple priests had not taught them.

My father talked to the men about what the temple priests left out of the Oracle's writings. He taught them about the Oracle's wise wife, who was his first councilor. He told my favorite story, one almost forgotten in the lands where the God in the Flame and the Oracle were supreme, of the Oracle's oldest daughter, the general who had dressed in armor to defend her father's temple city.

At last my father's cough returned ferociously. As the healer brought him a cup of syrup, my father waved to me. "Teky, read to them," he said, his voice hoarse. "Read to them from the Book of the Distaff." He raised his voice to the men. "This is not in your copies of the Oracle's Books," he said, and coughed for long moments. He swallowed a mouthful of syrup, then continued, "It is this the temple priests do not want you to hear. Tekalimy will read to you."

"A woman!" someone in the back of the room cried. "Reading!"

My father half-rose from his cushions. "Have you heard nothing of what I have said?" he demanded. His cheeks were flushed with his rising fever. I reached out to calm him, to press him back down to his cushions, but he shook off my hand. "Without our women we are only half of ourselves! If our women are unclean, we are half-unclean! Teky! Read!"

I stood, trembling, the book open and heavy in my hands. Never had I read before so many men. Never had I seen so many angry pairs of eyes, all burning me where I stood. Who was I? Would someone here betray me when the Council of Priests sent a new man here?

Then I remembered my words just that morning to Fadal. Under the black veil that covered my mouth, I smiled. Who could identify me? I was another set of black veils among a town full of them. Away from my father, I was simply another pair of eyes, another pair of feet.

As for those men's eyes burning me, they touched only my veils. I was safe inside them, looking out. They could no more know what was in my heart than they could know my face.

I began to read the Oracle's words. "'If you look at the god and see only the sun, you see only half the god,'" I read. My voice shook, then steadied. I had been reading these words all my life. "'If you look at humanity and see only man, you see only half of your soul. Attend to women as you attend to men, with heart and mind intent.'" From the corner of my eye I could see my father nod as, coughing softly, he drank the rest of his medicine.

I read until he raised his hand, then closed the book. As he leaned forward to question the men on what they had heard, I retired with the book in my hands, as I often did. I went no farther than my aunt's kitchen. She was the only one there. "Come," she said, and took me to a stable down the street. There I found women and girls, the families of the men who talked now with my father. They, too, had come for learning, summoned by my aunt and cousins, who had prepared them for me. They, too, were shaken by the events in the temple. While I had read to the men, they had listened in the shadows and outside the windows. Now my aunt and my cousins gave out slates and chalk or worn copies of The Book of the Sword: The Lessons of the Law.

"The Book of the Sword?" asked one newcomer, frightened. "Are you mad? It is forbidden to us!"

I opened the book to the Lesson of Family and read, "'Only by reading will the word of the God in the Flame blaze clearly in the eyes of all. If your wife does not read, you must teach her. It is your sacred duty, and the sacred duty of your wife, to teach your children to read. Without reading, we are all without light in the dark, without fire in the cold.'" I closed the book and said to the newcomer, "This is the beginning to the most important lesson in The Book of the Sword: the lesson of The Rights of Women Under the Law of the God. How many of you can read?"

They raised their hands. My aunt and cousins had been busy: half of them could. Now, without my telling them, those who could moved to share books with those who could not as I read the first lesson for all to hear. From the letters that made it up, the others would begin to learn to read, but they would also hear their rights as set out by the Oracle. Even temple priests would have to acknowledge them if these women petitioned the courts for their rights under The Book of the Sword.

"'If a woman shall bear a man's children and he divorces her, he is forbidden to turn her out of his house penniless. If he does so, she may appeal to the court of the temple,'" I read. I heard chalk squeak as the women wrote that down. "All men know this. The god did not wish us to be without power. The god did not tell the Oracle to make us powerless," I explained. Father did not know I used the Lessons of the Law. I was supposed only to teach them to read. But he had never said what I was to use, and he could hardly quarrel with how I taught when he was not there to hear me.

I did not say more than that. I had to be careful. I had to let them think about the words, and I had to leave time for them to concentrate on forming the letters. I also knew that I could not press them too hard. Four years ago a woman had complained to her husband that I was trying to turn the women against the men. That was when my mother was still alive. She was too shy to teach, but she had whipped me over the woman's complaint.

"Our lives are on the razor's edge!" she had scolded me after the beating. "Because you are clever, because you are the pearl of his eye, your father trusted you, but you go too far! You cannot bully people into change, Teky! We are like our land, with the very stones to serve us for veils. Rain change on us too much, too fast, and we do not drink it up. We flood, destroying everything in our way. Your lectures will bring death on us, on your father and me, and on you. Now. Will you teach them to read, just read, or will I tell your father you cannot be trusted with our lives?"

But don't you *see*? I had wanted to ask her then, and I still asked her ghost. Don't you see that the women need to know what is there? That The Book of the Sword already holds rights that the temple priests have to respect? I could show the women how to stand up for their rights.

But I bowed to my mother and told myself I would just take more time to make the women see how to do it, that was all. Not push them. Not lecture them. Only read to them what was in the Book and trust them to think about it, as my father trusted me to teach them to read. As even my mother trusted me to teach them again, after a while. As she trusted me to look after my father.

I crouched to help a girl perfect her writing of the word "law." My problem was that I wanted to help them *all,* my father, the women, the girls. They would have laughed at me, had they known. One sixteen-year-old girl, not even married, they would say. You can't even look after yourself!

Fadal would say that. Fadal, who thought my veils were chains. Poor Fadal, whose only way to deal with being a woman was to try to be something she was not.

As the shock of the temple's destruction grew in the town, the attendance at my father's lessons grew every day, and so did the attendance at mine. A week passed, then two. We had never stayed so long in one place. It worried and pleased me. A longer stay meant the chances were greater that those who ruled the temple priests in distant Kenibupur might hear of our activities. At the same time, the healer was able to banish most of that cough from my father's chest, which was all to the good. For the first time I saw the girls who started their first letters under my eye master their first short sentences. We could celebrate my oldest cousin's betrothal. I even dreamed of attending her wedding, but that was not to be. As the winds began to scour the mountain passes, word came that new temple priests were coming to serve the town again. My father took it as a sign to be on our way.

We left better provided for than we had been in years, three weeks after the day I talked to Fadal. Our donkey's packs were heavy. I carried my share of the weight, too. One of the men who had studied with us sent us to his family's village, where we would be welcome. He told us as well of caves along the road where we could shelter at night. It was like settling into a shabby, familiar pair of sandals.

I built the fire at the mouth of the cave that first night. Once it was going, my father helped me to cook supper, and he cleaned our dishes in the nearby stream. Afterward we sat in silence, watching the flames. Finally I asked him what I had so often asked as a child, "Do you see the God in the Flame?"

He sounded amused when he said, "I see the god in your bright eyes, Teky." After a while he sighed and remarked, "It is strange, to be traveling again, is it not?"

I nodded. "My aunt's home is a good place to live."

"I have been thinking. If something happens to me . . ."

I started to protest. Father held up his hand, his old signal for me to be silent. I hated it when he talked that way; he knew I hated it.

"If something happens to me, return to your aunt's house. She will arrange a good match for you, every bit as good as the one she arranged for your cousin." My father nodded as if he agreed with himself. "We talked about it. She knows what to do."

"Now, see here, my boy," I began in Omi Heza's old voice, thinking to joke him out of his decision.

He raised a hand. "Hush, Teky. This is no laughing matter." He took up The Book of the Distaff and began to read.

I continued to watch the fire, but instead of warmth, a creeping veil of cold eased up my back, my shoulders, and over my head and face. Go to my aunt's house, and wait to be married? When all I had done for the last five years of my life was this? Walk the roads of our country, talk to women and girls, men and boys, hear their stories, cook and eat with them, visit their homes, sew and weave with them, change their babies, and hold the hands of their grandfathers and grandmothers? I had cobbled sandals, made round bread, collected honey, milked cows and goats and sheep and even mares. In one village I had twisted rope; in others I helped to bring animals in from dust storms. In the mountains in the spring I had waded up to my waist in floodwater to save a child who had strayed. In stick huts in forests I had brewed medicines. In three cities I sold fruit and honey in the marketplace. In a hundred marketplaces, big and small, I studied with my parents and learned to dicker with merchants on my own. In my short sixteen years I had eaten hummus made at least thirty different ways. Sitting by this small fire with my back to a hollow in a hill, I could feel my world shrink to the size of a sun-dried brick house, of a village wall. To know only the same faces for the rest of my life, with only a light seasoning of new ones . . .

I think I slept where I sat, because the flames parted at their bases, opening like a teardrop to reveal orange coals that rippled with heat and bits of blue fire. Dreaming, I knew the god had come.

"Did you hear?" I asked the god as if he, she, were one of my cousins who had been sitting close by. "He just . . . he decided. He didn't ask me; he just decided. Why didn't he even tell me what he was thinking?"

"He is a man," said both halves of the god, woman and man. "He has never been stripped of his voice, so he does not know how it feels to be stripped of it, even a little. Now I, I understand it very well. I have been stripped of half of my voice for centuries of your time. My man voice thunders clearly—wrongly, sometimes, thanks to the priests who decided which words of my Oracle they would repeat—but clearly. But no one hears my woman voice anymore. I would like my woman voice back. You would like *your* voice back. And this man who loves you will never realize it. Don't you ever wonder who *will* realize it, Tekalimy?"

"Teky, Teky." My father was shaking my shoulder. "You are sleeping where you sit. Go to bed. I will bank the fire."

I looked up at him, blinking, my eyes hot and dry. They felt as if I had never closed them. "What if I do not want to go to my aunt and have a husband, Father?" I asked, my voice very tiny.

"Don't be silly," he said, kissing my cheek. "What else would you do? Go to bed."

I looked at the fire. If the flames had parted, they were joined again now.

As I unrolled my blankets and covered myself up, I admitted he had made a good point. What else would I do?

The next village already knew of the destruction of the

Hartunjur temple. As soon as the priest finished each night's lesson and banked the fire, many of the men who heard him came to the man who housed my father and me, to hear my father teach, to hear me read, and to talk with my father about what the reading meant. That first night, as I did in a strange town, I went to our host's wife. As always, I found her in her kitchen, having tea with friends. Hurriedly they fastened their veils. Among strangers, even women, we all kept our veils on during these meetings. We needed only one weak or frightened soul to report our true names and faces to the priests for there to be a burning that would be remembered for centuries.

"Excuse me," I said politely, keeping my eyes down, "but I know it is hard to hear at the windows and doors. There is no reason why your thirst should go unslaked while men drink. Would you like for me to read more of the Books to you?"

Someone gasped. They all drew back as if I were a viper.

"How did you know we listened?" my hostess demanded. She trembled all over.

I passed my hand across the veil over my mouth, the sign that showed I was smiling. "We survive in a man's world by learning all we can," I reminded them, just as I had reminded my father in my grandmother's voice. This was an old, old ritual for me. I followed it in every new village. "Knowledge keeps us ahead of them and better able to guide them, is it not true, my sisters? Will you not drink more from the Oracle's well of knowledge?" I asked, and raised the Books in my hand.

And so we fell back into our routine, which was the

same, but changed. The story of Qiom and Fadal raced ahead of us. It was autumn, then winter, but people traveled, just as my father and I traveled. Temple priests were more suspicious of newcomers as the story grew in its spreading. We no longer dared stay for more than a few days in each village, though those who came to hear us grew in numbers. For my father, the change was noticeable, though not startling. But for me . . .

For every three new men who came to hear my father, I met five new women and girls. In some villages, it might be seven and eight more women than I might have seen before. In December we stayed in a town for ten days, the longest stay since Hartunjur. I remembered it not only because a man and five boys came to hear *me,* leaving my father's lesson when I did, but because it was there that my father's cough returned.

We left the town because a delegation from the temple court at Kenibupur was expected to arrive within days, to honor the town by celebrating the Longest Night festival there. We dared not stay with so many temple priests on their way. Instead, despite my father's worsening health, we took the road to the next village. I had thought the boys in that place would be different. They would not be so bored, or so used to following their mothers, as to be curious about my lessons. I was wrong. Two grown men from that tiny village joined three boys to hear my teaching on the Oracle's law concerning their wives and daughters.

We traveled on three days later, with the priest practically snuffling at our host's door. My father's voice was ragged and cracked from coughing, despite the good healer who had attended him there. Putting her herbs and medicines away, she had shaken her head at my father. When he glanced over to see if I had seen, I pretended to do something else. He *must* get well, I told the god. Who will teach them if he dies?

That night I heard the god's voices again and saw the field of veiled women. "What do you see?" asked the god.

"People who can do nothing for my father," I said in bitterness, and turned my back on them.

"Then you are blind," said the god.

Two villages later, I was teaching the women, all of their children, and an old man about a daughter's right of inheritance when a boy came to fetch me. My father had lost his voice as he was teaching. "You will answer the questions for me, Teky," he whispered in my ear.

"I think you should stop!" I whispered back, frightened. His chest clattered softly like dried leaves stirred by the wind. "You are ill, you should rest."

"When will another of us wandering priests come?" he whispered. "You will tell them my answers *now.*"

"Why do the temple priests keep The Book of the Distaff from us?" a man wanted to know when my father made a sign for another question. "Why risk offending the God in the Flame and the Oracle's spirit?"

"Because people who are ignorant are more easily led," I replied, making my voice as strong as I could. They could not see me waver. "The god has not punished them, so they believe the god will never punish them. And they know that fear makes people easily led. If they teach you that your women are devilish forces, mysterious and not to be trusted, you will fear them, and you will turn to your priests to protect you from these veiled creatures."

"Is that your father who speaks?" an old man demanded angrily. "Or is it you, taking advantage of a sick man?"

My father raised his hands. He pointed to himself.

"My father says that the words are his. *I* tell you that I have heard this answer many dozens of times," I replied as the other men chuckled. "Many men have asked it."

I had to give my lesson in reading and the law during the noon hour the next day. My father's voice came back for a short time that night, then failed. Once again he needed me to speak for him. The same was true of the third night.

The god came back and showed me the veiled women. "Wake up, Teky!" she said, he said, as one. "There are your sisters, your mothers, your aunts, your cousins. What do you see?"

"People I can barely snatch the time to teach!" I cried. "People who have rights under The Book of the Sword that is in every temple! People who don't have to show the priests a Book they will get burned for possessing if they want justice!"

"So this is progress," the god told me. "But you have yet to give the simplest answer of all. It is truly there, in what you told Fadal, Teky. Only speak the answer that matters, and I will take you into my service. You will become my new Oracle, the one to speak my truth completely."

"I don't want to be an Oracle," I muttered. "I just want to teach my sisters their rights under the law."

A hand on my shoulder joggled me awake. "I am sorry,"

our host whispered. He did not have to say more. Somehow the temple priest suspected what we did in his village. Each night I packed our bags in readiness. As our host helped my father to dress, I pulled on the rest of my clothes and loaded our donkey. Our host led us out a hidden gate, giving us directions to the next village.

We walked until the sun was up, then stopped to drink hot tea from our flasks. My father turned his face up to the sun and smiled. "Blessed is the flame," he said. "Blessed are we who can see by its light." Then he began to cough, until he couldn't walk. In the end, I took a number of our belongings on my back, and he rode our donkey, to save his strength.

To my fear, the next village was two days' travel down the road. Snow caught us at noon, slowing us down. It was well after dark when we reached the small hut that had been set up for the wandering priesthood. By then I had been forced to give my father poppy to ease the pain of his coughing. He was spitting up blood. Worse, when we reached the hut, I found he could not rest lying flat. He could not breathe. The healers had warned me, had said that only a great wizard could heal him when he got this ill. I arranged our packs until he could doze sitting up. "Drink," I said, offering him a cup of the brewed medicinal tea.

My father opened his eyes.

"Mother?" he whispered, his beautiful voice only a ghost in his chest.

So I put on Omi Heza's voice for him, becoming my grandmother to give him poppy and broth, to read his favorite parts of both Books to him, until he slept. Then I sat next to him and the fire, holding his too-hot fingers to my cheek as I watched the flames.

This time I do not think I was sleeping. The flames danced for me, then pulled apart at the base to form a teardrop-shaped opening floored in embers.

The god spoke again in its twined voices. "Teky, three times we have asked, and three times you have given the wrong answer. One more chance do we give you to enter our service, to return the balance to our faithful. If you truly wish to carry on the work you have begun, then what do you see?"

And there they were, tall, short, plump, dark, pale, old and young and in between, a mass of black, with eyes so bright I thought they might burn me. Last time the god had said the answer lay in my talk with Fadal. Poor Fadal, who believed the veils were chains, until I made him—her—reconsider it, briefly, at least.

I looked at those fields of women, my sisters.

"Power," I said.

The teardrop opening to the fire's heart collapsed. I lifted my head. The heart was dark, as if something great had drawn the life from the fire.

The life was gone somewhere else, too. My father's hand was cold against my cheek.

Through that long night I wept and said the prayers. I rebuilt the fire to sew his shroud, and the next day I built his pyre and sent his spirit flying in the flames to the god we both loved. I gathered wood to replace all I had used, then went back inside to decide what I could do with my life.

It was nearly midnight when I remembered my father wished me to return to my aunt.

"I don't want to go," I said aloud. The donkey snorted and glared at me.

I looked at the fire and remembered the god had said she—he—would help me. The next village did expect a wandering priest. There had been female wandering priests before, but . . . I looked at my trembling hands: a girl's smooth, young hands. Then I considered the power of the veil and my last words to my father, spoken in my grandmother's voice.

I had a bit of mirror in one of my packs. I scraped some ash from the hearth onto a plate and considered the look of age.

Two days, and much practice, later, I let a young man help me up onto a platform my hosts had set for me in their barn. "Is that all right, Omi Heza?" he asked me nervously. I had wrapped myself in my grandmother's name like an extra veil, for strength.

I looked at a sea of male faces. It was so familiar, and yet it was not, because my father was not behind me.

"You cannot teach us!" cried some man. "You are a woman!"

"And if you were my grandson, I would give you my cane for disrespect!" I cried. Suddenly light spilled all around me, and other voices, a woman's and a man's, spoke entwined around mine. "Do you doubt I speak with the god's voices? Will you walk farther from the true flame?"

As silence spread—as the men knelt, as that dreadful light began to fade—I said in my own, old-woman voice, "And bring the women and girls in here. I am too old to go on teaching once to the men and boys, and once to them. From now on, I teach all together, as the balance is meant to be."

Three days later, with a thirteen-year-old boy to be my new companion, I set forth, bound for the next village. I rode my donkey, as befitted my age.

Nawat

In the Copper Isles, a tale is told of a crow who fell in love with a mortal woman and changed to human shape, as all crows can change, for her. Their love was sealed in the fire and blood of the Great Revolution that carried Queen Dovasary Balitang to the throne of the Isles. In that time crows, humans, and the black globe-creatures called darkings joined the rebel armies. Together they restored the native humans called raka to rule over their islands once more. This crow and his human love stood at Queen Dovasary's left hand, where all secrets were kept.

Some secrets reveal themselves after a handful of months. At the usual time following that revelation, Nawat Crow held one of his shrieking wife, Aly's, hands as she gripped an arm of the birthing chair with the other. Nawat was so tense that feathers kept popping from his human skin, which made the midwife uneasy. Aly, who usually noticed such things, had a mind only for her own efforts. With each strong pain she screamed, "I don't want eggs! I don't want eggs!"

Since humans came inconveniently arrayed with arms, legs, and a head, all of which might get stuck as they left their laboring mother, Nawat thought that any woman would be glad to birth a nice, well-shaped egg. Aly had never come to see his point of view. Once, in her sixth month, as he tried to explain it yet again, she had vomited on an expensive silk rug. After that she had forbidden him to discuss the subject.

Now, in a lull between pains, she settled herself in the chair, looked up at him, and plucked a feather from his temple. "Ow!" Nawat cried. He rubbed the sore spot. "Don't pull out big feathers, Aly!" He showed her the blood on his fingers. "It may not seem dangerous to you just now, but this would be serious if I was crow-shaped!"

Her face was red and dripping sweat, her hair soaked through. She waved the feather at him, tears rolling down her cheeks. "You're half-changed. You don't want to be with me. You want to go back to being a crow. You think I'm sweaty and ugly and horrible"—she began to sob—"and I *am*!"

Ah, thought Nawat, this. Pregnancy had not been kind to his dear one. He wrapped an arm around her shoulders, ignoring her halfhearted attempts to shove him away. "You are so beautiful, as beautiful as sunrise and sunset," he whispered. Holding the fingers of his free hand like a beak, he groomed her limp reddish blond hair with them. "I would not trade being your husband for all the sparkly things in the Isles. I will not return to crow shape and leave you. I—"

The groan began deep in her chest, deeper than any of the cries before. The raka midwife, Mistress Penolong, looked up from between Aly's legs. "Now then, girl, do your work," she said, her black eyes sharp. "Push."

"No eggs," Nawat heard his love mutter as she braced herself. He got in position to help her. "No eggs no eggs no *eggs . . .*"

She bellowed, her face turning purple. Nawat propped her up, silent, holding her tight.

"Here's a crown," the midwife said.

Aly tried to sit up straight against the back of the chair. "Is it an egg crown?"

Mistress Penolong snapped at Aly, "Give over these fantasies and *push*!"

Aly pushed. Nawat held her up, his eyes on her face more than her body. He had not confessed any of his fears to Aly, who had plenty of her own. She was the talker of the two of them. That amused him, because her work required that she keep so many secrets. She had to be the most chattery spymaster in all the Eastern Lands, without revealing anything important to anyone but Nawat or the queen. And it was only to Nawat that she had spoken her fears of dying in childbirth, as so many women did.

Not that she looked as if she might die today. If Nawat had to wager on such a thing, he would bet that Aly would kill the Black God of Death if he came for her at this moment.

"Now," ordered the midwife. "Now, now . . ."

Aly roared, the midwife shouted in triumph, and a baby's howls rose above both. "Finally!" Aly cried with relief.

Nawat reached for the cloth soaking in the basin and used it to wipe the sweat from the back of Aly's neck. She was relaxing now, a satisfied look on her face. Mistress Penolong was passing their child to her assistant, who did something with her finger, then with cloths. The bundle wailed over the indignities of birth.

The midwife smiled up at Aly and Nawat. "My lady, my lord, you have a daughter," she said.

Her assistant handed the mite to Aly, who cuddled her. "Have you a name?" the young woman asked Aly. Nawat brushed Aly's cheek with his hand. This they had settled long ago. Aly smiled up at him, though the smile quickly turned to a grimace. "Ochobai," she said. "For a teacher and leader who left us for the Peaceful Realms."

Mistress Penolong and her assistants bowed their heads and drew the sign of life on their breasts. In raka tradition it was bad luck to name a child exactly after someone living or recently dead, but everyone would know the baby's name was a tribute to a leader of the recent revolution.

Honor to the mage Ochobu aside, Nawat thought his chick was very ugly, all red and crumpled. He saw no pin-feathers, beak, or claws on Ochobai. Perhaps those things would come later.

"You don't like her," Aly said accusingly.

Nawat reached a finger down to Ochobai. "I don't know her," he explained.

His daughter gripped his finger with one hand, hanging on hard. Something inside Nawat turned warm. Ochobai had a crow's grip. She would not drop any prize she found. And this was not just a crow's hold that she had. He smiled at Aly. "She holds on like you."

He reached inside the child with his crow senses and

instantly knew something that only he could teach the nestli—the *baby,* he reminded himself. Aly stirred on the birthing chair, her face twisting in discomfort again. "May I take her?" Nawat asked.

Aly nodded. "I didn't think afterbirth felt like another baby," she told the midwife as Nawat lifted Ochobai from Aly's arms.

Nawat took the child to the window and opened a shutter. "You are too young to know," he murmured, "but I will help you. When our people relieve ourselves, we go to the edge of the nest and eliminate *outside* it." He undid the newborn's blankets—they were far too tight—and her diaper, draping them over his shoulder. None of the women noticed: they were busy around Aly. They did not see Nawat hold Ochobai outside the window as the infant peed.

The crows of the great flock of the city, perched in every tree within view, cawed wildly to welcome Nawat's child. Then they saw that he held a human infant, not a nestling. Immediately they went quiet. Nawat sensed them talking silently with one another, but he had more on his mind than the disapproval of the Rajmuat flock.

"Good," he said to Ochobai when she was done. He wiped her with the cloth he'd used on her mother, and then did up her diaper again. He was grateful that it was an ordinary day in the Isles—hot and sticky. Without feathers, his tiny daughter might have caught cold. "I'll tell the servants what to do," he said as the baby waved her hands. "There's no reason they can't teach you properly, even if they aren't crows."

Aly let out a cry. "What's wrong? This *hurts!*"

"You know we spoke of twins, my lady," the midwife told her calmly. "Here comes your second child."

Aly grimaced. "I was just praying it would be one, despite everything. My mother's bloodline runs to twins. Time to stop whining, then."

Nawat looked at Ochobai. The little one waved her arms blindly, her eyes squeezed shut. Shouldn't this nestling want grubs or insects right now? Inside her he felt the beginnings of hunger. He reached into his breeches pocket and found a worm he'd been saving for Aly. Although she had refused the insects he'd brought when he first courted her, Aly hadn't been able to get enough shovel-headed worms or white-spotted caterpillars during her pregnancy. Nawat had smuggled a few into the birthing chamber in case his wife got hungry.

He dangled the worm over Ochobai's face as he walked back to the birthing chair. If the little one reached for it, Nawat would chew it up for her. That was his plan, but between muscle contractions his love saw what he was doing.

"Nawat!" she screeched as she thrust a second child out of her womb. She reached out and seized the worm. "Goddess's great—*heart,* what are you doing?!"

"Nestlings are hungry," he explained. Their new boy was even bloodier and more wrinkled than Ochobai. Nawat smiled at Aly. "Junim has come," he said, using the name they had chosen for a son. "You had better take Ochobai. I must carry Junim—"

But he was too late to take the boy to the window. Before Mistress Penolong had cut the cord that tied him to his mother, little Junim had peed in her face.

"This is common," one assistant explained to the horrified Aly. "It will happen again."

Not if *I* am near, Nawat thought, eyeing Junim. "Our kind does not pee within the nest," he said aloud.

Another assistant cleaned the boy as she smiled at Nawat. "These are *human* babies," she said, as if Nawat were not very clever. "It's different for them."

Ochobai screeched, her small face screwed up in fury. Nawat felt her sharp need to eat and looked at his wife. "You took the only food I had," he said with reproach.

Aly reached for Ochobai, sitting up on the stool. "She's a *baby,* not a nestling," she replied. "Human babies *nurse.*"

"I forgot," Nawat replied as he gave their daughter to her. "I have seen it, but it looks uncomfortable. Bugs are much easier."

Aly shook her head at him. "Crow," she said lovingly. She cradled Ochobai in her right arm and guided her nipple to the infant's mouth. Ochobai latched on to her mother, which drew a yelp from Aly. After a moment Aly said, "I thought this didn't hurt. It's hurting. Not like the pains, but—ow!" Aly tried to take the baby from her breast. That proved to be even more painful than leaving her there, because Ochobai would not let go.

The assistant who had told Nawat that his children were human left the room.

"You are too much like your namesake," Aly whispered to her daughter. Then she winced again. "She was the most obstinate old woman I ever met." Aly gasped and glared at the midwife, who was still crouched between her legs. "Mistress Penolong, you said the afterbirth wasn't so bad! Don't I have enough problems at *this* end?"

The midwife was frowning. "The afterbirth is *not* supposed to give you such pain." She felt Aly's abdomen.

Ochobai spat out her mother's nipple and began to wail, her tiny voice piercing Nawat's skull. Aly looked at her breast. "No wonder it hurt!" she said, pointing. "I've a blood blister there. A big one!"

"Your little one must not have gotten the whole nipple into her mouth," the midwife said. "You will need to have that breast healed before you can nurse there painlessly." She reached into Aly's body between her legs.

Nawat looked away. He was not shy, but he felt there were some places that hands did not belong, not up to the forearm. He was already unnerved enough by Aly's casual attitude toward her nakedness among all these strangers. Of course, he thought, if I had spent a day with nearly all of my openings in plain view to a room full of persons, maybe I would not care by now, either.

The assistant who had left returned with a raka wet nurse Aly had spoken to weeks before. Nawat searched his memory for the newcomer's name: Terai, that was it.

"Ah, she didn't have her mouth in the right place," Terai remarked the moment she saw Aly, the blood blister, and the screaming infant. "Plenty of them do that, my lady. I've an ointment for that blister that will mend it."

The sarong over Terai's bosom was stained with leaking milk. She popped a large brown breast from her clothes and walked over to Ochobai and her parents. "Now I'll take the little one," she said, holding out her hands. Though Ochobai and the lad Junim were both crying loudly now, Nawat heard Terai's voice clearly. "I know you didn't truly want a wet nurse, my lady—"

"I wanted to nurse my baby myself," Aly wailed. Despite her protest, she was already handing Ochobai up to Terai.

The woman nodded to the screaming Junim. "Give that one a try," she advised. "On the other breast." She put Ochobai to her own nipple. Immediately the baby began to suck.

"Traitoress," Aly murmured, settling Junim in her hold. "Oh!" Junim had found her nipple without any help from anyone and was nursing with determination. Aly kissed her son's head in gratitude. Then she murmured, "With twins, I suppose I'll need help. Mother said she needed a wet nurse for my twin and—Hag's sacred *toenails,* that hurt! That's just as bad as having the babies!" she shouted at Mistress Penolong.

Nawat let out a squawk. "Is it the feeding? I thought you said they didn't have teeth as fledglings!" he accused, glaring at the midwife's people, then at his son. He reached to take Junim from Aly, using his crow senses to discover if the infant had ill intent toward his mother.

Aly said, "It wasn't him, love, it was—" She pointed at her still-splayed legs and Mistress Penolong.

The woman's attention was focused on Aly's birth canal. "More oil," she ordered her assistants. "Clean the blade *now,* and we'll need more cloths!" She wrenched the bottle of oil from the girl who offered it to her and poured it over her hands. The third assistant had already emptied and rinsed the basin where Junim had taken his first bath, and was filling it again with water.

"Stop your screeching, if you don't want that baby you're feeding to yell all his days!" the midwife scolded, looking up at Aly. "You may be the queen's left hand and her good friend, but it seems to me you don't know monkey *sampah* about the important things. Didn't your mother teach you to keep a serene heart as you nurse?"

To everyone's surprise except Nawat's, who had heard many stories of Aly's lioness of a mother, Aly broke out into a great, ringing belly laugh. Her laugh went on and on. Finally she managed to gasp, "My mother is as serene as a *volcano*!" before she laughed again. Now the midwife, the assistants, and Terai were laughing, or giggling, as their natures let them. Nawat was glad to see his mate laugh in that way she had when she had been working too hard and worrying too much. She would shed a hundred cares in such an outburst.

He also saw that Junim and Ochobai now slept contentedly against the breasts that had fed them. He reached over to stroke Junim's head, since the boy was closest, and smiled at little Ochobai. Aly stiffened against him with a gasp, whispering words she normally used far from the proper women who worked here in the queen's wing.

"*Here's* what's been causing this trouble!" Mistress Penolong said with pleasure. "Good thing you've got a wet nurse after all, my lady!" She lifted up a small, wriggling body that had a wet, lacy white veil over its face. "This one will be a seer, with this caul," she said as her assistants whispered prayers to the Mother Goddess. Gently the midwife cut the caul away from the infant's face, until her chief assistant could take it. Looking at Aly, the midwife said, "You have another daughter. I believe you are done now, save for the afterbirth."

Aly looked back and up at Nawat. She seemed pleased and alarmed. "What other names did we think about? I don't remember."

Nawat smiled and smoothed her sweat-soaked hair back from her face. They had chosen several names when Aly continued to fret about laying eggs. Three had been dedicated to close friends killed in the recent revolution. "Ulasu," he reminded her.

"Ulasu," Aly said. She let an assistant place her newest daughter in her free arm after the umbilical cord was cut and tied off by Mistress Penolong.

Junim was done feeding. Now an assistant took him to the long table at the side of the room. Nawat had a hand on Ulasu, checking that the child did not subject her mother to a bath of infant pee. The most he felt in this newest nestling was her confusion about the thing Aly wanted her to do. "I'm trying to feed you," Aly whispered. Nawat felt a hand in the pocket where he kept the worms. He turned his head and pretended not to notice as Aly quickly ate a handful.

Nawat *did* see that the assistant who had taken Junim had not only placed a diaper on the boy, but was wrapping him snugly in a blanket, top to toe.

"Stop that!" Nawat cried. Angry as he was, he did not forget to wait until Aly was sitting up before he removed his support of her back. Only then did he stalk over to the table. "What is this? He has to flap his wings! If you bind him tight like this, you risk breaking the bones! We're not made like you!" He snatched Junim from the assistant and began to pull at the snug blankets.

"But everyone swaddles babies," the assistant said. "It's good for them!" She looked at Ochobai. "You took off her blankets!"

Nawat glared at her. "No wonder humans never grow feathers or wings, if you bind your children when they are born."

"Nawat," Aly called.

He turned, the boy in his hold. Junim waved his fists as he smacked his lips. Nawat's anger did not seem to disturb the boy, any more than Nawat's stripping away of his wrappings upset him. Ochobai, however, was waking up in Terai's arms. She was unhappy. She was telling all of them that she was unhappy. "Aly, you cannot let them cripple our children!" Nawat called over Ochobai's howls. "One day he will take crow shape. If the bones shift while he is swaddled, they will break!"

The midwife rose to glare at Nawat. "I let you into this birthing room out of courtesy."

"She is my mate and these are our nestlings," retorted Nawat. "Crows need no midwives."

Aly sighed. Terai handed Ochobai to the shortest of the midwife's assistants and drew Ulasu out of Aly's grip. Without the baby to hold, Aly leaned forward and rested her head on her hands.

"Don't you move your behind from that chair, my lady!" snapped the midwife. "You've got the afterbirth yet to come. A brawl in this room won't help with that!"

Aly looked up as she sat back once more. Nawat instantly recognized the look in her eyes. Aly had so many faces that even he had trouble keeping track of them all, but this one he knew well. This was Aly-Smoother-of-Feathers, smiling and serene, with a bag of tricks behind her back. "Mistress Penolong, my husband is a crow. He has been so from birth. He has only been human since meeting me, and he changes to crow shape often to lead his war band of hunters. We did speak of this before, you and I. Is it not possible that Nawat may know more about our children, about how they are inside, than we do? I thought you had understood that, when we talked about our arrangements."

Nawat believed that such a talk, given in Aly's warmest voice, with her kindest smile, would have melted anyone, even when Aly was splashed with blood and whatever else was involved in giving birth.

Mistress Penolong, though, could have been made of the strongest oak. "My lady, my lord, I have helped more children into this world than I care to remember, and I say, if these little ones are not swaddled, they will grow crooked in their limbs!"

Aly nodded, wearing her sympathy face. Nawat understood that she had to conduct a long negotiation. In the meantime, he could tell his son had to pee again. While the assistants observed Aly, and Terai fed Ulasu and hushed Ochobai, Nawat carried Junim to the window so he could do what was necessary outside the nest. This time the watching crows made no sound at all. They had expected a human nestling and they did not like it. Nawat showed them a rude human gesture when Junim was done, then took his boy inside.

Aly got her way with Mistress Penolong after more debate. The triplets would not be swaddled. Nawat had never doubted that, not after his mate had turned her skills on the midwife. Aly was the realm's chief spy and mortal trickster, after all. Kyprioth, chief of the tricksters and cousin to the crows, had brought her here and made her his servant. Aly could persuade almost anyone of anything.

The youngest of the assistants was lighting the room's lamps when the mass of the afterbirth slid from Aly's womb and onto the cloth the midwife had laid underneath her. The midwife wiped Aly down with yet another oil. Once the afterbirth was placed in a bowl and set aside to be offered to the Great Mother, the assistants helped Aly to her feet and wrapped her in a sarong. One of them opened a door that had been closed the entire day. As the assistants helped Aly to the new door, the midwife held up a hand. The wet nurse, who cradled two of the infants, had not moved.

"Take your children to the nursery, Master Crow," ordered Mistress Penolong. A light seemed to come from her, a light as pale as the moon. "The cleansing bath is a matter for the mother, her attendants, and her goddesses. Men, even crow-men, are forbidden."

Aly looked back over her shoulder. "It's all right, love," she said. Her hair, spilling out of its pins, was not its normal reddish sun color, but tangled and black with sweat, her face pale with strain. Black shadows circled her hazel eyes. To Nawat she was still the beautiful creature who had called to his heart one morning as he followed the trickster Kyprioth because he was bored. "It's all right," she repeated, returning the smile that had come to his face. "It's a human ceremony. I'm in good hands."

Nawat saw the assistants exchange smiles of their own. His Aly had a way of winning friends. He stepped back as the women passed through that open door. The midwife closed it behind them all, but not before Nawat had seen that pale light still around her, lighting up the hall beyond.

"Lord Crow?" Terai asked as Nawat wondered which gods were abroad that night. "Where is your nursery? I would like to set these young ones down. And I will need to send for my own child, and some clothes."

Nawat blinked. The nursery—was it even ready for two additional nestlings and the servants the queen felt Aly's household should have? "This way," he told Terai, leading her through the door that all of them had used that weary day. He still carried Ochobai, who had fallen asleep at last, a frown on her tiny face. The wet nurse had Junim and Ulasu in her arms. Ulasu was getting her second meal since her birth, while her brother napped.

Spotting a round shadow on the stairs, Nawat asked Terai, "What do you know of darkings?"

The wet nurse frowned at him. "They are said to be black bug gods that serve the queen. The Great God

Kyprioth gave them to Her Majesty to help her defeat the luarin masters."

The shadow halted and reared up on its bottom. "Not bugs!" it squeaked in outrage. "Bugs tasty snack! Darkings people!"

Nawat thought that Terai must be a very accomplished wet nurse. Though she was clearly startled and even backed up a step, the infants in her arms remained calm.

"They are still here," Nawat explained. "We hope you can live with them. They report to Aly all of the time."

Terai looked at the darking. "It looks like a cupful of dark wine."

"Wine not think or talk or spy," the darking replied. It looked up at Nawat with a head-knob it had shaped for itself. "Trick say nursery ready. Where Aly?"

"Aly is taking a bath. Tell Trick we're coming with babies, all right? And thank you," Nawat said with a nod. The darking shrank back into a ball and continued along its way.

"Are they all like that?" Terai asked uncomfortably.

Nawat smiled at her. "That one was quiet as darkings go. Just be firm with them."

As they climbed the stairs to their third-floor rooms, Nawat turned his thoughts to practical matters. He and Aly had chosen only one cradle, because they had a large, round bed made like a nest. If Aly had laid eggs after all, she could have kept them warm in their bed. Now they would need two more cradles for these human nestlings. Perhaps he might be able to talk Aly into placing them in one large cradle, like proper little crows, or even bringing them into the nest-bed. But there should be two more nursemaids in addition to the one Aly had already hired. Sadly, she was needed at her spying work and Nawat was often away from home.

Nawat asked Terai, "You said you have a child?"

She smiled at him. "My lord, how do you think I come to be in milk?" she asked. "You will need a second wet nurse, though, so we are never in danger of going dry. I know someone."

Here, at least, Nawat was on solid ground. "You must ask our door guard to escort you to Atisa in the morning," he explained. "Have you spoken with her yourself?"

Terai shivered. Everyone remembered Aly's lieutenant after a conversation with her, and everyone in the Crow household had to speak to Atisa at least once before they worked for Aly and Nawat. Only then would Aly meet with them and confirm Atisa's choices. No one lied successfully to Aly. She saw every falsehood, except those of the crow shape-changers. "Atisa said I was fit to be wet nurse to your family," Terai told Nawat when her shivers were done.

"Give her your recommendation for a second wet nurse," Nawat said. "My mate—my *wife* and I have enemies. Atisa is the one who ensures that none get close to us. You must tell her we will require two more nursemaids." Two more babies than expected would not only need more care, but also more bodyguards. Atisa would pick women who had fighting skills as well as the ability to burp babies. "She probably knows already, though," Nawat admitted.

They reached the door to the suite of rooms that housed the Crow family. The man and the woman in army uniforms at the door brought their spears and their bodies straight in a salute to their commander, though their eyes flicked over the three small bundles in undyed wool blankets. Then the woman reached for the grip on the double door and opened it. As Nawat and Terai passed through, Nawat heard the man, the human, whisper, "Congratulations, *lurah*." (Chief.)

The woman, who was a crow when needed, murmured, "What, no eggs?"

"I am a failure as a mate," Nawat joked in reply.

The door opened onto their sitting room. The queen had placed them in the royal tower itself. Nawat had approved. The height would be a good perch when the nestlings tried their wings. He knew that might take longer than usual, since they had entered the world in human form.

The thought made him stumble as he led the wet nurse across the sitting room. A single hop gave Nawat his balance again; a cheerful grin comforted Terai, who had gasped in alarm. Inside, Nawat was not at all cheerful or comforted. There had been a tug in that thought about his children taking longer to fly—or was it that they had been born human? He was not certain which idea had made him start, but the feeling itself was what his people called "the god pulling a feather." It was a warning of trouble to come, a signal for a crow to be vigilant. He looked at the infant in his arms. What danger would come to her and her nest mates?

Ochobai was awake. She looked vaguely in his direction, but he knew she only did so to look *somewhere.* When he was learning to be of use to Aly, the village mothers had let him watch over their young. They had told him how much their nestlings could see and what their noises and movements meant.

"That way is your mama's workroom," he said, as much for the wet nurse as for Ochobai. "No one goes there without Mama's permission. If anyone tries to enter, the door will burn their hands. Here is the bedroom that Mama and I share."

"What a strange bed!" Terai remarked. "The wood's carved like—"

"A nest," replied Nawat. "It was Aly's gift to me on our wedding." Inside the sheer insect curtains the blankets and pillows were arranged just as he and Aly liked them, in a circle around the mattress. Nawat was glad to see that everything was in order. Aly would be tired when she came home. She would want to fall into her usual comfortable bed.

Inside the nets, he saw darkness rise from a carved bowl set in the wall above the pillows. "Aly not screaming now?" asked Aly's personal darking, Trick. It had been unable to bear the sounds of childbirth.

"Aly is fine. She's taking a bath," Nawat assured it as Terai stared at him.

"Who are you talking to?" she wanted to know.

Nawat opened a mosquito curtain and pointed. "Trick, this is Terai. Terai, Trick."

"Hello, Terai," the darking piped.

"Trick is Aly's friend," Nawat explained. He ushered Terai to a second door. "And this," he said, "is to be your domain." They walked through the open door into a well-lit room. Nawat halted, startled again. Three nursemaids, one of them the woman Aly had chosen herself, were tidying the room. They arranged diapers on changing tables, set washbasins where they would be needed, put linens and drying cloths on the tall shelves, and in all ways prepared everything for the addition of more infants and servants than they had expected at first. Cots and chairs were already set up for the new staff.

The cradle situation was also under control. There was the cradle he and Aly had chosen, its insect net open. Rifou, one of Nawat's distant crow-cousins and a promising carpenter, had carved the name "Ochobai" on the beautifully decorated piece of teak that hung on the foot of the cradle. Another cradle, plainly made but of good wood, had a net already but waited for a carved piece that read "Junim." That lay on the floor next to Rifou. The crow-man, still in his uniform, sat cross-legged before the cradles, cutting the third sign. His glossy black hair swung forward, hiding his face. His hands, as brown as Nawat's, but scarred from learning the carpenter's work, carved Ulasu's name in graceful letters.

"Rifou, I give thanks, but it will do no harm if they do not have signs," Nawat said to his cousin. Rifou was several years older. Even though Nawat was his commander, Nawat always took care to be polite with him. "They have different-colored strings on their wrists."

"I needed something to do," Rifou muttered. "I'll work on *proper* nests for the new ones when I have finished these. Proper *human* nests, that is."

Nawat did not like the mix of tones of his cousin's voice or the darkness that lay over his spirit. Rifou's human mate, Bala, crouched beside him. Her eyes were red and swollen from weeping.

"Cousin, please look at me so I may introduce your new kindred to you," Nawat said. He wanted to see the face that Rifou was so determined to hide.

Rifou hesitated, as if he thought to refuse. Then he turned and stared up at Nawat. His face, too, was red and puffy, but not from tears. Ointment lent a greasy shine to several deep holes on his cheeks. They were peck marks.

"I am *kaaaakitkik,*" Rifou said without emotion. "I have been cast out. The great Rajmuat flock said I have become more human than crow."

The extra wet nurse had come. Aly, the nestlings, and the new staff were asleep when Nawat flew from his bedroom window out over Rajmuat. Damp air rose from the City of Ten Thousand Gardens, as some ambassador had named it to Queen Dove. Nawat would have traded all 5,354 of them—one test for crows in his war band was to count Rajmuat's gardens, even the little ones—for a week in the dry air of Lombyn, the northern island where he and Aly had met.

He had taken no escort. Even Aly did not know where he was bound, though unless she was entirely exhausted, more than he'd ever seen her, she at least knew he'd gone. This was crow business, though. After their rude reception of his nestlings—they left before Nawat had a chance to show them Ulasu—the Rajmuat flock had interfered with Nawat's adult flock, his war band. He needed to learn the exact nature of the problem that had brought them to meddle with another crow's people.

He found them in their roosting trees, on the hills that

overlooked the humans' great burying place. The moonlight gilded the forest of pale stone monuments below. The roosting trees grew tall outside the wooden fence on the graveyard. Priests renewed the spells that kept the crows from eliminating dung and urine onto the stones each month, but they knew better than to go near the trees themselves. Those were sacred to the crows. Each great flock had its own place, and bad things befell anyone who intruded upon it, so humans thought. However powerful the mage who cast the graveyard's protective spells, the magic never lasted much longer than a month. Kyprioth the Trickster favored his crows too much to order them to respect the human dead.

As Nawat flew over the ten-acre burial ground, the crows' sentinels cried out that another crow approached. Always in the last two years Nawat had been treated as flock, with no warning given when he came close to them. What had changed? Did he carry the scent of birth blood on his feathers, and had they mistaken it for some other kind of blood? Rather than risk an attack by the flock, Nawat landed at the top of the steps to the temple dedicated to Batiduran the Python, the raka god of the dead.

He waited there, taking deep breaths for calm. He did not like it here, and he did not want to be so far from home if Aly woke. Neither did he want to be courting the favor of these arrogant city crows if his nestlings were being diapered instead of learning to use the edge of the nest. At the same time, as the head of Rifou's flock, he owed a duty to his war-brother and cousin. The Rajmuat flock must see that they could not attack his people.

One advantage of the city's water-thick air was that it

carried sound quite a distance. The voices of crows passing word to the heart of the flock came to Nawat's ears, as did the sleepy complaints of Ahwess, their king, and Gemomo, their queen. Soon the treetops, black against the moonlit sky, seemed to rise like an incoming wave. The peak of the wave traveled on, until twenty crows flew into the open. Eighteen landed among the gravestones. Two settled on the open ground at the foot of the temple steps. Ahwess and Gemomo clacked their beaks at Nawat, angry that he had taken the high ground.

Nawat spread his wings to say he meant for them to remain below him. He stayed that way for a short time, then folded his wings and stepped back, opening a large square of space on the temple porch, should the other two crows want it.

The royal pair hesitated. They didn't want to accept Nawat's charity, but it was worse to stay below him. They opened their wings and flapped up, over the stairs, to land on the porch beside Nawat. Then they settled themselves, angrily poking their beaks among their feathers to ensure that none had gotten lost or out of order on the way.

Finally Gemomo settled. "What is it, outlander?" she demanded. "What news or schemes have you that will not wait for the sun?"

"Neither," said Nawat flatly. "Who gave you the right to judge Rifou? He is part of *my* flock, not yours. You harried him away. Your people pecked him. I want an explanation. I want satisfaction. I want an apology for Rifou." Each time he said "I want," he ruffled his feathers a little more, to make himself look more powerful than his opponents. Among humans Nawat was a tall, slender, well-muscled young man, not one to make anybody feel threatened. Among crows, his human muscles were an influence on his crow size. He was strong and powerful, more so than the aging Ahwess and Gemomo. He used that strength now for Rifou.

"Threaten as you like," Ahwess said, his voice gravelly and harsh. "You would be dead before you laid a claw on either of us. You and your company of misfits may call yourselves a flock if you like, but you fool no one! The true crow flocks may cast out any crow that has forgotten what it means to be one of our people."

"Look at Rifou!" Gemomo snapped. "Cutting wood instead of hunting food. He does not nest or roost. He teases no animals or humans. He does not molt or eat carrion. He has turned his back on his people. He was warned, and he ignored the warning. Once one flock casts him out, *all* will do so."

"He isn't alone!" cried one of the crows who had accompanied the monarchs. "That clutch *you* call a flock—they get more corrupt every day!"

"Silence," Ahwess called without looking at the offender. He eyed Nawat. "It was one thing during the war. Our cousin the god told us to fight at the side of the humans, to return the rule of this place to the brown-skinned raka, our other cousins. We did so."

"The war is over," Gemomo told Nawat. "The humans can do without us. We never needed to involve ourselves in their messes. But your people have not returned to their flocks."

"My war band still has work to do," Nawat said hotly. "Traitors continue to plot and rebel against the Crown. Sometimes my flock is the first to discover it. My humans and crows work beautifully together to get work and spying done!"

"Let what is human stay in human hands," Ahwess retorted. "What one flock casts out, all will cast out. Many of your crows are close to the point of no return, from crow to not-crow." He took off, flying back to the trees. The crows in the burial ground did not move, but waited for their queen.

She walked over to Nawat and slashed him with her beak. He jerked away, but the smack of her beak on his made his eyes water with pain. "Don't count on Cousin Kyprioth's favor protecting you," Gemomo said, her voice flat. "You are in the most danger with your human mate and nestlings. You are watched, Nawat. If you fail a crow's test, any test that makes a crow different from a human, you will never be part of a flock again. Not ours, not your family's in the north." She took to the air.

All of the Rajmuat crows returned to the roosting trees. Only when their noises softened to those of sleeping birds did Nawat seize the air with his wings and slowly climb into the sky.

The flock leaders' threat was a grim one. To the birds that lived in flocks, there was nothing worse than being outcast. Not to have the splendor of a thousand wings beating around him, not to have the certainty that he would be welcome in a gathering of crows . . . If any of his war band were cast out of the conventional flocks, if *he* were cast out, what family would they have? Would the war band, Aly, and the nestlings be enough? Would his human friends make up for the great community of the flock? It didn't seem possible. Suddenly he knew how Aly must feel, so far from her own family and country.

Softly he landed on his window ledge. He shoved the insect net aside and hopped lightly to his bedroom floor. Waiting there, gritting his teeth through the many discomforts of the change to human form, he listened for the sound of Aly's breathing. He did not hear it. Aly was not in their bed.

Despite the pain he knew would come, Nawat forced his body to complete the change in a hurry, holding wing-hands over his mouth to smother any pain sounds he made. Aching, he took the sarong he'd left on his side of the nest and wrapped it around his hips. Reaching up to brush his hair back from his face, he discovered that it was still half feathers. It would have to change on its own. He was too angry to work on any of the feathers that remained on his head and body. Queen Dove had told Aly's people, *Aly* had told her people, and *Nawat* had told them, to leave Aly alone after the birthing for a week at least. If they had brought some foolish piece of spy business to her, something Atisa or Taybur Sibigat could handle easily, they would get the rough edge of his tongue and assignment to the smallest rock visible at low tide.

Soft voices were speaking in the nursery, and low, flickering lights burned there. Nawat walked through the open door, ready to scold loudly enough to chase someone out a window. Four women turned to look at him in surprise. Three were seated on low stools: Terai and her wet-nurse friend, both with babies at their breasts, and the chief nursemaid. His wife sat on the floor, with pillows under her bottom and at her back so she could lean against the wall. She was nursing Ochobai. Nawat could tell, knowing the scents of each triplet. Terai was feeding not only Junim but also her own child, a lusty six-month-old who had arrived just before bedtime. The younger wet nurse, who had brought Terai's son to the palace, had Ulasu in her lap. She was the one who had lost a child, Nawat remembered.

The women and the infants were not alone. Darkings perched everywhere. They were on the edges of the triplets' cradles. Two more sat on Aly's bare feet, while one stretched a thumb-sized ball on a long neck from her shoulder. Its eyes, if it had possessed them, would have been fixed on Ochobai. A big man with curly, gray-streaked hair had taken one of the hardier chairs in the room. He wore the uniform of the queen's personal guard. Darkings rode his shoulders and sat in his lap.

"Forgive us," Taybur Sibigat said to Nawat in his softest voice. "They wouldn't leave me alone until they had seen the triplets for themselves, and the queen is beside herself with curiosity. Secret is showing them to her." The big man pointed to the darking on Aly's shoulder. "She will come herself tomorrow, of course, but she didn't want to bring a horde of courtiers here tonight."

"Many babies," piped one of the darkings on the cradles.

"Only three." Aly said it wearily. Nawat had the feeling that she'd said it several times already. "The bigger one belongs to Terai. As for triplets, it does happen, from time to time."

"Darkings never see before," another of the creatures remarked. "Only ducks have so many."

"Chickens," said another darking.

"Geese," added a third.

"Before we name all of the animals you know who have more than one child," Taybur said, his voice quiet but firm, "it is time to leave. These babies need to sleep."

As if to make a liar of him, Ochobai spat her mother's nipple from her mouth and began to wail. Instantly the other babies roused to do the same. Several of the darkings fled immediately, using the crack under the door to escape the alarming sound. Others remained to help, or so it seemed, though Nawat was not quite certain. He had realized long ago that darkings liked it when they confused bigger and stricter humans.

Aly tucked herself against the wall, as she often did when the darkings came in numbers and stayed to misbehave. Nawat often wondered if two years of working for Kyprioth the Trickster God had not left her with some of his nature, not that Nawat minded. She did enjoy havoc more than she had when they first met. The only sober thing she did now was hand Ochobai up to him.

Nawat took his firstborn. He knew immediately that she was about to release the results of that day's feedings. As the wet nurses and Taybur dealt with crying infants and cheering darkings, Nawat slipped the diaper from his older daughter and, leaning outside, held her beyond the window in the crook of one elbow. He remembered to keep her legs away from the noxious splatter of dung that exploded from her. Once she was finished and he had cleaned her off, he set her naked in her cradle.

The wet nurses and the freshly roused nursemaids did not appreciate the darkings' presence. That was to be expected. Although there were more of the blobs than there had been when they joined the rebellion two years before, many palace residents did not know when they had seen one. Like Terai, they usually mistook the darkings for shadows or spots. The discovery that they liked mischief after dark was not a happy one.

Some of the darkings chose to try their skills in the nursery. By the time they had arranged things with the women, fetched clean linens, avoided Taybur as he gathered up those who wished to leave, and kept everyone's attention, Nawat had carried Ulasu, then Junim, to the window. As Nawat placed his son in his cradle, he whispered to the closest darking, "Thank you."

"Always help Aly and Nawat," the darking whispered cheerfully. "Human females don't like window messes?"

Nawat shook his head.

"We help," the darking told him. "You see."

Thus twenty or so darkings remained when Taybur kissed Aly's cheek and left. Normally the big captain would have shaken Nawat's hand, but Taybur's arms and hands were fully occupied by gleeful blobs who chattered as he left the room. Secret, the queen's darking, had pride of place on Taybur's head.

"They really are safe?" asked the younger wet nurse. Her eyes were on the darkings.

"Far safer than most humans," Aly said. She drew her legs under her and pushed away from the wall, trying to stand. Nawat went to her and picked her up carefully, remembering that she was sore. Aly looked into his face. "I *can* walk, you know," she chided. "Farm women are out working in the fields the day after they give birth."

"But I like to carry you," Nawat said, ignoring the nurses' giggles as he bore Aly to their nest in the other room. Someone—the youngest of them from her step—placed a lamp on a table, then closed the door behind her. Nawat eased Aly from her gaudy silk robe and placed her in the nest, behind the insect curtains.

"I did not frighten you, being away when you woke?" he asked as he blew out the lamp and shed his sarong.

"Why should you?" she asked with a yawn. "You're out often. You did worry me when you came back. Is everything all right?"

"All is well," he lied. She had turned on her side, away from him, so he could tell untruth to her back, as he could not lie to her face. Aly's magical Gift for seeing falsehoods was often a problem but not, happily, tonight.

Trick, now a long rope with a head at the end, dropped down from the ornately carved bowl that was its home. "No more screaming-Aly?" it wanted to know. "No more hurting-Aly?"

"No more," Aly replied sleepily. "We have babies now, Trick. Three of them."

"But no hurting-Aly," the darking repeated stubbornly.

"Hurting-Aly's screams hurt Trick's heart." The moment Aly had begun labor, Trick had vanished. Normally the only time Trick would let itself be separated from Aly was at night.

"All better," Aly told it with a happy sigh. "Do you even have a heart, Trick?"

"Don't know." Trick dropped onto the rim of the nest, then to the floor. "Going out," it said cheerfully. "See babies. Talk to darkings."

"Be careful," Aly said, as she always did.

Nawat waited until a plop by the door told him the darking was gone before he asked, "Aly?"

"Hm?" She was nearly asleep.

He cuddled her, wrapping one arm under the still-surprising curves of her chest. "Would you love me if I was not a crow? If I had no flock, if I was outcast?"

Her chuckle moved through her flesh like ripples in a pond. "Nawat, you would always be a crow. Even if you were frozen in man shape all your days, you would be a crow. And I would still love you even if we'd had eggs instead of triplets."

That was something to think about. Could he still be a crow without a true flock? The word for what he was in crow language did not mean a single creature. It meant one of a flock—the family nest, then the lesser flock of relatives, then the great flock that turned the sky black. Only Aly would say he could be a crow without a flock.

He lay awake, listening to his mate's breathing, listening for the cawing of his newborns. He could do nothing about his own fate, but the crows of his war band had to be told. They were in danger. Rifou was a warning to all of them.

* * *

In the nursery the next morning, he found six-darking teams handing infants to nursemaids. Other darkings drew the insect curtains back from the room's many windows. One of the babies—Ulasu by scent—was at a table, apparently having received a clean diaper. The nursemaid who stood over the child held a light blanket. She glanced at Nawat, then at Terai, who pursed her lips and shook her head. The nursemaid lightly wrapped the baby rather than swaddling her, then carried Ulasu to her crib.

The darkings called greetings to Nawat as the women curtsied. "No curtsies, no bows to me," Nawat said, cross. "I am no peacock lord or bird-of-paradise noblewoman. I am a plain old crow."

"You are a plain old crow who the queen made a captain and a war leader of the realm," Aly said, coming in from the sitting room. She was already dressed. "They'll get in trouble if someone besides us sees they don't salute you." She nodded as the women curtsied to her. "Or me." Today she wore a sarong in glorious reds, yellows, and oranges. Her hair was pinned up at the back of her head. Nawat wished, as he often did, that there was a sparkly rock big enough to tell her how much light and cheer she brought to his life.

Ulasu made a noise; Aly went to her. Nawat was patting one of Junim's fists with his finger when an arrow-feeling struck him. This had nothing to do with his children. He had these feelings often. They came when there was trouble with the crows of his war band. Worse, Rifou was at the heart of it, screaming like a nestling.

The nursemaids screeched themselves when Nawat fast-changed into crow form. Aly only came over to give his sarong to him. He would need it when he changed back. He gripped it in one claw and drew his beak up the side of her leg. She ran her fingernails through his crown feathers before he threw himself at the nearest window.

His war band was quartered a fast glide from their tower. Nawat dropped into the shadows at the west end of the crow barracks less than a minute after he'd left his family. As he resumed human shape, he watched the palace wake. Mists rose from the cool shadows under the trees, meeting air that had already turned warm. Birds stretched. Before his beak changed, Nawat called up to any late sleepers outside the barracks and within them.

He expected Parleen to answer from the open window on the barracks' second floor. She was Aly's friend, a born crow who kept a true nest inside the war band's home. Her nestling, Keeket, was always hungry and would be screeching for breakfast, yet Nawat did not hear him.

There was no reply from Parleen, either, though her nest was beside the window. Nawat frowned, made sure that his sarong would stay on his lean hips, and walked into the crow barracks.

The band was up and gathered near the pot where humans and those in human form cooked their morning rice. Empty bowls showed they had finished their meal. Most of the band sat with something to occupy themselves, sharpening blades, oiling them or oiling leather, doing stretching exercises. The ones in crow form occupied the perches just behind the benches. When they saw Nawat, they jumped to the floor, changing shape as they went. None of their human comrades so much as blinked to see forty-odd naked people suddenly join them. The easily shocked were always weeded out in the first week after they entered the band.

"Where is Parleen?" Nawat asked.

No one would meet his eyes. Finally someone said, "She left before dawn, *lurah.*"

"Crows from the Rajmuat flock came," someone else said. It was the woman who slept across from Parleen and her nest. "They talked to us. They said if we become much more human, we will be outcasts, like Rifou. Parleen went with them. She said she did not wish to be part human anymore."

Nawat looked at his people. "What about her nestling? What about Keeket?"

"They carried him with them," another of the crows replied. "I followed, and—" Tears trickled down her cheeks. "Outside, they saw Keeket had one leg shorter than the other and his back was twisted. They dropped him onto the burying stones. I would have brought him back if he'd lived, but they killed him with the drop. I left him with the dead."

"You know why we did not cull him, Nawat. Parleen thought he would heal as he grew. So did I." Parleen's mate, Taihi, pushed forward through the crow folk. "But the crows of Rajmuat follow crow law. A deformed nestling must be culled. We didn't do it, and Keeket died anyway. They sent a messenger to name me outcast. Parleen told Gemomo I forced her to keep him."

Nawat's heart ached. The thought of that child, broken

on the stones that had looked so cold in the moonlight, was too much. Yet he would have done it, if Keeket had been his, though he had not said so to Aly. Aly was Parleen's friend and godsmother to Keeket. She had talked his parents out of culling, meaning well. She didn't understand that culling was easier on the parents when they took care of it as soon as the deformed young hatched, before they had come to love it. "Why did you not go with Parleen?" he asked Taihi. "You could have defended yourself. You might have been spared casting out and given a last chance."

Keeket's father stared at Nawat. "*This* is my flock now, our people," he replied. "I can't return to being a crow in a wild flock. There are too many thoughts in my head. How would I get hot cooked food, or see plays, or hear human music? And mating is so—"

"Short," someone muttered.

"Boring," a woman added.

"Humans have a much better way of mating," a third crow-man said.

"If I'd had a human wife, Keeket would be alive now," Taihi said angrily. His face twisted and he turned away from the others. Two human women of the war band went to comfort him. The crow-women huddled with each other.

The door at the east end of the barracks smashed open. Rifou's wife, Bala, was there, her eyes red with weeping. Taybur Sibigat stood with her, unshaven, his hair unruly.

"Rifou hanged himself last night!" Bala cried before Taybur could stop her. "He did it because those vile birds turned on him!" She collapsed in her grief.

* * *

Nawat stayed with his people long after the noon meal, talking to each of them, crows and humans. The crows were badly shaken. Parleen was not the only one to leave the war band before dawn: five others had gone out of fear that they might become outcasts from a true flock. The humans did their best to console their sword-brothers and -sisters, feeding them and preening them with their fingers.

When he felt he could leave his people, Nawat went to see Taybur. The guard captain had recovered the bodies of Rifou and Keeket and had told Nawat he could find them, and Taybur, at the Black God's temple. Nawat arranged for their funerals with the priests, then learned the facts of Rifou's death from his friend.

"What happens if the Rajmuat flock throws you out?" Taybur asked, letting his darking travel from one arm to the other as they left the death-god's temple. "I would think it's a greater risk for *you* than for any of your people."

"I'm not worried," Nawat said, determined to put the best face on things. "I know of nothing that would make me break crow law."

Taybur arched an eyebrow at him. "Whistling in the dark?"

"No, truly. My little ones are fine and healthy and I will teach them crow ways. My war band and I will be sure to find work that takes us far from those caked-rump croakers," Nawat assured Taybur. "And if I catch them talking with my people without me again, I shall teach them respect." He meant it. He would wage war against them if he must, to keep the outsiders from wreaking the kind of havoc they had done with his flock today.

He understood that the ties between crows and humans in his flock frightened the Rajmuat crows. They disliked change. They wanted things to be the way they had been for their ancestors. Nawat and his war band were too new, and too different.

That understanding did not mean that Nawat would not do what was necessary to make them keep their beaks to themselves. There would be no more Rifous or Keekets. Everyone would hold to crow law and crow tradition while staying out of the rival flock's way. He would see to that.

This state of anger and energy sustained him up until the moment the guards opened the door to his rooms. A small darking that sported a strand of tiny red beads within its body stood there, obviously leaving as Nawat arrived.

"Not fun today," it called as it rolled around him and outside.

Nawat did not have to ask what it meant. The noise from the nursery was unmistakable. He strode in, scowling. "What is the meaning of this?" he called.

He had meant for the answer to be silence. That was how it went with his war band. Here, it only caused all four infants, counting Terai's baby, to scream louder. The darkings that held two bounced them, which made one stop crying to giggle—it was Junim, Nawat saw—while Terai's baby howled and began to hiccup. Two nursemaids and the younger wet nurse were cleaning a mess off the floor while Ulasu waved her fists and wailed.

Aly's hair was a complete tangle. It hung around her face and down her back. She tried in vain to toss it out of her eyes while keeping her grip on Ochobai. Their firstborn screamed loudest of all.

"I don't understand!" Aly cried. "She hates me!"

"Her diaper may be full, my lady," Terai said grimly. She glanced at Nawat. "I trust your day away from us has been a bright and sunny one, my lord."

Somehow Nawat did not believe she meant it in the way the words fitted together. "Darkings, set Terai's boy down. Where is Trick?"

"Trick run away when Aly yell," a darking—Nawat couldn't see which one—replied. Those that tended the largest infant obeyed Nawat's order, placing the wailing child in a new crib that had come during the day. The moment he felt a solid bed beneath him, the boy stopped crying.

"Don't bounce him anymore," Nawat ordered those darkings. "He doesn't like it."

"Junim likes," pointed out a darking who wore bright orchid petals under its skin. It braced Junim's head while its fellows bounced the rest of the lad gently.

"Then that is something we know about Junim," Nawat told them. "It may not be true of all babies." While he spoke to the darkings in and around Junim's crib, the women finished cleaning up and restored their area to order. Terai handed the sobbing Ulasu to the other wet nurse. The infant fell silent as the young raka cradled her in her arms.

Ochobai's howls split into howls and gasps. "I suppose you're going to wave your magic—*feathers* at this one and make her all sugar and cream," Aly said crossly. "I suppose you've had a splendid day with the war band while we appease these hungry, pissing, manure-making, screaming *things*!"

Nawat gaped at the wife who had been so at ease that morning. Terai leaned over to whisper in his ear. "The humors that help her bring children to term are still in her body, my lord. With no children to work upon, they affect her temper and feelings. You must be easy with her. A nursemaid is fetching medicine from the midwife." Her voice was anxious as she gripped Nawat's shoulder. "This is normal in a mother, sir. You *must* treat her well."

Nawat blinked at the head wet nurse. "I never treat her otherwise," he said quietly. Looking around, he called, "Trick! Come here, or I will send you to Lombyn Isle to herd sparrows!"

Nawat went to Aly and took Ochobai from his mate. Tucking the sobbing, weeping infant in one arm, he gently began to draw his fingers through poor Aly's hair, tugging knots free and letting the loose pins fall to the floor. "I enjoyed no splendid day, dear heart," he explained, kissing tears from her eyes. "We had two deaths. I could send no message that would make sense or that would not frighten you. My people needed me."

She turned her face against his shoulder. "I'm sorry. I thought you didn't want to look at me in daylight."

"You are beautiful," Nawat whispered, cuddling the weeping Ochobai against his side. The infant was getting quieter.

"My baby hates me," Aly said, pointing to Ochobai. "She hits my breast when she nurses. When I hold her, she cries."

"She does not know you yet," Nawat said. "Would you like mango rice? You always feel better when you have mango rice." A black head-blob rose over Aly's shoulder: Trick. Nawat glared at the darking. "Trick will fetch it for you, since Trick left you in distress."

"Trick hate to see Aly cry," the darking replied, hanging its head. "Aly cry almost all day."

Aly clung to her earlier thoughts. "I hated my mother, but at least I waited until I was old enough to know who she was *before* I hated her," she said, and sniffed. "Ochobai hates me right away."

Trick bounced in shock. "Baby not hate Aly!" it cried. "Baby hate being baby!"

Nawat thought the darking was probably right. "Ochobai is too young to know what hate is," he told Aly soothingly. "She loves you. She just is not sure that she loves nursing, or being outside her wonderful mother."

Aly began to sob. "You think I'm an idiot."

One of the nursemaids slipped behind Aly with a brush and gently began to work on her hair. The messenger arrived with the medicine from the queen's healer. Nawat persuaded Aly to take some, with a promise of mango rice to be delivered soon. Trick rolled out of the room, on its way to fetch a kitchen servant with Aly's favorite dish. Calmer, Aly let the attentive nursemaid take her to the bedroom for a wash and a change of clothes.

"She will improve," Terai said over Nawat's shoulder. "Having a child is complicated for the body. Many women are unable to shake it off right away. Your lady is very lucky to be under the care of the best mages in the Isles."

Thinking of everything that had changed within Aly's

skin and outside it during her pregnancy, Nawat shivered. "Men do not know when we are well off," he murmured, kissing Ochobai's forehead. The baby struck him in the nose.

Terai looked at him strangely. "You are an odd man," she remarked at last.

"I am a crow," Nawat said without thinking. "Did the queen visit?" Aly's upset would not have been helped if Queen Dove had seen her in disarray. She believed that the queen depended on her to be cool and unshakable, when Nawat knew that Dove liked Aly to laugh and joke with her. It was something few members of the court did with the fearsomely intelligent queen.

Terai shook her head, to Nawat's relief. "The Duchess Winnamine came in Her Majesty's place," she said. "She told us that Her Majesty would wait until my lady felt up to guests."

Nawat chuckled. Trust their friend Winnamine to know what was right! He would send a darking to thank her. He knew that properly he should send a note on some of Aly's elegant paper, but since everyone called his writing crow tracks, he would rather that a darking carried his message in his real voice.

He distracted Terai by pointing to a nursemaid who struggled to pull a bundle of diapers from a group of darkings. The blob folk thought it was a game. As the wet nurse, who obviously had taken command of the nursery, went to establish order, Nawat carried Ochobai to the nearest open window. He had her blanket and diaper off in one smooth movement, now that he knew the trick of both, as his firstborn batted his chin with miniature fists. He dangled her from the open window as she released her body's waste, then brought her back inside so he could use the diaper to clean her. As he did, she managed to dig one fist into his eye.

By the time Aly returned to the nursery, groomed and calm, servants had brought supper for everyone, including Aly's promised treat. The adults even had a quiet time in which to eat while the infants dozed.

Within a week Aly was nearly her former self, if her former self had been breast-feeding three infants. While Terai and the other wet nurse shared those duties, everyone impressed upon the new mother and her mate that a mother's first milk, before the heavier milk came in, had particular strength in guarding children from illness. It was important that Aly feed each triplet equally, though the breast that Ochobai had blistered that first day was off limits briefly while the midwife's salve healed it. In that time, those darkings who had taken an interest in baby care learned to amuse their charges, lift them so they were more easily taken from their cribs, hold the insect netting around the cribs at night, and announce dirty diapers. They fetched things for wet nurses and maids alike, conveyed orders to other areas of the palace, and made Aly laugh. For that alone Nawat would have considered them well worth the confusion they caused on occasion.

Aly soon heard of the death of Keeket. Nawat had not hoped to keep it from her for long, not when she was the chief of the realm's spies. He learned of her discovery when she woke him from a nap—they were both living on naps, the triplets taking their sleep in two-hour doses only—by shoving him.

"They *killed* that nestling, and you didn't tell me!" she snapped. Nawat checked: the door to the nursery was closed.

"Bad Nawat!" piped Trick, looped around Aly's neck as a thin rope.

"You said crows take care of ones that are hurt," Aly said, giving Nawat a second shove. He struggled to sit up. "You said they nurse them like humans do."

"If they're slashed, or hurt in a way that heals," Nawat said. "But a defective nestling must be culled. It hardly ever happens." Only now, as he sat up, did he see that Aly was crying. Of course she would cry for her friend and for her godschild.

"I'm sorry," he said, abashed. "I should have told you sooner, but I could find no time that was good."

Aly raised her hands as if to hit Nawat, and collapsed against him instead, sobbing. Trick slid off her neck. "Bad Nawat," it whispered before it dropped to the floor and wriggled out of the room. "Badbad."

"Keep doing that and I'll feed you to one of my band as a worm," Nawat whispered loudly. He cuddled Aly and kissed her head.

"I can't stand being this way," Aly said at last. "Weepy and yelling. Mother would laugh. She always said I'd be more sympathetic once I had children of my own."

"You will get better," Nawat consoled her. "Terai says, and she knows."

"Until then, promise me you will never drop our children

to their deaths, or give them to a flock to kill," Aly said, gripping him by the arms. "You must *promise,* Nawat."

"Aly, this is foolish!" he cried, offended at last. "Our children are fine, healthy nestlings! I would no more cull them than I would you! Just because I am a crow does not mean that I have no human feelings!"

She stared at him for much too long, her green-hazel eyes intent. At last she threw up her hands. "Megrims and vapors, that's what my nursemaid at home called them," she said. "I try to get a grip, but my inside is far too close to my outside these days. My da would be so ashamed. He taught me better."

"I like your emotions where I may see them," Nawat told her. "It is good to know how you feel in truth, for a change, without talking around you too much."

"But you always know how I feel in truth," Aly protested. "That's why I married you."

"I don't mind it when it is easier," explained Nawat with a kiss.

A wail from the nursery brought them both out of bed. Ochobai was awake and hungry, which meant the others would soon be wailing, too.

Ochobai may have consistently been the first to wake and scream for a meal, but it was Junim who caused the nursery women to flutter and whisper two days later. Aly was in her office deep in the palace for the first time, but Nawat was present when the women set up a stir. Looking around from the game of bounce-me that he played with Ulasu, he asked, "What is the matter?"

"Junim turned over," the younger wet nurse said, pointing to Nawat's son. The boy was on the floor with Terai's crawling child and Ochobai. Instead of lying on his belly to look around, as he'd been doing when Nawat picked up Ulasu, Junim now rested on his back, gazing with interest at the new world he'd found.

"I turn over all of the time," Nawat said to Ulasu, giving the baby a slight jiggle. She chuckled and drooled on her father. "No one gets excited when I do it."

"Only very clever babies do so when they are just a week old," Terai said patiently. "Most wait a couple of months, or three."

Nawat shrugged at Ulasu. "I don't think it's clever," he replied. "Crow nestlings stand right away, long before humans do. The belly is too vulnerable."

The women glared at him. "Most fathers are proud of what their children do," Terai informed Nawat. "One day these little ones will hear you compare them unfavorably to crow-children. It will hurt them."

Nawat smiled at her from his position on the floor. "One day they will learn to become crows. They will understand what they have been missing."

Junim blew a spit-bubble, and new scents reached Nawat. The crow father sighed inwardly. His son was about to pee. There would be no easy way for Nawat to hand off Ulasu and gather up Junim, now the object of so much attention from the women, in time to make it to the window unobserved. That meant that Junim was soiling his diaper. He would soon begin to smell.

Nawat sat up, keeping Ulasu upright in his hands. How was he to teach his children the proper ways with so many humans to look on? If only humans didn't have such foolish ideas!

Junim did not remain the sole master of the front-to-back rollover for long. Within two days Ulasu was doing it as well. Ochobai tried and tried, until she managed it two weeks after the triplets' birth.

While the women congratulated Ochobai and told her what a big girl she was, and how much more clever all the triplets were than other children, a messenger entered the nursery with a sealed document. Seeing Nawat, she trotted over to give it to him. It bore the seal of both the queen and Aly's Department of Information.

Orders, Nawat thought. His quiet time with the nestlings was over. He broke the seals and began to read. Once he had mastered the contents of the message, he went to the crow barracks to get his war band ready.

That night, in bed with Aly, he told her of Ochobai's new skill and his own preparations to travel north. "Everything's in order," he finished. "I think Ochobai will miss me."

"Those smugglers," Aly murmured. "I wish we could send the army, but it's not enough trouble to justify the expense. Especially not when the army's preparing for the monsoon. It's been so nice, having you here all the time. I don't know about Ochobai, but *I* will miss you."

"My crows ache for a long flight and time away from Rajmuat," he told her. "My humans feel the same. The Rajmuat flock has kept a watch here. It makes my war band tense."

He'd seen the city crows observing his visits to the window with an infant in his hands. He didn't appreciate their spying on him, either. "If all goes well, the journey will be short. These smugglers think we do not know they are there. We will take them by surprise. Since the rains are late, I've already sent my crows out. Our ship leaves before dawn."

"No," Aly said, wrapping her arms around him.

Trick, watching from its bowl overhead, sighed. "Now she will mope," the darking said. "She always mopes when you are away."

"Everyone says she is perfectly fine when I am gone!" Nawat protested.

"I work hard to make them think that," Aly whispered, burying her face in Nawat's hair.

Nawat was gone less than a week. When he returned, Ochobai saw him first and cried out. She set off a chorus of noise from Ulasu, Junim, and even Terai's boy, who knew actual words and could yell "Nawat!" Nawat gathered Ochobai up and gave her a sparkling rock he'd brought from the northern tip of the island. He handed a monkey doll to Terai's son, who snatched it gleefully.

"No, no stones," cried a nursemaid, swooping down on them. "She'll put it in her soft little mouth and hurt herself!"

The moment the stone was taken from her hands, Ochobai began to shriek. "Does this mean I am not to give Junim his shell, or Ulasu her feather?" he shouted over his daughter, frowning at the woman. "Must I take the doll away, too?"

Terai moved into his view, as stately as an eagle. "Babies

put things in their mouths, my lord," she said calmly into Nawat's ear. "They even try to swallow them. The doll is a splendid gift for my boy, and I thank you."

"Crow nestlings inspect objects, and learn from them," Nawat retorted. "How do you know my infants will not do the same?"

He did not wait for an answer, but carried the wailing Ochobai to the nest he shared with Aly. There he rocked and bounced his oldest daughter until she began to calm, and to think of filling her diaper. They made it to the window just in time.

As he cleaned her, Nawat had a feeling, the same one he'd gotten from her once or twice before. It was something in the smell of her dung, he thought, but closer sniffing as he wiped her did not reveal the scent. Once he'd cleaned her off, he ran his nose all over the baby while she pummeled his head with her fists and tugged his hair. Deep in thought, Nawat replaced her diaper from those kept in the bedroom, then carried Ochobai out to the nursery.

The darkings, nursemaids, and wet nurses, often confused by his behavior, watched him curiously. He removed first Junim's diaper, then Ulasu's, and gave each infant as thorough a sniffing as he had given Ochobai. He thought they smelled sweeter than their older sister, but the scent was so faint, and so elusive, that he couldn't be certain it was real.

As he replaced the diapers, he finally realized everyone was staring at him. He smiled. "Getting reacquainted," he said. "They don't have feathers for me to preen, so I do this."

It wasn't even half a lie. Crows did have greetings after they returned to the nest. "How have Aly and the little ones fared?"

It was a good distraction. It kept his children's caregivers talking until kitchen servants arrived with supper for the nursery folk. Seeing that Nawat was there, they set another place at the table for him. Nawat ate with the women. Afterward he remained to play with the children and talk to their caregivers.

There was no sign of Aly. Terai said that Aly had not been present for the last feeding, an hour before Nawat had arrived. It was three hours later, time for the next meal, and Ochobai was starting to fuss. Aly rarely missed two meals in a row if she could help it. She had confided to him that she felt like a bad mother if she always left it to the wet nurses to feed her children. Not only that, but she liked nursing, now that the bumps in the road were smoothed.

Nawat unpacked his bags as the wet nurses fed the infants, setting gifts for Aly on the bed. He was taking the gifts for the wet nurses and the nursemaids out to them when he saw that his wife had come at last. Aly stood in the middle of the nursery, her hands folded neatly before her. Today she wore a sarong in greens and browns that made her look like a tree spirit with very forbidding eyes. The room felt much colder to Nawat. The maids and wet nurses all had their faces averted. The darkings, except for Trick, who rode as Aly's necklace, had vanished.

Aly took a breath. "Nawat. I would like a word with you, if you please. Elsewhere."

Nawat followed Aly, wondering what had pulled her tail feathers. Normally she threw herself at him when he came home, and let him spin her around. If she was not brooding eggs, they had other fun as well. Something was wrong, because she did not take him into her office in their rooms, as he expected, to scold him in private. Today she led him downstairs to the second level and around the outer wall to her official offices as the queen's spymaster.

As they walked in silence, Aly slightly in the lead, Nawat began to get irritated. He was no longer an unschooled island crow, to be ordered about this way—he was her mate and war leader of one of the queen's finest commands. Surely he deserved an explanation!

Aly entered the offices that served her and her spies. At the moment they were empty: everyone was at supper. It was when they walked into Aly's private office that Nawat found that some people were *not* taking their evening meal. Queen Dove sat on one of the chairs, her small cat-face expressionless. The hanging gems on the points of her fanned crown shivered in the candlelight: her body was quivering. At her left shoulder stood Taybur, at her right Duchess Winnamine, their own faces unreadable. Darkings pooled at the queen's feet.

Nawat bowed deeply; Aly curtsied. "Your Majesty," Nawat said.

"Nawat Crow," Queen Dove said quietly. "There is a thing I hoped you might be able to explain to me."

"I am always at Your Majesty's service," Nawat replied cautiously. The queen's gems shook harder than ever. The entire population of the royal palace knew this to be a sign that Queen Dove was most displeased. The harder the gems swayed on the delicate crowns worn by the Isles' queen, the worse the trouble was for someone. Had one of his people offended Dove in some way?

"I have come from a most embarrassing interview with the Tyran ambassador," Dove said, her soft voice measured. "Apparently he and his aides took Moon Orchid Walk on their way out of the enclosure not long ago. As they passed the northeastern side of our residence, the Tyran ambassador stepped aside to admire a blossom. The god must have guided him. The splash of dung that might have drenched him struck his secretary instead."

Uh-oh, Nawat thought, bowing his head. I was certain no one was out there.

"Of course," Dove continued in that same quiet tone, "their party was quite startled. They looked to see what sort of bird had anointed the poor man. Imagine their surprise when they saw a pair of arms pull a naked infant into an open window of our residence. Imagine *my* surprise when the ambassador told me all this!"

Nawat understood the reason for Dove's quivering gems now. She was furious with *him.*

The young queen got to her feet. The darkings moved away from her in an arc. "I had to apologize to that condescending moneybags for the insult to his delegation when I am trying to get a *very* big loan to repair the damage that was done during the rebellion. I offered my own maids to help his secretary bathe the stain away, silks from my own storehouse to replace the ruined clothes, and the best of our shaving and hair oils." Small red patches had appeared on her cheeks. "Once I had rid myself of him, I sent for word from my household. My gardeners tell me they have been cleaning dung from that spot since your children were born. Aly says she knows nothing of it!"

"Crows don't foul their nests, Your Majesty," Nawat replied calmly. He had never seen Dove so angry, but she was reasonable. She would understand where Aly and the women of the nursery had not understood. "We go to the edge and eliminate outside it. Aly and the nursemaids insist on cloth diapers, but they're smelly and unnatural. I clean our babies right away. They don't get the rashes that make Terai's son cry, and they don't stink like he does."

Dove sighed. "It could have been the ambassador from Carthak, Nawat. They once started a war because they thought the presents for an imperial birthday weren't impressive enough to be anything but an insult. That's how they added Zallara to the Empire. Or it could have been one of the Yamani embassy—any of them. Then the defiled person, because they think anyone contaminated with the dung of others is defiled—that defiled person would have to kill himself immediately, probably on my doorstep. Then the emperor would have to avenge his relative, because everyone in the embassy is related to him somehow, except for the people who haul away the contents of their privies!"

"Oh," Nawat said, applying one of Aly's first lessons in diplomacy to himself. *When faced with angry nobility or royalty,* she had explained, *be still.*

"Yes. Oh." Dove sank onto her chair. Her lips twitched.

"You should have seen his face. . . ." She made herself look stern again. "I have to show him that I'm punishing you, so get yourself and your band ready for a lot of stupid small tasks. And I can't believe it's healthy to stick your babies outside when the monsoons are coming."

Crows live outside, Nawat wanted to reply, but he remained still instead and bowed to his queen. She rose and left the chamber, her darkings following her like a train. Taybur and the duchess nodded to Aly and left in the queen's wake. Nawat could not help but notice that the guard captain's body was shaking. Was Taybur getting ill?

Aly cleared up his confusion by whispering after Taybur, *"It's not funny!"*

After the door closed behind the queen and her companions, Nawat considered what had just taken place. He'd received his first reprimand from the queen. There would be tasks, but he had heard that such things were also usually accompanied by other punishments, such as a demotion in rank, or a reduction in salary. Technically, he had no rank. His war band operated on its own rules with Nawat as *lurah,* leader. Nawat dealt with the queen's generals, admirals, and captains, but only she had the power to command him. She had spoken as if command of his flock remained his. As to reducing his salary . . .

"Do I get a salary?" he asked his mate.

"What!" Aly shrieked behind him. Nawat turned to stare at her. She looked as though he'd turned into a kraken.

"Why do you raise your voice?" he asked, though if the truth was to be told, he had a good idea.

"You embarrass the queen—and our family!—with

people we are asking for *money,* with the representatives of a foreign nation, a nation that might take offense, and you want to know why I might raise my voice?" she demanded, though she also asked it more quietly. "Nawat, what am I to do with you? Human babies wear diapers, and ambassadors are living symbols of their realms!"

He crossed his arms over his chest, feeling as stubborn as his mate. "Crow nestlings go outside the nest. Those diaper things are a filthy habit. And they smell. I am sorry Ochobai splooted on the secretary next to the ambassador."

"There's another thing," she said, ignoring his apology. "You've been holding our children out the window all this time?"

"Only when no one sees."

"Are you *mad*?" Aly demanded. "What if your hold slipped? Our nestlings would be as dead as poor little Keeket from this height!" She frowned. "Actually, I'm surprised you got the ambassador's secretary from so high."

Nawat beamed. "Ochobai has very good aim," he explained. "She doesn't even foul the outside of the nest."

Aly started to grin, then glared at him again. "This isn't funny!"

"No, it's important," Nawat agreed. "It shows her muscles are healthy. *She* is healthy."

"She can be healthy in diapers, like a normal child," Aly retorted.

"My children must be crows!" Nawat cried, his voice harsh. "They must learn the things that crows learn when I am with them! You knew this when we married, Aly! They may look like humans, but they are half *crow*!" He was so upset that he began to sprout feathers: they itched and pulled under his clothes and dragged at his hair until they fought their way free.

"Crows!" he shouted, and left her. He would not make sense once he got so angry. Had she forgotten the Rajmuat flock? Did she want that fate for their nestlings, or for him?

Sometimes it is hard to be married to Aly, he told himself, not for the first time, as he ran downstairs and outside. Barely acknowledging the guards, he stalked through a gate in the Royal Enclosure. Sometimes she forgets that we are not her Tortall family. I cannot turn myself into a human knight or a human spymaster like her parents. At least Dove is only upset because we soiled a foreigner.

He turned down the path to the small lake near the Royal Enclosure. The beautiful pavilions that stood in the three coves held no interest for him. Instead he found a rock that stood over the turtle beach and sat there until dark, nibbling grasshoppers, dragonflies, and beetles as he watched the fish. Aly would never let him eat beetles at home; she said the way they crunched gave her the shivers.

When he saw the lamplighters come down the paths, Nawat rose and stretched with a sigh. His feathers were gone, had been gone for two hours at least. Ochobai was probably crying for him right now. She usually napped after her late-afternoon pee, and when she woke, after she'd fed, she wanted her father, even if she did hit him. Junim would be circled by cooing maids, while the darkings cuddled

Ulasu—if they did not actually talk to her. It was time to see if Aly still wanted him as a mate.

He certainly did not expect what he found in the nursery. Aly was directing the maids in the placement of three big pottery jars, one next to each crib. She looked at Nawat and smiled ruefully.

"Sometimes I am so busy quarreling that I forget there is always a solution, if I take time to think," she said with a blush. "I don't know how you can put up with such a difficult wife. Will these do? It isn't the same as dangling our children out the window—but really, isn't this safer?"

Nawat looked from her to the jars. They were widemouthed and glazed, with handles for the maids to grip. With care, he could hold the nestlings over them easily.

He went over to his wife and kissed her well. "You are so clever," he murmured as the nursery women sighed romantically. Then Ochobai began to scream. Nawat laughed and went to pick up his daughter.

The queen was a woman of her word. She issued a number of orders for Nawat's band that could as well have been handled by the army or navy. The group went up the coast or out to tiny islands that were marked only on the most precise maps. As if to help the queen prove that the father responsible for the Tyran secretary's embarrassment would be well punished, the belated rainy season began. The crows were forced to ride or sail with the humans or risk being blown out to sea. Generally Nawat's humans considered the little tasks a very good joke, but the crows still fretted about the danger of outcast status. They sulked.

"*We* have no babies to show the world we are teaching them crow ways," Nawat heard one of his people say to another.

"We could sit on the palace roof and mate-feed each other," suggested her friend. "But will that be enough? How do we know they're watching?"

Nawat pretended to ignore them. He asked himself the same questions, and he had no answers. To help put an end to the unpleasant trips, he presented the humiliated secretary with ten precious yards of a silk woven on only one of the Isles, a hard-to-get and expensive gift. It was pronounced a suitable apology by the ambassador, and the war band was allowed to relax.

On a rare day at home, Nawat decided not to eat the last of a worm snack. Instead, while Aly was in her office near the queen's rooms, and the nursery women were cleaning, he took Junim into the bedroom to play. The boy was alert and fascinated by the new toy his father took from his pocket. He giggled and swiped at the thrashing worm that Nawat dangled over his head.

"Catch, Junim," Nawat whispered. "Catch the treat!"

A couple of the darkings provided comments.

"Too low."

"Almost had it that time."

"Uh-oh."

Nawat thought "uh-oh" was a grab that almost got the worm until the darkings shot out of the bedroom. Without turning to face his mate, Nawat said, "Would you like it? I'm full."

When she said nothing, Nawat added, "I know they

aren't supposed to have anything but mother's milk. I wasn't feeding, only playing."

Aly's sigh made his heart hurt. "I didn't think it would be this hard. I thought, the longer you were with me, the more you would be . . ."

A coal of anger started to burn in his heart. When she did not finish her sentence, he said, "Go on. You thought I'd be more human by now." He called for his feathers in his hair and along his bare arms. When he did it on purpose, he could control how much change took place and where. Junim gasped as the long shafts grew from Nawat's scalp and skin. The infant's face crinkled. He grinned hugely, showing pink gums, and reached not for the worm, but for his father. Nawat turned to look at his wife, tilted his head back like a bird, and dropped the worm down his gullet.

Aly walked out.

Picking up Junim, Nawat grimaced as he swallowed the worm. Just now he would pull out a wing feather before he would admit it to Aly, but he really preferred to eat things as a human. The taste was much better when he could chew and savor. Bouncing the boy in his arms, Nawat carried him into the nursery and turned him over to Terai. Even though Ochobai was crying, Nawat left the rooms.

He bedded down with his war band that night. No one said a word about it. He worked on his own gear, sharpening the weapons he used as a human and oiling his leathers. He looked around at every squeak, thinking it was one of the triplets demanding attention—it was an annoying habit he had developed since their birth. He tried to sleep in the barracks, but every time he closed his eyes, he thought he heard Ochobai's cranky wail. Instead he changed to crow shape and took a turn at rooftop watch, despite the rain that poured from the skies. Even the weather couldn't distract him from his family.

When the next member of the band flew up to relieve him, Nawat didn't return to the barracks. Instead he flew straight to the Royal Enclosure. The mosquito nets on the windows of their room and around their bed were up, but the bed was made and unwrinkled. Nawat changed into human form and went to the clothespress where the drying cloths were kept.

"Aly working," Trick said from its bowl home over the bed. "Aly told me go away. She in bad mood. Are you in bad mood?"

Nawat sighed as he dried himself off. "I'm in a crow mood, Trick." It was a lie. Crows didn't get depressed unless a mate or a nestling died. Only humans got depressed over emotions.

Trick squeaked. "Crows drop darkings from high up!"

"It's not that kind of crow mood. Don't worry about it." Nawat went to a shelf for a sarong and picked one from the stack. When it didn't even cover his behind, he realized he'd gone to the diaper shelf without thinking. He folded the diaper carefully and replaced it, then went to the right shelf, for the right clothes. Normally he could manage well in the dark, even with human eyes, because he remembered where everything was. "Is she getting tired of me, Trick?"

"No fair," Trick said testily. "No fair, talk about Aly like that."

Nawat combed his wet hair back from his face with his fingers. "I'm sorry. I didn't mean it."

He was almost to the nursery door when he heard the darking say, "Nawat good friend to Aly. Aly good friend to Nawat. Everyone grumpy during rains."

The darking's words struck Nawat near the heart. The little creatures only gave advice when they cared deeply about the recipients.

"You're a good friend to us, too," he said at last, when he had mastered his voice. He opened the nursery door.

Just two shaded lamps were lit. Everyone was sleeping, not a state he wanted to interrupt. The one thing the entire Crow household had agreed upon, that first week after the triplets were born, was that sleep was sacred. The infants left them few unbroken periods of it, so all of them napped when they could.

Nawat heard a stirring of body and cloth, then the slightest indrawn breath. Without a sound he dashed to Ochobai's crib. Her eyes were open and so was her mouth. "You knew your da had come, didn't you?" His voice was barely audible in his own ears as he picked her up and checked her diaper with an expert hand. She was dry, a miracle of its own.

He wrapped her loosely in her warmest blanket, the rains having chilled the air. Rather than wake anyone, he sprouted a feather, plucked it with a wince, and left it in the cradle to let the nursery workers know who had the baby. He covered Ochobai's mouth on her first angry yell and trotted out of the rooms with her. Only after the guards closed the front door behind them did Nawat take away his hand to free Ochobai's furious wails.

"Good lungs." One of the guards was Bala. "She might be a herald one day."

The other guard chuckled. "Any howler monkey in your bloodlines, sir?"

Nawat grinned and carried Ochobai away from the residential part of the Gray Palace, down the stairs, and out into a colonnade that overlooked the garden between palace and temples. The torches gave scant light to the trees and buildings beyond, but he could hear the falling rain and smell grass and wet dirt. Ochobai sobbed briefly against her father's shoulder and fell quiet. She gripped a fistful of his hair and yanked.

Nawat bore the painful tug. "You're an ungrateful little sploot," he said, giving her the war band's name for dung and pee shot out of the nest. "All you do is hit me, scream in my ear, burp mother's milk on my clothes, pull my feathers, pull my hair. . . ."

Ochobai flailed the hand that gripped his hair, tugging it back and forth.

"Junim and Ulasu are *glad* to see me," Nawat said. "They smile. They do cute things. They blow little bubbles. You punched me in the eye once. More than once." He was getting that feeling again, the wrong feeling. It came from his little girl. It was inside her, the wrongness. Now that he was alone with her, without distractions, two months after her birth, he felt it cleanly. It was the sense he had always gotten from Keeket, the one that had made him want to cull the nestling.

Slowly Nawat slid to the foot of the inside colonnade wall, his legs in front of him. He placed Ochobai on his thighs, holding her with his hands curved around her sides. For once she remained quiet, willing to look around at the torches and her father.

Nawat bent over her, letting his crow senses spread through his nestling. He closed his eyes as he found what was wrong not now, but in its seeds at the heart of her bones and organs. Spread through her tiny body, Nawat followed the ghostly path of her future shape.

It would go slowly, so very slowly. She might be ten or fourteen when she stopped growing at the height her brother and sister would be at the age of eight or nine. He saw the curves that would develop in her leg and arm bones, the way her hands would get heavy, the cage her ribs would form for her organs.

He had seen the dwarfs of the human world. One served Queen Dove as keeper of her birds. Others performed with the Players who kept her court entertained at state dinners. He'd seen two of them begging in the street on his arrival in Rajmuat. Later he'd learned that both were spies for Dove's rebels. A family of cloth merchants in the city had two dwarfs in their shops, a weaver and a little boy.

Something about the shape of Ochobai's future bones made him remember the winter after he'd taken man shape to court Aly. He was living in Tanair village with Falthin the bowyer. Across the street, the miller's daughter gave birth in February to the tiniest of babies, one that weighed barely two pounds. For all its size, the baby was fully developed, not one of the unfortunates who came before its time. It was simply . . . very small, and very wrong. Nawat had stayed away from it. He'd feared he might peck it, though it was not his nestling or his responsibility.

It had died suddenly, two weeks after it was born. The family buried it after dark, with no priest to say words. Nawat had always wondered if they had done a human kind of culling, killing the baby before it grew, but no one ever spoke of it again. Even its mother said nothing, once she began to appear in public.

That baby had been wrong from birth, as crows saw it. From the patterns in Ochobai's body and bones, it might be a year or two before a human mage realized that she did not grow well. With crows, it would be different. Nawat was her father. It stood to reason that he would be the first to pin down the wrongness in his daughter. But in a matter of months, perhaps only weeks, other crows would begin to feel it. They would know that Ochobai had to be culled. They would wonder why Nawat had not taken care of it, when she was in his nest. They would look at the dwarfs of the city, working and playing, having children, and they would know that Nawat was acting like a human, not a crow.

He would be cast from the flock, from the great family of crows. The Rajmuat flock would drive him away, and the flock of his blood family back on Lombyn Isle. He could imagine their beaks tearing at his flesh, their claws digging into his hair and back.

He lifted Ochobai and stood. It would be better if he did it right away. If he used the fountain, he could tell Aly the baby had slipped from his hands. . . .

Aly.

If he culled one of their children, she would never forgive him. Even if he made it look like an accident. He had tried not to lie to Aly, who had the magical Gift of Seeing lies and other things. The fact that he was a crow confused her Gift; sometimes he *could* lie to her, but he didn't know if he could do such a big lie without her detection.

It didn't matter if Aly could See his lie or not. It would be in his heart, rotting away his love for her. How could he give up Aly of the sparkly eyes and glittering smile, Aly of the dancing hands and feet? That was the way he had first seen her, tending a flock of goats. The stubble of hair on her head had shone red-gold in the sun. She moved like a butterfly. She joked with him as if they were friends before he ever changed his shape. She was so much more than a human who treated a crow with respect, even at the start.

Nawat turned away from garden, fountain, and colonnade. Aly would not believe that Nawat was foolish enough to take the baby into the rain, or so slow that Ochobai would drown before he pulled her from the water.

He would cull Ochobai properly, from the nest. He could say he was sleepy and forgot the jars, so he took her to the window. It would be quick, quicker than Keeket. He would stay a proper crow, and lose his mate.

Small fists dug at his chest as he climbed the stairs from ground floor to third. Nawat looked down into Ochobai's face. She had gone quiet as she struck him over and over. Did she know what he planned to do?

She looked no different from Ulasu and Junim as they

explored something of interest. Ochobai's interest just now seemed to lie in pummeling her father. She did it with determination.

She does everything with determination, thought Nawat. Like Aly.

He ground his teeth together, forcing himself not to think of Ochobai as anything but a nestling with a disease that would be a problem to the flock. He would be helping her. Perhaps she cried so much from pain in her bones, though the midwife said she was healthy. As far as the midwife, Aly, and every other human were concerned, Nawat would be killing a perfectly normal baby.

Ochobai looked up at him and made a sound. She screwed her face up in a yawn. Nawat stopped, her beauty stabbing him all the way through the heart. Ochobai was his favorite, though he wasn't supposed to have one. From the beginning he was the only person of all the triplets' attendants who could quiet Ochobai mid-tantrum. He loved her from her downy puff of dark hair to the tiny nails on her hands and feet. Her grip on his finger was more ferocious than that of her brother and sister, the power in her lungs more piercing even than that of Terai's older baby. How could he drop this pink nestling, his first, sixty feet to the hard stone flags of Moon Orchid Walk?

She woke him up when he'd come home from missions for the queen, tired of flight, and tired of humans. She spat her mother's milk in his face, on his clothes, in his hair. When she had filled a diaper, she smelled horrible. She had gotten baby dung on his hands and chest. In the bath, she splashed so much that she got soapy water in his eyes, nose, mouth, and ears. She hated every toy he gave her.

The guards let them inside the rooms. Everyone was still asleep: Ochobai had not roused them by screaming for her midnight meal.

Nor did she now. She did need the jar—or the window, Nawat thought, his gut in a knot. Do it now, while it is quiet, while no one is awake. Before the Rajmuat flock knows I have not culled her.

Taking her blanket and diaper off, he looked inside her again. There was the wrongness: the part that made all of him that was a crow want to shriek and claw. It battered against his rib cage, demanding that he cull this malformed nestling *now.* It was flock law; it was *crow* law.

Nawat was sprouting feathers as he carried Ochobai to the window farthest from the sleeping women and the door to Aly's room. He ignored them and the claws that formed at the tips of his fingers. Holding the nestling in one arm, he pulled the mosquito net aside with the other and leaned over the stone sill.

He was about to stretch out the arm with the nestling when Ochobai grabbed two fistfuls of chest feathers and gave them her hardest yank. The crow-man looked at his nestling. Ochobai met his gaze. She yanked his feathers again without looking away.

The crow did not think of his mate. It was Nawat who saw those fearless baby eyes. Did Ochobai even know what he intended to do? How could she, an infant barely two months old?

If he killed her, he would be killing the baby who was

already showing a stubborn streak equal to her mother's. He would kill the daughter who slept between him and Aly more often than her siblings, because she was calmer with her parents. He thought of those small punches to his nose and his eyes again, but they were not insults. They were Ochobai, fighting two other babies to be the first into the world.

He held her with both hands. "You're not going to be wrong," he whispered. "Different, yes. Many of the dwarfs are different, and they have lives and families and work. They are no stranger than merpeople or Stormwings or centaurs. You will need to be a fighter." He cuddled her against his chest. "I am a fool. I cannot undo what I have become, no more than your mother can un-bear you."

A trickle of wetness down his leg told Nawat he had brought Ochobai inside before she had done the business *she,* at least, was there for. "I am well served," he said, kissing the crown of her head. "If I gave you a fright, you have paid me back." He realized that when he'd had his change of heart his feathers had retreated. Only Ochobai still clung to a few. "You have paid me back *royally,*" Nawat murmured with a wince, feeling sore spots where she had ripped the feathers from his chest. He carried her back to her crib for cleaning with the diaper he had not thought she would need again.

When she was tidy, Nawat carried the naked infant into his bedroom. Aly was awake instantly. Smelling the milk on her mother's nightgown, Ochobai began to fuss.

"Oh, poor baby," Aly murmured, holding out her arms. "I'll take her, Nawat." As soon as Ochobai began to nurse, Nawat washed off Ochobai's urine. Once he was clean, he got into the bed with a burping cloth in one hand and a clean diaper in the other.

"I'm sorry about . . . before," Aly murmured. "So very sorry. I'm all at odds and ends. It seems as if I take it out on you because what you say touches me in places where I have no defenses."

"Hush," Nawat said, putting a finger to her lips. "I have something you must know, something that will touch you there, and not because of me. Ochobai, Aly. She will not be like Ulasu or Junim. She will be a dwarf."

Aly looked up at him, her eyes wide in the dark. Through the open door to the nursery, Nawat glimpsed a maid as she lit several lamps. Junim and Ulasu had begun to wail for a meal. Terai and the other wet nurse moved to the cradles as Nawat watched.

"There's no sign," Aly said at last, her voice soft in the dark. "Mistress Penolong said nothing. She did enough spells over my womb while I was carrying. Surely she would know."

"Sometimes it does not show for years," Nawat replied as the other triplets went quiet outside. "But crows—we know when a nestling will not fledge into an adult like all the rest. We always know."

"And then you throw them out of the nest, or drop them to the ground, like Keeket," Aly said. She slid a hand under her pillow, where she always kept a dagger. "You *cull* them."

"Yes," Nawat said calmly, keeping his eyes on the scene in the nursery. He had not forgotten that Aly was a dangerous woman. He had to trust her. "Humans will allow a child that is not perfect, or *some* humans will." He thought of the tiny baby that had died in a cold winter, buried without witnesses. "I thought I was a good crow, fit for the Rajmuat flock. Instead I am only a crow fit for my own war band, and for you, I hope."

Aly looked at him. He could feel it, coming from her, the special attention that was her magical Gift. She was trying to See if he lied. "But you will be cast out," she said.

Nawat dared to stroke his daughter's soft hair. Aly did not stop him. That was a good sign.

"I will be cast out of the great, cruel Rajmuat flock," he said. "My war band has faced it, and so will I. We can live with that. It would kill me to lose Aly and my favorite daughter."

"You're not supposed to have favorites!" she whispered softly. "You're supposed to love them all equally!" She slid her hand out from under her pillow with a sigh. "Maybe when you get to know the other two better," she suggested.

Ochobai had finished her snack. She pinched her mother's breast to let her know that.

"A dwarf," Aly said, and kissed her daughter's forehead. "We will learn, then, all of us. We'll teach you to *keep* fighting." She handed the baby to Nawat. "We'll bring other dwarfs into this household. And no one will mock you for who you are."

"They will," Nawat said as he placed Ochobai against his shoulder. "Humans are like crows in that way. Ochobai will teach them better." He patted her back.

Ochobai belched wetly onto the cloth.

* * *

In the morning, Nawat went to the crow barracks to tell his war band he, too, would soon be outcast. He wanted to give them a last chance to leave if they still cared to go. He also wanted to make certain none of them would try to cull his firstborn. He took Ochobai with him, because she began to scream when he tried to leave her behind. Now he waited for his band's response with the baby in the curve of his arm. He watched each of the born crows, daring them silently to utter a word about his dwarf child.

Instead Bala looked at another of the born humans. "You lose," she said. "Pay up." She held out her hand.

The man grumbled and dug in his purse until he found six coins, all of which he set on her palm. "We had a wager on," he explained to Nawat as other members of the band handed over coins to Bala and one of the other women. "Bunch of us thought you'd get yourself made outcast over Lady Aly. These two thought it'd be one of the babies." He nodded at the pair who were taking in money.

"Did no one bet on me remaining a crow in flock standing?" asked Nawat, outraged.

All of his people looked at him and shook their heads slowly. "We *are* a bit worried about the Rajmuat flock coming after us, though, *lurah,*" his second-in-command told Nawat. "They can be real nasty."

Nawat bounced his daughter, who cackled. "I'm going to talk it over with them," he explained. "I have a bargain I'll offer. The Rajmuat flock leaves us be, and we don't hire mages to witch the roosting trees."

Everyone gaped at him. Roosting trees were sacred. "You'd *do* that?" Bala asked, eyes wide.

Nawat grinned at her and then at Ochobai. "I'm a crow, aren't I? Cousin to the Trickster God himself." He lifted his daughter in the air and wriggled her until she drooled on him. "We're *both* crows."

Suddenly the crows of the war band began to caw in triumph. The humans jumped to their feet, waving and pointing. In all the fuss, Nawat finally understood he was to look at the back of Ochobai's head.

A small quill had sprouted there, the sign of a nestling's first feather.

The Dragon's Tale

Bored. I was bored, bored, bored. If I could speak in the human tongues I heard below, I could have made "bored" into a chant. I hated it that I could not speak to humans or animals. I could not even speak mind-to-mind, as Mama Daine does with the beast-People. Many humans called me a mindless animal or even a monster. It made me want to claw them head to toe, though I am not that sort in general. If I could talk to them, they would know I was intelligent and friendly. I could walk among them and explain myself. Instead I had to sit up on this overlook, waiting for my foster parents to introduce me to yet another village full of humans who had never met a dragon before.

I could have stayed in the realms of the gods with Daine and Numair's human children and their grandparents instead of coming here. I could have spent these long days playing with them and the god animals. I could have even visited my own relatives. Instead I thought that it would be fun to visit Carthak with my foster parents. Thak City and the palaces, new and old, were interesting. Humans create pretty buildings. The Carthakis in particular make splendid mosaics. There were ships to see, statues, fireworks, human magic displays, and the emperor and his empress. I liked the onetime princess Kalasin, who was empress at that time.

Then Emperor Kaddar decided it would be wonderful to travel some of his country with Numair and Daine. Kalasin had to stay in the new palace and govern while Kaddar took to the road. I remained with Daine, Numair, and Kaddar as we journeyed east, where Kaddar stopped at every oasis and town to talk. The village of Imoun looked to be an ordinary stop on that trip. It was a small clump of humans who lived beside the river Louya and the Demai Mountains.

We had arrived halfway through the afternoon. The soldiers helped us set up Daine and Numair's tent above the camp, on a spot where it overlooked the rest of our tents. When they were done, I walked up to a flat stone outcrop where I could watch the rest of the day unfold. I don't know why I bothered. It was the same as it had been for the last twenty villages. The soldiers put up the platform, then covered it in carpets and decorated it with pillows and bolsters. The important humans would talk with Kaddar there later. More soldiers placed magical globe lights on posts around the platform, so everyone would be able to see when it got dark. Villagers built fires around the platform to warm the humans once the sun went down.

I never watched the setting-up from close by. Early on I had learned that I was always getting in the way of those who set up the platform and everything around it, even when I tried not to. The guards would complain to Papa Numair about me. The villagers only screamed and ran. Finally Kaddar asked me nicely to stay away. It's not Kaddar's fault that his people had never encountered anyone like me.

The soldiers got better. Some of them did. Some of them still treated me like Daine and Numair's pet, though my humans had explained many times that I was as clever as any two-legger. A few of the soldiers learned for themselves that I did indeed understand what they said.

Although I was brooding, I had not forgotten the world around me. I heard the horse that was climbing to my position. I knew who it was without looking, because I recognized the sound of his breathing. When Spots reached me, I pointed to the line where all of our other horses were tethered. They were happy to stay there, finished with their day's work. Then I made a fist and shook it at him. I wasn't angry. I was reminding him of how the horse guards would react when they found that Numair's very own gelding was gone again. They were lucky that Daine's pony, Cloud, had refused to come because it had meant a boat trip and Cloud hates those. Cloud and Spots together got into all kinds of mischief.

I don't care if they are angry, Spots told me. Though I am as mute as a stupid rock with animals, they can talk with me. *Daine will defend me. She knows that I like to look around. And who else can keep Numair in the saddle?*

He was right. Years ago Spots had learned to counter Numair when he let go of the rein or moved off balance. He was also good at pulling my foster father away from cliff edges and other hazards that Numair tended to find.

Once Spots had been like any other horse, only more patient and sweet tempered than most because Numair was his rider. I barely remember that Spots. Like any creature who lived near my foster mother, Daine, for a long-enough time, he grew more clever, as humans judge such things. Numair calls it "the Daine effect." Spots began to help my foster parents in their work. He watched me when I was small. That was when we found ways to talk to each other with sounds and gestures.

How long will we be here, do you suppose? Spots asked me. *It doesn't look like a very interesting place.*

I shrugged. I didn't know how many days we were going to stay. No one ever asked what I wanted. Spots nudged me with his nose and stuck his lower lip out.

I glared at him. I was *not* pouting.

"Kit, I can hear you scratching rock down at our tent." Daine walked up the slope to us, tying her curling brown hair in a horsetail. "It's a dreadful noise. I thought you were chewing stones. Oh, Spots, you undid your tether again. You know it makes the horse minders nervous when you do that." She cocked her head, listening as Spots replied, mind-to-mind. She slung his rein up over his back so he wouldn't trip on it. "I know Kitten digs at the stone because she's unhappy." Daine sat beside me and reached over to pat the rock. I looked. I had gotten so cross, watching the humans prepare for more talking, that I had gouged my claws deep into the rock at my side several times.

"It looks like you're trying to slice it for bread," Daine told me.

I gave her my sorry-chirp and leaned against her. I wished so much that I could talk to her in more than noises! Spots stretched around Daine and nuzzled the back of my head.

"You're bored, aren't you, poor thing?" asked Daine.

"At least Spots can talk to the other horses. Which reminds me," she said, turning to look at him. "Back to the ranks with *you,* magical escaping horse. The soldiers fear they'll be punished if one of the mounts vanishes."

Spots snorted, but he did walk, slowly, back down to the tethering lines.

I was still shocked by what Daine had said about me. How did she always *know* how I felt?

"At home you usually have something to busy yourself with," she said, running her cool fingers over my snout. "We might have left you in the capital, but the only person there who knows you well is Empress Kalasin. *She* can hardly take you about."

I whistled my agreement. Kalasin had to rule the Empire.

"We thought we'd see more of the sights, didn't we?" Daine asked. "But this, Kit, it's a wonderful thing, for Kaddar to meet with his people. Normally he'd travel with all manner of ceremony, and the local folk would be too frightened to say a word to him. With me and Numair to guard, and only a hundred soldiers instead of a thousand, he's approachable. They will talk to him and tell him the truth."

I made my rudest noise. Human truth telling was a mixed quantity at best. There were always untruths and evasions of some kind mixed in.

Daine looked sideways at me. "Oh, all right. As much truth as folk will tell their emperor. It's a good thing Numair and I are the only ones who speak Kitten. *You* are not suited to a life of diplomacy."

I made a lesser rude noise. Dragons do not use diplomacy. We are not good at it.

I heard the new visitors before I saw them. Daine and I looked down. Twenty fluffy-tailed mice had come to meet her. This sort of thing always happened when Daine was about. I loved it.

"Well, look at you!" Daine said, opening the pouch at her belt. She *always* carried food for small animals with her. "Kit, see how our friends have more red in their fur than the ones we met twenty miles back?" A few of the mice climbed up on Daine, holding on to her shirt or sitting on her shoulders, arms, and legs. She offered them dried raisins and sunflower seeds, inquiring mind-to-mind after their families and winter food supplies. A pair of the braver mice climbed up on me, which made me happy. Too often I remind small prey animals of a snake or a cat. Lately they had been more accepting. Perhaps a bit of Daine's beast-People kindness had begun to cling to me, reassuring them.

At last the mice said their farewells and ran into the rocks. Daine straightened with a grimace and looked at the sky. Dark was coming. Soldiers were lighting the fires below. The platform was finished. I smelled good things being prepared by the villagers and the emperor's cooks.

"I'll make sure a dish is brought to our tent for you," Daine told me.

I cawed at her. I hated the tent, and Daine knew it!

"We got here too late to take you about and show you to the local folk; you know we did," Daine said. "And two-leggers *always* startle more when they see you after dark. I'm sorry. Just stay in the tent for tonight. Tomorrow I'll introduce you to the village."

I knew she was right, but what was there to do in the tent? I gave her my saddest whistle and walked away. I had already gone through everything in Numair's mage kit and in Daine's. I had even read all of the books they had brought along.

Humans were so *stupid.* They likened me to a crocodile or some kind of lizard, though surely they should have known that those creatures did not have silver claws or rudimentary wings, let alone the ability to change color. They also did not stand on their haunches and chirp in a reassuring way, indicating that they would like to be friends. My muzzle was far more delicate than that of a crocodile, and my teeth stayed inside it! I was slender and fine boned. I was only forty-five inches long in those days, and fifteen inches of that was tail. Yet somehow there were always humans who were terrified by the sight of me. To cater to such idiots, I was kept to my foster parents' tent when there was no time to introduce me in a new place.

It was hard to stay inside. I could hear music and laughter, the welcome that came before the boring speeches. One of the emperor's soldiers—one of my friends—brought me a bowl of stew. I chirped happily at him: he'd remembered I liked honey-nut pastries and gave two. After he left, I was alone. My boredom soon reached the point at which I might shriek if I didn't do something. Since Daine only liked me to shriek during combat, I was really doing the right thing for Daine if I took a walk instead.

I wriggled under the back flap of the tent. On that side lay mountains, their ridges and peaks sharp in the light of the half-moon. A small herd of screwhorn antelope was climbing to higher pastures, away from the noise. They were just as visible to my dragon eyes as they would have been with no moon at all.

When I could no longer see the antelope, I concentrated on my scales. I changed color according to my mood; my parents knew that. They did not know that, over the long journey, I had learned to change colors deliberately. I let my magic spread out and around me, collecting the shades of shadowed sand, reddish limestone, black lava rock, gray-green brush, and moonlit air. I drew the colors back into patches over my scales. Then I set out for the village.

I was about to pass through the gate when I heard the very distant sound of young humans whispering together. Since I am always curious, I followed the faint noise around the outside of the wall, away from the meeting of the emperor and his people. Soon the voices were clearer. They belonged to boys, excited ones.

"Look! She's at it again!"

"She don't learn."

"You got rocks? Gimme some."

Four boys crouched in the shadows around the ruins of a shed. They were barefoot, their clothes mostly patched. I halted, secure in my camouflage, waiting to see what had their attention. The village garbage heap lay in a dip in the ground nine yards or so away from the boys. A young woman was sifting through the heap, collecting pieces of food and stowing them in a basket on her arm, working by feel and scant moonlight. Magic burned at the heart of her, the stuff called the Gift that humans put to use like a servant. Could she not make money with her Gift, as so many mages do, and buy food?

The thinnest of the boys crept forward and threw the first rock. He missed by a foot.

The other three ran up to hurl stones at the woman. One hit her shoulder; another struck her leg; the third missed. She dropped the vegetable she'd been holding, but she made no sound. Instead she knelt and scrabbled to get the vegetable into her basket. The boys threw more stones. All four hit this time. She half-turned, catching them on her shoulders and back. Then she grabbed one and threw it sharply, striking the thinnest boy hard in the belly. While the others took care of him, she scrambled to her feet and ran, ignoring their shouts of anger.

The boys gave chase. I followed on all fours, trying to think of what I could do that would stop them without permanently injuring them. In normal battles no one cares if I split someone's skull or shatter his bones with a whistle. I can throw fire, but that is just as fatal. These were human children. Daine, Numair, and Kaddar would have been very angry with me if I killed children.

The open ground before us gleamed in the dim moonlight. Here the mountains reached into the flatlands with long, stony black fingers that dug into the pale earth, leaving bays of light-colored dirt and brush between them. The woman ran for the bays, clutching her basket to her chest. The boys were hard on her trail. In addition to calling her vile names, they said that she had no business stealing their garbage. I wished I could ask the woman, or them, what they meant. Perhaps it was some odd local custom. Everywhere else I had been, garbage was made of things humans had no more use for.

Suddenly the race ended. While the woman ran from my sight between two black stone fingers, the boys began to act very strangely. They separated and ran about, skirting areas as if there were obstacles in the way. They never strayed from the open ground between the garbage heap and the rocks.

At last they came together, panting and exhausted. I crouched flat, listening.

"We searched those rocks everywhere, but she vanished!" the thin one said.

"Every time we think we got Afra cornered, she goes into the Maze," said another, a male with a long scar on his face.

The Maze? I wondered. I had seen no maze, though the boys *had* moved on the open ground as if they walked such a thing.

"You'd think the rock itself hid her," grumbled the third boy.

The four of them drew the sign against evil on their chests. "I tole you Afra was a witch," said the one whose clothes were a little better than the other boys'. "Witches do that. They vanish right in front of you."

That was pure nonsense. Numair is one of the greatest mages in all the world. *He* cannot do it unless the spell is already prepared. The female Afra had used no spells at all that I had seen. Her Gift was visible to me, but she had not employed it, nor did she wear any spell charms.

"We have to warn the emperor!" the scarred one said. "Afra might cast a spell against his life!"

The four turds raced away, eager to tell a man guarded by my foster parents that their witch, who was too generous to singe *them,* was a danger to him. Like most humans, they didn't realize that an emperor would never venture so far from his palaces unless he was very well guarded. I *did* think that perhaps the boys had seen Numair and had mistaken him for someone who was silly. Many people do.

I followed Afra into the rocky bays where she had gone to hide. I wanted to learn if she knew of the power that had not only made her escape route invisible to the boys, but made them believe they had walked some kind of maze.

Ten feet from the first stony finger, I walked into magic of a kind I had never encountered before. My experience of magic even at that time was great, yet this was unknown to me. I had not found it in visits to the realms of the gods or to the Dragonlands. Nor had I felt anything like it in all my dealings with humans, Gifted or born with any form of wild magic. Even the spirits of mountains, trees, rivers, and streams had nothing like this.

Numair says that magic is a sense for dragons as much as smell and hearing. The strangeness of this new power made my scales prickle.

I called it "new," but it was that only to me. Even while the strange force trickled across my face and made my licking tongue quiver, I could tell it was old. It might even have been older than my grandfather Diamondflame, who owns to several thousands of years. Where did this power come from? Who had placed it here?

I took a deep breath. The scent of the power entered my nose and burned, making my eyes water. I tried a smaller breath and thanked the Dragongods that Afra carried rotting food. That stench fought the magic's scent. I took three steps. That strange power thrust at me, trying to stop me. I whistled at it softly, pushing back with my own air-carried magic. My power balanced against that older one as I walked forward.

Three feet. I slammed into a solid wall of magic that flared a hot white in my eyes. My softer whistle did nothing to that. I was too impatient to work my way up through lesser whistles. I used a mid-level squawk, good for shattering drawbridges. It was enough, too, for this barrier, which melted. I walked on into a third magic that poured down between two rocks, a flash flood that blazed green with red and blue sparks. I had no time to think. I yowled at the top of my lungs, fearing what might happen if I failed.

The flood vanished.

Far in the distance I heard humans cry out, demanding to know what was going on. (I heard them talk later about a leopard.) High in the mountains to the east, beyond the humans' sense of hearing, I heard a rockslide. I cringed. If Daine shaped her ears to those of an animal that heard well, I was in *serious* trouble.

When nothing more happened and no humans came, I went on, following my nose. The scent of rotting garbage led me to a cave set in a mass of orange stone, partway up a black rock divide. Its opening was tucked around a bend in the trail, easily missed if no one knew it was there. Flat stones lay before the cave, so no footprints would ever give a dweller away. Light from a lamp or candle shone from its depths. She had to feel safe there.

I poked my head inside.

She gasped, then cried, "Monster! Get out!"

She was quick to find a rock and throw it at me, painfully quick. It struck my head. I ducked out and waited, holding my paws to the nasty bruise on my forehead. After a moment, I shielded myself in protective spells and looked inside. She screamed and threw a blaze of her Gift at me. I backed out again. Her Gift had not touched me, but I understood why she was so frightened and why she needed any food that she could find. Her baby had begun to cry.

It was time to think matters through. Turning what I now knew over in my head, I returned to the imperial camp. I needed to obtain a few things.

I had just come back from my scavenging when I heard Daine and Numair. The long talk was over; they were returning. I smoothed a layer of spells over the items I had procured. When my mage parents looked at my nest of blankets, they would see only the back of the tent behind me, not the other things. It was tricky to work out something that would fool Daine and Numair, but I'd done it.

They would have been glad to help if I had let them know about Afra, but they always helped. I didn't need that. I wanted to do it by myself, in part because I was bored, in part to prove to them—to myself—that I could. I needed something of my own to do. If I had not tamed Afra by the time we had to leave, I would let my parents know about her.

I curled up in my blankets and pretended to sleep just as they entered our tent. They spoke quietly while preparing for bed. They said that the villagers had told Emperor Kaddar about a number of problems. They were hard for local folk to handle all at once, but their emperor and his companions could take care of them easily, if they cared to do so. Kaddar had walked into the trap. Knowing Kaddar, he had seen the trap and entered it anyway. He and his men would seek a robber gang that operated in the mountain pass five miles to the east. Daine would see to illnesses among the village herds while Numair cleared the river channel of the waterweeds that choked it. I knew we might be there for as long as a week, even two. That would give me more time to work with Afra.

In the morning, when dawn just brushed the mountains and my parents slept, I tied my things in a small bundle. Disguised in the colors of barely lit earth and stone, I returned to the place where the boys had acted as if they were lost in a maze of boulders.

When the first shock of alien magic crackled against mine, I was ready. In the pale light, I saw it only as a blurring of everything that lay beyond. From sandy earth with its patches of scrub brush to the black mountain stone, the strange power remade it into softness. It gave this land a more forgiving face.

When I touched it, the magic ran over my scales. It felt different than it had the night before. This time it was like a thousand tiny hands explored me from crest to tail tip. I banished that thought. Grandfather Diamondflame and Numair would scold me for letting imagination color what I observed. I walked slowly into the magic's growing resistance, seeing the boys' tracks from last night and then my own footprints, off to my right.

Next I met the second, more resistant wall. I didn't see it. I simply walked into it and felt it give a little as I stopped. Again there was something new, like a pause, as if the magic waited to see what I would do. I shook the peculiar thought from my skull. It was a leftover from sixteen years among humans.

I had spent the night considering my encounters with this magic. I did not want to risk using sounds by daylight, for fear of drawing attention. If the villagers got frightened enough, they would call on Kaddar, who would call on my foster father. When Numair found this magic, I would no longer have the riddle to solve for myself. I didn't doubt that my papa could probably shatter these barriers easily.

Resting a paw against this barrier, I called up the spell I had prepared and blew it forward. The only sound I made was a long, soft hiss. The magic flowed out between my teeth, eating the barrier like acid. It vanished before my spell could devour it all, and I went forward with my bundle.

I was ready for that third defense, the flood of magic, but it never came. Had I exhausted it last night? I wished I knew who had set these protections. Surely whoever it was had died long ago. Perhaps the mage had been an Ysandir, one of the ancient race alive at the same time that human civilization was beginning to grow. That might account for the total strangeness of the magic's feel. It did not account for Afra's ability to pass it without effort, however.

With no more barriers to fight, I found a hidden place near the cave where I left my bundle. I reviewed my plan. After last night, I knew I could not rely on the cute tricks that worked with those who knew me best.

First I had to investigate. I wrapped myself in silence, then climbed up into the rocks and over to Afra's cave. She would not hear my lightest claw scratch or the slide of my scales. Then I positioned myself above the entrance to listen. It was so delightful, where I lay. Unlike the black rock, this orange stone was fine grained and warm, far warmer than it should have been with sunrise just begun. I had an odd fancy that the stone was breathing, which was impossible. Grandfather Diamondflame would have scolded me roundly for so foolish an idea. Yet I could not stop myself from stroking that warm stone like a pet as I listened for what Afra might be doing deep within her cave.

Light smoke flowed up from the entry and over my nose. I sniffed: mint tea. Other smells disguised those of rotten food: garlic, ginger, and onion. I smelled another thing, one I knew from the times after Daine gave birth to my human sister and brother. It was mother's milk. Afra was nursing her baby. She would not be leaving her hiding place right away.

I backed away from the cave entrance, then halted. I wanted to stay right there, spread over the warm and breathing stone. I didn't understand. I was no lizard, to doze my life away on any sun-washed rock!

Finally I ordered myself to stop being a fluffbrain, a

word Daine often used. I went back to my bundle. From it I chose some of the food I had stolen and carried it to the front of the cave. There I left my offering: a small goat cheese, dates, olives, and several rounds of bread.

Then I returned to my hiding place, sheltered by chilly, normal black rock. I could not hear the sounds inside the cave as well as before, but the black stone did not give me strange ideas, either. I drew my camouflage spell around me, just in case, and waited.

Soon I heard Afra's footsteps as she came to the cave's entrance. With my camouflage in place, I eased up to a spot from which I could see her. She stepped into the daylight, sure of the power that hid her retreat in the rocks. She was so confident that she almost crushed my gift before she saw it was there. Then she jumped back into the cave, vanishing into the darkness.

I waited. Soon she returned, crouching in the shelter of the cave's mouth, peering around like a frightened creature. She had a rock in each hand. Only her head moved. She was listening for any noise.

In the distance I heard the village goats and sheep as their shepherds took them to graze in the lands not hidden by the barriers. A rooster in the village suddenly remembered that he had duties of his own. As he cried his name, other roosters joined in.

Afra's eyes strayed more and more to the bundle of food. I wondered if her nose was as dead as most humans' or if she could smell the cheese, at least. I scolded myself for not bringing hot meat. She would have smelled that.

She licked her lips. She *could* smell the cheese.

Slowly she put down her rocks. She rubbed her hands as her Gift moved into her fingers. She wasn't able to do magic without some gestures, then. For anything subtle, she would need to write the signs in the air. She would require special herbs, oils, or stones for more. Did she have them? It would be good to know.

She wrote a sign for safety before her face. In the sunlight I could see the color of her Gift at last. I rocked back on my heels. Afra's sign was shaped in pale blue light, outlined in pale green. I nearly whistled my excitement, then caught myself. None of my human friends except Papa had magic in two colors. Numair's books spoke of such people, but he said he'd never met anyone else. He would be so glad to meet Afra once I had tamed her!

Had she borrowed her baby's power? I asked myself. Perhaps *this* explained how she had passed through the magic that turned the village boys around, but not her.

Afra completed her spell and set it in motion. It fell onto the food, oozing over it. Within a breath it had vanished, sinking into everything. The scales stood on the back of my neck. I hoped it wouldn't harm the food. Cheese in particular reacts badly to some kinds of magic.

Afra waited, looking all around, still wary. Then she darted forward, seized the food, and ran back into the cave. I guessed that if her spell didn't react, it proved there was no magic on the bundle. I could not see her, but I could hear as she thrust a handful of something into her mouth and chewed. She continued to eat greedily out of my sight as I slowly took the remainder of my stolen goods from my bundle. Daine and I had cared for many starving creatures, so I feared I knew what came next. I had hoped Afra would have better judgment than to stuff herself right away, but I had been wrong. Carefully, retracting my hind claws so they would make no sound on the stone, I carried my next offering to the cave's entrance and left it there. Then I ran back to my hiding spot.

I was just in time. Afra raced from the cave, her hand to her mouth. She made it to a pocket of sand in the rocks across from me before she spewed everything she had eaten. I cursed myself silently. I should have given her just a mouthful of food to start. She had been living on *garbage,* and I had given her a meal of good fruit and cheese.

She stood there, her back to me, after she'd finished the last of her heaves. I could see bone against her skin where it was not covered by her garment. How was she feeding that baby? She must be giving everything to it and keeping nothing for herself.

A blade of pain stabbed me, an un-dragon-like hurt. Diamondflame says that sentiment is weakness. Maybe I have been among humans for too long. Or maybe I can never forget that my birth mother had given everything for me.

Finally Afra straightened, wiping her mouth on her wrist. She knelt and buried her vomit well. I wondered if the magic kept wolves away, if there were wolves in these mountains. I knew there were leopards. Did she use her spells to protect the cave at night, or did the strange magic keep the large killers away, as it did humans?

Afra stumbled back to the cave, unsteady with weakness, and halted when she saw my new gift. She turned. Now she had to know that I had been close, to put that food there, and that maybe I was still close, watching. She scanned the rocks and the ground, searching for any sign of me. I had not left her even my footprints as clues.

It was my first chance to give her a good look. She had the bronze skin of the northern Carthakis, snapping black eyes, and coarse black hair that she tied back with a shred of cloth. She was young and so thin, with strong muscles that stood against her skin. She was trembling, though I could not tell if it was from long weakness or from just vomiting.

Suddenly she bent and took my second gift of food. She hurried into the cave with it.

I relaxed. I had given her two chicken-and-almond turnovers. I had stolen them, like everything else, from the emperor's cooks. They were mild and should not make her ill if she ate them slowly.

She would need vegetables, fruits, and meat. I would have to find a way to carry more, somehow. In particular, she had also vomited up the cheese. Daine's midwife had been very strict with her on the subject of milk and cheese for a nursing mother. She said they needed that more than any other food and that goat's milk was the best.

I wondered if I could steal a goat.

Daine found me before I even reached our tent. "Kitten, where were you?" she cried, running up to me. "I've been looking everywhere! We were going to the village, remember?"

I sat up on my hind legs and gave her my cutest wide-eyed look, with a chirp.

Daine glared at me. "None of that, mistress. You've been up to something. You can't fool your ma, remember?"

She was right. It was very discouraging. I settled back on my haunches and looked more seriously at her. I sighed, then clasped my forepaws.

"So you'll tell me when you can. Will it get you in trouble with these folk?" she asked me.

Afra didn't live in the village. The boys had chased her away with stones. She did not belong to the village and they did not want her there. I shook my head for Daine. The matter of the goat might be hard to explain, but I hadn't taken one yet, so I was not lying.

Daine bent down and picked me up. "Is there anything I can do?" she asked as she carried me to the tent.

I shook my head. This was still my discovery.

We had breakfast with Numair before the villagers came for my parents. When we three walked out of our tent, the strangers flinched at the sight of me and drew the Sign on their chests.

Daine stiffened. "This is Skysong, our dragon," she told them, her voice cold. "When our home was attacked, mages who opened a gate to the Divine Realms drew her mother through just as she was about to give birth." She was careful not to say that it was their old emperor who had sponsored the attack. "I helped Flamewing deliver her little one, but Flamewing herself died protecting us. She left her child in our care. Kitten—that's what we call her—is as friendly as can be. She's saved many lives, human and animal alike."

"Her face looks like a crocodile's," said one of the females, an old and wrinkly one.

Daine drew herself up. Numair settled her with a hand on her shoulder. "Kitten is a dragon," he said to the old woman. "They are more intelligent than even we humans. She understands every word that you say."

"Why doesn't she answer, then?" one of the males wanted to know.

"She is too young," Numair replied. "You will be centuries in the ground when she is able to talk."

That caused them to whisper among themselves. I never understood why people would be awed by that, when they were so unpleasant about my looks. Besides, for all they knew, Numair could have been lying. Still, they accepted his word that I would live much longer than they would, which was quite true, unless I was murdered.

"If you wish your animals looked at, you will learn to like Kitten," Daine told them. "Where I go, she goes. She may even do your creatures more good than I will."

I didn't feel like doing good for anyone in the village walls after the way they had treated Afra.

"Well, Master Numair, we're to take you upriver, if you still wish to go," the male who'd led these humans said. "No horses, if it please you. The ground's too rocky along the riverbank as we head into the mountains. Can't even take a mule that way."

Poor Spots, I thought. He's stuck here again. I looked over at the horse lines to see how he did. Most of the soldiers' mounts were gone, along with the emperor's favorite riding horse. They were bandit hunting. Spots was talking with one of the horses that hauled the wagons. That would amuse him for a little while. He would escape his tether by midday.

Numair and the men left on foot. The women looked at Daine and me, then seemed to come to a silent agreement. "If you will come with us?" the female who had spoken to Daine asked. We all set forward, the talker on Daine's left, the other two behind her. I was on Daine's right. "Two days back Tahat's chickens got sick. We've locked them in their coop, but that will be useless if it is a curse on the village. We think there is a witch hereabouts."

My ears pricked up. Did they mean Afra? I looked at Daine, and I had to snort. Her lips and nostrils had tightened right up. It would follow that in this village, whose humans had already irritated her by insulting me, she would first be asked to look at chickens. Her grandfather's chickens, the ones she had grown up knowing, were the nastiest, trickiest birds she had ever met in her life. Now, even though she had met dozens of perfectly decent chickens, she could not bring herself to like them. She was certain that their pleasantness to her was just another chicken trick.

If she had hated geese, I would have been more understanding. Geese have made *my* life a misery.

While Daine listened to the chickens' troubles, I let Tahat's children sneak up on me and poke me with their fingers. When a neighbor boy tried to use a stick, I snatched it from him and hissed. That amused the women who were not watching Daine. They seemed to like me better for it. Tahat, who was too worried about her flock to be afraid of me, even brought me a small dish of milk.

Daine saw that and warmed to her. "It's no curse, only

bird pox," she said. "You were right to contain them before it spread to the other chickens. I can deal with it." She looked up at the female who seemed to be the leader. "Will you help me?"

I hardly noticed when one of the older children tugged my tail. There were chickens all over the village. I could hear them. If Daine had to check them for this illness, she would not be paying attention to my activities.

First she had to make friends with the village's chief mage. While she had some kind of tea with that man, I busied myself by acquiring a few things: a round of cheese, four eggs, a woman's robe, two lamb sausages, and more fruit. Covered with camouflage spells and keeping to back paths, I carried those things one at a time outside the open gate, where I piled them against the wall. I hid them with still more camouflage, this time a concealment from sight, covered with the seeming of a nest of vipers. I didn't want the dogs to eat my loot.

Last of all I found an empty grain sack. I rolled it up and carried it outside the gate. First I was careful to wrap the eggs well in the robe. If they broke there, they could be washed out. I knew Afra must have a water source, or she could not have survived in the cave at all.

Once I had filled my sack with all I had taken, I realized I had listened to my ambition instead of my sense. I could not carry it. I was much too small. The path from the gate to our tent, or even partway to the invisible maze where Afra hid, was mostly open ground. If I dragged the sack—I was strong enough to do so, despite my size—folk would see the clear trail that the sack would leave in the dirt.

I whistled my vexation. I had a spell I shaped of breath and will to brush away any marks I left on occasions like this. It did take a great deal of concentration. That was easy enough when I was on horseback with Daine, which was the last time I had needed it. It would be tiring if I had to keep an eye open for humans, hold camouflage magic over my sack and me, and drag that sack. I needed to quickly reach the rocks that were perfectly visible to me and invisible to humans.

Again I had to wonder how Afra had found the cave. Did her dual Gift make it possible for her to see through the old barriers on that piece of land? Was the power that hid the cave hers to begin with?

I shook my head as I tied the sack shut with some cord I had found. If she had used her Gift to create an invisible maze in open scrub, I would have been able to see its colors by daylight. Moreover, I would have been able to shatter all of it with my middling squawk. Also, those boys had acted as if their maze had always been in that place. They were used to it.

Gripping the neck of the sack in my teeth, I wriggled until it lay over my shoulder. There was no one in view inside the gate or outside. I set out, keeping an eye on my surroundings. Far off to my left the soldiers who had stayed to guard the emperor's camp lazily went about their chores. They had shifted the picketed horses off to a line of trees by the river. I hated to think of my friend Spots cooking in the sun, like I was. No one was following as I struggled away from the gate. The bag slid to and fro as I went forward, so that I half-carried, half-dragged it. I was leaving an unmistakable track.

I halted briefly and took a deep, deep breath, then blew it into my cupped forepaw. I spun it around, blowing steadily, until I had a tornado as tall as I was. I drove it with my will, sending it over the unmistakable drag mark I'd left in my wake. Back and forth I swept it, then around and around, until the dirt no longer showed the trace of my sack. I kept the tornado with me as I trudged across the open ground. It swept over my trail, whisking my marks to nothing, until I crested a small rise in the ground and went down the far side. Once I was out of view of the road, I released my spinning winds. They scattered into the open air.

I collapsed onto the ground, letting go of my camouflage briefly to rest. How could Daine and Numair do more than two pieces of magic at the same time? I was worn out only by two, and by the effort of dragging my burden.

I hated being young. And I would be young so much longer than a human child.

I had to get up. There was too much risk of a human stumbling over me. The Carthaki sun was also a hammer on my scales. I rose, wove my camouflage spell again, and began to drag the sack toward the rocks.

I had gone scarcely a hundred yards, and had reached the point of telling myself that I was a poor excuse for a dragon, when a horse called to me. I turned to look. Spots was on my trail, his tether in his mouth. I released my camouflage, let go of the sack, and trilled a welcome. I was so happy to see him!

He trotted to me. *I followed your scent.* His slow, practical voice sounded amused in my mind. *I knew you would have found a way to get into trouble by now. Let go of that bag.* I did as I was bid, with relief. He gripped the neck of the sack and picked it up. It had been big for me. To Spots it wasn't nearly as heavy as one of Numair's book-stuffed saddlebags, which he had also carried in this way. *Why did you find something to do without bringing me?* Spots asked. *I always manage the heavy work for you.*

I hung my head. Then I made a fist, shook it at him, and pointed back at the camp. I still didn't want to get him into trouble. Then I touched a claw-tip to my chest and pointed to the walled village.

Yes, that is a great deal of walking for a small dragon, Spots said. He always understood me. *And I keep telling you,* I *will deal with the humans if they want to make trouble for me. It's time they learned that not all horses can be bullied.*

I saw the warlike look in his eye and shook my head. Spots had been getting some strange ideas lately. I squeaked an apology and took his rein in my paw. He nudged me to let me know that he didn't mind if I led him. Moving much faster now that I had his help with my burden, I took him to the rocks.

When we touched the strange magic of the first barrier, Spots shied and yanked on the rein. His yank threw me into the air. I came down with a thud. Spots put down the sack and nuzzled me in apology. *I'm sorry,* he told me, guilt in his mind-voice. *I didn't know there was magic here.* He gripped the sack again.

I showed him two of my claws.

Two magics, Spots said. *How splendid.*

I whistled a shield that covered him nose to tail. I loved him because he let me lead him onward into the magic, through the first barrier. He stood firm while I worked spells to get us through the second barrier. Each time he calmly went ahead when I chirped. I had not known until that day how much he trusted me.

Once we were through, we hurried to Afra's cave. I knew the sound of hooves ringing on stone would frighten her, but it was the fastest way to take the sack right to the cave's mouth. After we left it there, we retreated to a side trail to wait.

What do you have in there? Spots asked me.

With gestures and poses I explained it was a human female with an infant.

It would be easier to bring Daine or Numair, Spots reminded me. *Not that you ever choose the easy path. I prefer to leave humans to humans, myself.*

I only sniffed at him. Spots always said he liked his life to be boring, but he was always there when I got up to something.

Eventually the baby began to cry. It cried in loud whoops, then softer ones. I dug my claws into the stone, wishing the noise would stop. Just when I hoped the baby was done, it began to scream. That was when Afra came to take the sack.

She dragged it back into the cave, then called, "Who are you? Why do you help us? If you really wish to be my friend, show yourself!"

Afra didn't think that last night's monster was the one

who left food for her today. Yet why demand to see me? What good could it do? I looked up at Spots. He shrugged his withers, a human gesture he'd learned. He didn't know, either.

I didn't want to chatter or make friends. That baby needed its mother's milk, and the best way for its mother to make milk was for her to eat food, and to *drink* milk. That meant I still needed to steal a goat. She was wasting my time. I had only waited to be sure she took the sack at all.

"I know you are still here," she cried. "I heard your horse. You are quite close by; I listened to the hoofbeats."

Kraken spit, I thought.

Spots put his muzzle at the center of my back and pushed. *Do as she asks. We did not raise you to be rude.*

It was an easy thing for him to say. She had not hit him on the head and called him a monster.

I showed him my fist, meaning this would not go well. He nudged me again, until I fell onto all four legs. I glared up at him.

I mean it, Kitten, Spots told me. *Go.* He shoved my rump forward, nearly driving my muzzle into the dirt.

I ran as much away from him as toward the cave. The stubborn beast followed. He was determined that Afra should see me. Once he took up for someone, there was nothing he would not do for them. That included ordering me about.

Afra saw Spots first because he was taller. Her quick eyes took in his lack of a saddle or rider and his knotted tether. Then she saw me.

"You again!" she cried. She flung her hand out. A twining flare of magic, mixed pale blue and pale green ropes that would burn an ordinary mortal to the ground, sped from her fingers.

Afra's spell washed over me. It stung, a little. Then it flowed up, meeting the magical barrier overhead in bursts of gold sparkles. I wanted to grip some, but Afra was not done with me.

Brighter two-colored fires lashed from her hand. I could feel their strength—if they hit me, they would hurt. I raised a shield of my own power that would cover Spots and me. Her Gift splashed against it and was sucked into the magic overhead. It blazed gold.

The earth quivered, an anxious horse about to break free of all control. *Uh-oh,* Spots said. *Did you feel that?*

I looked at Afra. She was intent on working another spell. The earth shook hard, knocking her down. The stones beside the mouth of the cave trembled. If the shake got harder, there was danger to the cave.

Spots and I raced forward together without needing to check with one another. We were old campaigners; we knew what had to be done. The ground rolled. Spots scrambled for footing as small stones fell and hit Afra. Spots lunged and got a mouthful of her robe as I raced past him into the cave. Afra screamed as a large rock fell behind me, half-blocking the cave's mouth.

For a moment I could not move. Inside the cave a welcoming warmth enclosed me. It reminded me of how I felt when Daine held me. I thought I heard a whispering song in a strange language I almost knew. Dazed, I touched the cave wall. It was glassy and warm, an assembly of tiny beads. I wanted to stay there forever.

Then the baby screamed. Somehow I forced myself to break that spell of love and safety to walk deeper into the cave. Another shake inspired me to run, my night vision showing me all the dangers. Afra had a small fire going in the chamber she had turned into her home. I buried that in case falling rock scattered hot embers everywhere. The baby lay beside the fire, swaddled and tucked into a carry basket. I whistled a lifting spell until I could wriggle my forepaws into the straps. Then, as another shiver rocked the ground under my feet, I began to run, or rather, to slog.

I never expected a small baby and a straw carry basket to weigh so much. I was frantic to get out before the cave dropped on us, yet I also wanted to stay and be a baby myself, curled up against the mother spirit in the stone. Each time I stopped to catch my breath, I had to force myself to move on. Fortunately, though I did not think so then, the baby's screams constantly reminded me to keep going. I could not wait to get it off of my back, or sides, wherever it had slipped. By the time we came to the rock that half-covered the entrance, the basket hung off of my neck, yanking me sideways.

Eyeing the rock and the opening it had left, I crawled out of the straps. Grabbing them in my forepaws, I backed into the opening, tugging the basket after me. It was half-out when it stuck. I was squealing curses when Afra said, "I am sorry that I called you a monster. Please—let me get him out."

I slid off the rock with gratitude and let Afra lift her

child into the open. My poor forelegs ached. My back muscles complained. I wanted to go back into that comforting cave, which was deadly folly in an earthquake.

Spots came over to nuzzle me. I looked up at my friend and moaned. He pushed me a little harder with his nose. *Don't complain,* he told me. *You aren't bleeding.*

Afra had her baby out of the carry basket. She held it, bouncing it as she talked softly. It finally stopped screaming.

The hard ground shakes had also halted, though I could feel the same deep shiver that I had felt yesterday, on the rock over the cave's mouth.

"We should get to clearer ground," Afra said. "In case the earthquake returns."

I nodded.

"There is a place by the spring where I get water. But I cannot leave the food that you brought." She looked at the opening in the cave entrance, biting her lower lip. Then she placed the baby on the ground beside me. "Watch him, please. If something happens . . ." She shook her head and ran like a fool to the cave. She wriggled into the opening and was gone.

I squealed in irritation. I could have gone for those things! I looked at Spots, thinking that he could mind the baby.

She asked you *to watch him,* Spots said. *If you go into the cave with her, she will panic, thinking the baby is alone but for a stupid horse.*

I had to do as she had told me, since she was beginning to see that I was no monster. I muttered to myself. I knew he was right. He often is.

Spots walked over to the baby and began to nudge him to and fro, rocking him. The baby liked it. He was chuckling, as if a horse rocked him every day. Then he looked at me. I jerked back, thinking he would scream in fear, but he only watched me as he rocked, his eyes big.

Afra returned with my sack. She must have put some of her own things inside, because it was heavier, judging by the way she carried it. She set it down and watched Spots rock her son.

"I don't suppose you two would hire on as nursemaids?" she asked. "I'll take Uday now." She gathered her son up and tucked him into the carry basket, asking him, "Did you like that, Uday? Did you?" He chuckled for her, too. Carefully she settled the basket over her shoulders. While she tightened the straps, Spots made faces for Uday. I gave Spots' foreleg a push, for showing off.

Afra picked up the heavy sack. She looked at me. "It's not far, the spring. Would your friend mind if I put this on his back? I know it's slippery with no saddle, but I can hold it there."

Spots nodded at her.

Afra looked at him, then at me. "What are you?" she asked. Her lips quivered. Her eyes were wet. She turned to hoist the bag onto Spots' back. I feared for those eggs inside the robe. They seemed to be doomed.

"I do not weep in the ordinary way of things," Afra said, her voice defensive. "But it has been so hard, with everyone's hand turned against me. And now you two come—it was you with the food, before?" She looked at me. Her eyes were dry again. I nodded to her. "Why? What are you, and why are you doing these things?"

I made a cradle of my forearms and rocked them.

"The baby, yes," Afra said.

Then I ran in place and pretended to be throwing rocks at her. I started to walk around as if I followed a maze, looking confused.

She frowned for a moment. Then her face smoothed. "You saw the boys chase me!"

I nodded.

"Well, you're kindhearted, both of you. Come. The spring's this way." She pointed out the path for Spots, soon discovering that if she spoke the directions there was no need to point. That was just as well, because the sack did slide all over his back. She was kept busy just holding it there.

We followed the gully where Spots and I had waited for Afra to take the sack. The path twisted out of view, making a wide curve around the cave's protecting stone. We entered a small bay where trees grew and a spring bubbled up through the ground to make a pond. One of the three rocky walls of the bay was part of the stone that made the cave, reddish orange and fine grained instead of rough brown-black. Plants sprouted in the cracks in the walls. Birds fluttered to the tops of the trees as we arrived.

Spots let Afra take the sack from him before he trotted over to the water. He sniffed at it. *Is the water safe?* he asked me. *I suppose it is, if she has been drinking it, but it never hurts to be sure.*

I tested it with a drop of my magic. The water gleamed and rippled for a moment, proof that it was very good. Spots dipped his head and began to drink. I, too, was thirsty. I gulped until my belly sloshed.

While we slurped, Afra made camp. She set Uday up in his basket so he might watch us, then took everything from the sack. It was as I feared—the eggs were ruined. Afra looked at them, crushed messes in the folds of the robe. She covered her mouth, but I could tell that she was trying not to giggle. Finally she could not help herself. She gave way, and her laughter made Uday chuckle. She was different when she laughed.

Spots brought the soiled robe over to me. We were both shaking our heads over the ruined eggs when Afra picked the robe up. "It's a shame about the eggs, but you brought me two sausages and a brick of pressed dates. You're going to make me fat." She smiled when she said it.

A stream left the pond and flowed out through the rear of our bay of rocks. Afra went to it with the robe. I followed her while Spots cropped the grass that grew around the pond's edges and watched Uday. Afra knelt beside some rocks in the stream and began to wash the egg from the robe. "I saw this on their headman's wife," she told me, scrubbing two handfuls of robe against one another. "If she knew I had it, she would screech the clouds down." She looked sideways at me. "If I were a better person, I would return it, but the nights are cold."

I retracted my claws and took an eggy spot of my own, swishing it in the stream to wet it before I tried to scrub the stuff out.

"The horse is odd, but at least he is still a horse. But you . . . there are no pale blue crocodiles or monitor lizards, and a crocodile would have eaten Uday. You must have come from someplace wonderful," Afra told me. "Not that my experience of the world is so wide. I have known only the mountain towns and villages." She traded her clean handful of cloth for a dirty one and looked at me. I was scrubbing as well as I could in the hope that she would tell me her story. "My home is back that way." She waved her hand toward the east. "My family had the Gift. My mother could charm metal, my father doctored animals. My sister was good at all-around magic. They believed I had no power. Then my woman's time came, and my Gift with it."

I nodded. It happened that way in about one person in ten, Numair said. Often it was an unpleasant surprise for the newly Gifted child.

"You have seen my Gift," Afra said, finding a new place to scrub. I rinsed mine, then found another spot to work on. "No one knew what to do, or how to teach a girl with two-colored magic. They took me to our lord. He gave them three gold pieces for me and told them to go home. That was how I became a slave."

I reared back on my haunches and hissed. The last emperor, Kaddar's uncle, had tried to make a slave of Daine once. He had caged and bespelled me. That was why there was a new palace in the capital. They could do little with the old one, once Daine and her friends were through with it.

Afra smiled crookedly. "Oh. You know what it's like. I bore it at first. They fed me well. But I could not make my magic do as they wished, so they beat me and took the food away." She began to wring out the robe. We had cleaned it entirely. "I would have done as I was told, if I had *known* how to control my Gift. I didn't. After a few beatings and enough lost meals, I'd borne enough. That was how I learned that if I wanted to be free of shackles or ropes badly enough, my magic would do away with them." She shrugged. "I stole some things and I ran away. I traveled with a caravan for a time, dancing for coins." She spread the robe on some rocks to dry in the sun and she shook her head. "There was a man traveling with us. Sadly, he had a wife in one of the towns. I did not know that until Uday was growing in my belly."

I stood, watching her. She spoke well. Perhaps she had learned it at the lord's house. If I looked at her without the struggle of getting her to eat, or worrying about her magic, if I only thought of her as a human, like Daine's friends, how old could she be? Her face was not strained with fear or anger as she sat on a rock and looked back at me.

"I joined another caravan, but once my belly was big, I could not dance anymore," she told me. "You understand every word, by the rivers and springs, you do. I cannot see feelings in the face of a lizard or snake, but I can tell you are sad. Don't be sad for me. I have whored and stolen, and done both of those among people who had taken pity on me and gave me work." She pointed toward the village on the other side of the rocks. "Why do you think those boys were so happy to stone me? I got caught at my thieving and thrown out. The villagers had warned me about the maze of stone, but I never even saw it. I found the cave instead. I felt safe there, and that is where I managed to have Uday without bungling things too badly." She looked at her worn straw sandals. She was about fifteen, I decided. Nearly my age, just a baby. I knew human females are supposed to be old enough to marry and have families by the time they are sixteen, or even fourteen, but that never seemed right.

I could not play any more games with Afra, trying to keep her to myself. When she trusted me enough, I would take her to my parents. They would know what to do. Numair would welcome her for her rare Gift. Daine would welcome her because once she, too, had been a girl on her own. Afra and her baby would be as safe with my foster parents as I was.

"I think I will sleep," Afra told me suddenly. "I have learned to fight using my Gift, but it tires me. Or maybe it is nursing a baby and fighting with my Gift both." She walked back to Uday's carry bag and curled up beside him, without even a blanket. I looked at Spots, thinking that there were extra blankets in Numair and Daine's tent.

Once Afra slept, Spots and I left her there. Afra could also use one of Daine's scarves, and perhaps a few other items. They wouldn't mind, once they knew the entire story. I was sure of that.

Spots hid behind the tent while I packed up the things I had decided to take from Daine and Numair. Once I was ready, I whistled Spots around to the front of the tent. This time I used some of Daine's scarves and sashes to tie the bundle to his back. He was helpful about kneeling to help me reach everything. I was just finished when we heard a man's footsteps on the hillside.

It's one of the horse guards, Spots said. *The one who*

thinks I should stay tied up all of the time. He thinks he knows better than Daine and Numair what to do for me. I am tired of being polite. Will you destroy his rope for me?

All through this trip I had watched Spots struggle with this stupid human, who would not learn that Spots could manage himself. I gladly would have done even more than destroy a rope.

"There you are," the soldier told Spots, his face hard. "All morning and all through my noontide meal I've been lookin' for you, you cursed contrary beast." He had his lariat at his side and was swinging the noose easily. "I don't know how you got away from the lines, but you'll not do so *again*!" He flung the noose just as Spots turned out of its path. The noose missed. I shrieked—it was one of my new ones—and noose, line, and coiled rope went all to ash. The soldier swore, hugging his scorched hand to his chest. Then Spots danced up and swung his head hard, right into the man's chest. The man stumbled, fell, and began to roll down the steep slope to the imperial camp. Spots and I fled, Spots soon getting ahead of me.

When I looked back and could not see the soldier, I whistled up my tornado and swept the hillside. I kept the spinning wind trailing me until I reached Spots. He was waiting patiently for me at the edge of the first barrier spell. I let the tornado go and leaned against my friend's leg. He still had the bundle.

He nudged me gently. *Thank you. I must ask Daine to speak to him again and make certain that he listens this time. The other soldiers have learned, but he is too stupid.*

I crooned my understanding and reached out, feeling the barrier. It gave under my paws, making them tingle.

Spots took a step forward. *What is this?* he asked. His skin twitched all over, but he could move through the magic, whipping his tail as if he were beset by flies. *I am no mage, so something has changed this barrier, Kitten.*

The second barrier stopped him. It also felt different. It flowed over my outstretched paw like cool soup. I felt no little hands exploring me, and I missed them. Confused, I made a shield for Spots and hissed a spell at the barrier. My breath barely touched it before it vanished.

I followed Spots into the rocks, feeling baffled. These barrier spells were *old.* Why were they changing now?

Afra was still asleep, but Uday was not. He was amusing himself, playing with magical bubbles that were dark pink, pale green, and bright yellow, all swirling together. Afra's son's magic was even stranger than her own. I felt grateful that if she did not know of Uday's Gift, I would not be the one to tell her. Since her power had brought her such trouble, I could not see her welcoming it for her baby. Maybe Numair would teach her how to be glad of their Gifts.

Spots stayed to guard them. I clambered up onto the orange rock to listen for goats. My luck was in: the herd was grazing not too far away, near the edge of the barrier around the rocks. Swiftly I clambered over that warm, welcoming orange stone to find them. I was soon in the oddest state of mind. Flashes of green, orange, red, blue, and brown fires filled my vision, then faded. The lands before me were shaped the same, but their covering was different. The areas that did not sprout stone were green with trees and brush, and populated with big animals. There was an *enormous* shaggy cow—why would I imagine a giant cow? There were zebras, too, like King Jonathan and Emperor Kaddar have in their menageries. That was senseless. Zebras could not thrive in these desert lands. Still, I saw the land as green, so perhaps zebras would do well here.

When I ducked to avoid a large imagination bat, I tumbled down a groove in the orange stone. Luckily for me, the groove was long and cushioned with brush that grew in the earth collected there. I was also grateful that no one was there to see me, except for a family of rock hyraxes. They had a good laugh at my expense. I bared my teeth at them, which made them run away. Then I felt small as well as stupid.

At the foot of the stone was open ground where the magical barrier ended. I barely felt the magic's tingle on my scales as I passed through it. Beyond lay slopes of the black lava rock spotted with brush on its sides. Goats. I was back in the real world, looking for goats.

Pausing on the level ground, I listened for a goat bell and heard one nearby, over the ridge. I trotted over to the black rock and began to climb. Then I halted. The bell was coming closer, and with it, human voices. Hurriedly I drew camouflage colors over myself, blending in with the rock and the scrub. Then I crept forward to listen.

"I don't want to give up my afternoon's grazing so this mage can look at the beasts," I heard a human boy whine. "Make her come out to look at them—" I heard the sound of a slap. "Ow! Ma!"

"She is the emperor's friend! As well ask His Imperial

Majesty to call on you! Gods all above, why did you curse me with a son whose head rattles like a gourd?" a woman cried. The goatherd and his mother climbed down from the pasture on the other side of the rock where I sat. The herd of goats followed them, so obedient I could have sworn they were spelled. Knowing goats as I do, I wouldn't have been surprised if they knew I wished to steal one, and delighted in twitching their tails as they trotted by, bound for the village gate.

The goatherd turned to make certain that he had them all and choked. "Ma! Ma, look!"

His mother, a good-sized woman in a head cloth and robe, turned, ready to cuff him. Her hand froze in midair. Only long training for and in battle kept me in my place, hoping that I had not made a mistake in my camouflage. No, they were not staring at me, but at the orange stone to my right and at the open ground before it. The goats were baffled and frightened by the humans' confusion. They began to bleat their fear.

"That wasn't there before!" the woman said, drawing the Sign on her chest.

The boy did the same. "The rock Maze lay in that open ground. We never saw no orange rock!" He ventured forward, his staff outstretched.

"Careful!" his mother cried. "This is magic; it's folly to meddle with magic!"

The boy stopped just five yards from me and waved his staff, expecting something. He was not the only one. He should have touched the barrier there, and with each step forward that he took. When he stopped to tap the orange stone, he was six feet inside the barrier of magic I'd walked through each time I came here.

His mother could bear it no more. "Leave it!" she cried. "We're no mages! That's what ours are for—yes, and those grand ones the emperor has brought! Get away from there before you're hurt!"

The goatherd had blossomed more rolling sweat with each step he had taken beyond that five-yard point. I think he expected to walk straight into a cliff and break his toes. When his mother ordered him to come with her, he turned and raced to her side. They and the goats ran for the gate.

I shed my camouflage once they were inside the village walls and climbed down from my place on the black rock. Once on the sandy ground, I walked straight toward the round curve of orange stone. There was no sign whatever of the barrier. I even waved my paws through the air, seeking its power. I'd felt it—somewhat—on my way to find those goats. Where had it gone since then? No one had worked a spell big enough to destroy it. I would have sensed that.

Remembering the next barrier, I ran up the stone, which quivered under my paws: the earth was shuddering. At the top of the formation I braced myself to look at the black lava rocks around the orange, and at the village to the south of my position. Was I visible to anyone who might pass, if the barrier was gone? I had to be, if those humans had seen the orange stone. I camouflaged myself a second time, then moved on, seeking the next barrier as the stone beneath me trembled. I hadn't even noticed that it was gone when I'd passed this way before, wrapped in strange visions. *Why?* What had destroyed the barriers?

At last I reached Afra's clearing. She knelt beside the open bundle that had been on Spots' back, a small pot of one of Daine's healing creams in her hand. She put it down when she saw me. There were tearstains on her cheeks. "You go too far! The village mages have not tried to break the magic on this place because they believe there is none, only stones and desert. Now you have taken costly things! If the mages track these things here, who is to say they cannot shatter the spells that hide us?" She wiped sweat from her face with a hand that trembled. "And that you did this now, with the earth dancing again . . ."

If the village mages could have pierced the illusion of the maze of stone, they would have done so the first time Afra was spotted at their garbage heap. They didn't even know it was there. Numair was another matter, but now, with the barrier gone, we *needed* him to come, and Daine, too. Or we needed to go to him and Daine, out through the taller rocks, before the ground opened up under us. Afra could not stay here. The goatherd and his mother had to be spreading the news that the village had land this afternoon that had not existed that morning. People would be coming, if there wasn't an earthquake first.

I straightened the blankets that had served to bundle up what we had taken and began to put Afra's belongings in their center.

Kitten, what are you doing? Why are you packing? Spots pawed the ground, nervous. He knew how I behaved if we were safe and if we were not safe.

I hissed at him, the noise I used to mean "trouble," and pointed back in the direction from which I had come.

Spots snorted in disgust. *Why does this happen just as I begin to like a place?* He began to help me pack, choosing only the most important things to place on the blankets.

Afra stared at us. "What are you doing now? Are you *packing*?" She set down the cream. "Please! I'm frightened enough with the ground so restless, but this is the safest place for us to be. There's no tall stone here to fall over on us. Please stop! I have to be calm for Uday; surely you know that!"

I went over to her and gripped her wrist, then pulled her and pointed in the direction of the path back to the cave—and the imperial camp. I opened my mouth to explain that soon we would have curious villagers entering our sanctuary, but of course all that came out was baby chatter.

"Go back there?" Afra demanded, pulling free of my grip. "That place is surrounded by high rocks and cliffs. We'll be crushed!"

I shook my head. I was nearly screaming with frustration, cursing my lack of speech. I hunkered down on my hindquarters and placed a group of small stones together, some of them black, some orange. I put the orange ones in the center, as they seemed to be in the true rock formation. Then I drew a circle around them. The line was jagged. Afra was not the only one made edgy by the shaking ground, but we dragons are supposed to control ourselves.

Afra nodded. "The magic, yes." Spots continued to pack, rolling up the bundle of blankets.

I wiped away the line around the collection of rocks. Then I stabbed a claw into the area where I'd erased my line and glared at Afra.

She wiped sweat from her upper lip. "No. I don't believe you. The villagers told me that the rock maze has been there ever since their people can remember." I stabbed the ground again. Afra was still shaking her head when Uday woke and began to cry. "I have to feed my child," she whispered. She went to him while I threw the rocks into the pond.

I wanted to throw myself in after them—not to drown, only to cool my temper and my nerves. It made me half-mad to be unable to speak at a time like this! I could tell her about Daine and Numair, about how they would be able to help her and the baby! We wouldn't be dithering here, but on our way to safety!

Should I go get Daine? Spots asked me.

I was about to say yes, but the ground heaved under me. I shook my head and pointed to Afra and Uday, then made running motions with my claws. We had to get them away first.

Spots began to nudge Afra toward the way out of the clearing. Each time she turned away from his nose, back toward the pond, he would turn with her and begin to nudge again. He was very stubborn. I often wished I could tell him that I suspected he had a mule in his ancestry. I had so many jokes I could not tell him.

I walked around the pond to think of something, but all I could think was that we had to *go.* The water's surface rippled under the force of the quivering earth. Loose rocks tumbled everywhere. I reached deep into the ground with my power, feeling for the cracks in the earth that might open and swallow us, but I found none. That meant nothing. In

Numair's books I had read that the deadliest faults were miles underground.

When I returned, Afra had taken away everything that Spots had placed on the blankets. She then rolled up the blankets themselves to make a rough circle in the open, away from the rocks, where Uday might crawl in safety, free of his swaddlings.

I did shriek then, and scold. I had left to get myself under control, not to say I had conceded the fight! Spots walked over to my side to let Afra know he agreed with me. His white and brown withers were dark: he, too, was sweating, his fear of the shakes obvious in the way he planted his feet and watched the stone around us. I felt guilty. I had been so busy with my tantrum that I had not even asked my friend how he did.

Afra stood in front of Uday and said, "The barrier has kept me safe for longer than I have known you, strangers. We are safer in this open ground than we will be running through those canyons. Go if you wish, but Uday and I stay here."

I wanted to weep in frustration. Humans!

We did not leave them. I went to the far side of the pond and whistled cracking spells at the small rocks there, turning them to gravel, until I had myself under control. Then Spots and I gathered dead wood for a fire, lurching to and fro to get the wood that lay on the ground. Uday crowed and raised his arms for me when we came back, which touched me deeply. Afra, about to swaddle him again, gave me a nod, but the look in her eyes was wary.

I'd just started the fire when we heard the dogs. Afra jumped to her feet, then stumbled as the ground gave a hard shake. She looked at me. "They sound so close," she whispered.

I raised one claw and put it to my muzzle, to silence her. Then I clambered up over the orange boulders to see how near the villagers had come. The stone rocked beneath me for a moment and then settled. I raced forward before it had another spasm. Finally I saw the last rise, the one before the slope to where the barrier had once been.

This time I did not trip down the crack past the rock hyraxes, if they were still there. I crouched and called my magic, letting it rise as fire all around me. When the stone beneath me begin to scorch, I rose onto my hind legs and walked up the last rise.

The villagers stood at the foot of the orange stone. Three mages were in the lead, each with his Gift blazing in his hands, ready for use. Men and women stood around the mages with dogs on leashes. The dogs were barking and yowling. They knew they were supposed to be hunting *something.* They wanted to be taken off the leash so they could do their jobs. More villagers armed with bows and spears stood behind the leaders and dog handlers. From their reaction as I stood up, they had not expected anyone to meet them.

I went red with rage. When humans say that, they mean their faces go red. When I go red, it is my scales that turn that color, blotting out my normal blue-gold. I let my anger flow into my power, so that the air around me burned scarlet. Some of the villagers began to run. I stood all the way up on my hind feet, stretched my neck out as far as it would go, raised my head, and blew a long plume of spell breath, shaped as a stream of flame.

More people ran then, but they were not the right ones. "It is the witch's illusion!" cried the chief mage, who had spoken with Daine only that morning. "Now!" He and the other mages threw fist-sized balls of magic at me. They *hurt* as they struck, though my power devoured them. I screeched a breaking spell, shattering the weapons of those who had stayed to attack. Now most of them ran, too.

"Illusions don't wield magic," I heard a mage say.

"Again!" cried the chief mage, not caring.

I did not wait for a second attack. I could endure the hurt. My problem was my own magic. If it devoured more power, it might get too hot for me to bear.

I turned and galloped for Afra's camp, half-stumbling all the way. The earth, so calm while I had faced the villagers, now shook harder than ever. As I skidded down the last slope, the rock bucked like a stallion, pitching me into the pond. My magic evaporated. The cool water eased the heat that the use of so much power created. I actually rolled there for a moment before I remembered I could not swim.

I scrabbled at the bottom mud, trying to crawl up to the water's edge. Then two strong hands gripped my forelegs and pulled. I kicked back with my hind legs as Afra dragged me from the mud, water, and clinging strands of weed.

Sitting on the ground, Afra plucked some of it off of my back. "What are these for, if you can't fly?" she asked, passing a gentle hand over my tiny rudimentary wings.

I shook my head, sprinkling her with more water, and

cupped a paw around my ear. She heard the shouts of humans in the distance.

"You were right?" she whispered. "The barrier is truly gone?"

She did not wait for my answer but jumped to her feet and hurried to tie a bundle of her things to Spots' back. Even though she had not believed me about the barrier when I left, she had been worried enough about the dogs to pack.

She is quick to work when she is frightened, Spots said with approval. *She would do well in the army or the Queen's Riders, if she did not have to worry about Uday.* He pitched as the ground shook harder. I looked for Uday. He was swaddled and tucked in his carry basket once more.

The villagers were still coming. From the sound of their arguments, they feared their mages more than they feared being caught under a rock, at least for the moment.

Afra was hoisting Uday's carry basket onto her shoulders when I heard new voices in the canyons between us and the imperial camp. One male whined that the protection from earthquakes and falling rocks had best be good. Another cursed "that mad, thieving horse" and "that evil little dragon." The soldier who had tried to stop Spots was coming to reclaim him. At least one mage came with him, as well as more soldiers. Did I not have enough trouble on my scales?

Afra started to lead Spots toward the stream that flowed away from the pond. I grabbed her arm and towed her toward the trail that we had used to come here.

"No," she whispered, tugging her arm from my grip. "That goes toward the village."

I took her arm again and pulled harder.

"They'll *kill* me," she snapped. She yanked free.

She would not trust any symbol for mage, even if she knew one. I knew no symbol for emperor. I quickly drew a picture of a crown.

She staggered as the ground shook and clung to Spots' mane to keep her feet. "A king? Are you mad? We have no kings," she said, "only an— Oh, no. No, no." She shook her head, her eyes wild. "The emperor is the judge of all Carthak. He will return me to my master, if he doesn't execute me for all I've stolen!"

We were out of time. The chief mage was the first of the villagers to top the orange stone rise. "Witch!" he cried, pointing. "Thief!"

I got in front of Afra and threw up my best shield as spears of yellow fire sped from his fingers right at her. They struck my power and flew straight into the air. I rose on my hind legs as the other two mages and the remaining villagers joined the chief mage. The dogs were nowhere to be seen. They must have fled for home like sensible creatures.

The mages' Gifts shimmered and blazed around their hands, the chief mage's brightest by far. I wriggled my hind feet, seeking good purchase. Then I summoned my own magic, letting it crackle like lightning over my scales. I was almost blind with the rage that comes from using too much power. In my fury, I meant to cook those annoying humans where they stood.

"Kitten!" I heard Daine cry, her voice shocked. *"Bad* girl!"

I looked over my shoulder and released my magic into

the empty air. Daine stood behind me. She looked cross. She and Numair had come with the imperial soldiers I had heard. Numair held a protective shield of magic over all of them, keeping falling rocks from their heads back in the canyon. I could see its white sparks shimmer against its sheer black fire.

Daine looked at me, then at the villagers, her eyebrows knit in a frown. "Kit, you know better than to threaten humans. And I would like to know why these humans are threatening you and your friends!"

Numair surveyed all of us. "Your pardon, my dear, but the magical energies here are making my ears ring," he said in his usual mild way. "Something very big is about to happen within these stones."

That made my ears prick. Magic? Earthquakes weren't magical.

"Perhaps we should all return to the emperor's camp and finish this discussion?" Numair asked. "I am certain that Kitten did not adopt such a threatening posture without reason." His Gift flowed out from him to enclose Afra, Uday, Spots, and me, but not the villagers. My foster father had seen we were under attack from them.

Afra started to raise her hand, her magic gathering around her fingers, but I grabbed her wrist. I was fairly certain that, even with her two-colored magic, she would get hurt if she tried to fight Numair.

She stared at me, her eyes wide with fear. "Is that the emperor?" she whispered.

Spots and I shook our heads.

"Stand away!" screamed the village's chief mage. "This

woman is a witch and a thief! She is ours to deal with! Call your monster off!"

Daine's frown deepened. "Kit's no more a monster than you," she called back. "Though just now you're looking fair monstrous to me."

No one heard what the mage said next. The orange rock under him bucked and split. He and the other villagers were thrown, as I had been, into the pond. Chunks of rock dropped away from the orange stone. The villagers who escaped the pond tried to run down the canyon where the stream flowed, only to find boulders were blocking the way.

No one wanted to come near us. They stayed on the far side of the pond.

As more orange pieces rolled onto the open ground, darker stone was uncovered. The inner rock was brown, glassy stuff. Once most of the orange stone had fallen away, the brown stone began to jerk and rise. Its ridges shifted as larger, angled pieces appeared out of the mass of rock beyond our view. The assemblage of stone, oddly shaped, even sculpted, kept turning toward us. One piece set itself on the sand next to Daine and Numair.

I was looking at a lizard-like foreleg. It was made of a glossy brown stone filled with a multitude of different-colored fires that blazed in sheets, darts, and ripples under each stone scale.

The center section up above bent in a U as the dragon—it was a dragon—hauled its still-captive hindquarters from their stone casings under the earth. Then it had to pull its tail loose, the tail being trapped in a different section of rock.

I saw the foreleg press up. With a roar of shattering stone, the dragon forced its upper body free, then its tail.

Raining gravel and powdered rock, the opal dragon turned. It brought its head around and down to our level, regarding us with glowing crimson eyes. Their pupils, slit just like mine, were the deep green of emeralds. Free now of its prison, it was not so big as I'd thought. Numair was six feet and six inches; the dragon stood that tall at the shoulder. Head to hip it was sixteen feet. The tail I could not measure. This dragon carried it in curled loops on its back. I noticed its other peculiarity right away as well: it had no wings.

It said something that flattened me. I squeaked, in my body or my mind, I don't know which. I tried to meet its eyes. The dragon spoke again, using very different words and talking slowly. I shook my head in the hope that I could make my ears open up, but my ears were not the problem. The dragon spoke within my skull, expecting me to understand. The language was completely unfamiliar.

Daine raced over and picked me up. "Stop it!" she cried, glaring at the great creature. "She can't understand you! She's just a baby!"

I shook her off. I didn't mean to, but I was *trying* to understand this being. Was it a relative of mine? Didn't the dragon ancestors mention kindred of ours, dragons fashioned of stone, flame, and water, at the gathering I had attended when I was nine? I was busy playing with my cousins, but I had listened to some of the stories.

The dragon looked at Daine, then at me. It tried another

series of sounds, gentler ones. I heard something familiar, *Sleep,* and called back with my own mind, *Awake?*

The dragon flashed a look at the village's chief mage, who was trying to creep up on it. He shrank away, his hands blazing with his Gift. The dragon stretched its head out on its long neck and blew a puff of air straight at the mage. His Gift vanished from his hands. He gasped and plunged his hands into the pond.

The opal dragon looked at me and spoke within my mind, *Child?*

Dragon child, I thought to her. I knew this dragon was female. It was in the way that she said "child," as if she had mothered several. She had loved them and scolded them, watched them grow, tended their hurts, and seen them leave in search of their own lives. Somehow I had learned all that just from the way she had thought that one word to me.

The dragon waved her forepaw at the humans around us. *These? Tell.*

I explained about Emperor Kaddar's journey here. How I'd seen the boys stone Afra, and how Afra had led me to the cave in the rocks hidden by magic. I was almost to the end of how I'd tamed Afra with food when the dragon said, *That is sufficient for me to learn your speech.*

I stared at her.

It has been an age since I last heard the speech of my winged cousins. I had quite forgotten it. The opal dragon eyed the humans. *Other things have changed as well.* Some note in her voice was different. She was ready to talk to others. She asked, *Have you pestiferous creatures gotten any wiser?*

The villagers dropped to their knees, crying out or weeping. Their chief mage was the last to kneel. He quivered as if he could not help himself. Afra clung to Spots. I was so proud that she did not kneel.

Spots bared his teeth at the dragon. *Try your luck against me, big lizard,* he said. *I have fought giants and steel-feathered Stormwings. I have faced Kitten's family. No dragon, not even a stone one, will make me run.*

So I see, the dragon replied.

Neither Daine nor Numair had budged, though the emperor's soldiers were on their knees. My parents, like Spots, had met far larger dragons.

Numair stepped forward. "It depends on how you gauge such things, Great One," he said quietly, answering her question about humans. "I have met foolish dragons and badgers with great wisdom."

The dragon regarded him, then Daine. *Mages have improved,* she said.

"Would you favor us with an explanation?" Numair asked in his polite way. "We had no sense of you, or we would not have disturbed you."

You did not disturb me, the opal dragon told him. She turned her crimson eyes to Afra. *Nor did you, small mother. I layered my protective spells so that none of my kind, who had been plaguing me with questions and requests for* ages, *would find me. I wanted a nice, long nap. But I set the wards so that any mother or mother-to-be might find sanctuary behind my barriers. I welcomed you in my dreams.*

She snaked her long neck around Afra to peer at Uday.

A little uncertain, Afra half-turned so the dragon might get a better look at her son. *And I am quite charmed by* you, *small human.* Uday crowed in glee, as if he understood.

The dragon straightened so she could eye all of us again. *It was* this *young dragon who caused my waking. When first she entered my barriers, I began to rouse myself from sleep, bringing down my old wards and cracking the shell that time had formed over me. It has been more than two thousand circles around the sun since her kind and mine have spoken. Moreover, she is so young. I feared that you two-legged creatures might have captured her. You have been known to do that.*

Her gaze was so stern that the villagers, who had begun to rise, knelt again. The soldiers behind Numair and Daine quailed.

I am no captive! I told her. *Daine and Numair*—my mind added their images and voices to their names so the opal dragon would know them better—*are my parents. They adopted me. My kin allow it. Daine tried to save my dragon mother's life, and my mother left me with her. I have been managing very well among humans, thank you!*

Now the beautiful creature looked down her long muzzle at me. *In my day, infant dragons were not so forward,* she said, her mind-voice crackling.

I am not like the infant dragons you knew, I replied. *You said yourself it's been more than two thousand years since you spoke with any dragons.*

For a moment I thought I heard her sigh. She picked up a slab of orange stone that was three feet thick. *My nap lasted far longer than I had intended. I was very bored, and tired.*

You could come with us, I said. *It wouldn't be boring if you did.*

"Kitten—Skysong—means that it wouldn't be boring for *her,*" Numair said. "But surely, after such a nap, it *is* time you moved around a bit?"

"Numair!" Daine said, tugging on his sleeve. "The people in the city—well, people anywhere! If we have a dragon with us—a *big* one—if folk see her out and about . . ."

I slumped. I liked this dragon, for all that she was so much older and a snob. She was beautiful and funny. Daine was right, though. People screamed at the sight of me. What would they do if they saw her?

My children ceased to need me long before my nap. The time I showed you, young dragon, the time when these lands were green and the creatures were larger, was the last time I was happy. Somehow I could feel the dragon spoke to me alone. *I cannot—would not—take you from these strange friends, or your two-legged "parents." But I would be happy to come with you, if you would like.*

I squeaked and ran at her and wound between her forelegs. The glassy stone of her body was cool and pliable. She looked at Daine and Numair. *The skill of the dragon depends on the stone of our flesh,* she said so that everyone could hear. *We opal dragons are the mages of ideas, illusion, seeming, and invisibility. That is why my magical protections held for so long.*

Suddenly I could feel her, but I could not see her. No one could. Then I could not even feel her. I cheeped, sending my magic out, searching for her. Just as suddenly as she had vanished, she appeared again, beside Afra and Spots. Afra jumped; Uday began to wail. Spots' ears went back. The villagers decided it was time to run away.

"Now that's fair wonderful," Daine said with a smile. "You can hide in plain sight." She looked at Afra. "I didn't catch your name."

"I'm—Afra. This is Uday," Afra said, keeping an eye on the dragon. "Your little creature, there—she's been looking after us." She pointed to me, then Spots. "And the horse—he, too, has cared for us."

"Kitten is the dragon," Daine said, coming over to Afra. "Her ma named her Skysong, but she's got to grow into it. Spots is the horse. He's Numair's. I see Kitten found some of my things for you to use. She's a rare thief." She hugged Afra's shoulders, then looked at the dragon. "And your name, Great One?"

The opal dragon looked from Daine to me. *Why does this child not speak to you mind-to-mind, as she does to me?*

"She is too young. That's what her family told us," Daine replied. "It drives her half-mad. I think it's the only thing she dislikes about living among humans. She needs to talk with us, and she can't."

The dragon—my ancestress? my kinswoman?—went to the rocky hollow that had once been her bed and began to sift through the stones, tossing most of them aside. *I am Kawit, in the language of my people. Ah. Skysong, eat this.*

She turned about and offered me one of her discarded scales. It sparkled in the sun.

But it's too pretty to eat, I protested.

Eat it, Kawit ordered me.

I obeyed. Daine asked Kawit, "Will you teach me how you did that?"

The scale fizzed and tingled in my mouth, crunching among my teeth. Then it was gone.

I compliment you upon your raising of Skysong thus far, Veralidaine, Kawit said. *She is a valiant young one who will do whatever she must to care for her friends.* She nodded to Afra.

"How did you know my full name?" asked Daine, startled.

Because it is in all of me, I said. *My mother put Daine's name in all of me, so every dragon, god, and immortal would know who my new mother is. Kawit, would you tell her?*

"Oh, my," Daine said. She sat on a rock.

You have already told her, Kawit replied.

You hear me! I cried, and I ran to my mother. I jumped into her lap. *You hear me! Now we can talk and I won't have to make funny signs or noises!* Daine hugged me close. Once we stopped saying private things to each other, I looked at Spots. *Can you hear me, too?*

As well as if you were one of the beast-People, he replied, nibbling on some weeds. *I'm glad you are happy, but we managed perfectly well before.*

But now I will understand your jokes. I only used to guess at them, I explained. I looked up at Numair. *Papa, Afra has magic in two colors, and Uday in three. Afra needs someplace to be safe and well fed and not enslaved.*

"Why are you telling my secrets?" Afra cried, looking around. She hadn't noticed the villagers' departure before this. Even the soldiers who had come with Numair and Daine had fled.

"She tells only us," Numair said kindly. "And we are safe, because Daine and I are both mages. I wish Kitten had brought you to us sooner—"

"I suspect she wanted to look after Afra herself," Daine told him. "Seeing as how we'd given her nothing to do."

I felt myself turn pale yellow out of embarrassment. It was dreadful that my parents knew my mind so well.

She has something to do now, Kawit said. *I know nothing of this new world. She may be my guide, and my friend. I hope she will be my friend.*

I struggled to concentrate, so that only Kawit would hear my reply. *I would* love *to be your friend,* I said. *If you don't mind that I am very young.*

I like it, Kawit told me. *You make* me *feel younger.*

Daine sat me down and went to Afra. "May I see your baby?" she asked. Slowly Afra turned so Daine could lift Uday from his carry basket. "I have two of my own, but they are with their grandparents," Daine told Afra. "Please come with us. We'll send the soldiers back for the rest of your things." Holding Uday, she took Afra by one wrist and drew her toward the trail.

"But the dragon—Skysong—" Afra said, hesitating. "She drew a crown. The emperor is with you?"

"He's a nice young man," Numair said, coming to stand beside her. "Kitten said you have two-colored magic? How do you manage to keep one aspect from overpowering the other? My own, which is two colored, has always been integrated, as you see—" He showed her a ball of his black fire so she could look at the white sparkles in it.

Oh, no, I thought. If Numair starts to ask questions now, I will never get my own answered. *Papa, when are we going home?* I demanded, tugging on the leg of his breeches. He was already walking off with Daine and Afra. Spots trotted ahead of us. *Kawit, come! Papa, did you fix the river? Mama, are the chickens going to be all right? Are you going to scold those mages for trying to kill us? Will you tell the soldiers to leave Spots with Kawit and me instead of tying him up all of the time?*

That was just a start. I had a great many more things to say.

Lost

When Adria reached her father's deserted storeroom after school, she sat in a dark corner, hid her face against her knees, and cried. The new mathematics instructor had marked her work a failure. Worse, he had sent a note to her father after showing its contents to Adria.

Instructor Hillbrand told me that Adria is brilliant at mathematics, but in my view her past excellence has led her to laziness, Instructor Park had written. *I instructed the students to do all of the steps which lead to the solution. She will not give the intermediate steps, only the answer. She will not do all of the work that is required.*

Adria blew her nose on her handkerchief. She wasn't *trying* to be bad. The stupid in-between steps just wouldn't stay in her mind, not when the answer was so plain. She had explained that to Instructor Park, but he had only shaken his head. Then he had written the note.

What her parents would say—what her father would say! Her lips trembled and her eyes flooded. Please, gods, don't let Father be angry, she begged silently. She didn't know which was worse, waiting for one of her father's rages or having one break over her head. She hated being a coward.

She wiped her eyes and got to her feet. Regardless of her problem with the new teacher, she knew she would *definitely* be punished if she didn't get to her shop chores. She could see an open crate of brass lamps that had to be cleaned for sale. There was the sweeping to do as always, inkwells to be filled in the clerks' room, brushes to be rinsed off. She would do the lamps first, the inkwells and brushes when the clerks went to supper.

As she set up a table for her polish and rags, she worried the mathematics issue like a bad tooth. Instructor Hillbrand had never cared how she reached her answers. From the time she was very small, she had known the answer to any mathematics problem, long before the other children. She had been the wonder of the district and Father's darling. Instructor Hillbrand had even spoken of university training when she was older, though Father always said it would cost too much.

Then came Instructor Park, educated at the great university in Carthak. His mathematics for older students involved letters as well as numbers. There were steps toward the solution, and each student must do the steps as well as answer the problem. He would not accept the answer alone.

Adria polished an already shining lamp, crying again. She loved the new mathematics. The idea that letters could take the place of numbers opened a world of possibilities whose limits she could not see. Even after her scolding, she had asked the instructor about the mathematics that lay beyond their current studies. That conversation had not gone well.

"It is clever of you to deduce some of the future

applications, Adria," he had said with a kind smile. "But you overreach. First you must work your way through this course, and learn the discipline of the mathematics I will cover in these three months. Since you are already having difficulties, you should concentrate on the work at hand." As she had turned away, red with shame, he had added, "Besides, higher mathematics is taught at the universities. Surely your family prefers that you remain here, to work in their interest, on accounts."

After the possibilities she had glimpsed, that answer was as bad in its way as any whipping Father might give her. It was as if she had seen a star-covered sky, only to have Instructor Park tie a blindfold over her eyes.

She picked up another lamp and wiped her face on her sleeve again. That was when she heard a voice say, "Don't cry."

She gasped and looked around, frantic. "Who's there?"

"Me," the voice replied. It was a very small voice, and childlike.

Adria searched the big storeroom, forgetting the lamp in her hand. Unless the child, or any of the clerks who wanted to make fun of her, had packed himself in a crate or turned himself into a fancy jar or box, she was alone. Trembling, she went back to her rags and polish.

Doomed to be switched and mad as a rat in a trap, she thought as she scrubbed at a tarnished spot on the lamp.

"Why sad?" asked the voice.

She dropped the lamp. The lid rolled off into the shadows.

"Ow," the voice said.

Adria stared as smoke oozed out of the lamp. No, she thought, too fascinated to run or shriek. It wasn't smoke. It was more like liquid, but it was liquid that kept to a roundish shape, without sending random trickles outward.

The liquid rose and produced a headlike knob. A mouth opened and said, "Hello."

Mad as a rat in a trap, Adria thought again. Trembling, she knelt before the creature. It was a little bigger than her fist. "What are you?" she asked, trying to remember the lists of immortals and gods she'd memorized two years ago. None were little black blobs.

"Lost," the thing said.

"You're lost, or your name is lost?" she asked, twining her fingers in her polishing cloth. Her nerves were fizzling, but at the same time she was getting excited, as excited as she'd been when she had glimpsed the mathematics beyond what Instructor Park was teaching her.

"Lost," replied the creature. "All two."

"You are lost, and your name is Lost," Adria said, to confirm it. She liked to have things laid out plain.

"Yes. Name Lost, self lost."

"And you talk." Adria leaned in for a better look. Lost extended its head-knob toward her as if it inspected her in turn, though as far as she could tell—its "head" was no bigger than her thumb—Lost had no eyes. It did have several bright yellow threads within its glob of a body, threads that curved around like a whirlpool. On its front, or the part Adria assumed was its front, the creature bore a flake of copper like a brooch.

"Your name?" Lost asked.

Adria blinked as the tiny mouth in Lost's head moved. "Adria," she replied. "I'm a girl."

"I know girl," Lost replied with a slight note of reproof. "I lost, not stupid, Adria."

How does it make the sounds without teeth? she wondered. This was one of her questions that her family would find annoying, but Adria could not be content unless things made sense. They had to have a reason to be the way that they were. Even "it's magic" wasn't a good enough explanation. She had seen enough guild magic lessons and the work of marketplace mages to know that magic had rules. People with no teeth talked badly. People with teeth managed better. Lost had no teeth that she could see, yet spoke very well.

"Adria?"

She jumped, recognizing the voice of the head clerk, Minter. She scrambled to her feet, clutching the lamp that had served Lost for a home. She didn't notice the creature looping a long tentacle around the spout so it could pull itself up and into the lamp.

"Yes, sir?" she called in reply. "I'm in the storeroom."

Minter stuck his head into the room. "We're going to supper. Stop whatever you're doing and tend the desks, please." He didn't wait for her to agree. He never did.

Adria, keeping very still, listened to the sounds of the clerks as they left the building. Her mind whirled with amazement and thoughts. No one who lived on the river Drell could escape seeing the fabulous creatures that had begun to return to the world nearly twenty years before. Her father did business with a centaur tribe that lived north of the canal; winged horses made regular deliveries from the markets in the south, and ogres came to trade. Adria had even gotten the chance to pet a unicorn when she was eight.

But no one had ever mentioned black blob-things. Not in the legends, not in the market gossip. She looked for the creature on the floor, but there was no sign of it.

"Right here," Lost told her.

Adria jumped and dropped the lamp again.

The creature flowed out of its hiding place and turned its head-knob up to her. "Jumpy girl," it said flatly. "Calm down."

"I had a bad day," Adria replied defensively. "Unknown creatures appearing out of lamps don't help."

"Not unknown," it said patiently. "Darking. Tortallans know darkings."

"This isn't Tortall," she replied, going to make sure that the clerks' office was empty. It was, and the door to the shop where buying and selling took place was locked while the clerks were gone. She turned to find that Lost had followed her. "This is Tusaine. Tortall's on the other side of the river. I thought you said your name was Lost, not darkings."

"Darkings my kind," Lost explained. "I am Lost."

"You certainly are if you expected to be in Tortall," Adria murmured. "I don't know how I can help you get there. Unless I carry you to the ferry and you stow away. But I have chores, and I'm in trouble already. Chores come first." She had been looking blindly at the door while she thought of what she could do to help her new acquaintance. With a solution in mind, she turned to look at it. Once again Lost was absent from the floor. Panicked, Adria looked around the worktables until she saw the darking. It had made its way onto the single high table that was Minter's domain, and was poking its head into the inkwell.

"Don't do that!" She lunged for Lost and almost knocked the inkwell to the floor. Like a very long, shiny black inchworm, Lost extended its head to the side of the desk, then let its body drop to the next table. Its head followed, and it was a round, solid blob once more.

"Not right, girl so nervous," Lost told her with disapproval. "Who make you that way?"

"Nobody," Adria said defensively, clutching Minter's inkwell to her chest. "I—I have a lot of work, that's all, and I don't even know what you eat, or how to get you home."

"Eat everything," Lost replied. It thought a moment, then added, "Almost. Don't want to go back. This more interesting. I help with chores."

"You don't have hands."

Lost produced a pair of arms, and hands to go with them. Then it produced five more arms and hands. "Darkings full of surprises," it said. Adria would have sworn it sounded smug. "Work now?"

Adria had never laughed so hard doing chores in her life as she did once Lost began to help her. She hadn't believed the small thing could do much of use, but she also hadn't understood how far its arms could stretch, or how strong those arms were. She suspected the darking of sipping the water it used to wash the brushes, but the inky liquid seemed to do it no harm. It lifted inkpots out of the way as Adria scrubbed around them, and stacked slates as neatly as if that were its life's work. The heavy account books used by the senior clerks were too much for its strength. Adria handled those, shifting them to clean the desks beneath, and then restoring them to their proper places.

She stopped, as she always did, to look at Minter's book. "This one is my favorite," she explained to Lost, running her fingers over the page with today's entries. "Minter has been here since before I was even born. He taught me my first numbers. He even got Father to let me attend the merchants' school. Look how exact the letters are, and the sums. No blots, no mistakes."

"Fun," the darking said in a voice that told Adria he thought Minter's pages were no such thing. She smiled. Her school friends didn't think numbers were fun, either. Carefully she ran her dusting cloth over the closed book and raised it back up to Minter's table. When the volume, the heaviest of the account books, began to slip from Adria's hold, Lost put up an arm to steady it until the girl had a better grip.

They had just placed it on the desk when they heard keys in the door opening to the shop. Adria gasped. She seized Lost and stuffed it into the pocket of her dress, holding it there.

"Ow," she heard it say.

The door opened to reveal not the clerks, but Adria's father. She could tell from the set of his jaw that his teeth were clenched. His brown eyes were harder than the slates.

"There you are," he said, his voice quiet. He locked the door behind him and hung the keys from his belt. Adria backed up a step, though she knew he despised anyone who showed cowardice. Her father took a folded paper from the purse that hung beside his keys. Adria recognized it as Instructor Park's note. "What is this?" her father demanded. "You defy the teacher? You shame our house? You have become so conceited with Master Hillbrand's praise that you think you do not need to study!"

"No, Father," Adria said, shaking from top to toe. "I can't remember the steps, they aren't important—"

"They aren't important?" he demanded, leaning toward her. Adria stepped back again. He seized her by the shoulder. "Stand still when I talk to you! You think you know better than an instructor who studied at the university in Carthak, who was brought here at great expense to instruct you children? Who do you think you are?"

The darking was fighting Adria's hold on it. Adria clutched it tighter, hoping she wasn't strangling it. She would not let the creature out. She wasn't even sure why. She couldn't think of anything when her father towered over her, bellowing at her.

"There are older people, better people, who would have done anything for this chance!" Her father shoved her into the workroom. "They would take it with humility. Now you shame us all with your presumption! My rivals will question my judgment because my daughter forgets her proper place. Over and over I have told you that we can show no weakness in this world, and yet you cannot maintain the proper diffidence, the proper decorum."

Adria lowered her head, feeling sick and battered. He could go on like this for hours, or what seemed like hours. By the time he was finished, she would promise anything, if only he would stop talking at her. She would believe anything. He was the wisest man she knew, someone who had learned all of his neighbors' secrets and weaknesses. Every time she tried to make him proud, she failed.

He had fallen silent. Adria flinched, not sure why he had stopped before she began to beg him to tell her what she could do to make all right with him. Then she heard what he heard: the jingle of keys at the shop door. The clerks were coming back.

He pointed his finger at her. "No supper. No food tomorrow. You will apologize to your teacher, before the class. I will hear of it if you do not. Present yourself to me after supper tomorrow, your work here and your work for school done completely. Then we shall talk about meals." He walked back into the clerks' office, pulling the workroom door shut behind him.

A series of squeaks and thumps in her pocket reminded Adria of Lost's plight. She pulled her hand out, her fingers cramped around the darking. It had bulged through the gaps, but not all of it had escaped completely from her grip. She opened her cramped fingers.

It plopped onto the floor. "Ow!" it cried. "Ow, ow, ow!"

She tried to shush it. When it continued to shout, she scooped it up in her cupped hands, enclosing it completely. She could move faster than Lost, it seemed.

She opened her fingers a crack and held her hands before her mouth. "Promise to be quiet," she whispered.

"I ow," the darking replied.

"I'm sorry about the ow," Adria said quietly. "Promise you'll be quiet or I'll lock you in a box, I swear it."

"Will father come back?"

"He might, yes, and he must see me working, Lost, promise!"

"Promise," the darking said after a moment.

Adria put it on the floor and grabbed her cloths and polish. She went at the brass work with desperate speed, one ear always on the clerks' door.

Only after she had finished the work and locked the storeroom after her did Adria begin to talk to Lost again. "I didn't let you out of my pocket because I was afraid he might take you," she told her new friend as she walked down the street. "He might not realize you're a person when he's in one of his tempers. It's my fault, I shouldn't make him angry—"

"Not your fault!" Lost squeaked, its voice the loudest Adria had heard. "You are young, he is old! He must know how to keep temper! I know that and I am only here . . ." It paused, clearly thinking, then produced several fingers around its head—"*this* many years!"

Adria blinked down at the creature that rode half-in, half-out of her pocket. "It's too dark for me to count." She didn't like this idea, that there was nothing she could do to change her father's rages. All her life she had believed that if she only did the right things in the proper order, he would be pleased. The possibility set before her by Lost was frightening. It meant Adria could never make Father happy.

"Besides, he too slow to catch me," Lost said.

"He's very quick," Adria said, thinking of the times her father had caught her unaware.

Lost made a very rude and realistic noise. Even though she was worn out, Adria still had enough of her wits to note that the darking must have spent plenty of time around humans and animals to imitate it. She hadn't noticed the proper opening for that sound on the darking itself.

"Father slow and stupid," Lost said. "No match for darkings."

Adria looked around, alarmed. "There are more of you?" It was hard enough to keep Lost a secret. It would be impossible to hide others of its kind. Knowing the market, and the trade in rare and magical creatures, she feared for the life of her new friend and any like it.

"Not *here,*" Lost told her scornfully.

Adria sighed her relief.

"Not right, young one be so jumpy," Lost remarked yet again. "Young things should play, have games."

"Where did you learn that?" Adria wanted to know, thinking to tease a bit of real information from her new companion.

"Places" was the frustrating reply.

Her weary steps had brought her at last to the tradesmen's gate in the wall around the family's house. It wasn't barred yet. One of the stable boys was drowsing just inside. He answered her quiet knock, rubbing his eyes. Once she had passed through, he barred the door and ambled back to his bed in the loft. Adria let herself into the house through the servants' door. She looked into the kitchen. The cook and the housekeeper were awake yet, gossiping as the cook ground spices and the housekeeper mended linen. The housekeeper shook her head when Adria looked in. She had already received her orders from Adria's father with regard to supper.

The girl went on up to her room. She dug into the clothes chest for the bread she tucked away each morning after breakfast, in case the day went badly. Lost ate two small bites, then crawled up the wall, snail-like, to stare out her window. It was still there when she fell into a deep, exhausted sleep.

Adria woke at dawn to a view of black with yellow threads twisted in a column just below the surface. She sat bolt upright with a gasp.

Lost's head popped out of its body, right above the copper flake where it should have had a neck. "Jumpy!" it snapped, as if she had just woken it from a nap. "Young people—"

"Shouldn't be so jumpy, I know," Adria replied, rubbing her eyes. "Do you tell your children this?"

"Darkings not have children," Lost explained as Adria ducked behind her privy screen. "Darkings split when more wanted. Saves time."

"But then you're all alike," Adria said.

"No. New experiences make new darking. New learnings make new darking. New likings come, and dislikings. Have to learn quick. Human rules, immortal rules, god rules, all hard on us. Too many killed at first."

Adria stared around the screen at it, her washcloth in hand. "You've seen gods up close?"

Lost shivered all over. "Too close. Gods and immortals too quick. Ogre step on me once. Make me flat for weeks."

Adria chuckled as she finished washing up. The mental picture of a flat Lost trying to scold her was a good one.

When she came out from behind the screen in her shift, she halted, shocked. Two sausage rolls and a peach lay on the bed. "Where did those come from?" she asked as her belly growled. Never before had anyone, not even Mama, risked smuggling food to her when she was in disgrace.

"I bring," Lost replied, its voice smug. "Bad to go hungry. Numbers won't glow in head if you hungry."

"But . . . ," she whispered, confused. The peach alone was bigger than the darking. "How?"

"Secret." Lost was clearly pleased with itself. "Eat. Your belly talks."

"Not here," she said as she stuffed the food into her book bag. "If anyone catches us with this, the kitchen staff will get in trouble. Outside!"

She finished getting ready for the day in a hurry, her mouth watering at the smell of the sausage on her fingers. With Lost tucked in her pocket, she tiptoed down the back stairs. The kitchen servants were already awake, preparing breakfast for the household. None of them would look at her, knowing that she was going hungry. Adria ducked her head and trotted out of the house. So afraid was she of getting caught that she waited until she was a block away before she took a sausage roll from her bag and gobbled it down. She did not forget to give Lost as much as the darking would eat.

When they reached a small square where local households came for their morning water, Adria sat on a stone bench to eat the other roll and the peach with more decorum. She and Lost watched the sleepy-eyed maids, daughters, sons, and wives draw their buckets of water, listening to the bits of gossip that came their way. Finished and full,

Adria rinsed her hands in the trough of water by the well, shyly nodding to people she recognized. Then she hoisted her book bag on her shoulder and walked toward the river.

She liked the city at this hour, when people were getting ready for the day. The mist from the river kept things cool, but it was retreating, taking its pearly curtain away like a street-corner mage. Shopkeepers opened their shutters and called out greetings to passersby, not urging them to spend money, just welcoming the new day. Horsemen were slower and kinder at this hour, waiting for people to cross instead of half-riding them down. It was for these moments of unexpected kindness that Adria loved her city in the early morning, and it was why she walked out at this hour to watch them, stolen breakfast or no.

"School now?" Lost asked when they had been walking in silence for a while.

"Oh, I'm sorry, no, it doesn't begin for a couple of hours. I go for long walks in the mornings," Adria explained. "It's time to myself, to think, and . . . you'll say I'm silly."

"No," Lost said.

It was such a complete "no" that she believed it. She opened her mouth and told Lost the thing she had never told anyone, not her favorite sister, not her friends at school, not Instructor Hillbrand.

"I like to look at the places where things are being built. I like to see how they put up houses, and temples, and such. The . . . the way engineers and builders fit timber and stone together, how they get the roofs up. They use mathematics for that, did you know?"

"Darkings not build things," Lost explained. Then it added, "Yet."

"I wish I could," Adria said as they came to the road that ran beside the Lily Canal. "Engineers are almost like gods, making things that will last forever." The canal was the oldest in the city. It carried anything that could be transported on the Drell all the way inland right to the governor's palace. A bee to the biggest flower in the garden, Adria headed straight for the new bridge.

Not that it was truly a bridge, not yet. A year had been spent already driving pylons into each side of the canal, pylons that were wide and strong enough to support what all of her elders, including her father, said was the maddest idea ever to gain Crown funding. A group of young engineers claimed they could build a bridge that would rise up, at need, to let river ships pass down the canal. Adria had been coming here since the day the building crews had blocked the river off from the canal and begun to dig.

They would not be at work for a while. At night the river gates were opened for small-boat traffic on the canal, enough to ferry goods to the city's heart. The gates had been closed two hours before dawn, and it would take the water another hour to drain enough that the bridge crews could get at their tasks. The foremen were at their stations already, checking for changes to their orders. The master builders were there, too, consulting over their plans. And for the last two weeks the woman engineer had also been present, seated cross-legged on a large crate that overlooked the shrinking thread of water below.

Her materials were scattered around her: the pad of stitched-together parchments, a bottle of ink and a brush for permanent record-keeping, a pile of maps, and the bottle of red ink and the brush she used to mark them. Today she also held the slate and chalk she used for temporary calculations. The first week she had been there, Adria had crept closer and closer from behind, trying to see what she did. Twice Adria had seen the engineer write on the pad, tear off the sheet she had written on, and wave it in the air. Both times a man from the work crew had come to take it to the builders. Unless the woman did that, however, Adria had quickly discovered that if the engineer was concentrating on her work, she noticed nothing else, not the dogs that piddled on the edge of the crate, not the street urchins who threw rotting vegetables at her until Adria had found the courage to run them off. Not the curious town girls.

The second week, Adria was a foot away on tiptoe, reading the strings of numbers and letters the engineer had scrawled on the slate. She did not immediately notice when the engineer shifted the slate a little to her right, so Adria had a better view. Adria jumped back as soon as she *did* realize that she had been discovered, and fled home in alarm. After long hours of internal debate, she had returned the next morning, to find the engineer in the same place, making careful notes on parchment. The slate, full of equations, was placed at her side, positioned so that Adria, standing behind her, could read it easily. The invitation had been too tempting to pass up.

Without a word between them, the engineer continued to let Adria see what she was doing. Adria had spent several days giddy with the discovery that the new bridge was to be built in two sections, with the flat parts to be lifted like castle drawbridges so ships could pass through. The mathematics was harder to grasp. It depended in part on a kind of figuring Adria did not know, though she saw plenty of the new school mathematics in the engineer's calculations. Some of it was in strange new marks.

Then she remembered where she had seen the runelike marks before. Instructor Hillbrand had left her in his office for half an hour once while she completed a test. Finished and bored, she had begun to look through one of the instructor's well-used texts. On one page she saw the angles of a triangle described and the rune called sine that helped the student calculate the size of the angles. When Hillbrand had returned, he'd taken the book away, telling her she would be ready for it in a year or two. That was before Instructor Park came to say Hillbrand had taught her all wrong.

Yet here was sine again, with the rune for square roots, and equations. The woman's chalk, or her ink brush, spat them out rapidly, filling slate or paper with them. Adria soon began to piece together parts of equations. She was praying for the courage to ask the woman about the parts Adria hadn't worked her way through when Lost came.

"Be quiet and watch," she told Lost now when she saw that the woman was at her usual place. "Not a peep. She lets me watch her work. I don't want to be turned away."

"I be good," Lost replied.

Adria carefully steadied her book bag so it made no noise and advanced until she stood a foot behind the crate and the woman. Looking over the friendly stranger's shoulder, she saw that the engineer was writing a series of numbers and letters, using sketches of cranes, pulleys, and weights to illustrate the figures. Swiftly the engineer made her marks, dipped the brush, and continued, leaving no drops or blots. Adria wished her own schoolwork was so tidy.

Then she stopped thinking about the look of the page and concentrated on what the engineer did. With the drawings to illustrate the problems, the mathematics began to explain itself. The strange oval cut in half at the top of the page was the angle of the ramp and the angle of the height to which a bridge had to be raised to clear an average ship. The equation beneath that one calculated the speed at which the bridge could be safely lowered without accident. A chance equation, scrawled in chalk on the slate beside the woman, was the key to a half page of calculations.

One page had filled up. Today the engineer did not tear it from the pad. Instead she cut it away with the tip of her belt knife, then anchored it under the slate. Wetting her brush afresh, she began a new page.

Adria, excited, was now figuring with her as she wrote, new insight following each calculation the engineer put down. These covered the weights necessary to pull the halves of the bridge up and to hold them up. If Adria understood correctly, each stone weight could be increased with lesser ones to a point, before it was necessary to switch to heavier rope cables and larger stones. Days of rain or snow changed the load of the bridge. The engineer was calculating the difference for the seasons.

The woman had covered half a page more when Adria forgot herself. She pointed over the engineer's shoulder and said, "No, no—it's *three* x divided by five, not four."

"Oops," said Lost.

"Maiden tears, you're right," the woman said, and half turned to look at Adria. "And when did you learn trigonometry?"

Adria backed up, suddenly convinced she had opened the door to disaster. She didn't know what manner of disaster, she only knew it was coming.

"Stop it," Lost ordered.

Adria halted. The engineer said nothing but waited, her hazel eyes level.

Finally Adria stammered, "What's tri—trigo—?"

The engineer turned the rest of the way around, catching her ink jar before it tumbled over. "Don't tell me you *guessed* the answer!"

"No," Adria replied, stung at the suggestion. "I worked it out, going by the calculations that went before. The only possible answer was three x divided by five."

"Then tell me again, where did a chit your age learn trigonometry? Don't lie to me, now."

"Adria not lie!" cried Lost, leaping from her pocket. It plopped to the ground in front of the girl. Adria gasped and lunged for it, but the darking dodged her. It added, "Adria too honest."

The engineer pulled at her lower lip with her teeth and released it. "Mother, bless your servant," she murmured. "What is a darking doing in Tusaine?"

"You know what Lost is!" Adria said, shocked.

The woman smiled. "Anyone who studies at the university in Corus knows what a darking looks like." She turned to Lost. "What is your name, noble defender of shy mathematicians?"

"Lost," it replied, as Adria blushed to hear herself called a mathematician.

She was also more than a little alarmed to learn that darkings came from the Tortallan capital. Her homeland was currently at peace with its larger neighbor, but things had not always been that way. There was an old saying, "Warbirds fly in any weather."

"Lost, is it?" the engineer asked. "Not spying?"

"Lost," repeated the darking. "Too silly to spy."

"What a comfort to your friend," the engineer said, looking at Adria. "I hear darkings are brutally honest. If they're keeping a secret, they'll tell you that's what they're doing. They won't lie." She turned back to her paper. "Well, then, I correct this figure, and what do I do next? Come on, girl. Move the slate—mind my paper, there, unless you saw any mistakes on that?"

Adria shook her head. Then she realized the engineer could not see her and said, "No, mistress, I didn't. But I shouldn't—"

Lost had inchwormed over to the crate and up its side. It looped itself around the chalk and erasure cloth for the slate. "Her name Adria," it told the engineer before it lowered chalk and cloth to the ground.

Slowly, shaking with nervousness, Adria walked over

and took up the slate and the parchment under it. Gingerly she sat on the edge of the crate.

"Master Hillbrand said you would be timid," the woman remarked as she wetted her brush once again.

"Master Hillbrand!" Adria cried, jumping to her feet. Lost, who had been trying to climb into her lap, fell to the ground.

"It's polite to visit your advisor when you come to his new town," the engineer said, glancing at Adria. "Did you know he'd taught in Corus as well as Carthak?"

The girl nodded.

"Why he came to this hole in the hedge . . . No offense. Anyway, I paid him a call when I arrived for this job. He told me you came this way in the mornings, and I might see you, but he never mentioned you're as shy as a fawn. I'm Keraine Waterstone, by the way," the engineer said. "I'm *not* shy."

Adria smiled. "I noticed," she said quietly. She curtsied. "It's an honor, Mistress Waterstone."

"Just Keraine, all right? Now, sit and look at these." Keraine eyed Lost, who had climbed onto the crate. "Would you want to see, Master Lost?"

Lost produced its head-knob and shook it. "Mathematics not fun."

"No, Lost!" protested Adria. "You see, it's a game!" She sat in the space it had left between it and the engineer. "Now, watch."

Lost was soon able to leave Adria and Keraine to their discussion, as Adria got so absorbed in the way trigonometry unfolded in her mind that she forgot to include the darking.

Keraine kept pace for the most part, but when Adria tried to follow some of her newest ideas to their next revelation, the engineer held up a hand.

"No, that's too theoretical for me!" she protested for the fourth time, laughing. "You've gone past the boundaries of what I studied! Others went on to advanced mathematics, but not me. Where did you learn this?"

"But I've only seen this as I've watched you," Adria protested. "I'm just thinking aloud. Doesn't it *have* to be this way? Other factors would change the calculations, but you didn't include them."

Keraine produced a flask and took a drink from it. "Barley water with lemon," she said, offering it to Adria. "I've talked myself dry."

Adria accepted it with murmured thanks. The liquid was cool in her throat. She was pouring some into her hand for Lost when the marketplace clock began to chime. Terror flooded her, buzzing in her veins and turning to heat in her belly. How could she not have heard the bell before this?

"Uh-oh?" Lost asked, peering up into her face.

"You look like a ghost just bit your heart," said Keraine.

"School began two hours ago," Adria whispered. "How could I not hear the bells?"

"I will write a letter to your headmaster," Keraine said, preparing to cut a fresh sheet of parchment loose. "I will say I asked you to help me."

Adria shook her head. "They will tell Father. My father is very strict about my attendance at school."

"Father bad," Lost announced flatly.

"No, no! He knows what is best for me," Adria

protested. Inside her a voice, one that had been only a whisper before Lost came to add its doubts, said, Father only cares how he looks to other merchants.

Adria brushed the chalk from her hands and mumbled something to thank Keraine. Then she grabbed her book bag and raced down the canal road to the guild school, Lost clinging to her ankle to keep from being left behind.

When she reported to the head instructor, the man waved Adria away. "Your family has already been notified, Student Fairingrove. You will report to those studies which remain of your program for the day. Tomorrow we shall discuss with your father if you should remain in merchant studies or change to a convent school."

Adria's throat closed up tight. She had already gone far beyond the mathematics that was required of convent girls, who learned only what was needed to keep household books. She had hoped—she had dreamed—that her success in mathematics would be so great that her father would consent to her ultimate dream, to study in the great universities of Tortall or Carthak, even though she knew it was just a dream. Now she risked the loss even of Instructor Park's class.

She reported to Carthaki history, but she barely heard the lecture or the questions, earning her a red mark from that instructor. She moved through the rest of her day in that manner, her mind racing along the same tracks: How could she appease Father? How could she convince him to give her another chance? Could she appeal to her mother? But Mother had not said a word against her father's will since Adria could remember.

I'll go and clean the upper storeroom, the one I've been putting off, she resolved at last. Lessons were over. She nodded to her friends, hoping they would understand why she hadn't spoken with them that day, and trotted out into the street. I'll do that, every last bit, and then I'll decide. If he sees how hard I work, maybe he won't take me out of school. She looked at her hands. They were shaking badly.

Out of sight of the students and instructors now, Lost rose from Adria's pocket, twined around her arm, and climbed snakelike up to her shoulder. "Please talk," the darking urged. "All afternoon you only shake. You still shake. Run away if news so bad. Come to Tortall. Nobody make you shake there."

Adria smiled for the first time that day. "I'm too frightened to run off," she replied. "I've never even left this town."

"Time to go, then," Lost said, but Adria shook her head. The roads and woods beyond the city were filled with killer centaurs, bandits, giant spiders with human heads, and other monsters. She'd heard the stories all her life from merchants who came to buy and sell at the shop. Girls who took the road risked murder, kidnapping, rape. Father had made sure Adria and her sisters knew of every daughter of their acquaintances who got caught in a servant's arms, who ran away to a bad end, or who disgraced their families. Every daughter, every son.

She wanted to sit down and cry all over again, but if she was going to clean the storeroom better than she had before, she had to work. She had to start now.

Lost cleaned the downstairs storeroom with her. The darking made her smile as it swung or rolled or inched from task to task. It sang to her in its piping voice, songs with words in languages she'd never heard. "Where did you learn so much?" she asked, stopping to catch her breath after shifting some crates.

"Other darkings," Lost replied, hanging from a beam overhead. "What one know, all know."

"Isn't that confusing?" she asked, grabbing her buckets. It was time to attack that unused storeroom. "Having so many voices inside you? Or is that not how it works?"

"Not confusing. How we *are.* You two-leggers lonely," Lost said, swinging from one temporary tentacle to another along the beams as it caught up with her. "Darkings never lonely."

Adria bit her lip. She had been so lonely since Instructor Hillbrand had left the school.

When they reached the upstairs storeroom, she threw open the shutters. To her surprise, the late-afternoon light revealed signs of a recent dusting on the counter. There was a tattered cushion on the lone stool in the room. A man's boot prints showed clearly in the thick dust on the floor. When Adria began to sweep under the counter, she pulled out a branch of half-burned candles that had been hidden there.

Lost vanished into those same shadows. "Books here," she heard it call.

"Why would books be here?" she asked, getting down on her knees. "Lost, if there's a rat under there—"

"No rat," her friend replied. "Rats afraid of darkings. We get big, yell 'Boo!' Rat scamper. Fun!"

Adria chuckled softly, then smothered a gasp as her fingers touched what felt like leather. The darking was right.

Someone had put books under the counter, where no one would see them. She gripped the spine of the topmost volume and pulled it out onto her lap. It was a common account book, like those in the clerks' office downstairs but with black leather binding instead of red.

"Who would put these here?" she asked herself more than Lost. "It doesn't make sense." She couldn't see what was written where she sat. She struggled to her feet, keeping the heavy book in her hands.

"Me too," Lost called from the floor.

She could barely tell the difference between it and the dark wood. Setting the book on the counter, she scooped up her friend, giving it a quick ride to the book. "Whee!" Lost squealed.

Adria set the darking on the counter and opened the book. The writing in it was her father's.

"Why does he hide these up here?" she whispered to herself.

Adria slowly leafed through the pages. These were accounts. Moreover, they were *current* accounts, with dates that began that January and ended the day before.

Uneasy, she rubbed her forehead. She remembered pages from the books downstairs. She couldn't help it. As she worked, she looked at them and tried her own calculations against those of the clerks. Her favorite books to view were Minter's. Seeing his familiar neat columns and calculations took her back to the days when mathematics was fun, not something Father used in his unending war with his competitors.

This book was like those Minter kept for her father, but

different. There were extra columns and extra lines, costs and goods that were not in the books reviewed by the royal inspectors. Adria remembered yesterday's totals. They were a little below the usual day's profit, as had been the case for a week. According to *this* account, with these extra goods, her father's accounts showed their business making profits a third higher than those recorded downstairs.

She continued to read swiftly. The goods labeled "sand" were plainly no such thing, not at the prices her father gave them. Nor were the goods he called "bronze ingots." The "glass bottles" were the most expensive items of all, priced far above anything the shop ever carried. There was only one answer. Her father was smuggling. The downstairs books were for show. These recorded his real profits.

"Now what?" inquired Lost as Adria set that book aside and picked up the next one in the stack.

"Don't know," she replied, unaware that she was suddenly talking like a darking. "Strange."

"Strange what?"

"Hush," Adria whispered, reading the notations in this book, dated last year. There was another volume for the two years before that, and a fourth for the three years earlier yet. "Whatever Father is smuggling, he worked his way up," she whispered to Lost. "See here? Only a little bit at first. More and more as time moved on, until every shipment that comes to him carries smuggled goods in the cargo." She shivered.

"Cold?" Lost asked.

"Frightened," Adria replied.

"You frightened before."

"Frightened for all of us, Lost," Adria said. There were

old, oily marks—finger marks—on the paper. "The Crown skins smugglers." She put her nose close to one of the marks and sniffed. A tiny black blob, Lost's head, did the same thing, even making the same noise.

"Frankincense," she whispered. Her father didn't sell frankincense in the shop. That must be one of the smuggled items.

"Adria!"

She cringed.

"Mithros curse you, girl, I know you're hiding here!" her father cried from the storeroom below. "The longer you avoid me in this stinking, cowardly way, the worse it will go for you!"

"Father bad," Lost said mulishly. "Time to go."

"I have nowhere *to* go!" Adria whispered. She dragged herself to her feet. Then she looked at the book in her hand. How could he have put their family's livelihood in such danger? Didn't he care for them at all?

Swallowing often, trying to keep herself from throwing up out of sheer terror, she made herself walk toward the steps. She didn't want Father to find her up here. Whether she showed him the evidence of his crimes or not, she didn't want to be trapped in this musty room with no way to escape.

"Adria!" Father shouted yet again.

She put one foot on the stair, then another. A small weight struck her back and clung. "I right here," Lost whispered.

The darking's voice put a little strength in her shaky ankles. She walked faster. At the foot of the stair she placed the smuggling book on a crate in the shadows, then moved into the light of the main storeroom.

Her father stood near the front door, looking into the clerks' office. When he heard Adria's steps, he closed the door and faced her. "There you are." He strode quickly to her and gripped her by one arm. "How *dare* you hide from me? Stand straight and look me in the face. No sniveling." His voice was quiet. That was a very bad sign.

"Father, please forgive me," Adria whispered. "I know I was wrong to be late for school. I'll never do it again—"

"As Mithros witnesses, you *will* never do so again," her father snapped. "You will never be given such a chance."

"Father, please don't send me to convent school," Adria begged. "I swear, I'll never be late again, I'll work here all through the holidays—"

Her father's gray eyes opened wide. "Convent school? You have shown you are unfit for any schooling!"

"None?" cried Adria. "But I was late only once! How—"

He slapped her.

The force of his blow knocked her sideways into a stack of crates. Adria leaned there, one hand on her throbbing cheek, staring at him. He had never struck her before, or any of her sisters, though he had hit her brothers when they were younger.

He pulled his arm back for another slap.

"Stop!" A ribbon of black darted over Adria's shoulder and onto the floor. It rose, spreading to form a thin, filmy wall. "No more hurt! No more yell!" Lost produced its head-knob on a long, skinny neck and put its face right in front of the man's. There it spread until it could have covered the human's face. Softly the darking added, *"Or no more breathe."*

Adria's father now took a step back. For a short time none of them spoke or moved. Then the man said, "So a monster has enchanted my obedient child. A monster that has taught her to lie."

"Only one monster here," Lost replied.

Her father's words were the strangest thing Adria had heard him say. He sounded nearly mad, which made her shiver. "I'm not bespelled," she said quietly, trying to explain without making him think she defied him. "Lost isn't a monster. It's a darking, from Tortall." Adria moved so she stood beside her friend. Lost shrank in until it was a ribbon, then hopped to twine around her arm. She turned her hand so the darking could put a blob of itself in her palm. "See? It's the most gentle creature in the world." She stroked the darking's head-knob with a finger that trembled.

Her father took another step back. "It's a monster from an enemy realm. You should have brought it to me the moment you found it. Already the thing was working its wiles on you."

He wasn't listening. Adria tried again. "Father, there's an engineer working on the new canal who can vouch for Lost," she said. "She's the reason I was late this morning. She's named Keraine Waterstone."

Her father reached for the flat, hard length of wood used to lever crates off carts. He clutched the lever with both hands and came closer to Adria and Lost. "Let go of that thing, my girl," he ordered.

Adria wrapped both hands around the darking, gripping its tail with one hand to keep it from smothering her father. Now it was her turn to back away, toward the door at the rear of the storeroom. "Father, don't!"

"Do not defy me again. Hand the monster over."

Adria trembled. It was so hard to keep defying him, but he was finally asking too much. She shook her head. "Lost is my friend."

Her father swung the lever at her. Adria dodged. Lost took advantage of her distraction to leap free of her hands. It wrapped itself around the lever board and yanked the tool from her father's grip. The man stumbled, off balance, as Lost flung the board into the shadows. Adria caught the darking as it jumped back to her.

"Master Fairingrove?" a voice, Minter's voice, called from the door to the clerks' workroom. "You have visitors. I tried to bar them, but their . . . creatures managed to open the door."

Already Adria's father was collecting himself, straightening his tunic, checking his hair. He advanced to the door to the front offices, smiling. He never showed his angry, roaring self to anyone but family, Adria realized as she shivered near the rear exit. For years she had thought the roaring Father was the false one, the handsome, smiling Father the real one. Suddenly it came to her that the roaring Father was the Father she would always have, the one who waited inside the smiling Father. Even if she somehow cajoled him into letting her continue lessons, sooner or later she would do something to offend him. She would skip a task or drop something. He could take her food, or her few treasures. Worse, now she had Lost, whom he'd sworn to kill.

"Lost, you have to get away," she whispered. "Go back to Tortall. You can do it. Just get a ride with a caravan. They won't even know you're with them. Don't pretend you're too silly to work it out. I know you better now."

"No," that soft voice said by her ear. "Lost and Adria friends. Darkings never leave friends."

"He'll kill you!"

"I hide."

Adria's belly surged. She ran into the shadows to vomit, though only water came up. Apart from the breakfast Lost had stolen for them, she'd eaten nothing that day. She waited there, thinking, ignoring the voices by the shop door. Lost was tucked under her ear, its small body warm.

That answers that, she thought wearily. Monsters on the road or no, we have to run. Lost was right. I cannot stay with Father. He will take everything that makes me happy.

Slowly, walking like an old woman, she went out into the light. She had the rear door open when Lost began to bounce on her shoulder. "No, no! Wait! Darkings here!"

"But we have to run away," whispered Adria. "I have to pack."

"Help come, Adria! Help here now! Go to Father!" Lost threw itself to the floor and bounced before her.

She sighed. More than anything, she wanted to leave this big, echoing room where she had worked so had, but she owed Lost for saving her a beating. She couldn't believe her darking friend was a monster who would lead her astray, as Father said, so she followed it toward the collection of people at the shop door.

The sight of a familiar head brought her to a stop

halfway there—not her father's, whose back was to her, or Minter's, who had returned to the clerks' office, but Hillbrand's. There was something new about her former instructor, she saw. A black blob that glittered with silver dust sat on his shoulder, one tentacle-arm slung over his ear in a friendly way.

Hillbrand's face lit with a smile when he saw Adria. "But here she is," he said, looking at Adria's father. "You told us she had gone home."

"We *said* he lied," tiny voices chorused. As Minter and Adria's father turned to look at her, Adria could see that Keraine Waterstone was there, too. A pair of darkings rode with her, one in the crook of her arm, one on the pack she had slung over her shoulder.

Three more darkings! Adria thought, startled. "How did they get here?" she asked Lost, her lips barely moving. It had jumped up to her wrist.

"What one darking knows, all know," Lost whispered to Adria. "I told them, bring help." It twined itself around the length of her arm.

"My daughter's presence makes no difference," Adria's father said coldly. "You can have no possible interest in her. You have retired from the school, Master Hillbrand, and I am taking Adria from it. She is spoiled and unfit. Tomorrow she leaves for my cousin's farm."

"Are you mad?" Keraine asked, eyes wide. "Forgive me, we've only just met, but is it possible you're unaware of your daughter's talents?"

"My daughter does tricks with numbers that make her think she may do as she pleases," replied the man Adria decided to think of as Master Fairingrove, not Father. "It was amusing when she was a child. I indulged her, and now she does not attend classes, she defies her teacher. She lies. She disobeys. She is completely out of hand."

"Sir—Master Fairingrove, I am Keraine Waterstone," Keraine said. "I am an advisor engineer for the company that is building a drawbridge over your canal. I have studied in Carthak and in Corus. I know a powerful talent when I see one. I met Adria late this morning. She and I worked on equations I've been doing for a series of bridges."

"Ridiculous!" scoffed Master Fairingrove. "You expect me to believe such a lie?"

Keraine's cheeks turned crimson. She grabbed a chain at her neck and hauled it over her head, then held it out to Adria's father. A gold disk swung at the chain's end. "I am a master of the guild of builders," she told him hotly. "If you wish to contest my judgment, you may do so before the Guildmaster, when the guild convenes on Wednesday!"

"Ha ha!" chuckled Lost to itself.

Adria swallowed a gasp. The guilds frowned on anyone who accused their masters without evidence. Her father had standing in the merchants' guild, but his rank was bronze. The merchants would not back him the way the builders would protect one of their own who wore gold, even if that one was a stranger.

"Well!" Keraine said when it was plain that Master Fairingrove would neither touch her medal nor answer her. She draped the chain over her head once more, but this time she did not tuck her insignia under her clothes. "You say you mean to send Adria to some farm?"

"She may have bedazzled you, but *I* am her father. I will see to it she learns proper behavior," Master Fairingrove said, his voice tight. "The old man spoiled her"—he glared at Hillbrand—"and now she will not heed her betters."

Hillbrand snorted. "Instructor Park is not Adria's better," he said with scorn. "He is a third-rater who teaches here instead of Carthak because he has neither ability nor patrons. I fear I did not help you with him, Adria," he explained, meeting her eyes. "I told him that he should let you work ahead and come to me for special instruction. My friends at the school have let me know he took against you instead. The more he saw you could do, the more jealous he became."

Adria tried to smile, to tell her old friend she understood, though she *didn't* understand. It made no sense for a teacher—an adult, a university graduate!—to dislike her.

"Jealous! Of a child!" scoffed Master Fairingrove.

"Bad man," said the glitter-covered darking on Hillbrand's shoulder.

Master Fairingrove flinched. Hillbrand reached up to stroke the small creature. "Now, Silvery, that was rude," he chided gently.

"True," piped the darking in the crook of Keraine's arm. "True," echoed the one in her pack.

Adria saw Master Fairingrove's hands clench into fists. "Please hush," she begged, afraid of what her father might do. He seemed to have taken against all darkings, not only Lost. "Darkings, please." Lost made an arm and patted Adria's cheek gently with it.

"Adria doesn't need a *farm,*" Keraine announced. "She

needs the university in Corus. They'll be able to keep up with her there. I know several good families who will be glad to take her in."

"You raise her hopes for nothing," Master Fairingrove said, crossing his arms over his chest. "I will not pay for a *girl* to attend university, not the fees, not whatever these people will ask to clothe, house, and feed her. In any event, she is far too young. The masters there would never accept her."

"But they will," Hillbrand said gently. "She has two graduates in good standing to vouch for her—Keraine and me—and she will pass the examinations easily. As for expense, I have no children, and quite a large sum in savings. I always meant to leave it to Adria. I will just do it sooner. In fact, I believe I will take her to Corus myself."

"You will *not,*" Adria's father said, his voice thick with fury. "She is *mine.*"

"Adria no slave!" cried Lost, raising its head from Adria's shoulder. "Adria belong to Adria!"

"No slavery here," called the darking seated on Keraine's elbow. "You not own her."

Adria barely heard them. She was thinking, working on the solution of her life. This was an equation made up of feelings and knowledge of Master Fairingrove. She had been prepared to run away to nothing. Now she had something, if she found a way to change her father's mind. Her old self, the one who would do anything to please him, struggled and failed under the weight of all she had learned about him today. If she had been ready to run away with nothing, surely she could fight for this gift of her dreams.

She bit her lip, then forced herself to cry gaily, "Don't

worry, Father!" She ran to the shadowed area by the stair to the old storeroom and retrieved the account book she had hidden there.

"This help?" Lost asked, concerned.

"Don't know," Adria replied in a whisper. Back she went, going all the way to the adults this time. She offered the volume to her father. "Father, it's all right. I finished checking the books. You don't need me to help anymore! Unless you want me to have the guild auditors review my work?"

She met her father's eyes, keeping her own wide and innocent. He stared first at her, then, frowning, at the account book. He turned pale when he realized that it had a black cover. He realized she was threatening to take his secret to the guild.

"I'll have that, my girl," he said at last.

Lost rolled onto the book. "Adria goes free," it said. "Or all darkings in city know what we know now."

"What one darking knows, all know," called the one that rode on Keraine's shoulder.

Lost put out an arm and tapped the book. "All know."

Master Fairingrove took a deep breath. Adria could tell he was fighting to contain his temper. "I had not known your work was . . . done, Adria. That is . . . *very* different. Go with your educated new friends, if you like. You get no blessing from me."

Lost rolled back to Adria's arm, whispering "Huzza, huzza, huzza!" as she gave the book to her father. Once she was free of it, she went over to Keraine and Hillbrand.

"May she go home to say goodbye to her mother and siblings?" asked Hillbrand.

"She may not," said Fairingrove. "I will have her things sent to your home in the morning. She is no longer a member of my family." He looked at them as if they were beggars. "I will thank all of you, including your monsters, to leave my property. The back way." He pointed to the rear door.

As they walked out, Keraine put an arm around Adria's shoulders. "I am so sorry," she whispered. Her darkings hung down, chattering softly with Lost. "I never thought he would be so . . ."

Adria shook her head. "It's all right," she whispered. She would have Lost take a note to her mother, warning her about her father's smuggling.

"No, it isn't all right," Hillbrand said, stealing the torch that lit the storeroom entrance. "But it will be, eventually."

Five days later, three travelers got onto the ferry to Tortall. The two women wore scarves against the strong wind that came downriver from the north, while the man who traveled with them wore the hood of his coat up over his head. One of the ferrymen, trying to coax a horse aboard, told the man to watch where he went. The ferryman reaped a surprise when a black blob the size of two fists put together, covered with silver dust, popped out of the man's hood and piped that they *were* minding where they went! Hillbrand apologized hurriedly for his companion and sat in a protected corner with Adria and Keraine. The four darkings pooled in Adria's lap, chuckling over the start that Silvery had given the ferryman, while Keraine dug in her pack.

Looking at the darkings, Adria had to smile. It was impossible to mope in their presence, and she loved them for coming to her aid. From them she had learned that Lost had asked friends to find Keraine and tell her that Adria needed help. Keraine had thought it would be better to bring in Master Hillbrand, who Master Fairingrove already knew. When she mentioned her idea to the darkings who had found her, they had called for a third, Silvery, to fetch Hillbrand.

In the time Adria, Keraine, and Hillbrand had spent with the four darkings, they had not gotten a straight answer as to how many others of their kind were actually in the city. The answer that gave all of them goose bumps was "Enough." That was when Keraine decided to quickly finish her work on the bridge so she could leave for Corus with Hillbrand and Adria.

"If something is brewing, it may be better that any Tortallans are gone when it boils," Hillbrand had remarked when Keraine announced her decision to come with them.

"Ah!" the engineer said now, producing the item she searched for. "Something to read during your journey to a *proper* school."

Hillbrand took the book from Keraine. "It was a guild school that educated you for university," he said mildly. "You never complained before. Ah. Yasmadad's *Principles of Trigonometry.* Aren't you rushing things?"

"*Rushing* things?" cried Keraine. "With snippets she picked up somewhere, she was reinventing trigonometry right in front of me, I told you!"

While the older pair talked, Adria opened the tattered book to the first page. There were the symbols, what she'd thought of as runes, for sine and cosine. Four black knobs on long necks arranged themselves around the edges of the book as the darkings looked on. "What trig'nom'ry good for?" asked the one called Puff, who managed to hold a cloudweed puff in its body.

"Building things," Adria said, leafing through the book and halting at the pictures. "Bridges, houses, towers. It's the first step."

"Building things," the four darkings said with a sigh, as if they were having visions of wonderful structures.

Adria glanced back at her city as the ferry drew away from it. She looked only once. Then she turned her eyes forward, toward her home-to-be.

A tentacle tugged on her sleeve. "Adria," Lost said. "Teach us."

"I'm learning myself," she protested, but she bent over the book and began to read softly to her class of four.

Time of Proving

Arimu of the Wind People was halfway through her Year of Proving when she found the creature at the bottom of a Dustlands canyon. She was on her way back to her camp with combs of honey when she heard a roaring moan. Since she was a careful girl, she tethered her camels in a safe place, then went to see what made such an unearthly noise.

There, in a stream, she discovered what looked like a bull wearing blue silk drapes and brass trinkets. He lay there as if he'd been thrown from the cliffs as a sacrifice to the gods. But that made no sense. Arimu knew this country. No one lived here to make any sacrifices.

She approached the bull, her spear raised. He looked half-dead—she would put him out of his misery. A crippled animal would never survive here.

The bull turned his head. Arimu froze. He glared straight at her. When could a bull look a human straight in the eye?

He croaked something, as if he spoke to her.

Nonsense, Arimu told herself. Bulls can't talk!

The bull made other noises. These, too, sounded like speech.

"Stop it," she ordered, before she realized she spoke to him as she would a human.

She had heard *stories* of bull people. His feet were human-like and bleeding from cuts. So were his hands. His chest was powerful, to hold up his large head. And now she understood the problem with his eyes. They pointed forward like a human's.

The blue silk rags had once been embroidered trousers and a jacket. The many rings on his horns were gold, not brass. Some were jeweled. He was no sacrifice. No one threw gold and gems into a canyon.

He was still talking. Finally he spoke in a market language she knew. "Help . . . me. Please."

Arimu scratched her head. How could she explain? She doubted he knew the customs of the Dustlands nomads. Someone of her tribe would have mentioned knowing bull-men or cow-women.

"You . . . understand," he said, and coughed. "I beg you, by the laws that govern all civilized people, to help me." He spat into the dust. "You *are* civilized, are you not?"

Arimu leaned on her spear. "I am civilized by the laws of the Wind People, the children of the Dustlands," she replied. "Who are *your* people? How did you get here?"

"I ran," said the bull-man. He looked at his scraped hands. "When I did not run, I walked, and when I could not walk, I crawled. I was on holiday when I was captured like an *animal.* An animal! Hunters from the Merchant City cast a sleeping spell on me, and put me in a cage. They released me in a canyon maze, far from here, to hunt me, camping in silk tents at night while I starved! I stole a horse, but it finally threw me. I just kept running away. Look at me!" He lifted his rags. His hands left bloody streaks on them. There were tears in his eyes.

"I am a Tenth-Rank Scholar," he said woefully. "I was studying to become a Ninth-Rank Scholar. I wanted a little holiday, and now look. I don't even know where I am." He drew away. "Where are your people? Are *they* going to hunt me?"

Arimu smiled crookedly. "The Wind People are in the north. I am the only human you will see for miles."

He still looked nervous. "You will rob me. Only I know how to take my rings from my horns. If you cut my horns from my head, a dreadful curse will descend on you." He began to chant in some foreign language, only to begin coughing. At last he caught his breath. "Please help me."

Arimu sighed. "The Wind People do not give knowledge away. Once we did. Then, when we were poor, we were driven from rich homes east of the Andrenor into tents in the Dustlands. We no longer *give* anything to outsiders. When I go home in six months, I will be asked to tell the full tale of my time here. I cannot lie, and I cannot break my people's law."

The bull-man reached up to a horn, wrapped his hand around a jeweled ring, and gave it a complex twist. It popped open. He slid it off and tossed it to her. "What will this buy?"

She inspected it. When she saw it was real gold and jewels, she put her spear aside and came to look at him more closely.

"It buys you medicine and care for your wounds," she said. The bottoms of his feet were cut to ribbons, his knees and hands nearly so. He took another gold ring from his horns and gave it to her. "This buys you a ride to my camp. The wounds first. I can't bandage them all, but I can clean them." She set her pack down at a distance, so he couldn't grab it, and took out what she would need. "Do you have a name?"

He lay back with a groan, then spoke a mouthful of syllables. "You would say Sunflower," he added.

Arimu smiled as she cleaned his cuts. "Well, Sunflower, tell me if it hurts too much," she said to warn him as she swabbed a six-inch gouge in one of his great thighs. He grunted a reply; sweat rolled from his hide. His feet twitched as she plucked thorns from between his toes; she ordered him to hold still. Seeing a stone embedded in his heel, she pulled it out. He wheezed and relaxed. When she looked up, his eyes had rolled back in his head. He had fainted.

"Just as well," she muttered in her own tongue.

By the time she was done, he was awake enough to get onto her strongest camel. She tied him down when the pain of that effort made him faint again. Slowly she led both camels up a tiny trail to the canyon's rim. Twice Sunflower's camel nearly fell off the path, dragged down by his shifting weight. Arimu got so frightened that she promised the rings he'd paid her to the goddess Dansiga, if she let them reach the top in safety.

They camped that night on the canyon's rim. In the morning Sunflower showed improvement. Though he was too weak to walk, he had plenty of questions, demanding to know the names and uses of every plant he noticed. Once they camped that night, Arimu gave him a tiny knife and a stick, and asked him to whittle some tinder while she got firewood. When she returned, he had cut himself three times.

"Scholars don't whittle," he said when she scolded.

"How will you live to go home?" she demanded as she cleaned his wounds. "It's nearly autumn. You'll need to build fires at night. They don't just start themselves."

"I'll learn quickly enough," Sunflower said.

Arimu wasn't so sure. She remembered his infant-soft hands and feet. What did he know of the kind of work needed to survive in a desert autumn?

As she got the fire going, he resumed his questions. This time, they were about her.

"They turn you out on your own at *thirteen*?" he asked, horrified, when she explained about the Year of Proving.

"If I want to lead my people," she said, watching the flatbread as it baked on a stone. She boasted, "It's the path of greatest honor, if I succeed. I came to a part of the Dustlands where the Wind People have never gone, to map land we have never walked. If I survive the year and bring my maps home, my people will have new places with water, grazing, and hunting. We will have new places to live free of our enemies."

Sunflower snorted. "How far away can your people be, not to have maps of this place?"

Arimu smiled up at him. She did feel smug about her choice. "Spring City. Here." Using the map she carried with her, she pointed to the location of Spring City and to the ruined tower where she lived now.

"You're mad," he said. "You'll get eaten, or lost."

"Not as long as I have a good map and the stars." She pointed to the sky. "The North Star never moves. I know the constellations and where they are at every season. All children of the Wind People learn these things as soon as they are able to learn. What are *you* taught?"

"How to read, and write elegantly," Sunflower replied dreamily. "How to play the lotus flute and the harp. The principles of music and poetry and law."

"Where did you learn such useless things and not fire starting?" Arimu wanted to know.

Sunflower touched the map southwest of the Dustlands, on the seacoast. "We call it Wheeler."

"The Veiled City," she whispered. "But it's a legend."

"It's veiled against those who mean us harm," he corrected her. "So we cannot be invaded and enslaved."

"But you wanted a holiday," Arimu said.

Sunflower heaved an immense sigh. "I *wanted* an adventure. And so I left the veils. I got my adventure, and a person who wants me to pay for everything, and asks what use are poetry and music."

Arimu knew her duty to Sunflower. She meant to do it, even if she made him pay according to the customs of her people. "If you're to get home alive, you must know some things," she explained as she helped him down the steps into her lair under the old tower called Karn Wyeat.

"But I feel your kind of learning will not make me as happy as my kind of learning," Sunflower replied mournfully.

"You'll be happy when you're home." Arimu helped him to sit, then built a small fire of tinder and twigs and lit it. "There's the firewood," she said, pointing. "All you need do is add wood to keep the fire going. I'll tend the camels."

She returned to a smoke-filled room. Once she aired it out, he explained that he had begun to look through a book she had found in the ruined karn. When he saw the fire was dying, he had thrown tinder onto it. Then, when it had blazed too high, he had scattered water on it, dampening the tinder and making it smoke.

More than once in the weeks that followed, Arimu wondered if that had been a sign from Dansiga that Sunflower could not survive on his own. He let meals burn. He let fires die. He knew wonderful stories for every constellation but had no idea of their summer or winter positions, which could guide his travels. She found him watching a sandstorm advance, as if it were an interesting display. She barely got him back to the karn with both their skins in one piece.

She taught him the uses of honey and spiderwebs as medicines first, then which plants were edible. She even showed him how to build a fire using dried dung and brush.

"Why?" he asked her, recoiling from the smell. "There is wood here."

"Because you don't want to follow the Andrenor to the coast," she told him.

He shuddered. "Follow the river to the Labyrinth and Merchant City? I may be a dreamer and an idiot"—names she had called him after the sandstorm—"but I don't want to be captured again!"

"Then you will have to cross the desert. Trees are scarce west of here. It's mostly brush, so you'll have *something* to use, but you must know how to use it."

"Oh," he said mournfully. He drew closer to the fire. "Honored Teacher, teach me to cook food over burned animal droppings."

She grinned, put out the small fire, and began again.

While Sunflower mended their clothes—children of his people were also taught to sew—Arimu made a straw hat that would fit around his horns and a pack. He copied her map with brushstrokes that made it into a work of art. When he was strong enough to venture farther from the karn, she tried to show him how to find water and food.

He was not very good at it.

One by one, Sunflower paid Arimu every ring from his horns. The next day, he put on his hat and the pack. He tucked the copy of the map in his rope belt. "You have taught me all you can by the laws of your people," he said. "I thank you. When I am home, I will compose a song in your name and sing it before the elders. . . . What is this?" he asked as she thrust a small pouch at him.

"I did not give full value for the sapphires in that pair of rings two days ago," she told him. "This makes us even."

He dumped the pouch's contents onto his brown hand: her spare flint and steel. He failed at making a fire with sticks as often as he succeeded.

"Thank you," he whispered. "Your goddess Dansiga blessed me when she put me in your path. I will make an offering of songs to her as well."

She had told him that the Wind People hated goodbyes.

He walked up the steps and out of the karn. Arimu followed and watched as he checked the sun's position and headed west. He used the trail they had already scouted. It would take him into a valley where a stream flowed south.

She told herself, He can follow that safely for at least four days. If he doesn't fall in and lose his food. If he doesn't forget to check the rocks for snakes before he sits. Unless he sees a bird he doesn't recognize and follows it out of that valley and gets lost, or steps in a bog. Or he loses the pack, or . . .

I have taught him all I can under the Wind People's laws, she thought angrily. He has nothing more to pay me. He is an outsider, a bull-man. I owe him nothing.

He is no more fitted to find his way to the Veiled City than a baby.

What is a Year of Proving about, if it proves I am a heartless person?

"Wait!" she cried. "Sunflower, wait!" She ran to catch him. She grabbed his sleeve, panting. "I want maps. Good ones, like the one you made for yourself, of our whole route south. I want trade goods to take back to my people. And you have to mind what I say." She glared up at him, daring him to say anything that would make her ashamed of her softness.

Instead he just smiled. "This will be so much better," he said. "And I can teach *you* what poetry is for. *That* is a fair trade."

They shook hands on their bargain.

Plain Magic

Only once in my life was I glad that my family was large. Until I was fourteen, the tale of my days was one of hand-me-down clothes and toys that barely lasted a month by the time they reached me, and a place to spread my blankets on the floor between my older sisters' beds. Then came the news that the dragon that had been destroying towns to the north was just two days' flight away.

It was time to pack. Everyone had to choose what might be carried to the caves in the mountains and what must be left behind.

With a houseful of frightened older girls and their children—my sisters were married, living with us until their men could build homes of their own—my mother had no use for me. After she had ordered me out of the way for the third time, she thrust bread and cheese into my hands and told me to go.

"Don't stray from the village," she ordered. "Who can say where that dragon is?"

I thought that we would know if he was near, since he was supposed to be as big as three bulls, but nobody argued with my mother. I put my food in a string bag and left our house.

At first I thought I would go to the woods, as I liked to do, but my father saw me and told me to stay close to home. Then I went in search of my friends. All of them had been put to work packing, getting ready to run when the dragon came. Bored and lonely, I wandered into the village and found an unexpected arrival. A peddler had come and had set up in the square across from the fountain.

Her cart was scarlet with designs picked out in yellow paint on the wheels. One whole side of the cart was lowered to form a broad tray. On it were neatly stacked goods: bolts of cloth in a dozen colors, neat rolls of beautiful lace, cloth dolls as small as my fingers or as big as my hand, spools of thread, and balls of yarn. The peddler had placed a wooden bench next to the tray. She sat there, busily embroidering a square of cloth.

She wasn't much to look at—brown and dry and thin, with dark hair tied back under a scarf. Her dress was plain brown cotton with small, dark buttons. She wore skirts as short as those of a girl my age, hanging just a few inches below the knee. They revealed scuffed, flat-heeled boots, as well worn and dusty as everything else about her. I guessed her age at a little over thirty.

There was a dragon coming, maybe, but it was still my lucky day. Normally my parents frowned on my speaking to people who came from the big world outside our village, but they were busy. I could talk to this stranger all I wanted.

I told her my name, Tonya. She gave me hers, Lindri. I

asked about what she had to sell, and she answered. She even showed me the silks she kept tucked away in the cart, for customers with fatter purses than our villagers had. The silks came from odd-sounding places, where the dyes were ten times more vivid than any we had. Lindri had been to those lands. She described them so beautifully I could almost see them.

She embroidered as she talked. Her needle darted through the cloth as if it were alive, shaping a garden of flowers on what would be a sleeve. I had never been very interested in needlework, but Lindri made it seem fascinating. I didn't realize I was staring at the design until she patted my cheek smartly, waking me from a daze.

"Don't watch so long," she said with a grin. "They say there's a plain kind of magic in needlework—do you want to end up a slave to it, like me?"

I winced. "Don't talk of magic or slavery to me," I growled. "I've no idea of what I'm doing, but people here still keep asking me for charms for everything under the sun."

Lindri raised her brows. "You have magic?"

I nodded.

"Surely your teacher is showing you how to work."

I laughed, bitterness choking me. "Wizard Halen? It's like pulling teeth to get him to teach me what little I *do* know. He's so afraid I'll be better than him that he won't even teach me to read."

We continued to talk about nonmagical things. When the noon hour came, I shared my bread and cheese with

Lindri, who added some apples, jam made of a berry I had never tasted before, and mugs of cider.

While we ate, four-year-old Krista emerged from her house across the square. Bit by bit she wandered closer as we finished our meal. At last she reached the lowered tray. She stared at the brightly colored balls of yarn, with her finger in her half-open mouth, as if the balls held the answer to some great secret.

Lindri smiled at her. "Hello, young one. Can I do something for you?"

Krista was shy. She turned to run, stumbled, and fell with a shriek. When I picked her up, I had to bite my lip to keep from gasping. She had cut her palm on a rock in the street. The bones of her hand showed through the deep, ugly gash.

"Hush, hush." Lindri took the screaming Krista from me, brushing her off with an efficient hand. "So much noise. Let me see."

To my surprise, Krista stopped wailing. She held the bleeding hand up for Lindri to examine. Blood welled thickly from the cut, and I shivered with fear. Rot was almost impossible to avoid with such a deep wound. The chances were that pretty Krista would lose her hand.

"That's bad, I suppose," Lindri said. "But it could be a lot worse." She took the girl to a water barrel fixed to the rear of the cart, holding Krista's hand beneath the spout as she rinsed the wound clean. She whisked a strip of linen from the piles on the tray and sat down, settling Krista in her lap.

"If you're brave about this," Lindri told her, "you may have one of the red balls of yarn for your very own."

Krista stuck the fingers of her good hand in her mouth and held out the injured hand. Lindri bandaged the cut neatly and quickly. She finished by tying the loose ends in an oddly shaped knot directly over the wound, tapping the knot lightly with her fingers when she was done.

"All fixed," she told Krista, putting a crimson ball of yarn into the child's good hand. "Keep the bandage clean, mind. When you take it off, you'll be as good as new."

As Krista ran home, I frowned at Lindri. It would have been rude for me to say so to an adult, but I thought it was cruel for Lindri to lie to Krista. The child would know it was a lie when she could no longer use the hand, or worse, was forced to have it cut off.

Lindri smiled at me. "You'll see that I'm right," she said, as if she knew what I had been thinking. "Now, tell me about the dragon who's been preying on this valley."

No one could have disobeyed the soft note of command in Lindri's voice. "It first attacked villages below the northern mountains," I began. "That was about two weeks ago. It's been coming south ever since. It doesn't burn every town in its way, but it's burned enough. People who flee it come through here because we're the last village before the pass out of the valley. But you'd know that if you came up from the south."

"That's right," Lindri replied. "I drove through the pass this morning."

Mistress Fane, the miller's wife, came up to us and pointed to a bolt of cloth. "I'd like to see more of that, if you please," she ordered Lindri. The woman could never ask for anything politely.

"No one knows why it burns some villages and not others," I went on as Mistress Fane inspected another bolt of cloth, and a third. "It was spotted near here two days ago, but we don't know if it'll attack us or not. Everyone hopes it will just go away."

Mistress Fane bought the pink cloth she had been looking at, which filled me with glee. She looked awful in pink.

Lindri picked up her embroidery again. "Why are your people still here?"

"We're too poor," I told her. It felt odd to say such things to a stranger—I was very proud—but Lindri had a listening way about her. I went on as I watched her needle flash through her cloth. "All most of us have is our farms. We can't take them with us, and we've no money to start fresh someplace else." I sighed. "I'd *like* to start someplace else."

Lindri glanced at me. "Adventurous, are you, Tonya?"

I felt as if she'd taken a leash off my tongue. Out spilled my dreams of leaving the valley someday, of seeing new lands and meeting new people, of simply being somewhere *different.* Then I remembered. I was Tonya, the headman's daughter. The only place I was likely to go to was my future husband's home. It was silly to talk of my dreams to Lindri, who had seen the world beyond the mountains. It was silly and it was senseless, because soon she would leave, and I would still be here.

"Where are you going now?" I asked.

She looked at the sun, which slid toward the western

horizon, and traded her embroidery for knitting. "North," she replied briefly. "To the mountains, I expect."

"You can't!" I protested, shocked. "It's dangerous. Wild animals live there. More dragons, and bears taller than a tall man, and giant cats—"

Lindri shrugged. "I like animals. They rarely bother you unless you bother them first."

I was about to argue further when Riv interrupted us. He had come in early from putting his sheep up for the night, probably to get news of the dragon. "Excuse me," he said politely, picking up a small square of folded lace. "I want to know how much this is."

Lindri looked him over. "One silver minim."

"For just this little bit?" Riv asked, eyeing the lace. It was beautiful, filmy white stuff. I had an idea that the price Lindri had given him was less than what she would charge somewhere else. He handed the square to her. "Hold this, please? I want to look at the rest." He went to the small stacks of lace at the far end of the tray.

"He seems like a nice young man," Lindri remarked softly. "What can you tell me about him?"

"He's getting married next month," I whispered, keeping an eye on Riv. "His girl Aura is my best friend. She's standing over by the fountain, the one with the basket on her arm. Riv's chief shepherd, but he hasn't been chief through a spring shearing, so he hasn't any money. And all Aura ever wanted was a lace veil when she marries, like the city ladies have."

Lindri was tugging on the edges of the lace Riv had given her, which worried me. What if she got it dirty?

"Nobody else here got a lace veil," I went on. "So people say Aura thinks she's better than everyone else. But it's not true! She just wants something pretty."

Riv came back. "See anything you'd rather have?" Lindri asked.

He offered her a silver minim, his face beet colored with shame. "No. This is fine." He was trying to smile, but it didn't look right. "It isn't a whole veil, but—well, it's very pretty," he finished.

Lindri pocketed the coin and gave Riv the folded square. "Enjoy it," she told Riv, smiling. "And may your marriage be happy."

Boys had come to set torches around the square. The whole village would be coming here soon, to get the latest news of the dragon. As the torches caught, they threw their wavering light over Riv as he walked back to Aura.

"It's just not fair," I muttered as he offered her the lace. "Old, mean people like Miller Fane and his wife have nice things, but Aura and Riv—"

Riv fumbled the lace and caught it just in time. Then the lace began to unfold, and I gasped. Length after length spilled from Riv's hands like a waterfall, shimmering white in the glow from the torches. Riv had to raise his hands higher and higher to keep the white stuff from touching the ground, while Aura laughed and cried at the same time.

They tried to make Lindri take it back, but she refused. "That's the piece you bought," she told Riv firmly. "Ask Tonya if it ever left my hands after you gave it to me."

And that was the biggest puzzle of all. I had talked to her the whole time, and the only thing she did with that lace was tug on it. I *knew* it had been a folded square of one or two thicknesses when Riv selected it, but I couldn't prove it. They went away at last, Aura crying on Riv's shoulder as he carefully refolded the lace.

Lindri shook her head, straightening the goods on her tray. "People should inspect strange goods carefully," she murmured. "They never know what they've purchased, otherwise."

I was about to ask what Riv *had* bought when my father came as the village headman to meet Lindri. The other two elders, Priest Rand and my teacher, Wizard Halen, soon joined us. As Rand said polite things to Lindri, Halen started to inspect her wares. Suddenly he picked up a square of linen. "There is something odd about this piece," he began.

Lindri snatched it from his fingers. "Don't touch unless you plan to buy," she snapped. "No one purchases dirty goods."

Wizard Halen's eyes narrowed. He was about to speak when my brother Selm galloped into the square. Normally Selm was calm and slow going, but when he reined up before our father, he was in as much of a lather as his horse.

"I saw it settle on Tower Rock!" he gasped. "Long and bronze, like we were told!"

People came quickly to the square as the word spread, until everyone was there, including my entire family, Riv, Aura, my other friends, and Krista and her parents. Miller Fane and his wife arrived with their horse-drawn cart—the only one in the village—piled high with their things. They could afford to run, to start fresh somewhere else.

Everyone listened as my father, the priest, and the wizard explained the problem for what seemed like the thousandth time. Were there any choices but flight?

Wizard Halen said, "I may have found a way."

"Tell us, then," Tanner Clyd yelled.

Just then Krista's mother saw the bandage on her girl's hand was dirty and bedraggled. I watched her tug at the strange knot Lindri had used. At last she gave up trying to undo the knot and cut it with her belt knife.

"I have read the various remedies for a plague of dragons," Halen said loudly. His squeaky voice quavered with the effort.

Of course, I thought unhappily. He's been at his precious books. We had fought so often over his teaching me to read that I had finally given up asking.

Halen went on. "A spear made of silver, of course, wielded by a virtuous man—"

Someone called, "If there was enough silver here to make a spear, Wizard, you'd have had it all by now."

My father scowled. "The wizard is trying to aid us," he said. "Listen to him."

Halen looked smug. "A dragon may also be lured to its death in a pit of fire, or buried in a river of ice." He tugged his nose for a moment. "But there is a fourth way to be rid of a dragon, and I have found it at last."

"Is it as impossible as the others?" Miller Fane wanted to know. "There are no pits of fire or rivers of ice here!"

People muttered agreement. Halen waited until they were quiet before he replied, "It is not impossible, but it is costly. You may think it better to flee."

"Where will we go?" Krista's mother cried. She stopped

unwinding the bandage from her daughter's palm. "We have lived here for generations! No one has the coin to build new homes!"

Everyone shouted agreement.

"You must give the dragon something," Halen announced. "You must assuage his hunger."

"Oh, no," Lindri whispered tiredly.

I missed Halen's next words because I was staring at Krista. Her mother had the bandage off at last. She was turning the little one's palm back and forth in the torchlight, trying to see the cut. So was I. The ugly gash that had marred Krista's hand when Lindri bandaged it was gone.

". . . a young girl," I heard Wizard Halen say. "Unmarried. A virgin."

Everyone was silent. To offer the beast one of our own . . . A woman began to cry.

"You must draw lots," Halen went on. "You must be fair."

"Drivel." Everyone turned to stare at Lindri, who stood beside her cart, hands on hips. "Absolute nonsense. Do you seriously think a dragon can taste the difference between a virgin and an old man?"

"You are a stranger here," Miller Fane called. "Speak to our wizard with respect."

"Your wizard doesn't know what he's talking about," Lindri told him calmly and clearly. "Dragons hate the taste of human flesh."

"Legend is filled with the sacrifices made to dragons!" Halen was turning red. Just when he had everyone's attention and respect, this peddler woman was trying to make him look like a fool.

"Of course they'll eat a human if a human is staked out like a goat," Lindri replied. "They aren't very smart. This one will eat your virgin, and then he'll be sick. A dragon flames only when he is ill. He'll pass over your homes because he has fed, and then he'll burn the next village he sees to the ground. You will have killed a girl needlessly, and others will die or lose their homes. All for the lack of a little sense on your part, *Wizard.*"

My father was dark with anger. "You have said more than enough," he told Lindri. "You are a guest, and Halen is an elder. Be silent, or our young men will see you on your way."

Lindri eyed my father for a moment, as if she could see through his face into his head. I was angry and ashamed. *I* knew what he was like, but he was my father. What right did a stranger have to look at him as if he were a fool?

Lindri shrugged and sat down. My father stared at us, waiting for another sign of rebellion, then turned to Halen. "How young must they be?"

The wizard swelled with pride. Lindri had been silenced, and now everyone waited for him to tell us what to do. "They must be of marriageable age, and no younger than twelve," he announced.

There were just seven girls of that age—the village was very small. We seven were separated from the others as Carpenter Daws cut a rod into six long pieces and a short one. The wizard made a bag out of my mother's shawl, and the pieces were dumped inside. The priest said a prayer. Then we were told to each step up and take a piece of wood without looking. Lindri was silent, knitting busily.

I got the short piece. When I held it up, everyone looked at my father. They wanted to see if he would try to save me, either because I was his daughter or because after Halen I was the best magic worker in the village. They didn't know my father. I wish *I* hadn't known him as well as I did.

My mother was sobbing quietly. My sisters gathered around her and led her home. Not one of them met my eyes. I looked for my brothers and brothers-in-law in the crowd. They, too, looked away.

"Tonya is the one," my father said. "We will take her to the north meadow tomorrow and leave her there for the dragon."

Aura ran up to me and hugged me fiercely, weeping. I felt distant and strange, as I had since I had seen that short piece of wood. When Riv kissed my cheek and drew Aura away from me, I felt numbly glad. I knew I ought to say something, to them or the elders or someone, but I couldn't think.

Lindri came up to me and put a hand on my shoulder. "You're brave, Tonya," she whispered. "Be brave awhile more." She returned to her cart, climbing inside and closing the door behind her.

My father, along with two of my brothers, took me to a shed by the north meadow for the rest of the night. Selm was the one who hesitated when they would have closed the door and locked me in.

"We don't want to do this," he said, almost as if he were pleading with me. "You're my sister, and I—" He seemed to think better of telling me he loved me. "We have to do this," he told me, hanging his head. "We've no choice." He closed the door. I heard the bolt slide home.

I lay awake all night, staring at the shadowy roof and listening to the men who guarded the shed. None of this felt real, not even the rocks that pressed into my back.

At last I could see bits of pale light through the cracks in the walls. My father, Halen, and Priest Rand came for me.

The post was already standing in the middle of the north meadow. They had found shackles somewhere and hung them from the post. The priest locked them around my hands, muttering a fast prayer as he kept an eye on distant Tower Rock. When a touch of sun showed over the horizon, they left me at the run and hid in the woods at the meadow's edge.

My numbness evaporated. Giddy with sudden fright, I faced Tower Rock and the humped form that sat on top of it. Once the monster's in the air, I thought, he'll be here fast. It'll be over before I can feel it.

At least, I prayed it would be so.

Then I heard the jingle of a horse's harness, the clop of hooves, and the creak of wood. Lindri stopped her cart a little way from me, and her piebald gelding put his head down to graze. The elders yelled for her to get away, but they were too afraid to leave the protection of the trees to stop her.

Baffled, I stared at Lindri as she walked over to me. Little things about her struck me as suddenly very important. Her hair was freshly washed and braided. She was wearing a clean blue dress with white embroideries, and she had wiped yesterday's dust off her boots. She glanced at Tower Rock, her eyes as clear and alert as if she'd been up for hours. As the distant dragon unfurled its wings, Lindri gathered my shackles in her hands.

"This has gone far enough," she said, looking the chains over. "If they'd listened to me, you would have been spared a very bad night. I'm sorry for that."

She tapped each lock with her fingers, just as she had tapped the knot on Krista's bandage. The shackles sprang open. Then she pulled a length of twine from her pocket. "Go, Tonya. I'll tend to the dragon."

It was all too strange. I should have been frightened and hysterical. Instead I quivered with excitement. I went only as far as her cart to wait, stroking the piebald's nose and warming my cold hands in his mane. My father and the others were still shouting. I ignored them, just as Lindri had.

She faced north, looking just as calm as she had while we gossiped the day before. Only her fingers moved, tying multitudes of knots in her twine. They formed clumps that grew far greater than the amount of string I had seen her take out. Like Riv's lace, the knots spilled from her working hands to the ground in billows. As the dragon leaped into the air from Tower Rock, Lindri bent, gathered the masses of knots into her hands, and straightened.

I glanced back at the woods. Wizard Halen screamed curses, jumping up and down in a fury. My father was staring at Lindri, white faced. The priest had fallen to his knees and was muttering prayers.

I turned in time to see the dragon as it glided low over the meadow, claws outstretched. Lindri waited until he was directly overhead. She crouched, then leaped, hurling her bundle of knots into the air. They spread until I could see clearly she had shaped a huge net. Like a living thing, the net wrapped itself around the dragon, wings, snout, claws, and all. The great lizard screeched with alarm as it tumbled to the ground, landing with a thump on the meadow.

As I looked on, the net drew itself tighter and tighter, pulling the dragon's limbs and wings close to its body. It was beautiful, long, and muscular, with copper-bronze scales, gold claws, and deep amber eyes. It was as long as two bulls and as big around as one—a far cry from the three-bull size that people had claimed for it. Pressing its wings against the clinging net, it cried softly, until I began to feel sorry for the thing that might have eaten me.

Lindri approached, tugging a fresh length of twine until it was a rope. Reaching through the net, she slid her rope around the dragon's neck, making a leash. The dragon stopped its struggle, rubbing its muzzle against Lindri's hands. She spoke to it quietly before she pulled her hands free of the net. Now the creature sat and waited, eyeing her curiously.

She grasped a thread of the net and tugged. The web of knotted string fell apart and shrank, leaving her holding only a piece of twine. She tucked that into her pocket and wound the free end of the dragon's leash around her wrist.

My father and the others had left the safety of the trees and were advancing warily. Lindri waited for them, rocking on her heels as the dragon butted her affectionately with its head.

"You tricked us!" Halen screeched when he was close enough that she could hear. "You never told us—" He couldn't seem to remember what she hadn't told them. His face turned mottled purple as he opened and closed his mouth soundlessly.

"You didn't believe me when I told you something about their habits," Lindri said calmly as she rubbed the dragon's muzzle. The elders stopped twenty feet away from her, refusing to draw closer. "Would you have believed me if I told you about this?"

When they didn't answer, she led the dragon to her cart and hitched it at the back. The gelding looked at the lizard in a bored way, as if dragons always brought up the rear.

Perhaps dragons always did.

"What will you do with it now?" My father sounded nervous. I looked away from him. Any love I felt for him had gone in the night, but I hated to see him trying to be humble to her now. "We meant you no harm—"

Lindri climbed onto the driver's seat of her cart and picked up the reins. "He's lost," she said briefly. "I'm taking him home to his mountains."

"Lost?" Halen whispered.

"He would never have come this far if he hadn't been lost in the first place." Her mouth curled scornfully. "Neither would he have done so much damage if folk like you hadn't insisted on feeding him their children." She looked down at me. "Why don't you come with me, Tonya? I'll take you someplace where you can get a proper magical education."

I seized the edge of her seat. "I don't want to learn someplace else," I told her. "I want to study with you. I want to learn what *you* can teach me."

Lindri raised her brows, her gray eyes puzzled. "This? It's just plain magic, Tonya. Nothing spectacular."

I glanced at the dragon following the cart, attached only by what had once been a piece of string. He—she had said it was a he—nibbled curiously at the wooden step under the rear door. "It's spectacular enough," I told her.

Lindri laughed. Suddenly I could see she wasn't old at all—she was barely a handful of years older than I. "Come up, then," she said, offering her hand. "What I have to teach you, I will."

Mimic

When I rattled down the ladder and into our kitchen, my younger brother, Peng, greeted me with his usual complaint: "When do I get to take the herd?" He must have thought if he got me early, I might not be awake enough to give him my usual answer.

"No, Peng." I slung my pack onto the table and tucked the wrapped food set on the counter into it for later in the day. "I don't know why you keep asking, when my answer is always the same. You do good work with the cows."

Ma shook her head as she handed me a breakfast bowl of rice mixed with dried pork. I think she was getting tired of this argument between Peng and me.

"There's plenty of folk to work the cows," whined Peng. "You had your first flock when you were younger than me. Grandpa will take you for his apprentice any day, he says so all the time."

I shoveled rice into my mouth. I didn't want to say that I would cling to the freedom of the hillsides and my flock of sheep as long as I could. Study with Grandpa would mean hours indoors, away from the sun, the winds, and the wild creatures. It would mean stuffy rooms and dusty books with only stuffed animals and dusty skeletons to look at.

"Your grandfather says there are other shamans without magic," Ma said. "They use talismans and amulets made by those with power, or they borrow from their neighbors who have power."

I glared at her, but Ma only shrugged. She was one of Grandpa's helpers, a healer with no magic. She was happy with that.

"Unless the chief herdsman says different," I told Peng, washing out my bowl and setting it to dry, "that flock is mine." I slung my pack over my shoulder. Ma handed my staff and water bottle to me and kissed my cheek. As I left our house, I heard her tell Peng, "Your turn, my son. The cows are waiting."

The early larks greeted me as I stopped to fill my bottle at the stream that ran by Grandpa's house. I stopped to pour some of my fresh water into the wide drinking dish before the Shrine of the Compact. I visited the shrine daily. Its roof was made with feathers that the valley birds let fall, gathered by our people and placed here. Every day the roof was different. Today it seemed that someone had found a molting cardinal: bright red feathers graced the roof.

The shrine was also proof that, long ago, there had been plenty of magic in our village. In those days we were able to shape an agreement with all the birds who lived here. We would care for them and they for us, through all of time. There hadn't been such big magics done in this valley in ages, but we had this, at least, to remind us that one great magic still worked here every day.

I turned away from the shrine and walked to Grandpa's workshop. He was awake and poking up his fire. I didn't speak to him in case he was thinking of a new medicine or surgery, but went straight to the shelf where he kept the big jar of ointment for wounds. I was running out.

When I finished refilling my jar, I turned to find Grandpa scowling at me. I sighed: first Peng, now him.

"It's too nice to argue," I said before he spoke. "The birds are awake and calling. Thank you for the ointment!" I kissed his cheek and ran outside.

"Butterfly!" he called after me. "What will you do when the snows come?"

I didn't shout back. It would have been rude. Besides, he knew what I did when the snows came. I spun wool and went outside as often as I could. The sheep still needed attention, and they didn't fuss at me about doing something with my life. I was *living* my life!

I whistled Brighteyes and Chipper from the barn where the herding dogs spent their summer nights. My two came, tails wagging, still licking their breakfast from their chops. Together we went to our sheepfold and opened the gate. The sheep, lazy things, just stared at us. The dogs ran in to get them moving. "The birds are already awake, sleepyheads!" I told the sheep. Some of them gave rude, blatting answers as they filed past me.

Hundreds of songs, not just those of the larks, rose from the trees that surrounded our village and fields. The daytime flocks were waking up, getting ready for their part of the contract: hunting the flying insects that plagued our workers as the day turned warm. The crows took to the skies first, a great black cloud of them. Half soared over my head, making a great racket as they went searching for food on the plain. Half flew the other way, bound for the woods and fields on the far side of the river that cut our valley in two. Only when they were gone and I could hear the prettier songs again did I take out my flute to play my reply to the songbirds.

On we went, sheep, dogs, and me. Brighteyes barked as she trotted beside the sheep. She thought the music was for her. Chipper ignored us as he guarded the flock on the other side. He was young and very serious about herding.

We followed a stream up along the flank of Taka Hill. Taka was my favorite place to graze the sheep, and we hadn't been up there in a week. It was broad and tall, with plenty of wide dips filled with grass. On the east side it ended in a cliff. From there, I could look out over the Great Plain, beyond the hills that marked our valley's eastern flank.

The early ground mists had burned off. The sun turned the plains grasses to gold and gave long shadows to the herds of buffalo and antelope that grazed there. They were safe from our hunters for now. Winter was a good three months off, time enough for the little animals to grow strong on summer greens. The only thing the wild herds had to fear, or us, for that matter, was the terrible summer storms. One of them flashed lightning in the distance, at the very edge of my vision. I don't know what it was that made me shiver—those rapid spears of fire out on the immense plain, or the single gray finger of a tornado that reached from clouds to ground.

Only when the tornado vanished and the storm was gone from my view did I turn to view my own, smaller world. I loved our valley. Unlike the longer valleys to the north and south, strung like beads along the foothills of the Heavenly Fire Mountains, our valley held only our village, fields, and orchards. The Birdsong River and its companion road split it in two along its length. A second road divided the valley in half across the middle, bringing us travelers from the cities on the far side of the plain and from the mountains in the west. From the hill where I stood I had a king's view of it all.

The rest of the village was awake. Out came the other shepherds and their flocks, and the goatherds. The goatherds went into the hills on the western side of the river, closer to the mountains. Other shepherds waved as they passed us on the way into the hills south of the pass and the road at my feet. The cowherds moved out on the heels of the smaller animals. They led our cattle through the pass onto the edge of the Great Plain. With men and dogs on guard, the cows would graze as their wild cousins did. Small flocks of birds followed the herds to feed on bugs and warn against enemies. None of the other villages in neighboring valleys had such a useful arrangement. They said we were stupid to feed the birds in addition to what they took as they hunted.

With my sheep settled across the hill, away from the cliff, I took out my spindle and my bag of wool. Spinning thread, I walked around the edges of the herd. The sheep were in a good mood. Even the lambs were well behaved after a few chasing games.

Noontime came with its hard, hot sun. Brighteyes,

Chipper, and I moved the sheep to cooler grazing under the trees by the stream. I piped a hello to the birds there, who sang their own greetings in reply. I opened our lunch. First, because they looked so sad, I fed the dogs chopped-meat patties that Ma had fixed for them.

"I didn't fall for the drooping ears, though," I said as I put their food on the ground. "I give you this because it's time to eat, not because you made me feel sorry for you." Brighteyes wagged her tail and barked, then gobbled her lunch. Chipper simply ate. Pa said he didn't know what would happen when Chipper got too old to run with the sheep. The way he ate, without a herd to keep him busy, Chip might turn into a ball with a tail.

As the dogs fed, I ate my own lunch. Then I broke up some cakes and tossed the crumbs out on the ground in front of me.

The birds here were friends. Most had been brought to me by the fieldworkers and herders. All had been in danger once. They'd had broken wings or legs, or their nests had fallen from trees. Grandpa had taught me what to do for them. Now I tended injured birds on my own. I always kept back some of my food for those who had returned to the sky. They would visit me wherever I took my sheep, happy for a free meal, as I was happy for the company.

While everyone pecked at crumbs, I sat back and played my flute. The birds lit all around me, peeping and singing along.

Suddenly they shrieked and fled into the shelter of the trees. Brighteyes and Chipper snarled, staring at the sky. I leaped to my feet. It was the golden eagle who hunted our hills. It had prey in its claws and was flying toward us, on its way home.

I had a score to settle with that eagle. He must have come from a nest outside our valley, because he ignored the compact between our village and the birds. He had taken a lamb in the early spring. It was time for him to learn I was no one to meddle with. I set a rock in my sling and let fly. The eagle screamed at me and flew higher. I loaded the sling a second time and spun it through the air, choosing my moment. I didn't really want to kill the great thief. He was trying to live, like me. I just wanted him to stay away from my sheep! I loosed my stone.

The eagle shrieked as my rock drove through his tail feathers, knocking two of them free. They spun on their drop to the earth.

"Ha!" I yelled, and set another stone in the sling. "Take that, sheep-stealer!" I let fly again.

The eagle veered away, losing a wing feather. Better, I had alarmed him so badly that he dropped his catch. I ran to get it, in case it was still alive.

Luckily, the prey fell straight into some brush. I heard it squawk and thrash as I searched the branches for it. I pried its claws away from the tough stems, talking softly. It calmed as I worked, and stopped struggling. Finally I drew back from the bushes, scratched and bloody, and got a real look at the eagle's prize.

If it was a bird, it was the ugliest bird I had ever seen. An ailment, maybe, had stripped away its feathers, leaving only brownish pink skin stretched tight over its ribs. Two long flaps of skin over a couple of long, slender bones joined its sides and arms, like a bat's wings, but it wasn't furry like a bat. Its forepaws were little more than hooks on the long arm bone. Its hind paws were like a lizard's, with toes that ended in hooked claws, but lizards had no wings, and bats did not have beaded skin. I ran my finger along the thing's back. It was as long as my forearm, not counting its tail, and there were small bumps along its spine. Could it be a dragon? They were bigger in the stories, bigger than barns. Could it be a baby dragon? Surely this baby was too small to one day grow large enough to carry a bull away.

It panted in my hands, eyes closed, as I examined it. One forearm was broken. A flap of skin on its right arm hung open, the wound bleeding. I guessed the eagle's talons had made that and the long cut in its left side.

"You tried to fight, didn't you?" I asked. I cradled it in my arms gently, pressing the bloody wounds to halt the bleeding. It still did not struggle, as if it knew I meant it no harm. "You are very brave," I said as I carried it to my pack. "Now, I'm sorry to say I must hurt you a little to make you feel better. I have to sew you up so you won't bleed anymore." I sat cross-legged by my pack and opened it one-handed, the other hand still pressed to the worst cut in the lizard's side. I opened my medicine kit, setting out all I would need, including the cloth I used as a worktable in the fields. I did everything slowly to keep from frightening my patient. When I placed it on the cloth, it stayed still, panting softly. I wished all the animals I had cared for had been like this one—they had fought unless they were too sick to struggle.

"You are so good," I told it. "Brighteyes, isn't this a good fellow?" Looking around, I saw that Brighteyes had left. She and Chipper were minding the sheep. They were used to watching the flock as I doctored.

After wetting a square of cloth with water from my bottle, I touched the damp cloth to the cut in the lizard's side. It let out a sharp peep and opened its eyes.

"I'm sorry," I said. "I did warn you it might hurt. I have to clean all the blood away." Then I got a good look into its eyes. They were bright copper, the shade of fresh-worked metal, with long black pupils. Those were not bat eyes. I wondered if they gave off heat, and scolded myself for so foolish an idea. It blinked, and I blinked, too. Now its eyes lost their hold on me.

The lizard shrilled and bumped my hand with its nose. It seemed to be telling me to go ahead.

Gently I cleaned its wounds, where the bleeding had stopped. It was wonderfully well behaved, though I must be hurting it. As I stitched the cuts, it began to trill in a high, sweet voice. I stopped, but the lizard only looked at me and continued to sing. I resumed my work as it did, splinting the broken bone in the wing once the open wounds were stitched. I learned to be careful of those finger-hooks: they were sharp. My last step was to put Grandpa's healing ointment on the stitches.

Only when I was done did the lizard's song end. I wiped my forehead on my arm and looked up, to see that the trees around us were filled with birds. The sheep and the dogs had gathered near us on the ground. The creature looked around and gave one final, drawn-out whistle. Finally it stretched out on the cloth and went to sleep.

The birds took off when they realized the newcomer was done with its song. I covered it with a clean, dry cloth and walked down to the stream with the dogs. Now that I'd cared for its wounds, the question of what it was returned to baffle me. I *knew* our valley's lizards. This creature was like none of them. I had seen pet lizards brought by travelers to sell to mountain and city dwellers, lizards with frills around their necks, or chins covered with spikes, or strange-colored scales. None of those lizards did more than hiss, let alone sing. None were so ugly as this creature, with its pink-brown skin and lumpy head and spine.

As I washed my hands and arms in the stream, I thanked the gods for sparing its life. Then I checked the flock, making sure no sheep had wandered off. After confirming that everyone was present, I left the dogs to mind the herd and returned to my belongings. A crow I had healed once—I knew him from his white-splotched tail—stood over the lizard, his black wings spread to shelter the wounded creature from the sun. When I came near, the crow squawked and flapped away. I stopped for a moment, breathless with wonder. How had the crow known to do that? And why had he done it for this stranger?

The lizard raised its head and looked at me, those copper eyes bright even in the afternoon sun. It opened its mouth and cawed, exactly as the crow had done.

I laughed and crouched beside it. "That's so clever! Are you a mimic?" I asked. The creature cocked its head, opened its mouth a second time, and barked just like Brighteyes did. I sat back on my heels, startled. It seemed far more normal for a lizard to copy a bird's sound than a dog's. Here was another puzzle to add to that of a crow sheltering a strange creature. "Then shall I call you Mimic?"

The lizard trilled a lark's musical song. I lifted it free of its resting place. "Mimic you shall be, whatever you are. And will you mind if I say you are a he? You seem like a boy to me, getting into trouble and falling out of it."

He was patient as I inspected him. The stitches looked good. His bleeding had stopped. The ointment I had placed on his hurts was still there. "You *are* very good," I told him. "You didn't lick it off. The sheep always try that."

Mimic smacked his jaws.

"Are you hungry?" I had meat patties left for the dogs. I took one out and broke it in half. When I offered a piece to Mimic, a forked blue tongue flicked from his mouth, picked up several bits of meat, and vanished into his mouth again.

Three more trips for his tongue, and the half-patty was gone. Mimic looked at me and squawked. I hurried to feed him the second half. Once he was done, I poured water from my bottle into one cupped hand. When he had drunk his fill, he went back to sleep.

I shifted him onto my pack, then carried both into deeper shade. While he slept, I worked up a harness so I might carry him home, fashioning it from splints of bamboo and cloth ties. Toward sunset he began to stir. Gently I tucked him into the harness and strapped him to my pack. The ties held him in place but did not touch his splinted wing or rub his stitched wounds.

Securing him, I felt heat rising under his skin. I had expected a fever, but it still made me nervous. What treatment could work for this unknown animal? I needed to take him to Grandpa. For a moment I hesitated. My grandfather did not care for lizards as I did. In fact, he'd ordered me not to bring them to him anymore.

I shook my head. Grandpa would relent, once he saw how odd Mimic was. How could he resist those beautiful copper eyes?

"I can't believe you're not panicking," I said to Mimic as I tested the harness cords yet another time. I tucked bits of wool under them, so they wouldn't chafe. "Any other creature would thrash like mad. Now, be nice and don't try to open your good wing, all right?"

Our eyes met. For a moment I had the idea that Mimic wanted to say he *would* be good and keep as still as possible. I giggled at the folly of the idea and carefully lifted my pack to my shoulders. With the dogs on either side of us, I whistled for the sheep and walked down to the trail. It was time for the part of the compact I loved best.

I explained it to Mimic, since he was a newcomer. "Long ago, the shaman who led my ancestors to settle here made a compact with the birds of the valley," I explained. "If they agreed to guard our fields, fruit trees, and gardens from insects, each day when everyone headed home for supper, the seed-eating birds could help themselves to grain, and the others could have the insects. In the winter, any birds who stayed here instead of flying south were welcome to grain from our own stores." Mimic cawed like a crow in my ear. "Well, crows eat scraps," I told him. "Isn't it wonderful?

When more birds come, they guard us as we work, so we hardly get any itchy bites. And they help the other animals with fleas and ticks. Nobody told them, they just figured it out, and did it." Mimic made a chuckling sound that got *me* to chuckle. "There are other villages all along these foothills. Their people laugh at us. They make their children drive the birds away from the fields. They don't believe our crops are bigger than theirs, that we lose very little to insects. That that makes up for what the birds take."

I heard the voice of the big gong at the heart of the village. That was the signal for the fieldworkers to go home. Already the cattlemen were coming through the pass, on their way to the barns. "Now watch," I told Mimic as the last workers and cowmen passed down the road into the village. "This is the good part."

Hundreds of birds rose in flocks from the valley's many trees. They settled in the fruit trees, the grain, and the gardens for their share of seed and insects. Once they were full, they would return to their home trees. And they sang, their many songs mingling into one beauty. The village cats came and sat in the road as they always did, to watch. As far as anyone knew, the truce between cats and birds at the day's end was also part of the great magical pact.

Once the home trees were empty, the crows returned from the plains and foothills, making their noise. They sounded like a village meeting, only *much* louder. I wondered if they exchanged news about the things they saw, and traded gossip, the way the grown-ups did at our meetings.

Usually I waited to bring the flock in until everyone went quiet and twilight came on. Tonight, worried about the heat coming from Mimic, I called in the dogs and the sheep and took them down the trail. The birds in the path and the cats in the road moved out of our way to let us pass.

Once the sheep were in their fold and the dogs fed, I took Mimic to Grandpa. The lizard was starting to worry me. Here it was nigh on full dark, and Mimic was hot and restless. Lizards were day folk. They turned cold and sleepy at night. His fever was rising fast, and I knew nothing about lizard fevers.

Grandpa was napping when I barged into his workroom with Mimic. He jumped when I slammed the door. "Howshi bless the fields, haven't I *begged* you people not to do that!" he cried. Then he saw it was me, and he smiled. "Ri, don't do that to your old grandfather. I don't like to be cross with my tiger lily. What have you got on your back?"

With grumbling and moaning he pried himself from his chair and came over to help me remove my pack. When he saw what I carried, he went still. "I told you last time, Ri, no more lizards. They're vermin. This one's a *big* vermin."

I turned around and faced Grandpa, angry that he was being so cruel. "He's hurt, and he's getting sick. You can't turn him away! Look at him! He's a lizard with wings!"

"Then he's deformed and ought to be left to die peacefully," Grandpa said flatly.

"Might he be a dragon?" I asked. "You know, a little one that guards rocks? A baby?"

But Grandpa was already shaking his head. "No dragon I have ever seen could match your lizard. They are colorful, and their head horns and antennae are long and slender. Their scales shine, like they have been painted with lacquer.

This thing is big for a lizard, but dragon babies would have to be larger still. And it is dying."

"No," I whispered.

Grandpa heard me anyway. "Take it out and put it on the compost heap to wait for death. Or break its neck if you want to be truly merciful."

I set my pack on the long work counter, glaring at Grandpa. "You doctor Tuerh, even though you fight all the time and you think he cheats on weights at the mill."

"Tuerh is a human being. That's my calling—good or bad, I treat all humans. I make exceptions for our animals, who work hard, even the birds." Grandpa was glaring at me, his thick eyebrows half-hiding his eyes. "What are lizards good for? It's just a waste of work! Be sensible, Ri. You'd doctor rats if I let you."

I didn't tell Grandpa I did help the occasional rat, in secret.

"Look at this ugly thing," Grandpa went on. "It probably steals eggs from the nest—maybe even whole chickens. I mean it this time, I won't help."

I grabbed his tunic with both of my hands. "Please, Grandpa," I begged. "An eagle was going to kill him. He hasn't been stealing eggs. He's all skin and bone. You should hear him sing! Please?"

Everyone always said I was Grandpa's favorite. I took advantage of it, hanging on to his tunic until he sighed.

"One last time, girl," he told me. "If I can even help at all." His hands were knobby and stiff with bone disease, but their touch was feather-light when he lifted Mimic and his harness away from the pack. He set Mimic on the counter as

I lit two more lamps to help him see. I undid the knots that held my lizard to the harness.

"Ugly creature," Grandpa muttered. He bent over Mimic, squinting as he traced the long ribs of Mimic's splinted wing. "Not like a bird's wing, but a bat's. Each rib is a finger, each claw the nail. But this thing is too heavy. It'll never fly on these."

Mimic looked up and tweetled like a mountain thrush. His eyes were glassy.

"Interesting," Grandpa said. "Lizards don't whistle, or have wings." He raised Mimic to have a better view of the stitches I had made. "You've sewn it up well, my dear. But this lizard, it's too warm for this cool night. And see here. What do you make of these lumps on its head and back?"

I shook my head. I had assumed they were all part of Mimic.

Grandpa sighed. "I do *not* say this because I want to get rid of it." His eyes were grave. "It's dying already. The last time I saw a creature with so many lumps on his head—a squirrel, it was—the lumps grew until the squirrel could not raise his head. He died. This thing's fever is part of his last sickness."

"No," I said, digging in for another fight. "He got hurt when the eagle dropped him. Creatures always run a fever when they've been hurt a lot. The lumps don't mean anything." I'd expected Grandpa to say all manner of strange things, but not that Mimic and I were beaten before we'd begun.

Grandpa went to his collection of small skulls and picked one out that I'd never seen before. It had been hidden at the back of the shelf. When he handed it to me, I flinched. I wouldn't have known it was a squirrel's skull, so distorted was it with bony knobs.

"If you are kind, you will let it die without more suffering," Grandpa said.

Mimic turned to me and peeped. I had the idea that he was saying Grandpa was wrong. Grandpa was never wrong, but I didn't want to listen this time. "Do you know what kind of lizard he is?" I asked. "Maybe if we had the right food?"

Grandpa carefully ran his fingers over Mimic's beaded skin. "I've never seen the like of it before."

Mimic waved his good wing, catching its claws in my sleeve. I unhooked him, only to have him snag my sleeve again. I knew this time that he did it on purpose.

"He wants to live, Grandpa. Don't give up," I begged. "Maybe the bumps will come off. Maybe the eagle dropped him on his head—"

Grandpa rested a hand on my shoulder. "Ri, your heart is too big." He held his free hand a couple of inches over Mimic. "I can feel it burning up without touching him. We must free it of its pain."

"He *ate,*" I said, trying to put it like a healer, not a child. "Most of two fishes, and a meat patty. He kept them down, and all the water I could give him." But Grandpa was shaking his head.

Mimic looked at me. He was depending on *me.*

I remembered something Grandfather had done twice that I had witnessed. "A cold bath," I said, excited. "Twice when people have been really feverish you put them in the river and kept them there. You said it was a risk, but their fevers broke."

"Ri, this is a *lizard.*" Grandfather took my hands. "Humans carry heat with them. Lizards don't. The river will kill him. I only dared try such a cure with young people who were otherwise healthy."

I pulled out of his grip. "I'll keep Mimic with me tonight," I said, getting one of Grandfather's flat baskets. I thought Mimic would like it better than my harness for the short walk home. "He's stronger than you think. You'll see." I set a few rags in the basket to make it softer and carefully put my lizard inside.

"Very well," Grandpa said gruffly. "This is a thing you must learn on your own. If Mimic lives until morning—which I doubt—maybe you will see fit to do the merciful thing then."

I shouldered my pack, picked up Mimic's basket, and went home.

Mother only rolled up her eyes when she saw what I carried. She was used to my habit of bringing home sick or injured creatures. "Clean up, and put *that* in your room. It is not eating with us," she ordered me.

I took Mimic up the ladder one-handed. Once inside my little room, I replaced the rags in the basket with wool and set the nest beside a bowl of water. When I returned after supper with a dish of minced chicken, I found him half out of his bed. He lay over the rim of the basket, supporting himself on his good wing.

I knelt. "Didn't I tell you to stay put?" I asked. I slid my hands under him.

Mimic was burning hot. His eyes were glassy and he'd drunk all of his water. Carefully I set him back inside the basket. "Now stay there," I told him. "Let the basket hold up your splinted wing, so you don't have to. And relax!"

I filled his water bowl. He drank, but he refused the chicken and the cold meat patty I stole when no one was looking. I even let Peng try to feed him, but Mimic refused to eat. When Peng gave up in disgust and stomped back to his attic room, Mimic went to sleep, his bumpy head propped against my hand.

I left the food next to the basket, filled the water bowl again, then changed to my nightshirt. I was asleep the moment I pulled up the covers. Healing was hard, and harder still when it looked as if my patient would not live.

A sound in the night woke me. I waited, blinking, not sure what it was, until it was repeated. It was a dry, rasping noise. Pa had sounded louder but much the same when he'd been so sick last winter.

It was Mimic. He was hotter than ever and his water bowl was empty again. I lit my lamp and refilled the bowl, using my flask. When I tried to get Mimic to drink, though, the water ran out of his mouth. He opened his eyes just a little before he closed them again. His skin was dry. Bits were flaking away like fish scales.

I stared at him, kneeling beside his basket, and thinking, Don't die. I don't want you to die.

Then I got angry. *Really* angry. It wasn't *right.* It wasn't Mimic's fault the stupid eagle grabbed him, any more than it was his fault that I made the eagle drop him. It wasn't Mimic's fault that we didn't know what he was. But it would be my fault if I didn't try everything I knew.

I didn't even realize that I'd gotten up and was pulling on my tunic and pants while the last ideas were going through my head. I only grasped what I was about when I blew out my lamp, cradled Mimic in one arm, and climbed down the ladder.

Ma had banked the fire for the night only a little while before. It was easy to get a spill and light a downstairs lamp from the coals. I quietly left the house with the lamp and Mimic.

This time I followed the path that went around the back and through the vegetable gardens. It was a little longer than the path to the river near Grandpa's, but Grandpa didn't sleep well. Sometimes he worked spells late at night. I didn't want to have another argument with him.

"I know this may just kill you out of hand," I told Mimic in a whisper. "If it does, I hope you will forgive me in the Heaven of Healing when we meet after I die. But this is the only trick I have left. You *will* die if I don't try it." I couldn't even look down to see if he had opened his eyes. My lamp wasn't bright and the trail was twisty as we entered the trees.

We came out onto the long shelf of the tumbling river. The women washed clothes here during the day. There were plenty of stones on the river's edge, big ones the laundresses used to dry out wet things. Some of those rocks created pockets of water. One of those small pools would do for Mimic, I thought. It would keep him from being swept away by the hard currents midstream. I had a particular pool in mind. It might be not so deep that Mimic would drown, particularly if I held him.

We would not freeze, exactly—it was summer, after all—but neither would we be comfortable, if we lived. If Mimic lived.

I started praying to every god I thought might be even a little helpful as I set my lamp on the tallest stone by one of the small pools. Then I lay flat on the long rock close to the rippling surface and explored underwater with a free hand. It was a little deeper than I remembered; I would not be able to let go of Mimic. I had feared that. He would drown if he thrashed, maybe even break his already broken wing again. I'd hoped I wouldn't have to keep my hands in the icy water, but Mimic was more important.

I apologized to the fish I'd scared out of the pool and took a deep breath. "It's your last chance to tell me you're on the mend before I give you a horrible shock, Mimic," I whispered, cradling him on his back in my hands. He didn't move. I couldn't even hear if he wheezed, the river was so loud.

Once more I lay on my belly. This time I lowered my poor friend into the pool until only his muzzle stuck out.

Mimic gasped. His back arched, then went straight again. I would have thought he had died in that moment, but for the press and sink of his ribs against my palms. It continued, when I knew an ordinary lizard would be dead.

Whenever the backs of my hands went numb, I would lift one from the water and tuck it beneath me until it warmed, being entirely careful to hold Mimic without squeezing him with the other hand. Strangely, scarily, my palms were warm. Very warm. Mimic's cursed fever kept them warm. This was too new. I wanted to ask Grandpa if he had ever heard of a fever so great, but I wouldn't. I was angry with him for giving up on my friend.

Once I had feeling in the hand under me, I would hold Mimic in that, and warm the other. When my eyelids grew heavy, I lifted him from the water to see if I dreamed the warmth on my palms. He was still hot. I ignored the tears that rolled down my cheeks and placed him in the cold pool again.

To keep myself awake, I sang to him. I sang every song I knew. I brought him up twice more so I might drink from the pool, then returned him, because he was still deep in his fever. At last I tried to whistle birdsongs for him. I startled an owl into a reply. A second owl answered that one. I was trying to do the song of a lark when a lark *did* sing out, her voice loud and perfect.

Only it was still night. Our larks were asleep. I brought Mimic up. He looked at me and sang like a lark once more. His skin was cool when I pressed my cheek against him. For a moment I could only weep.

The next day Ma praised Mimic's improvement, though if she had known about our late-night trip to the river, she might have smacked my head. Instead she let me feed the lizard bits of fish soaked in broth. Then I bound him gently on the harness and took him with me on my day's work. We had to take the sheep to the pastures on the western side of the river because I had slept late. The other shepherds had gotten to the eastern hillside grazing before us, which meant we got the long walk across the bridge and past the marsh. I could have sworn I heard whispered complaints under the sheep's normal calls, but that had to be my imagination. No one who could talk was near us.

That afternoon the whispers continued, now speaking of rain. I knew it was silly to heed unreal chatter, but I put Mimic back on his harness and whistled for Brighteyes and Chipper to round up the herd. The day was near its close anyway and we had to consider the walk home. As we crossed the bridge into the village, I saw the first clouds swarming up over the eastern hills.

Heavy winds blew ahead of the storm. I raced home once I had settled dogs and sheep for the night. I seemed to have left the whispers with them. Inside our house the only voices I heard were those of my family, along with Mimic's occasional cheep or whistle. My parents admired Mimic's changed health all over again while Peng fed him some of my leftover meal. I had meant to show him to Grandpa after supper, but I was too worn out. Mimic and I went to bed early.

We went down the ladder in the morning, Mimic in his harness on my back, to find Grandpa eating breakfast with Ma. Pa had already left for his carpentry shop, while Peng was still getting dressed.

Grandpa glared at me from under his thick white brows. "I hear it lived."

"He," I said, gently placing Mimic's harness on my bench. "Mimic is a *he.*"

"It could be a cloud fish from the moon for all you know," Grandpa said. He got up and came around to undo Mimic's ties while Ma handed over my lunch and I tucked it into my pack. Although Grandpa's voice was hard, he was careful when he handled Mimic, and eye-popping shocked to feel Mimic's skin cool under his hands. My friend looked into Grandpa's eyes and gave the sweet, insistent tweeting of a warbler. Grandpa winced. Ma turned away, hiding her face. Mimic couldn't have known that my dead grandma's favorite bird was the warbler. Neither would he know that Grandma used to call warblers to her with their own song. Hearing that sound stabbed us all in the heart.

Grandpa put Mimic down, still gently, and left the house. I ate my breakfast without a word. Ma wiped her eyes on her sleeve and gave Mimic some bites of a ham that she was cutting up for soup.

Peng came thumping down the ladder. "What's going on?" he asked as I finished loading my pack. "Why is everyone so quiet?"

"Because you weren't here," I said. I pinched his nose and settled Mimic on his harness again.

Over the next four weeks Mimic improved in many ways. Though his bad wing was still in a splint and his good wing was bound to keep him from trying to fly, he startled me with short races. If either of the dogs—sometimes even the sheep, or a few of the lizards in the rocks—started to run, Mimic would be up and running with them. He could go very fast upright on his long hind feet if the distance was not a great one. He beat the sheep and the lizards by getting in front of them and blocking the way. The birds, including the crow who still sheltered Mimic from the sun as he slept, flew over to watch the races. They would set up a lot of noise, as if they were cheering. Brighteyes and Chipper would always win, given a decent start, because they could run longer distances. Then the birds would sing to Mimic, as if they consoled him.

"You'll do better when you can fly," I'd tell Mimic when he had to stop, panting as lizards did in the heat. No matter how many times I said it, Mimic sulked anyway. He liked to win.

Every day I took his good wing out of its binding so he might exercise it. All of the birds I had ever cared for would try to fly the moment they could move the healthy wing. That was why I bound it once he was well enough to walk around, as easy on his hind feet as if he always walked that way. Mimic never did try to fly with the whole wing, though. He would open it slowly all the way and close it, over and over, until I bound it to his side again. Not once did he flap it. Even so, I kept it bound unless he was exercising. I wouldn't put it past Mimic to try to trick me and escape, as a bird might if it could think so far ahead.

Grandpa had said Mimic was too heavy to fly, but Grandpa had also said he would never survive a cold bath. Why did the gods give my friend wings unless he could use them? It was hard to wait for the day when I was certain Mimic's broken wing was healed, so he might surprise Grandpa yet again.

By that time I was straining to hear the whispers that had begun after the night at the river, but when I thought I did hear them, I could not be sure that they were not simply a jumble of the valley's normal sounds. I had always listened as much as I watched. Any slight change in the winds, the sigh of trees and grasses, the rush of streams and rivers, the noise of sheep, birds, dogs, and village, might mean some change for good or bad. Everyone with a herd to guard paid attention to the world around them, though I'd heard my parents and other people say I was better at it than most. Peng and my friends only complained they could never sneak up on me.

The problem, when I worked to hear all the noise around me, was that too often things combined to make something that could sound like words. How was I to tell the difference between that and what I thought might be "berries here!" or "storm comes"?

It was a month of bad storms, for certain. One day Mimic and I saw three distant tornadoes touch angry fingers down on the Great Plain as the herds of buffalo and antelope wheeled and ran. That very night a tornado struck the valley west of us. The messenger who brought the news said it was like a child god had taken a big stick and drawn a line straight through the edge of his village, vanishing after it killed. Two families were never seen again, and another family lost their father and three children. All of us were called to the temple to pray for them and to thank the gods that we were spared.

There was a week when storms came every day, making everyone miserable. I tried to leave Mimic at home to save him from the wind and water, but he ran after us, so I let him come. He followed as I checked my poor sheep for foot rot. He stayed in the fold with me after dark and sang to the sheep while I treated them, for which I was grateful. I thought I heard whispers in the rustling of the sheep, the thump of their hooves, their grunts as I worked, and Mimic's song. But like as not I'd been so tired I had nodded off for a moment. Surely I had dreamed that the sheep thanked the ugly lizard for his songs while their human helped their feet. I shook off my drowsiness and concentrated on paring.

I begged extra fish from Ma for Mimic's supper that first night he sang, explaining how Mimic helped in the fold. She and Pa came the next night to witness it for themselves. After that I didn't have to beg extra food for him anymore. If my parents heard whispers, though, they said nothing about it.

The day came—a sunny one—when it was time to take the splint from Mimic's broken wing. As if they knew, the sheep, the birds, the dogs, and the lizards who took part in Mimic's races came to watch. I set him upon a rock with shaking hands and removed the ties and splints for good. Every other time I had done this, my patient had flown or run without so much as a squeak of farewell.

I examined Mimic's healed wing before I let him go. His claws were perfect. Broken bone and ripped skin alike had healed well, though Mimic would always have a scar where the rip had been. Silently, trying not to cry, I took the bindings from his good wing and stood back.

Mimic shook both wings. Then he stretched them out a couple of times, to the limit of their reach. He gave them a few good flaps. Once that was done, he folded them against his sides and squawked at me.

"Go ahead," I told him. "Fly. You know you want to."

He leaped onto my shoulder instead. Gripping my tunic sleeve with his hind claws, he used his foreclaws to climb batlike over my upper back, until he could drape himself along my shoulders, a lizardy scarf for me to wear. At last he sighed and belched breakfast smells into my face.

Was Grandpa right? Was Mimic too heavy to fly? But why did he have wings, in that case?

I tried something that had seemed to work with baby birds I had reared. First I had to lean over the rock again and get Mimic to climb down from my shoulders. Then I held him carefully, under his belly and without getting in the way of his wings. Slowly I raised and lowered him in the air. (It was not as easy with a creature as big as Mimic.) It was the birds' instinct to flap their wings as soon as they felt themselves fall. It was Mimic's instinct, too. He flapped briskly, but unlike the birds', his body didn't lift in my hold. He stayed in my hands, plump and solid.

I set him on the top of a tall rock and asked him to fly. Over the days that followed, I tried the branches of trees, other rocks, the edge of Taka Hill bluff, my bedroom window, and the bridge over the river. I asked him to do it from the trail overlooking the grain fields, so he could join the birds that night. He might flap his wings. He might stretch them. He would hop to the ground or my bed. He climbed down the trees, headfirst, his wing-claws working like a bat's and his hind feet keeping him from falling bottom-over-top. He croaked at me as if he wanted to know why we tried to do this every day.

He did not fly.

We were on Taka Hill once on a stormy day when, desperate, I tossed him into the wind. He glided to the ground with his wings outstretched, ran over to me, and bit my ankle. It only bled a little. I did take it as his way of saying he'd had enough. That same day he called me to the bluff overlooking the plain with a shriek. A tornado had touched down not so far away that I could admire it in comfort. It was close enough that I saw land and a couple of bison fly up around its deadly tip. If it hadn't been moving away from us, I would have grabbed Mimic and screamed for the dogs and sheep to run. We got a brief drubbing with hail as it was.

Only those of us in the eastern hills ever saw the storm or felt the hail that day—us and the cattlemen at the plain's edge. They were forced into the barns that our people had built on the plain ages ago. No one else in our valley even knew that the storm had passed so close.

At last we had sun and heat for a couple of weeks. The fields dried. Our farmers predicted that we would have a fine crop, the gods willing.

We were only days from the grain harvest the morning when Mimic and I woke to a heavy gray sky. It was going to rain again. If I'd had my way, I'd have stayed home, but sheep have to eat. The knowledge that I was going to be soaked again put me off my own feed. I skipped my breakfast, giving Mimic his and filling my pack.

"Be sensible," Ma told Peng and me. "Come in if you think it's bad." She looked worried.

I touched my forehead to her hand in love and laughed when she had to dust flour marks from my skin. Then Mimic and I trotted off to the fold. Mimic was restless. Normally he preferred to ride atop my pack on our way to the pastures. That day he went afoot, at least until the sheep were on the path up Taka Hill. Then he climbed onto the back of our bellwether. He was the most patient of the sheep when Mimic wanted to ride. He only looked at me as if to ask, What can a fellow do?

On top of the hill, the wind was gusting from the south, hard enough to make me wonder if coming here had been my best idea. The birds who flew up to join us fought the gusts all the way. They finally steered into the trees down by the stream. They did not try to reach the bluff, not when the wind knocked them back every time. I left the herd by the stream as well. There were dips and hollows in the ground where they could graze out of the wind.

No herds were out on the plain. My view was limited: rain fell in the distance, and gray clouds filled the sky above me. Lightning struck a few miles east. Even the air was different. It had turned a strange yellow color. I did not like it. Mimic was acting odd. He stood upright beside me, his eyes fixed on the cloud that had harbored lightning. When I shifted my leg to press against his side, I found that he was trembling slightly. We both flinched at the next flare of lightning. This one ripped like a river along the clouds, vanishing in the north.

When I heard the approach of our cows on the road below, I looked down. I was curious to see if the chief herdsman would take them on the plain today. Men, dogs, horses, and cattle bunched up where the road entered the pass through the hills. Everyone was looking at the dark skies.

The chief herdsman, my uncle Tao, walked ahead to the top of the pass to see how things were. Lightning jumped from the clouds above the plain, striking the earth in three places. This time I could hear the distant growl of thunder.

The storm was an hour's horseback ride away, moving faster than any horse.

When Tao came back to the herd, he was shaking his head. He motioned for everyone to go back the way they had come. They would cross our river to the pastures beyond. The cows and their guardians would be safer there than on the plain.

Uncle, the last to go, looked up and saw me high above. He made the same turn-around motion to me. I gave him a big wave to tell him I had seen. Just as I did so, a gust struck me hard in the back, almost knocking me off my feet. Mimic bawled like a calf, clinging to my pants to keep me from falling.

I turned to look at the plain. The rain was closing in. I could see the fire of lightning, but not the bottoms of the clouds. The air was turning from yellow to green, a very bad sign. I had only been caught on the edges of four such storms in my lifetime—all had been killers. It was time to get everyone home to safety.

I put my fingers to my mouth and blew the whistle that told my dogs to gather the sheep and take them home, now! I caught Mimic up in my arms and half-ran, half-stumbled as the rising winds pushed me. We reached the stream. Chipper was there, barking furiously to get the sheep together. They were baaing with fear, their own good sense telling them that the weather had taken a turn for the worse.

I shoved in among the restless sheep to put Mimic on the bellwether's back. "You'll be fine with him," I told Mimic when he squalled his objection. Already I could see that one of the ewes, her lamb, and my dog Brighteyes were missing. The wind picked up, blowing away my whistled signal to Chipper to take the herd down. I was about to try it again when a much louder echo of my whistle cut through the wind's roar. Mimic looked at me as if to say, I'm helping even if you want to get rid of me, before he gave my whistle, *loud,* a second time. Chipper drove the flock down the trail while I went in search of the missing ones.

Hail came—hurtful knobs of ice as big as pigeon eggs—just when I found Brighteyes and my missing sheep. Lamb and ewe had slid into a small gorge when the earthen lip crumbled under them. Brighteyes had gone after them. She was trying to tow the lamb out, but the silly thing thought the dog was trying to eat her. It fought Brighteyes, throwing her off balance. Sheep and dog alike were yelping their pain as the hail struck them. I wanted to join them in their cries, or better yet, hide until the hail was over, but that would not get any of us to shelter in a hurry.

I yanked the rope from my pack, secured it around the nearest tree, and used it to walk down the crumbling dirt side of the little gorge. First I brought the lamb up. It had gained weight since the last time I'd had to carry it over my shoulders. I dumped it at the base of the tree. "Don't you *dare* stray," I ordered, and went back for its mother.

I heard barking. I turned, wondering what had possessed Chipper to leave the herd and come back. Of course, it was Mimic. He stopped in front of the lamb, barking at it just as Chipper would have done to make it stay put.

"Thank you," I said, and went for Brighteyes. She only needed me to bring her halfway up; she scrambled over the rest of the gorge's wall.

The ewe waited patiently as I put on my leather gloves. I hoisted her over my shoulders with a grunt, thanking the gods that she was young and not one of the heavier ewes. I'd had to work for a couple of years to be able to lift a grown sheep. Only then was I trusted with a herd, just for times like this. At least the hail was done. I would have good-sized bruises when the day was over.

Step by step I pulled us up the side of the earthen gorge. We were nearly to the top when a crack of thunder sounded almost in my ear, deafening me. Stupidly, I took one hand off the rope to drag the ewe into place and slipped down. She jerked, her weight dragging me backward. I flailed until I got both hands on the rope again. Slowly, grinding my teeth, I bent until she was balanced again and began to climb. I was a third of the way from the top when someone began to pull us up. It was easier to climb with that help. When I threw the ewe and myself over the edge, there was Mimic with his teeth buried in the rope.

The ewe scrambled to her feet and ran to shove her lamb in the direction of home. Brighteyes went with them. She knew where the others were.

I went to Mimic. "How did you do that?" I asked, feeling as if the world had turned sideways. "You pulled us up—how did you do it?" I had the strangest idea that he was a little bigger, which had to be a dream brought on by too many knobs of hail striking my head. "You did that—and what about your teeth?" I whispered. My hands trembled. Mimic could not have done that, but he was the only one who could have done so. "What if you broke them? I would never forgive myself!" I knelt and drew his lips back. Patient as ever, he let me do it. His teeth were fine. Perfect, in fact. Like the rest of him, they seemed to be larger. "Maybe it's growth," I said, talking mostly to myself. "Sheep grow, why not you? No doubt you've been a little bigger each day, and I just never realized it until just now." But he still wasn't big enough to haul us out like that, unless there was some magic to him. I reminded myself that he could be no dragon: no antennae, no glorious colors, no scales, no great size, since even their little ones must be large.

Mimic only squeaked and rubbed his head against my hands. "I love you so much," I told him. The air was emerald green.

A roar like a thousand bears struck the valley. A fresh thunderclap deafened me. Rain lashed us, stinging every bare inch of my skin. My hearing returned, only to be overwhelmed by that roar. I forgot Mimic's new strength. We both ran until we could see the road and the pass. Mimic got there first. The rain that had pelted us must have stopped, because I saw everything so clearly.

The sky above the pass churned. Less than half a mile from where I stood, on the far side of the road, the clouds formed a shape like a top that pointed down in a slight curve.

That curve grew longer and longer as Mimic and I watched. I was terrified that if I tried to scramble over the dips and lumps to dash straight down the hill, or if I backtracked to the trail for its easier way down, the short-lived monster in that stem of cloud would attack me from behind. In my fear I even forgot to pray.

The tornado touched down in a cluster of pines that was older than my village. For ages they had crowned the hills on the western side of the pass. The tornado ripped a gaping wound in them, throwing tall trees into the air like a child in a tantrum. Now the tornado grew thicker, its winds screaming. Like a turtle, I pulled my shoulders up toward my head—I still held Mimic—trying to block some of that dreadful noise. I didn't realize I was screaming, too. The monster was moving north, down the hillside toward our fields.

Then I saw a thing that made me weep with wonder and grief. It was the birds. The birds in the trees—the ones who had joined the herd and me, and the others who lived in our valley, thousands of birds—they all took wing. I thought they fled the death that bore down on them, but I was wrong. They had come to fulfill the pact. They flew at the tornado, using their own magic to get as close as they could without being sucked in. When the winds thrust them back, the birds reached out with their claws and seized lengths of the furious air. Turning, their wings digging at the sky, they tried to drag the tornado up, back into the clouds.

The crows came next, their beaks open. They must have been screaming, but I could not hear. Other birds came with them, big and small, bright-colored and dark. They flew over my head from the plain, and from the direction of the river and the village. They, too, seized pieces of the tornado and fought to pull it back into the storm that had birthed it. The tornado's stem wobbled and shook, needing those pieces of itself as thousands of birds dragged them away. The tornado's roar sounded like curses to me. Lightning shot from the clouds—four, five, six bolts of it—murdering birds in its path as the thunder made my ears ring. More dropped from the sky, dead of exhaustion and wounds. The birds who still lived kept their hold on the monster.

A surge of clouds passed from the thunderheads down, through the stem of the funnel. Thunder crashed again. Suddenly the tornado was bigger, stronger. It flung off the birds, hurling them to the ground or into the trees.

Mimic began to thrash in my grip. I clung to him, terrified. Then he bit my arm hard. I dropped him. In all that noise a whisper said in my head, *I'm sorry.*

I sat down. I did it because Mimic jumped into the air, flapping his wings. With each beat, his wings got bigger. Bigger, and stronger. His body stretched and lengthened. His pink and brown skin cracked and peeled to reveal new skin, scaled and beaded in every color of red that could be imagined. The lumps on his spine and head swelled and burst. They revealed flame-shaped scales on his back, and horns and tendrils above his eyes. He opened his mouth. Light, not sound, came from his throat in a burst that lit up everything I could see. Inside that light, Mimic flew at the fat trunk of the tornado and seized it in his claws.

The birds rallied to help. Those who could returned to the air to grab any pieces of the tornado that escaped Mimic. They surrounded the great crimson dragon in a cloud of feathers and claws. All of them, dragon and birds, hauled the shrieking tornado back up into the clouds. Lightning wrapped around Mimic just before he vanished in those soft gray mounds. Its jagged spears rippled along his new crimson hide.

Then Mimic was gone from my view. So were the birds. I bowed my head on my knees and wept.

Suddenly a great roar made me scream in pain. I covered my ears and looked up. The part of the storm over our valley had blown apart at the center. The remaining clouds tumbled toward the mountains, in a great hurry to leave the place of their defeat.

As the storm fled, a large, mixed flock of birds flew or glided slowly to the earth. Many of them came to me, borne on the wings or in the claws of other birds. They had not survived their battle with the tornado unscarred. Looking at them, I could see I had a lot of work to do, right away.

I was not left to do it alone for very long. Our healers came up from the village to help.

Ma and Grandpa reached me first. I was splinting the wings of Mimic's friend, the crow who had always sheltered him from the sun. At least it was used to me and did not struggle as I worked.

"Ri, you're hurt," Ma said. "The bleeding's stopped, but—that looks like a bite." She poured water on the wound in my arm and then tugged away the sleeve that had dried over it. She was so gentle that I was able to keep fixing splints to the crow. I did my best not to flinch.

"We saw everything," Grandpa said as Ma took care of me. "Tuerh created a vision pool in the well, in case we had to flee the village. We saw what our friends did for us." He soothed the heron he was tending. "Where did the dragon come from, Ri? I have not seen one leave the mountains since I was a boy."

"The green dragon," Ma said as she put ointment on Mimic's bite and bandaged my arm. "I thought it was a story you made up, Pa."

"Never got a close look at it, only the underside," Grandpa said, the heron calm enough now that he could stitch the wound in its back. "The shadow glided over me and I looked up. Bright, bright green it was, and—" Grandpa looked beyond me, his eyes gone wide. *"Huge."*

Ma also stared that way. I turned around as the crow squawked its greetings to the newcomer. Mimic—now as long as three men laid flat, crowned with a pair of crescent-moon horns and six long, nimble antennae that never ceased their moving—clung to the hillside with his hind feet. They, too, had grown with the rest of him. His claws were the size of sickles and the color of red jade.

Forgive me, he said to me, touching Ma's bandage with the edge of one scarlet wing. *But you would not let go. I could not let the feathered cousins die.*

"You've *always* been a dragon?" I asked.

The crow shrieked, asking Mimic, *How long must I be this way? I know it will help, her tying my wings to sticks, but it's* boring, *and you know my people hate to be* bored—

Mimic reached for the crow with three of those very long, silvery antennae. Without thinking, I held the bird up.

Do not speak such things for Ri to hear, Mimic told the crow as he ran his new antennae over it. *She knows what you say now.*

My ties, made so carefully, dropped from the crow, along with the splints. It stood up in my hands and flapped its fresh-healed wings. *I apologize,* the crow said to me. Now I knew she was female. *You have been very good to us. Better than some, who chase us away from their nasty herb gardens, not that we would touch those bad-smelling things.* She flapped away, loosing a white blob of dung that struck Grandpa on his head.

As he yelled curses at the crow, I asked Mimic, "Did you mean for me to hear the speech of animals? Is it true, I started hearing real voices? I thought I might be crazy!"

It is a gift of the dragons, Mimic explained. He spoke not with his mouth, but with his mind. *You drank the river water that cured my fever, and took some of my essence with it. I did not mean to make it worse by biting you, but you would not release me. I am sorry. You will learn how to hear what you wish to hear and close out the rest. It is very confusing at first.*

I thought of being able to talk to the animals as I cared for them, and grinned. "I will learn," I told him. "It will make things so much easier. And you can help me now."

But Mimic was shaking his big head. The one copper eye that I could see was unhappy. *I cannot stay, Ri,* he told me. *I speak now so all of you will hear me.* Ma, Grandpa, and all of the healers who had come to help drew closer. *I know I must leave. I am much too big. Where will I sleep? I am not a bird. I would eat far more than the village could spare. And I can feel the herd animals trembling. They can smell me. They are terrified of me, even the sheep who were my friends. I have made the choice to grow. That means my time with you is over. My people are calling me to the mountains.*

"Why should you go to your people?" I asked, confused. "They haven't done anything for you!"

"I'd like to know that myself," Grandpa said. I could see that Mimic was making the other healers nervous. The birds who could walk were going to him, though, leaning against his hind feet. Mimic spread his immense wings to shelter them from the sun, as the crow had once sheltered him.

Dragons must be careful about breeding, Mimic told us. *There cannot be too many of our kind. When she mates, a female dragon lays her eggs far from the dragons' home. My mother placed her clutch on the other edge of the Great Plain. We are born knowing these things.* As if we could see through the hill, we turned to look. I shook myself and fixed my eyes on this new Mimic. *We are hatched looking in no way like dragons. Then we must prove ourselves worthy to be them. We must survive the journey across the plain. Few of us do. If it had not been for you, Ri, I would have perished.* Mimic bowed his great, shiny head and touched his nose to my face. He smelled of dry summer winds and the air before a storm.

"You still haven't explained how you went from lizard to dragon," Grandpa said. "You didn't grow that way. It was magic!"

It was the last step, Mimic replied. *It must be a choice. Life as a small one can be happy. We must decide that it is time to grow up. Time to take on the life of the dragon. My choice was simple. I could be a dragon, or I could watch my friends die.*

Mimic looked away toward the mountains. *My only regret is that I could not save more,* he said. *And I wish that I did not have to go. But I will continue to grow, you see.*

"You must go, indeed," Grandpa said. I hid my face in my hands. For a minute I hated them both for saying it so openly, as if it were nothing.

Mimic touched his great head to mine again. *I had to*

choose, Ri. I knew he spoke only inside my mind now. *It was time. But it is not all bad. When* you *choose, you will come to visit me, yes? You will be able to find me, and I will know you are coming. Just as you will hear the voices of the little brethren and know where their pain is. You are part dragon now.*

He backed away from all of us carefully, so none of the birds would be knocked over when he rose on his hind legs. Slowly he flapped his great wings once, twice, thrice. He leaped, scooping air under his wings. He shoved it back at us, making us stumble. Then he was airborne, climbing higher into the sky.

I said little for the rest of the day. I was too busy trying to sort all of the voices in my head as I patched, splinted, and sewed. I found if I stared at one bird, or one dog, as I did when I went to see how my herd and the dogs were faring, I could hear that creature's voice clearly. The others faded some. I practiced with the mice in the walls in our house—Ma was wrong; we had some. Then, when it got quieter, I thought about what Mimic had said.

It wasn't like *talking* with animals. Their thoughts were simpler. That much I had learned already, listening to the birds on the hill, the village's cats and dogs, the sheep in the fold, and the mice. Mimic had spoken to us like an equal, to me like a friend. He had been giving me advice without making me feel stupid, as my parents and Grandpa did. He wanted me to understand that here, in my valley, I would always be a child if I only did a child's work. Only the heads of the combined flocks were adults. Even they were sometimes treated as children, big children who knew a lot about the care and keeping of cows, sheep, and goats.

Before I went to bed, I talked to Peng. It took me a while to make my point, because he was already half-asleep. When he finally realized that I meant what I said, he almost strangled me with his hug. I slept well, dreaming of Mimic.

At breakfast Ma stared at me when I turned my shepherd kit over to Peng. He knew the signals for the dogs and the sheep, since he had gone out with me most of the spring for training. I finished my breakfast slowly after he left, grateful that Ma knew I would explain myself when I was ready. Once done, I walked down to Grandpa's place.

He was grinding herbs when I came into his workshop. Seeing me, he asked, "A bit late today, aren't you?"

"You never said what time I had to come here to learn," I replied.

Grandpa set his work aside and gave me his attention. Like Ma, he seemed to understand that the events of the day before called for big changes in my life.

"I don't know how good I'll ever be with people," I told Grandpa. "But I've got the dragon magic now. It helps me hear creatures. It may help me do other things. And I suppose it's time for me to grow up, just as Mimic did."

Did Grandpa know what I was thinking? He traveled out of the valley for new herbs, and sometimes he sent his pupils into the mountains to study. I thought of my friend, flapping his way up into the cloudy sky. I might have to walk to see him again, but at least I was taking my first step.

Huntress

My dad left for good when I was ten. My mom kicked him out. "Fine!" he yelled. "I've had it with you, your family, and all that screwy New Age Goddess crap! I shoulda left years ago! Now watch—you'll turn my own daughter against me!" He grabbed his bag and walked out. He didn't notice I was standing right there.

I should have said something. Instead I stared at my however-many-great-grandmother's portrait. It hung in front of where my dad had been standing. There was Whatever-Grandma in Victorian clothes, laced in tight, with that crescent moon tiara on her head. He was so clueless he didn't even see Mom's family was into the goddess stuff back then, before anyone ever said "New Age" with capital letters. But that was my dad.

After the divorce, he found a girlfriend. They got married and had a kid. Kevin was sweet, but I stopped visiting. They were always joking, asking if Mom and my aunts sacrificed any cats lately, or did I brew up some potion to get a boyfriend. I told Dad it wasn't funny and then that he was boring my socks off. Finally I just told him I couldn't visit, because I had practice. He bought it. Clueless, like I said.

But when it came to Mom's family portraits, and her religion, he wasn't the only one who thought it was just too weird. By the time I was in sixth grade, the friends I brought home were noticing the crescent tiaras and full moon pendants. They'd notice, and they'd ask, and I'd try to explain. I'd make them nervous. Then the jokes and whispers began. In seventh grade, the witch stuff blended in with whispers that I was too weird, even stuck up, maybe a slut. I didn't even know where that had come from, but sixth grade had taught me I couldn't fight any of it. I acted like I couldn't hear. I would read for lunch and recess, by myself in a corner of some room. I kept my head down. I didn't even try to make friends. I didn't see the point. Sooner or later I would have to take them home. There they'd see the portraits and the jewelry. They'd ask their questions. Back to square one.

The only good thing was track. I'd found out I was good at it in grade school. With a summer of practice and middle school coaches, no one on our team could catch me by the time the seventh-grade spring meets rolled around. I came in second in the district in all my events but one, and that one I won. Winning was like a taste in my mouth. Everyone I raced against was a possible source of whispers, but I couldn't hear them if they ran behind me. They'd have to catch me to make their words hurt.

In eighth grade, I won all of my middle school events at the all-district meet. A bunch of the high school coaches wanted me to come to their schools, but Mom had other plans. At the last meet of the year, she introduced me to the head coach from Christopher Academy. Christopher offered a full scholarship, if I wanted it.

Wanted it? Christopher was one of the top private schools in the city, with one of the top track teams in the country. If I did well there, I could write my college track ticket. Better: nobody in my school could afford it. Nobody. And nobody else was getting a scholarship. My teammates didn't talk to me, but I heard everything. They would have told the world if they had gotten into Christopher Academy. It was out of their reach. Christopher kids were like Beverly Hills kids on television, clean and expensive gods and goddesses. Nobody at my school would dare to talk to them. There wouldn't be any whispers in those expensive hallways.

When she saw I wanted this school and this chance, Mom went a little nuts. Over the summer, we moved from the old family apartment in the Village—and wasn't my aunt Cynthia happy to move in when we left—to a squinched-up little place on the Upper East Side. Mom took a second job, tending bar at night to cover those expenses. The new apartment was near the school and near Central Park, where the Christopher runners trained. I could practice with the team and not have to worry about taking the subway home after dark, Mom said, putting her altar up in a corner of her tiny bedroom. I felt guilty. Mom and her sisters were true believers in the family religion. She wasn't happy with just a medallion, not even a proper hunt-Goddess figure, instead of the shrine in our own place, but this was only for four years, I told myself. Maybe the new place wasn't so much, but I could have friends, and bring them over, and only have to explain horseshoes over the doorways.

Anyway, I wasn't a believer in the family Goddess after middle school. If their Goddess was so wonderful, why didn't she fix my life? She protected maidens, right? Wasn't I a maiden? My dad was right about that much—the worship was screwy.

After all that, ninth grade still wasn't exactly a popularity explosion. It was made clear to me that while I had a scholarship to run, ninth graders did not show up the upperclassmen. They trained and they waited for their turn, their chance. They ran with the team. If I heard it once during those first weeks, I heard it a dozen times: I belonged to the Christopher *team,* the Christopher tradition, the Christopher way of doing things. I warmed a bench and kept my mouth shut.

And there was another problem. Things had changed. I had changed. It wasn't easy for me to make friends since I'd stopped trying years ago. I still waited for whispers to begin, though months passed without them. It was like I thought the gossip was weeds that would sprout when my back was turned.

I did make two ninth-grade friends from the track team. We had lunch together, walked home together, sat together on the way to meets. We ran when Coach told us to. We cheered the upperclassmen and held down a leg on the relay team. We raced other ninth graders from other private schools, and we envied the older runners. The seniors weren't that interesting. Their eyes were locked on the Ivy Leagues. They didn't draw our attention the way a certain junior did.

Felix soaked up light in the halls and gave it off again, from his bronze and gold gelled hair to his tanned calves. He was so right, so perfect, that no one ever gave him a hard time for the long, single braid he wore just behind one ear. People gave him tokens to wear in it—beads, or ribbons, or chains—but he didn't take just anything. Just because he accepted someone's token one day didn't mean he wouldn't give it back to them the next. He wrote his own rules for the school, too. The staff let him do it most of the time, maybe because the auditorium had his last name over the doorway. It was listed five times on the brass plaque that announced the different heads of the school. Felix was what Christopher Academy was about, and his crowd was Christopher Academy, just like track was Christopher Academy.

He ran, but he didn't care about it. He'd slide out of boys' warm-up laps to come over and flirt with his sophomore and junior girls, or his "lionesses," as he called them. The first time I heard him say it, in April of my ninth-grade year, he said it to our coach as we circled the baseball diamond in our section of the park, our feet thudding on wet dirt.

"What do you think of my lionesses, Coach?" he called, keeping pace with his girlfriends in the middle of the pack. "Let's take them to the Serengeti, get some blood on them, show them how to hunt." He fiddled with a strip of camouflage cloth that was wound into his braid, running a finger over a dark spot on it.

"Ewww, Felix," cried Han, a Chinese girl who'd been lip-locked with him before practice. "Blood? No thanks!"

"Can't break oaths sworn in blood, sweetness," he told her, falling back as we ran by. "Isn't that right, Corey?" he asked, slapping me on the arm.

He knew who I was. He called me by my last name, like I was any other member of the team, any other rich Christopher kid.

I forgot to be careful. I forgot that I was new, that I had to be one of the team and earn my place. Trying to outrun the blush that burned my cheeks, I sped up. I cut through his precious lionesses as they jeered at him, telling him he scared me. I stretched my legs until I caught up to the senior girls. They glanced over, saw me, and glared. "Back of the pack, *freshman,*" one of them grumbled.

So I stopped being sensible. It was only practice. "Afraid you'll have to work for it?" I asked, and picked up my pace. They weren't really trying: it was a warm-up run. My cheeks burning now because they thought first place would be handed to them, I skittered behind the seniors, looking for a way through their bunched-up group. When they closed in tighter, I powered around them in the turn. By the time it dawned on them that they ought to show me who was boss, they couldn't catch me.

Stupid, I told myself, slowing after I thudded past the finish, my temper burned off. Stupid when you want friends, stupid when you don't want to stand out. Stupid when you're "with the team."

Across the field the boys were hooting at the runners. I turned around to see the lionesses, juniors and sophomores together, cut through and around the red-faced seniors. Red-headed Reed looked back at the seniors and yelled, "You snooze, you lose."

Coach glared at me, then walked toward the seniors, clapping her hands. "You thought it was going to be easy, these final meets of the year?" she yelled to the seniors as the lionesses caught up with me. "You'd catch a break because it's your last year in the high school leagues? Nobody cares! Younger girls are waiting to make their names, and they'll kick your asses. Two more laps before you quit for the day!"

"Showin' them, Corey," Reed said, tugging my braid.

"You rock," another one muttered.

The lionesses collected me after practice. I looked at my two friends, but they shook their heads and grinned. They wanted me to go, so I could tell them what it was like in the morning.

The way the lionesses acted it was no big deal, drinks and French fries at a diner on Madison Avenue, a sour-faced waitress watching as six of us jammed into a corner booth.

"Why don't you split up?" she wanted to know. "Make it easier on everybody?"

The older girls fell silent, staring at her. The air went funny. The waitress looked at them, then threw down the menus and left. The minute her back was turned, they began to laugh and nudge each other. "Shut *her* up," Reed said.

"Like that dealer," another muttered.

"Only he *ran,*" Beauvais, a platinum blonde, whispered. Reed elbowed Beauvais hard. She elbowed back but didn't say anything more as the waitress—a different waitress—came for our order.

I don't even remember if I talked very much, but I was there, with the kids everyone looked at. And the guys showed up, even Felix. I learned then that the guys were lions, to match the lionesses. Felix called them his "Pride" and said casually, "You should see them hunt."

Half of me wanted to stay, but half knew I was supposed to be home fifteen minutes ago. I had to run to be there when Aunt Lucy, who watched me while Mom worked, put dinner on the table. I expected a reaming, but my aunt was so happy I'd been with kids my age she didn't even yell. I pretended I didn't see her light a moon candle in thanks while I cleared the table. I guess I wasn't the only one who thought I was going to be a hermit all through high school.

After supper, we went for a walk. We talked with the neighbors for a while outside the building. I was playing with the baby of the couple downstairs, so I don't know how it started, but I heard the old guy who lived across the street say, "—just a dealer, so excuse me if I don't cry."

"Was it an overdose?" asked the baby's mom.

The old guy shook his head. "The cops say people were chasing him last night after dark, and he grabbed his chest and fell into the lake near the Ramble. Heart attack. A drug dealer, having a heart attack."

"Good riddance," said the baby's father. "But how could anybody see to chase him?"

"It was a full moon," Aunt Lucy and I said at the same time. She smiled at me and said, "Jinx," because we had echoed each other. She looked at the other grown-ups. "Plenty of light for a chase."

I shivered. The baby's mom saw and collected her from

me. "It's getting cold," she said. I didn't argue, though I don't think I had shivered because I was cold.

When I got to school in the morning, my life had definitely improved. Suddenly my two friends and I had more company at lunch. They liked that. I did, too.

I didn't exactly like it when, at the next meet, Coach pulled me out to run with the juniors and seniors. "You started this, you finish it, Corey," she muttered as she changed my place in the lineup. So I ran the way I did alone and made the two best runners sweat to beat me. The Pride thought it was cool. They cheered for me at meets. At the all-district competitions, when I had the hundred-meter and the three-hundred-meter events, Felix gave me an ornament from his braid to wear, a little golden sun. I came in second in the hundred, first in the three hundred. He wouldn't take his sun back. He kissed me and told me to wear it instead.

I told myself he kissed all the girls. Then I went out and got a top-of-the-ear piercing done just for that earring. Once it was there, I looked at myself in the mirror and let myself dream about him.

The night after the last practice, I was on my way home when I saw one of the Neighborhood Watch people taking down the sketch of a rapist who had been working the Upper East Side. This one, with his spiky eyebrow piercing, had given me the shivers for weeks. "What happened?" I asked her. I was going home to an empty apartment—Aunt Lucy had finally convinced Mom a girl who was almost sixteen didn't need a babysitter—so I was being lazy about getting there. "They caught him?"

"They caught him," the woman said with a grim smile, like she had been there. "The cops got an anonymous tip. He was at the bottom of Bethesda Terrace with a broken leg and a broken arm." I winced. That was a long, hard marble stair around the big fountain in Central Park. She told me, "Bastard said he was out for a run and he tripped. They found his rape kit under him, complete with souvenirs. He said a gang chased him. Good for them, that's what I say." She waved the flyers she'd already collected at me. "One down, plenty more to go."

I went on home, shaking my head. Who ever heard of a gang that chased somebody until they fell, then ran away? And who tipped off the cops? How did they know who he was?

I told the Pride about the rapist at lunch the next day.

"Cool gang," said Felix, laughing. He had a new addition to his braid that day, a spiky bar that could have been for an eyebrow piercing. "It captures criminals. A superhero gang. Maybe I can join. Do they wear cool jackets?"

We all cracked up. Maybe they called themselves the Pride, but I thought of bandannas and leather jackets and box cutters and low-rider cars when I thought "gang." These were trust fund babies. They were a world away from the ugly street and the gangs in the projects like the ones I knew. They were strong young animals dressed in light and fresh air, not dirt and blood.

"Hey, maybe it was us. We hang in the park when school's out," black-haired Jeffries said, tossing a rolled-up napkin from hand to hand. "Sure, it coulda been us. Except

I'd probably just give a rapist my dad's card. He's always telling me even slime deserves a defense, right?"

Beauvais shoved him. "Like your dad would defend a *rapist.*"

"One with money," Han said with a laugh.

I smelled mint as Felix leaned back and whispered in my ear, "Sometimes we hang out after dark."

I reached down for my backpack, hiding my chest so he wouldn't see his effect on me. "Isn't it dangerous?" When I sat up, I cradled my pack, just in case he looked at my too-perky tits.

"We go as a group," Jeffries said. "Our gang, remember?"

"Have to be safe," Reed told us, sprawled over her section of the table. "Parental units throw a fit if they find out you're out in the scary old park."

Felix ran a hand down my arm. Of course the bell rang and monitors came out to move us along to class. Felix grabbed my wrist and tugged me down till his lips brushed the little sun in the top of my ear. "The next full moon, come out with us," he whispered. "We meet at the East Ninety-seventh Street entrance and go for a run to the Loch, just the Pride. You want to really be one of us, be one of my lionesses, right? You'd maybe even replace Reed one day as queen of the hunt. So come. Not a word to anybody, Corey. Pride business. Nine o'clock, the night of the full moon."

I had laughed at the idea of the Pride as a gang. But as a way to erase the misery of the last few years? It was pure gold. The presidents of the new senior and junior classes for next year belonged to the Pride, as well as the captains of both track teams and both soccer teams. Okay, so Felix seemed to be the boyfriend of almost all the girls off and on. The guys didn't seem to mind. Rich kids were different. A little of Felix was better than none, maybe. Or maybe he'd settle for only me.

I wouldn't be alone anymore. I wouldn't be weird or strange. I'd belong, not as a happy outsider, like Mom and her family, but as a happy insider, smooth and tan and laughing, like my dad and his new family. As choices went, this one was easy.

So I was there, the night of the full moon, dressed to run, but dressed for Felix, too, in a black tank top and running shorts that hugged what I had. I thought about leaving my crescent pendant at home, but left it on. How many people knew what it was anymore? A lot of girls wore them as jewelry without knowing they had a religious meaning, or caring if they knew. I added a snake earring and a couple of gem studs, fixed a gold chain in my braid, and was ready to go. No bracelets, no ankle bracelets, not when I ran. I carried my phone, my water, a towel, and other things I hoped I might need in my backpack.

Felix and some of the other guys of the Pride looked me over and made happy noises. Felix backed a couple of them off with slaps on the chest that could have been serious. The lionesses wore shorts like me, or cropped cargo pants, short blouses, running shoes. The guys wore shorts and T-shirts, summer wear. When Reed finally showed, wearing cargo pants, we set out across the park, a group of about seven girls and eight guys. Other people were out; it was still early enough and the moon was starting to rise. We passed dog walkers and other runners, bicyclists, skateboarders, Rollerbladers, men sitting alone on benches with paper bags beside them, men seated alone on benches waiting, arms stretched out on the backs of the benches, legs spread wide, a warning in flesh not to come too close. The girls of the group moved inside, the guys outside, though no one seemed nervous or even like they paid attention. I wondered what Mom was doing now.

There were peepers chirping all around us from the trees that circled the meadows. We moved out onto the grass and toward the rocks that led to the oldest part of Central Park, where trees from the old island had been left to grow beside Olmsted's carefully chosen plantings. I could hear an owl somewhere close by. There were bugs everywhere, big ones, some of them. A moth fluttered past. A rippling shadow darted after it and surrounded it. The bat moved on, but not the moth. Central Park, which seemed so people-friendly when we did our practices there during the day, was showing its real face now. I touched my snake earring, thinking about the hidden world, the one my family knew.

We moved into a smaller meadow near the rocks and trees. "Our hunting ground," Felix said, looping an arm around my neck. "One of them, anyway. This one was our first ground. This is where we became a pride. A person could get lost back in those trees."

"A person could get found," said one of the guys. The boys laughed.

The girls didn't. They put their stuff in a heap and began to stretch, getting ready to run. "Put your gear down,"

Felix said. "We'll keep an eye on it. Used to be around here we couldn't do that, but things have changed late—"

"You." A big guy, ragged and swaying, lurched over to us. "You stinking kids. You play games with my friend and leave him in the street like *garbage*—"

Felix let me go and faced the homeless guy, fiddling with his long braid and its ornaments. "Which hunt was he?" Felix asked, sounding bored. "I guess you're talking about one of our hunts, loser."

"You made him run onto Fifth Avenue," the man accused. His eyes glittered in the moonlight as he watched the Pride fan out around him. Everywhere I saw shadowy figures moving, but none came to help or stop whatever was happening. This was a harder end of the park, closer to Spanish Harlem. I would never have come there alone.

"That one?" asked Jeffries with a yawn. "He wagged his dick at Han."

"My feelings were hurt," Han said with a pout. "It wasn't even a *good* dick."

"You chased him and got him killed," the big guy snarled. "I'm gonna fuck you up." He had knives, one in either hand. "Little rich bastards think you can run people to death."

My head spun as Felix put his arm around my neck again. "Okay, Corey, here's how it works," he explained, keeping his eyes on the big guy. "The lionesses have their claws. Right, girls?"

They held up their hands. They had slim knives I had never seen before, tucked between their fingers so a couple of blades jutted out of their fists, like claws. They were busily tying the blades to their palms with leather thongs so they wouldn't fall from their hands.

"We lions keep him from leaving the grass. The lionesses drive him to you. You have to mark his face without him killing you. Then you girls drive him into the rocks"—Felix pointed—"and the lions chase him down and finish him. You get the trophy to mark your initiation." Felix smiled down at me. "Here. Your first claw." He handed me a long, slender knife. "The trick is to run him till he's too exhausted to see straight. One of these scumbags, it's not hard. They don't have any lungs left because they're eaten up by crack, and their muscles suck because they're too lazy to work. Don't worry about cops. We have watchers, and they don't investigate this kind of thing very hard. They have a saying for it." He looked at the homeless man. "No Humans Involved."

My mouth felt stuffed with cotton. I wondered if I'd been drugged, except I'd been drinking from my own water bottle all the way there. "That's not funny."

"Sure it is," Felix told me. "One strong, healthy runner against a degenerate bum. It's hilarious."

"You killed his friend?" I asked. I could hear my voice shake.

"No," Felix replied. "The stupid mope ran out in traffic and got killed. Another useless mouth who isn't getting state aid. Corey, you're either a lioness or a mouse."

My brain clattered into gear. "The drug dealer that got chased. The rapist that got chased."

"Scum. Scum," Felix said patiently. His eyes sparkled oddly in the growing moonlight. "Girls, get this hump moving."

The lionesses surged forward, running out to circle around the homeless man. They looked small and slight against his shadowy bulk, but they surrounded him. He flailed with his knives. One girl darted in, then another. The man bellowed.

"No!" I cried, and dropped my knife. "This isn't an initiation. It's murder." I looked at him, wanting him to be gold again, not this white marble boy with eyes like ice. "Felix, are you crazy? I swear I won't tell, but I can't be in the Pride like this."

He made a cutting motion. The lionesses fell back, except for Reed. She pulled something from a pocket in her cargo pants and showed it to the homeless man. He put up his hands, letting his own knives drop. She had a gun. So that was how they made sure things always went their way. She motioned with it. The homeless guy ran, stumbling. He fell once and lurched to his feet.

"Don't hope he'll bring the cops, Corey," Felix said. "His kind knows better. And since you ruined our hunt with him, you'll take his place. Which is fine with us."

I stared at him.

"See, the cops will listen to you," Felix explained. "And frankly, most of us would rather have you for prey."

"You don't belong," Han said. "Not at the Academy. You don't understand how to wait your turn, making us eat your shit at the meets this spring. Sure, we laughed. We knew you'd be coming out here with us." She smiled and drew her knives gently down my chest. They didn't cut, this time.

My choices were clear. Argue or move, fast. I broke left, out of Felix's hold, away from Han. Three lionesses blocked my escape on that side. I whirled and darted in the opposite direction, jinking around Reed, then Jeffries, feeling my knees groan as my shoes bit into turf. I dashed for the rocks, but the lionesses swept out and around me, long limbed and beautiful, moonlight gleaming on their muscled arms and legs. I'd lost surprise, and I knew all of them were good enough to give me a good run. I set out for the longer meadow to see if I could outlast them.

Bad luck: two of the lions joined them. I couldn't outrun or outlast lions. I kept running, looking for a way out. All I found was an audience. People had come to line the meadow's edge, homeless people, kids our age and older in gang colors—real gang colors. Hard-faced women and men, and men on their own, smoking, drinking, watching. There for a show. They knew. They knew this went on, and they came to see.

Still, I had to run. I searched for an opening not covered by a watcher or a member of the Pride. I don't remember how the first lioness crept up on me, but I felt that sharp sting on my back. I stumbled, swerved, clapped my hand behind me, and brought it up before my face. It glittered with blood. I spun and fell, tripping a lioness whose dad was president of some investment bank. She had been trying to be the second to cut me. I scrambled to my feet and bolted forward again, weaving between two more of the lionesses. Now the fear was filling my legs, turning my knees to jelly.

The next to rake my arm was Reed, who I liked. I got out of her reach and stayed away to ask, "Why are you doing this?"

Her eyes were wide and dark and hot. Her teeth shone

in a moonlight grin. "Because I can," she said, and faked left, trying to drag my attention from Beauvais. I turned and dashed, tripped on a wrinkle in the ground, hit, and rolled to my feet, flailing with my arms and legs for balance. I felt a blade catch in my shoe. It almost yanked me off balance.

"Because you don't stay the best without *practice*." Someone scored a long shallow cut across my head and ear and forehead, coming out of my blind spot.

I bolted and came up against one of the huge boulders that marked the edge of the broken ground leading up into the trees. I scrabbled and crawled onto it, panting, as the Pride moved in, forming a half-circle around the base of the stone. Felix was there, toying with his braid. The lionesses stood with him, panting, some of them leaning on their knees. They were tired. I'd shown them some moves.

But my muscles were burning. I felt a bad shiver in my calves and hamstrings, a sign I was overworked. I ripped off my tank top, not caring if every creep in the park saw me in my sports bra. I tore the cloth into strips with hands that quaked. That shallow cut on the side of my head was the worst, dripping blood into the corner of my eye. I needed to get that covered up if I had to run again.

"Too bad you blew it, Corey," Felix said, his voice almost like sex. "Nobody's ever given the lionesses a run like this. The prey is usually blood sushi by now." He was getting off on this, maybe like he'd been getting off on the whole game of luring me in.

With my head and my arm bandaged, I grabbed my crescent pendant with one hand, squeezing it so hard the pointed ends bit into my palm, letting the pain clear my head. I wouldn't answer. I needed my breath for running. Screaming was useless. Screaming in Central Park at night was so useless. There, away from the park's roads, the only way I'd get lucky would be if horse cops or undercover cops were somewhere near, and I had a feeling that ring of creeps would warn Felix about them. They wouldn't want anyone to spoil the fun.

There was leaf and earth litter between my boulder and the one behind it. I carefully felt around at my side for what rocks or glass pieces might be there. I'd need them for weapons.

"Now, you can come down here and race the lionesses some more," Felix said. He threw a bottle of water up to me. "Or we can play the next level."

"Shit," I heard one panting lioness say.

"Pick door number two, Corey," another of them advised me, her voice hoarse.

I stared at him, then at the bottle. For a minute a black haze fizzed over my vision. My life, my *blood,* was a *game*? I reached for the bottle, ready to throw it straight back at his head and say "Fuck you"—but there was the gun. Reed had a gun.

I should drink the water. I'd lost so much fluid. But that was a bad idea, too. I wouldn't have put it past Felix to drug the water to slow me down. He couldn't gamble on the cops being somewhere else all night. He'd want to end this.

So I threw it at him after all. He dodged, but I struck Han in the shoulder. She swore at me. Felix only shook his head. "A waste. I didn't think you were a hothead, Corey."

I ignored him. I'd exhausted the mess of leaves beside

me. All I had to show for it was a handful of small stones. It wasn't good enough. I blinked tears away so they wouldn't see me wipe them off.

"Here's the deal. You come down here, or you can go up there." He pointed past me, into the rocks and trees of the wilder end of the park. "The lions will take over the hunt." They were already stepping back from the girls. Moonlight slid along the knives in their hands. "Hey, you might even find your way out up there. Or you might find a friend. Someone who's not with the Pride. Of course, they play kinda rough up here." He grinned as he unsheathed his knife. "And if the lions take you, we'll be wanting a little something extra for our trouble. Before we collect our trophy."

My stomach rolled. They would rape me, he meant. "I'll get out, and you will be so dead," I croaked.

"When they find the drugs in your backpack? And Reed's family says we were at their place tonight? Our word against yours, Corey. Those very disturbing things you told my lionesses during all those after-practice get-togethers . . ." He shook his head. "Sad. You scholarship kids can be so troubled. So out of your element."

And I had wanted to be one of them? "At least if I don't get out of this, I'll die clean," I mumbled to myself.

I looked at the meadow, and at the creeps. I looked at the lionesses. They were drinking water and adjusting their blades. I'd tried to break free out there. I wasn't sure I had the speed to do it now. The thought of letting any of that "audience" get their hands on me made my skin crawl. Turning my head, I looked back and up at the towering trees. Mom's family called these old parts of the park "godwoods." They said the old gods of the land still lived there.

Why was I thinking of their crap now? Look at me, trapped! Look at what their gods had done for me! Even the Goddess who was supposed to look after me had done nothing. There she rode in the sky, or so they'd always told me, just a flat white disk. I could count on nothing from her except scratches from the stupid pendant I wore! I began to cry in silent anger. Furious, I shook my blood-streaked fists at the moon.

That's when I saw the broken bottle at the edge of the litter on my boulder. I sat casually, dangling my legs over, hiding my side as I grabbed its long neck. It was warm in my hand. Finally, a weapon I could use to do some damage before the Pride cut me down. "Do I get a head start?" I demanded, wiping my eyes with my free arm. "You guys are fresh. I want it. I get into the trees before you so much as take the trail into the rocks."

Felix stared at me. "Damn, I wish you didn't have to die," he said finally. "You're a *real* lioness. A real—"

"What would you know of lionesses, you perfumed and gelded whelp?"

A moment ago, when I had looked at the open meadow, she had not been there. Now she strode across it like a queen, a tall, ice-blond woman in a white tank top and jogging shorts. Her long limbs were so pale they almost seemed to glow. Her ponytail picked up the moon's gleam as it bounced behind her. Even the woman's eyes were silver, colorless and icy as she looked the Pride over.

I don't know how she got there or what she thought she

was doing, but I couldn't have her stepping into my shit-storm. "Lady, get out of here!" I screamed, or tried to. My throat was too dry for more than a croak, and I coughed as I spoke. "Go on, get out of here, call the cops—do you have a cell phone on you? Run—get—"

She held up a long-fingered hand as she came to a halt ten feet from the nearest lioness. It was as if she had laid her hand on my mouth. I couldn't make another sound. "Hush, maiden. Your courtesy is well intended, but needless. Under the circumstances, it is gallant. I will not forget." She looked at the Pride, which swung out to encircle her. "You seek a hunt," she said. "I fear you will not give me a hunt that will satisfy, but times are corrupt. Tonight you shall be *my* prey."

Jeffries laughed. "Wait your turn, bitch."

She stooped and picked up a quiver, which she slung over her back, then an unstrung bow—a big one. I knew damned well they hadn't been on that grass before. "Once, you would have known to whom you spoke, and understood your death was before you," the woman told Jeffries. She took a bowstring from the pocket of her shorts. Everyone watched her. They had to. It wasn't possible to look anywhere else as she gracefully fitted one end of the string to the end of the bow she had placed between her running shoes. With hardly any effort she bent the heavy bow and slipped the string over the free end. "For your foulness, I shall not soil an arrow on you. I have better things for those of mongrel breeding."

Jeffries gasped. He always bragged on his family going back to European nobility and did not like her comment about his breeding. Ignoring him, she put two fingers to her lips and blew a whistle that had everyone clutching their ears. As its echoes faded, I heard sounds in the brush behind me and around me. Dogs trotted down from the rocks and trees. It was then, I think, that a few creeps decided life was better somewhere else. Some of those dogs were really big. They looked like they had Rottweiler or wolfhound in them, but it was all part of a mix. Whatever the full mix was, it was dangerous. They were lean, hard-looking animals, cautious as they came out onto open ground.

The closer they got to Her—by now I understood the truth of Her being—the lighter they were on their feet, until they frisked around Her like puppies, tails wagging. They were glad to see Her. They were strays, their coats tangled, some ribs showing, but they weren't stray-cautious once they could smell Her.

"Fuck this." Reed broke the spell. She had her gun out and had pointed it at Her. "I don't know who—"

Up came the bow. I didn't even see the hand that took an arrow from the quiver. I glimpsed the arrow on the string, the ripple of muscle as She drew the string to Her ear, and loosed. The arrow went through one of Reed's beautiful eyes. She fell, the gun still in her hand.

The Goddess looked at Felix and the Pride. "I said, *you are My prey now.* You thought to hunt one who is under My protection. Now meet My price. I give you the chance you gave to her—the trees. Linger but a moment more, and I shall lose My patience." She looked at the dogs. "My children, see that one?" She pointed to Jeffries. "Tear him to pieces."

That set the Pride free of Her spell, if She had cast one.

All of them, including Jeffries, bolted for the trees of the old forest. She let them go. Despite Her words, the dogs waited around Her feet, panting, scratching, rolling on the grass. She walked over, collected Reed's gun, and handed it up to me, along with the bottle of water Reed had carried in a holder at her waist. I took both with shaking hands and would not meet Her eyes. The Goddess did a few runner's stretches for Her legs, then chirped to the dogs. Running easily, the bow in one hand and an arrow in the other, She headed up into the rocks. The dogs fanned out around Her and caught up, all business now.

It was a long time before I found the nerve to come down and check Reed. She was dead, her skin as cold as marble. The arrow that had killed her had vanished. There wasn't even a mark where it had struck her.

I looked around. All of the creeps were gone. That was probably a good idea. The Goddess might have decided they were worth hunting next. There was no telling what might offend Her.

For a long time the only sounds I heard were the dogs' baying, and an occasional shriek, up among those old dark trees. I made myself collect my backpack and everything I had brought. At some point there would be cops. I didn't want them finding anything of mine and tracking me to my door like they did on television. I knew they wouldn't believe me, and I didn't want the psychiatrists, or the medication, or the attention. I just wanted to curl up in my bed and come up with ways to apologize to my mother's family for past disrespect.

Thinking of them, I checked my cell phone. There were no calls, though it was long past midnight. I wondered if Mom knew who I was running around with so late. The thought made me giggle. The giggle sounded a little strange, so I made myself quit. Then I sat down and waited. It never occurred to me to just go home. I hadn't been dismissed.

Sometime before dawn the dogs returned one by one. They were tired. After a look around, and a pee at the base of the rocks, they decided I was harmless. They lay down close to me and got to work licking the dark stains from their fur. Last to appear was their mistress, carrying a small terrier I had missed in all the confusion. His muzzle, too, was dark. He was more interested in trying to kiss Her face than in cleaning himself up.

I scrambled to my feet, though my legs were jelly from all my running. She would not catch *me* showing Her disrespect. She stopped in front of me.

"As I thought. They were better prey than hunters," She said in that chill and distant voice. "Here is my sign, to safeguard you on your way home." She pressed a blood-smeared thumb to my forehead and drew a crescent there. It felt as cold as Her voice. I swayed and tried not to faint, either from Her touch or from the thought that I now had Pride blood on me. "Tell your family they have served Me well. I am pleased." She dropped something on the ground between us.

I looked down at Felix's braid. "I didn't ask for this," I whispered. "Or for them to die."

She smiled. "I answer prayers as I will, maiden. Only remember the others who perished at their hands. Your enemies would have taken more, in time." She yawned and pulled the tie out of Her ponytail. Ivory hair cascaded down over her shoulders. "Good night to you, maiden. Or rather, good day."

I watched as She strolled across the meadow, still carrying Her terrier. A quick whistle called the rest of her pack. They followed Her, panting, tails wagging. Somewhere in the middle of that long expanse of grass, with no trees or rocks to hide them, they vanished.

Comments on the Short Story "Testing"

When I began college, I was in the middle of a five-year case of writer's block, so I made other career plans. I chose psychology, with an eye to working with kids, structuring most of my work-study jobs to that end as I took courses in education and social work as well as psychology. Just before the start of my junior year, my writing returned to me. After that, I forgot my original goal. I wrote.

After I finished the manuscript of a long, single adult novel titled *The Song of the Lioness,* I drifted until my dad and stepmother invited me to live with them in Idaho. A week following my arrival, I found a job in the only thing I was educated for: I became a housemother in a group home for teenage girls. Many events in "Testing" actually happened to me, though not all in the first week.

My girls were lively, inventive, and well defended. By the time I met them, their trust had been abused so often that it was hard for them to open up. I began a dialogue with them not through photographs, as X-ray does, but through storytelling. My first "serial" for the girls involved retelling my *Song* to them (I wasn't allowed to let them read my novel, which dealt with adult subjects). A year later, when my agent suggested that I break it up into four books for teenagers, I realized I already had.

I miss the girls still. They taught me so much, not just about writing for kids, but about the need for a sense of humor. I've been trying to pay them back ever since, not directly, since we all fell out of touch, but by writing for other kids who could use some fantasy in their lives.

Testing

I never realized how much I needed things to be *steady.* The Smithton Home for Girls wasn't paradise, but it was solid. Things had been the same ever since I arrived. Every other week we had Renee, who was the best housemother for a crew of ornery girls that you could imagine. She was perky, funny, energetic, knew the current groups and dances, and didn't yell at us to turn the music down during free time. We liked our other housemother, Shoshana, too, but in the spring of my first year at the Smithton Home for Girls, Shoshana got married and moved to Oregon.

They hired Dumptruck first. She was fortysomething and sloppy, had a voice that would break glass, and feet she always complained about. To go from Renee to her every other week was more than any of us could stand.

Then we found out Dumptruck hated lizards. Hated snakes. And the way she yelled when she found the newt in her bed . . . She killed the newt with her shoe and quit. Keisha cried about it for days. You wouldn't think a girl who was there for robbing convenience stores with her thirty-year-old boyfriend would care what happened to a slimy newt, but Keisha was nuts for animals.

Next came Sugar. She was younger, thin like a stick, with dry, straight hair and pale eyes that grabbed a girl and hung on to her. She carried a Bible wherever she went. We called her Sugar, after her strongest curse, "Oh, sugar!"

She told us to walk and talk quietly. She prayed before meals, which majorly chapped Maria Hightower. Maria's boyfriend taught her Native American religion before he got her pregnant and dumped her at a bus station. When Sugar insisted on prayer even after Maria explained about the Great Spirit, Corn Woman, and Coyote, Maria told us Coyote ought to teach Sugar respect.

By then we were tired of going from Renee, who made us feel good, to Sugar, who told us that the Smithton Home was our road to redemption. It was her not-so-subtle way of telling us that we'd all done stupid things to end up there.

Sugar was a little harder to get rid of than Dumptruck, but we managed. We painted some candles black and switched the King James Bible she kept in her purse for a book Elsie found, *The Satanic Bible.* We wrote "Satan" backward on the covers of our notebooks. Maria told her the baby the state made Maria give up for adoption was really sacrificed to the dark powers. Sugar ran like a rabbit.

I was drawing in my room a few days after Sugar left when Ana came to get me. "You got to hear this," she said. She led me to the office downstairs—Maria, Keisha, and Alouette were already listening at the closed door.

"—don't dare tell them they have control over which housemother stays or goes." That was Dr. Marsden—Dr. M, we called him—who ran the home. "If we ask them to go easy on new housemothers, they'll be in the power position, and they'll use it."

"Sooner or later we'll run out of housemothers, Ben." That was Rowena Washington. Ro was the in-house social worker. She took us to court, medical, and dental appointments, helped the housemothers to chaperone at things like fairs and movies, and helped Dr. M fill in when there was no alternate housemother. "Every time we advertise, we get fewer and fewer applicants."

"They'll stop the testing behavior," we heard Renee tell them. "School's about to start—pretty soon they'll be busy with that, and they won't have time to get rid of the new housemother."

A chair scraped, and we got out of there. Later, in the smoking corner of the house, we decided "testing behavior" sounded like a most cool term for what we were doing. We would have put any new housemother through the mill, just as the girls the year before me put Renee through it, but "testing behavior" made it sound like an important kind of game. We *had* to play.

Five days later we came home to find a strange girl sitting in the dining room with Renee. "This is Doreen Swanson," Renee told us. "She's going to be our new housemother." The girl—she was just out of college, we found out—smiled shyly as Renee started to introduce us.

I was shaking Doreen's hand when my throat started to close up. The minute she let go, I ran upstairs to my room and shut the door. I couldn't breathe. Sweat poured down my face; my knees wobbled so I could hardly stand. I dropped on my bed and covered my eyes with my arm, trying to get a grip. It was a panic attack, the first one in months. When I arrived at the home, Dr. M—who was a shrink as well as the director—put me on tranquilizers and had personal sessions with me for weeks to help me with them.

Now I did what we'd worked out. I held my breath, then let it out slowly, the way Ana had to when her asthma got rolling. After a while, my throat relaxed some. I'm in my room, I told myself, as Dr. M had suggested. I'm on my bed. My stuffed animals are in a pile in the corner. My picture of my mom is on my desk. My books are on the dresser.

By the time I had named all the things that were mine, that had always been mine, the shakes were fading and I could breathe almost normally. I could think, which was the next step. I was supposed to work out what had given me attacks before. I didn't even remember what my last ones here at the home were about. Before that, I got them in juvenile hall, in court, in cop cars and bus stations. I had one when the last guy who picked me up showed me his knife. Then it had actually been useful: he'd thought I was dying and dumped me out of his car. Those all made sense.

But this one came from nowhere, as far as I could tell. Those that hit without warning had been when I lived with my dad. Not while Mom was alive, not even when it was just me and him—no, wait. The first one came when I was maybe six. We had moved into a trailer home, our fourth house since Mom died. When I got off the bus, I couldn't remember which trailer was ours. I'd had to sit by the mailboxes, sweating and trying to breathe, till Dad came home from work.

I didn't have another until he divorced his second wife and brought a new girlfriend home a week later. She bent down and grinned at me, showing big teeth stained brown. That night I woke up trying to breathe after a dream where she ate me. She was gone a month later. This time only two days passed before Dad introduced me to his new girlfriend.

That was when the attacks came all the time, whenever we moved and whenever he moved in a new girlfriend or a new wife. Aunts and moms, he made me call them, each one seriously bent somehow. What kind of regular woman would decide she was in love with somebody enough to move in with them after a night at a bar? Some took drugs, some made me do all the housework, some knocked me around, some had relatives or even other boyfriends who shared their bad habits and added a few of their own. It wasn't until I ran away that first time that I got a night's sleep, in someone's tree house, with no panic attacks.

But for eight months at the Smithton Home, nothing had changed. Renee was there one week, Shoshana the next. The same faces, the same house. The same teachers, the same rules. The attacks slacked off, then stopped. Dr. M took me off tranquilizers. And now I'd had an attack, over the newest housemother. The newest new face.

Maybe she'll stay, I thought as I washed up. Please let her stay.

Doreen was sweet, really, tiny, pretty, and bashful. She survived all the tricks we played on her during her first week and only lost her temper a couple of times. We wanted her to stay, but that was when Lydia Carmody still lived at the home. Lydia had what the workers called "rage reaction." She would motor along quietly for about five weeks, then in the sixth week, boom! She would blow up and try to kill anyone who got in her way. She had her second explosion all over Doreen, who left with a broken arm and a broken nose. Lydia went to the state hospital. We were relieved about that but sad about Doreen, and I had two mild panic attacks.

Jalapeño didn't stay either. She had a temper, and she hated to be sassed. We got her to lose her grip twice in front of Dr. M, and she went to work someplace else. Mrs. Bertoldi didn't survive her week of probation. She said that raising teenage girls when she was thirty and raising them when she was fifty were two completely different things. Now I was waking up a couple of times a week, unable to breathe.

Penny was cool, *I* thought, but Elsie saw her sneak her boyfriend in through a downstairs window. That made Maria, Janice, and Alouette crazy, because if the housemother could have her boyfriend over, why couldn't we? They called Dr. M, and Penny was gone in a day.

The next one . . . The next one. We called her X-ray, for the way she seemed to look right through you with her pale eyes. She was medium in almost everything, medium height, medium skin, medium chubby measurements. She spoke just loudly enough to be heard by the people around her, no louder. The only thing that would make people look twice at her was her hair. Even its color was medium, somewhere between blond and brown, but it fell all the way to her waist. When she wasn't dressed up for the interviews or for meeting the board of directors, she wore pants and shirts in colors no one would ever remember. We thought she maybe came from a planet of invisible people.

During her observation week, when she followed Renee around to see how things were done, we kept an eye on her. She seemed okay. When we sang in the van—we sang a lot when Renee drove us—it turned out she knew some interesting songs we'd never heard before. She didn't even mind writing five copies of the lyrics out by hand, since the house computer was for house business or homework help, period. She didn't freak when Alouette sneaked up behind her and screamed in her ear, like Jalapeño did. On the coordination scale she rated about a minus fifty: even with Renee to help, we couldn't teach her to dance.

Keisha and I voted to leave her alone the night before she spent her first week on duty with us. I was so tired of the attacks, and I knew sooner or later somebody would notice I was showering sweat off in the middle of the night again. They'd tell Dr. M, who'd put me back on tranquilizers. I *hated* those things. At school our first tests were coming up. Torturing the housemother took a lot of work we could have used to study instead—and I wanted things to calm down. I wanted boring, excitement-less days back.

"No way," said Maria. "She can't walk in here like them others and expect us to love her because she's, you know, taken an *interest.*" Maria was the hardest of us and maybe the smartest. Her mom was a drunk, so she had looked after her brothers. That stopped when Children's Services put the kids in foster homes. The boys' family was okay, but Maria got a string of creeps, the same as Keisha and Elsie. I guess without her brothers to take care of, Maria ran a little wild, met her boyfriend, stole some cars, and got pregnant. "We can't fall for that I-love-you-cuz-I-just-*do* crap," she added.

"Why don't you just go and put a two-cent price tag on us?" demanded Ana, checking her hair for split ends. "Tell 'em we're *easy*?" Ana thought she was such a hardcase. All she ever did was sell pot at school until her folks got her busted.

"She gets tested the same as Renee got tested," Elsie said.

Testing X-ray won the vote. Keisha and I went to do homework while the others decided on a plan. The staff would be sure to warn X-ray of everything that was done to the other housemothers, particularly since we were all on restrictions for it. That meant no walking home from school: staff picked us up. That meant no TV during the week and no mall trips till after Christmas. Of course, restrictions meant we had more time to work on the newest housemother. You'd think they would have figured that out.

Finally it was the day of X-ray's first duty shift. The rest of the staff had gone home. "Let the game begin," Janice whispered in my ear as we walked into the house after a cigarette break. I rolled my eyes, but there was no way I wouldn't do my bit, panic attacks or no. I had to live with these guys.

There were snacks and juice on the dining room table, so we all grabbed chairs and sat. Alouette dropped into the chair across the table from X-ray. "Where are you from?" She challenged X-ray in the way she said it; she wanted X-ray not to answer the question and to say Lou was rude. "You're not from around here."

"I moved here two months ago," said X-ray, peeling an orange.

"Where from?" asked Lou.

"College," said X-ray, getting orange-skin oil on her face.

"And where was college?" That was Maria. She spoke in that bright, slow, hyper-interested tone that grown-ups who don't know better use on little kids.

I was sitting beside X-ray. Maybe I was the only one who saw the corner of her mouth quiver, as if she hid a smile. In the same understanding tone as Maria's, X-ray replied, "Philadelphia."

"Where were you from before that?" Elsie had a heap of Oreos in front of her. She was opening them, eating all the filling, and putting the cookies aside. She'd only eat the cookies when she'd sucked up all the filling.

"It depends," said X-ray. Keisha and Janice rolled their eyes. I saw X-ray glance at them, and there went that quiver at the corner of her mouth. "Right before college I lived in Singapore."

We all looked at each other. Who ever heard of someone living in Singapore? Who ever heard of a medium person like X-ray living anywhere cool?

"How'd you get there?" Janice asked. That wasn't part of the testing; she really wanted to know.

"My parents were in the State Department," replied X-ray. "We moved around a lot."

"So where were you born?" asked Keisha.

X-ray frowned, as if she had to think hard to remember. "Guam, but we went to Peru right after that. We lived there till I was four, and then again when I was in high school."

"Peru!" Janice leaned closer. "What was that like?"

Now X-ray did smile. "It was all right, except for the volcano."

Everybody began to yell, wanting to know about the volcano and Peru. I thought maybe she was lying when she talked about walking all day with an umbrella to keep the ash off and a scarf tied over her mouth and nose, but she showed us a picture in her wallet. It was definitely her; definitely she had the umbrella and the scarf. From the waist down she was covered in ashes. By the time she got done telling us about how nice it was before the volcano erupted, it was time to start supper.

Now Keisha and I weren't the only ones who didn't want to test X-ray. Janice wanted to know about the places she had lived; she didn't want X-ray leaving until she'd heard it all. Janice was always writing stories in notebooks and reading about far-off countries with goofy names, telling us she'd go to them when she got out of the home and became a rich writer. She thought she could get ideas from X-ray. Maria was determined to test, though, and when Maria was set on a thing, Ana, Lou, and Elsie would back her up.

"No warning her," Ana told us while we finished cleanup in the kitchen. At the home, the girls cooked and cleaned while the housemothers supervised. "We never warned nobody else."

Maria excused herself from homework at the dining room table later and went into the kitchen. When she came back, she had an open-faced sandwich made of peanut butter and marshmallow fluff. I watched as she squeezed behind X-ray's chair and stumbled. She brought the fluff-

and-butter side straight down on that long, long hair, then dragged it all the way from X-ray's neck to the ends.

She immediately began to apologize, saying she was sorry over and over. Maria was the best actress in the home, though we were all pretty good.

We held our breaths, waiting to see what X-ray would do. First she pulled her hair around in front of her and inspected it, a strange look in her eyes. "Oh, ick," she said finally. I could see she was breathing hard, and the corners of her mouth were tucked really tight, but she didn't blow up. Did Dr. M and Rowena warn her that blowing up got you a failing grade on the test?

She went to the big mirror in the entry hall, using it to look at her hair in back. "I know I need styling gel, but isn't this kind of extreme?" she finally asked.

We stared at her. What an odd thing to say!

"Aren't you mad?" asked Janice, wide-eyed.

"I'm not *happy,*" X-ray replied, twisting to get a better look at the back of her head. "But I've had worse."

"Oh yeah?" demanded Maria coldly. We all nodded. Who could believe that? "Like what?"

X-ray backed closer to the mirror, to see if she could improve her view. "Well, the girls in this tribe in Africa told me I wouldn't be cool till I did my hair like they did. They rubbed this orange clay all over my head and braided my hair. I couldn't even wash it out before we left the village, because it would have hurt their feelings."

We stared at each other, horrified. "For real?" Elsie wanted to know.

"I have pictures," said X-ray.

After a moment of respectful silence, Keisha asked, "So how can you ever get this junk out? You'll have to wash and wash and wash, and it'll be all gummy."

X-ray gave herself one last look in the mirror, sighed, and walked back into the dining room. "I just let it grow in college—I hate fussing with my hair. It begins to occur to me"—she looked at us, and something in her eyes made me wonder if she wasn't pretty sure Maria's stumble wasn't an accident—"maybe my hair is a liability in a job like this. I'll end up using time I should spend on the job keeping it out of my face." She sighed again. "I'll tuck it up and tie a scarf over it for now, and get it cut tomorrow."

We all traded looks. The plan was that she run upstairs and jump right in the shower. We could stay up late and she'd never know, while she tried to get that gunk out of her hair. Now we were stuck and she hadn't even yelled at us.

"I cut hair good," Lou commented suddenly. "I used to cut my sisters' hair at home." Maybe she even had. Lou never talked about her real family.

X-ray bit her lip and touched the back of her neck lightly. A hank of white-and-gold-streaked hair stuck to her fingers. She tugged them free. "You sure?"

"Absolutely positive," Lou told her.

We scattered, some of us to find newspapers, Janice to get the tall stool, and others to fetch a towel and comb and to giggle in the bathroom. X-ray brought the good scissors from the office.

"Of course, it was a really long time ago when I cut hair

last," said Lou as she chopped a big chunk right out of the middle of the mess. I saw X-ray's shoulders droop. Still, she didn't stop the party. Instead she told us about the photo safari that ended in that African village while Lou cut and Maria and I took turns wiping goo off the scissors. When Lou finished, we were all quiet. Poor old X-ray looked as if somebody had cut her hair with hedge clippers.

What she did when she saw herself in the mirror was important; we all knew that. It was like the moment when Maria smeared that mess over her hair: If she did a Jalapeño, we had her. If she started to cry, we had her. Particularly if she walked straight out the door, we had her. If she did the sweet silly thing and said it was a great cut, we'd know she was just another lying social worker pretending to be a friend. By the time we got to the Smithton Home, we had all had it up to here with people like that.

X-ray inspected the cut in Elsie's hand mirror, then went back out to the entry hall mirror. We followed her. Lou kept her hands over her mouth, trying not to crack up; Ana and Elsie were snorting. X-ray took her time viewing the damage. Again I saw the corners of her mouth tuck, first down and then, weirdly, up; her breath came faster for a while, then slowed. At last she said to Lou, "It could be worse—but not by much."

Lou ran upstairs, laughing so hard she couldn't breathe. X-ray shook her mangled head. "Let's clean up that mess and finish the homework," she told us. "And then it's getting on toward bedtime."

"Why aren't you mad?" demanded Maria. I think she

was angry that X-ray kept all her feelings hidden. "I'd be mad."

"I'm upset," X-ray said, looking straight at us. "I'm human, and I didn't want to look like a dazed porcupine this week, thanks all the same. Still, the damage is done; it can be fixed. If I didn't learn anything else growing up, I learned that you do better if you just deal and move on. When you keep meeting people from different cultures, you can get yourself in real trouble by losing your temper. Homework."

We got to studying, and she went upstairs. When she came back down, she had wrapped a scarf around her head and made it into a kind of turban. We knew then she wasn't going to wash her hair until we were asleep.

Lou came down with her; when we looked at Lou to see if X-ray had yelled at her, Lou shook her head. "She said I might want to get lessons before I cut any more hair," whispered Lou when X-ray went into the kitchen for some water.

The next morning when Rowena came to drive us to school, I was the only one downstairs, setting the dining room table. I heard Rowena gasp when X-ray let her in. "My God, girl, what happened to your head?" Sometime the night before X-ray had shampooed what hair she had left and gotten rid of the turban.

I couldn't hear X-ray's answer, but I heard Ro: "Dr. M is gonna be pissed."

"No," X-ray said flatly, loud enough that I could hear. "I asked Lou to cut my hair—I don't want her getting in trouble for something I asked her to do. Besides, once I get it trimmed, it'll be easier to take care of."

"But aren't you mad?" I heard Ro ask, just like one of us.

X-ray laughed. "When you get back, I'll tell you something worse that happened to my hair once."

I told the rest what she had said on the way to school. Lou seemed thoughtful, like maybe she was sorry she had done it now. If X-ray hadn't stood up for her, Lou would be on restrictions forever; we knew that.

But Maria was still the hardcase. "She's just trying to suck up and make us her little buddies," she told us as Ro was paying for gas. "You wait. It's all a fake."

When we got home from school that afternoon, we found X-ray with her hair trimmed and shaped short, like a boy's. She actually looked okay. And she had stopped off at home, because a scrapbook sat on the dining room table. It was open to a picture of her at our age. Orange clay caked her head, turning a pair of braids she wore into orange turds. We laughed till we cried.

Then Janice wanted to look at the rest of the book. Keisha and Elsie did, too, partly because they were interested—what was X-ray doing in *Morocco*?—partly because that was the next plan. I wanted to hear the stories, too, but I was in our latest test, never mind being up for two hours in the middle of the night with an attack. While the other girls kept X-ray busy, Maria, Lou, and I sneaked out the back door. Our yard was circled by a hedge six feet high. Nobody but girls or staff was allowed in there.

Our boyfriends were right outside the back gate. We'd set it up at school. Lou and her boyfriend ducked low until they were past the kitchen and dining room windows, then went to the far side of the yard, where they couldn't be seen from the house. Maria and I stayed close to the gate, talking with the guys. I was too nervous to kiss Pete in front of other people, and Maria and Chuck weren't that far along yet. They were actually talking about books when X-ray walked through the gate. She must have left the house through the front door and come around the yard so quietly that we didn't hear her.

I never thought someone who was so medium could go so cold. Chuck and Pete actually seemed to shrink, even though they were taller than she was. "We—" Pete began to say.

X-ray pointed at the gate. "Out," she said flatly.

Chuck and Pete left. X-ray walked over to Lou and her boyfriend. They were so busy she had to tap his shoulder. When he looked around and saw her, he actually backed away from Lou. X-ray pointed to the gate, and he left.

Back came X-ray with Lou. We all went inside. When we got as far as the dining room, the other girls looked at us with horror. They told us later she'd gone to answer the phone in the office. They never saw her leave the building.

"I'd like to think the rest of you didn't know about this, but I'm not so sure," X-ray told us. "In any event, up to your rooms till supper, all of you. And you know I have to report this to Dr. M." The way she said it, not even Janice tried to talk her out of it. We all knew the rules; there were no exceptions. And it had just occurred to us that medium, quiet X-ray could be strict.

On our way up the stairs Maria whispered in my ear, "She's quick, you gotta give her that."

We complained to each other. We swore we were running away. Elsie, who had a knack for being over-the-top, said the home was just as bad as prison, though we knew it was no such thing. Maria had been in prison for a week; Keisha had been in jail for a month before they placed her in the home. From what they said, we *never* wanted to go to a real prison.

We came down for supper, cleanup, and homework. By then Dr. M had arrived to give the lecture and hand down the punishment. After that, we went to our rooms.

Friday night was when the staff took us out for pizza, to the mall, or to a movie. With everybody on restrictions, Friday should have been a major pain, but it wasn't. X-ray showed us how to make stir-fry for supper. Then we had ice cream and she told us stories from the photos in her scrapbook.

"Why take so many pictures?" Maria asked as she paged through. "You have, like, all kinds just from Calcutta, and you were only there a week."

"I'm a photographer," X-ray said. "I like taking pictures. It gave me something to do when I didn't have friends to hang out with."

"So if you're a photographer, how come you're working here?" Ana wanted to know.

"Because everybody has to start somewhere, and I have to eat till I get rich and famous," X-ray told her. "I have to build my portfolio, to show what I can do. Besides, I took social work in college."

Maria ran a finger over a picture of a beggar who sat

beside a soda machine. "Would you show us how to take nice pictures like these?"

"Yeah!" cried Elsie. "That'd be cool!"

We begged X-ray to teach us. She looked us over with a wary eye. Maybe she was remembering we switched the sugar for salt at breakfast, or that her *Evita* CD, that she had played for us the day before, had gone missing. "Tell you what," she said finally. "You'll have to find your own cameras, even if they're the throwaway kind. We'll start with that, and I'll develop your photos on my time off. Beyond that, we'll see."

Now we looked at the pictures in her scrapbook differently, asking her how she'd taken them. Friday night ripped by. We hardly remembered to be mad because we were on restriction.

We had to wait for the next test till Sunday afternoon, when we took our nature walk. Keisha really fought that—she was afraid X-ray would kill an animal. We finally talked her around, and on the walk she found a nice garter snake. We left it in X-ray's bed. Then we had to wait till bedtime. X-ray stayed downstairs for hours, it felt like, writing in the log. Then she climbed upstairs. We all went to our doors to listen.

Nothing.

Nothing.

Nothing.

Her light went out, and still nothing. Some of us waited till midnight, thinking we'd hear the scream any minute. We didn't hear a thing.

Keisha could be so dumb. She and Maria were on the schedule to fix breakfast. As soon as they got to the kitchen, where X-ray was starting the coffee, Keisha said, "You killed it!"

"Nope," X-ray replied.

"I don't believe you," Keisha said. She started to cry. "You killed it."

Maria said X-ray sighed and went upstairs. When the rest of us came down to breakfast, there was a shoebox with airholes punched in it on the kitchen counter. The snake was curled up inside, under some paper towels, with a jar lid full of water next to it. "I'm taking it back where you got it," X-ray said when we sat down to eat. "And shame on you for yanking animals from their homes for a joke."

"That's it," Keisha told us when we piled into the van for school. "No more animal tests. X-ray's right."

"Get us all in trouble, why don't you," muttered Janice as Rowena got in.

X-ray didn't report us or the snake to Dr. M.

"Everybody listen," Maria said when we met for a planning session at lunchtime. "No more of the test stuff till Wednesday. We hit her with everything on her last day."

"Why?" Janice asked. "I like her."

"Me too," said Keisha.

I raised my hand. If X-ray stayed, maybe the attacks would stop. Things would be calm again.

Maria put her hands on her hips and glared at us. "We liked Penny, but she turned up wrong. And Mrs. Bertoldi just dumped us, 'cause we were extra work. We save it all for her last day, all right?"

So we were angels for three whole days, except for Maria and Ana getting in a fight over Maria's plum nail polish that Ana said was hers. And Lou sneaked a long-distance call to her dad, who she still thought was going to take her back. Ro caught me smoking behind the work shed—more restrictions. Janice thought someone stole her cheapoid camera and ran around accusing everybody, but when we looked, it turned up in the mess under her bed.

Wednesday afternoon, when we got back from school, we hit the ground running. Even Renee got tired some by Wednesday. In their first couple of weeks new housemothers were always wrung out by the end of their shift, which is why we had saved up. At snack time, supper time, and homework time, when we were supposed to be together in one room, a couple of us always made sure to be gone, so X-ray couldn't sit for five minutes without having to get up and hunt for missing girls. Our school friends called off and on all night, so X-ray kept having to run to the office to get the phone; they always hung up when she answered. Lou put a "Kick Me" sign on X-ray's back—just like Lou, so immature.

Just as homework time was ending, the phone in the office rang again. X-ray actually *growled.* We waited for her to walk into the office and close the door. Then Ana and Keisha, who were the strongest, grabbed the knob and hung on. Doors at the home opened in—with those two on the outside, there was no way X-ray could escape. She rattled the knob, tugged on it, banged on the door and yelled, "Girls, this isn't a good idea." Ana and Keisha hung on, giggling.

The office went quiet, and everyone but Ana and Keisha

ran upstairs to do what they had planned. I was disgusted by the whole thing and went into the dining room to finish my homework. I didn't hear—nobody heard—X-ray pull the chair over to the window and open it. We found out later that she climbed out, quiet like a ghost, slipped under the dining room window, slid out the back gate, and walked around. I saw her when she very quietly opened the front door with the home keys and let herself in. My jaw dropped. She held her finger up to her lips and walked, not tiptoe but still without a sound, down the hall. She waited until she was right behind Ana and Keisha before she said, "Did you girls need something?" as if they'd never locked her in. They screamed, and jumped, and ran upstairs. X-ray went back into the office.

We had a snack before we went to bed, and a last look at the scrapbook. I couldn't help but think that if she quit, we'd never know about the islands that were just tree-covered rocks, eaten away by waves at the base, rising out of a perfectly blue sea. She wouldn't explain who the men in blue head veils were, or the women who wore masks that were made of coins. We'd never find out how to get to the buildings that were carved into a pink stone cliff. I'm pretty sure Janice was thinking the same thing, because she lingered over the scrapbook, turning pages with a gloomy look on her face. X-ray had to gently take the book from her and tell her it was time to go to bed.

We lay awake with the lights out once more, waiting for X-ray. When she came upstairs, we all went to our doors to listen. "Yick," was her only comment when she tried the doorknob at her room and found oil on it. It wasn't even a *loud* "yick." She went inside.

We went to listen at her door, for what good it did us. She had to have found we'd soaped half of her toilet seat and honeyed the other half, just as she must have discovered we'd restuffed her pillow with old Easter grass and short-sheeted her bed. The problem was, if she did anything when she found all those surprises, it wasn't noisy. We heard a thing or two that might have been sighs—that was all. We gave up and went to bed once she turned out her light, after we did one last thing. We got macramé cord from the crafts room, a thick, braided rope of it. First we tied it around X-ray's doorknob, making sure it was tied tight. Then we pulled it across the hall, wrapping it first around Keisha's doorknob, then Maria's. We figured X-ray would go nuts when she found she couldn't get out.

I was up with an attack an hour before my alarm rang, so I showered and dressed. I figured it wasn't *so* bad: at least I could see what happened when X-ray tried to go downstairs. I tiptoed into Ana's room: if I watched through the door, holding it barely open, I'd get a view of X-ray's room. Ana didn't even stir when I came in—she slept like the dead.

I heard the muffled sound of the housemothers' alarm clock. Ten minutes later, I was half-asleep when I heard a knob rattle. X-ray's door opened a bare inch, no more. The cord shook twice, as if X-ray had really yanked on the door. Then it eased.

She *couldn't* give up so easily.

The cord tightened again as her door opened as far as it

would go. Then I saw a silvery gleam. A knife began to saw at the cord. Within seconds it fell to the floor, cut through. X-ray came out, looking tired. Calmly she folded up her penknife and stuck it in her pocket. Then she gathered the cord, undoing it from Keisha's and Maria's doors without a sound. She coiled it, yawned, stuck it in her pocket, and went downstairs.

When we went to breakfast, the coil of cord was in the middle of the dining room table, like a centerpiece.

She said goodbye when Ro came to take us to school, waving as we pulled out of the parking lot. Ana settled back in her seat. "She won't come back," she announced. "She's worn out."

"So am I," Janice muttered.

"Yeah," added Keisha.

A week later, on the drive home from school, I got an attack. I tried to stifle it, doubling over my books. Keisha, sitting beside me, poked my arm. "You're having one of those things, aincha?"

"Shut up," I wheezed.

"You better tell Dr. M," advised Maria from the seat in front of us. "You been doin' it a lot lately."

I gave her the finger. Maria didn't take it personally, lucky for me.

Ro pulled up in front of the home and we got out. Everybody else ran in ahead of me. They wanted to make sure that they had won and X-ray was gone. I walked in slowly, trying to calm down, thinking that if this was winning, I sure didn't want to lose.

They all stood by the dining room table, silent. A new scrapbook lay there. We heard banging noises and peeked into the kitchen. There was X-ray, cleaning out the garbage disposal we had jammed at breakfast.

We all pulled back into the dining room, looking at each other, wondering what everyone else would say. Finally Maria sighed. “Aw, hell,” she told us. “Let’s keep her.”

Not that we made it *easy* for X-ray to stay on.

Coming from Random House in 2011,
the third title in the
Beka Cooper trilogy:

Mastiff

For a sneak peek
at the next adventure in Tortall,
turn the page!

The following text is not final and is subject
to change in the printed book.

Published by Random House Children's Books,
a division of Random House, Inc., New York.

Excerpt from Saturday, June 9, 249

Now the Summer Palace appeared through the trees on my left, a long building with another open corridor on this side. There were balconies and turrets, and it had originally been very pretty white stone. Now soot streaks marred nearly every window frame. Part of this wing had collapsed into the cellars. Some of the windows stood open to the air. Others sported a single shutter, or half-burned ones. Tatters of burned draperies and furniture had been thrust from the windows to lie haphazard below. A chill ran clean down my spine and up into my skull. This was fearful business.

Achoo whimpered and scrabbled against the ties that held her to the packhorse. Something was frightening her.

"Would you release her?" I called to the men of the King's Own. "She needs to get down." The younger one rode to Achoo's horse to do as I asked while I looked around.

Between the palace and our road were gardens. Mayhap they'd been pretty, too, but now that I eyed them, and smelled them, I did not think they could ever be pretty again. Bodies lay among the flowers. Here were the missing Palace Guards, men of the King's Own, and the Black God knew how many servants, all sword-hacked or stabbed.

Lord Gershom swore. "Tunstall?"

Tunstall rode up to the older of our companions. "How many people have ridden this track before us?" he asked.

Achoo jumped to the ground. She ran over to my horse, her tail between her legs. She was nearabout spooked out of her fur.

I'd begun to slip from my horse when the man's voice stopped me. "A large group rode over this place last night in the dark. All of us were in it. And it is not this for which you are called. Come."

"Not this?" Lord Gershom demanded, but he set his horse in motion. The mage and I followed. Tunstall fell in with me as we passed. We heard my lord mutter, "What in Mithros's name can be worse?"

That same question worried Tunstall and me, for certain. I could not read Master Farmer's face yet.

"Is this what you meant?" I asked Pounce in a whisper.

It's the beginning, he replied.

Master Farmer looked at me. "So your cat talks," he remarked, as easy as if he rode by dead folk every day. "Doesn't it unsettle you?"

Easy, Beka, Pounce said in my mind, when I would have given the mage a tart answer. *He's frightened, too, for all he doesn't act it.*

"He's talked to me for years," I replied. "I'm used to it."

"Oh, good," Farmer replied. "I wouldn't want you to put a good face on it for me."

We rode past the flower gardens, but the landscape of the dead continued. They had fought in the trees here. Tunstall pointed to the far side of our road. There were footprints on a wide path that led down toward the sea. I nodded. Had the enemy come from there, or had people tried to escape taking that path? If Tunstall, Achoo, and I were supposed to make sense of this raid, we were sadly overmatched. I'd put at least five pairs on sommat as big as this, and more than one mage.

Thinking of mages, wouldn't that seaward path be magicked to the hilt? Wouldn't that wall down below be magicked just the same? Royalty came here for the summer. Surely those in charge of keeping them safe wouldn't leave their protection to a couple of walls and some guards.

Now we reached the pretty open circle where Their Majesties' guests might leave their chairs, horses, or wagons. This had been cleared of the dead. That there *had* been dead I was near certain from the splashes of blood on the ground. Men of the King's Own, all as grim as the others we had seen, took our horses. I called Achoo to heel—she was sniffing the bloody spots now that I was on the ground with her—and followed Tunstall, Master Farmer, and my lord inside.

Our guides did not come with us. Mayhap they did not want to face the soot-streaked, blood-splashed entry hall. We were turned over to a fleshy, white-haired cove who had mayhap been very well satisfied with his life a few days ago. Now I had to wonder if he would live out the month, for all that he wore a rich silk tunic and hose and a great gray pearl in one earlobe.

"Your people may wait in there, Gershom" was the first thing he said. He pointed to a side room well fitted with chairs and small tables. "You will come with me."

My lord gave us the nod and we did as we were told. The room had escaped both fire and murder. There were pretty mosaics bordering the walls at top and bottom, as well as inlaid at the window ledges. The shutters were well-carved cedar, open to the air outside. The chairs were beautifully carved, too, and made of cedarwood as well. I made note of it, because my friends would surely want to know what the inside of a palace, even a summer one, was like. There were silk cushions with silk tassels everywhere, even on the floor.

Pounce went over to one and idly batted a tassel. Achoo showed no interest in the furnishings. She went to the open door and whined.

"*Kemari,* Achoo," I told her. *"Dukduk."* She looked at me and hesitated. I pointed to a spot next to the chair I meant to take and repeated my commands.

"What language is that?" Master Farmer asked. "It sounds like Kyprish, but it's pretty mangled. Doesn't she respond to commands in Common?"

I'd placed his accent by the time he was done. He'd come from the roughest part of Whitethorn City, off east on the River Olorun.

Tunstall had listened to him with both eyebrows raised almost to his short hair. "Now, would you go about giving away all your mage secrets to some stranger who asked?" he wanted to know. "Cooper has secrets for the handling of a hound. It's the same thing."

I ducked my head to hide a grin and pretended to be tucking my breech leg more properly into my boot. Tunstall wanted to test the mage a little.

"What kind of mage are you?" he asked Master Farmer. "The scummer-don't-stink kind, or the pisses-wine kind?"

Master Farmer scratched his head. "The I-just-like-to-be-friendly kind, I think. Ma always told me I was the friendliest lad, just a help to everybody."

Tunstall advanced until he was but three inches from the mage. He was half a head taller than Master Farmer and heavier in the shoulders, chest, and legs. In his Dog uniform he was overpowering. "Don't expect that lovable-lout game to play with us. We're Lower City Dogs from Corus. We've seen it all, we've heard it all, and we've hobbled it all. What kind of name is Farmer, anyway?"

Farmer grinned. He looked like a fool. "It's my mage name."

Tunstall was about to spit on the beautiful rug when I cleared my throat and glared. I don't care where he spits normally, but not in the palace. He coughed instead. "Mithros's spear, what kind of cracknob picks a mage name like Farmer?"

The mage shrugged. "All the others kept saying how I walked and talked like I had my feet in the furrows and my head in the hayloft. I thought maybe there was something powerful, them all thinking the same thing, so I took Farmer as a mage name." He looked at me. "I've been wondering lately, though, do you think mayhap they were making fun of me?"

I scratched Achoo's ears. I was thinking that he couldn't possibly be as crackbrained as he talked, or else why would Lord Gershom have summoned him?

Tunstall shrugged as if he were settling his tunic more comfortably on his shoulders and stepped back. "Don't ask us," he said. "We're city Dogs."

"I was a city lad, once," Farmer said cheerfully. "I never had pets. At home we ate them. In the City of the Gods we sacrificed them for our magic." He crouched next to Achoo and me. This close, he smelled a little of spices and fresh air. "Is that why you bring your pets along? So no one will eat them?"

Try to eat me and you will regret it for what remains of your short life, Pounce said. I couldn't tell if Farmer heard. I didn't think so, not when he didn't even blink.

Achoo was thumping her tail just a bit, telling me she wanted to make friends with the dozy jabbernob. Pounce sauntered over to him and looked up into his face. Master Farmer stared at him for a moment. Then he said, "Now there's a pretty set of eyes. You don't often see a purple-eyed cat wandering about loose." He held out a hand. Pounce sniffed it for a moment, then bit one of his fingers. "And that's a lesson to me," said the mage, grinning. "Have you a name, Ebon Cat of the Amethyst Eyes?"

"I don't know what that means, but his name is Pounce," I said, frowning at the cat. "And he's not normally so rude." To make up for Pounce's bad manners, I said, "Achoo is no pet. She's a scent hound, as much a member of the Provost's Guard as Tunstall or me. And she's got more years on the street than me, too. *Bau,* Achoo." Since Achoo kept wagging her tail as she smelled Master Farmer's fingers, I said reluctantly, *"Kawan."* He seemed harmless enough. Lord Gershom trusted him. That had to be enough for me.

Achoo had rolled over so Master Farmer could scratch her belly when the door opened. The most beautiful lady I'd ever seen came in. She had masses of brown curls that hung down to her waist. A few jeweled pins hung from them. Her maids were lax, letting her go about with her hair undone like that. She had large golden brown eyes, a delicate nose, a soft mouth, and perfect skin. Her undertunic was white linen so fine it was almost sheer, her overtunic a light shade of amber with gold threads shot through it. Strips of gold embroidery were sewed to the front and the left side of the tunic, vines twining around signs for peace and fertility. Golden pearls hung from her ears, around her neck and wrists, and in a belt with a picture locket at the hanging end. Pearls were sewed to her gold slippers. Gold rings with emeralds and pearls were on her fingers, save for the heavy plain gold band on the ring finger of her left hand.

I write all this, remembering her beauty purely, though she was smutched with soot from top to toe. Even her face and hands were marked.

Tunstall had seen her before this at a closer distance than I, but we all knew her identity. We were kneeling before she had closed the door after her. "Your Majesty," the coves said. My throat would not work.

"Oh, please, please, get up," she said, her voice as soft as the rest of her. "I can't stand—not now. Please. Look, I'm sitting down." It was true, she'd settled in one of the chairs. A smile flitted on and off her mouth, which trembled whatever she did. In fact, she trembled from top to toe, the poor thing.

Pounce walked over and jumped into her lap without so much as a by-your-leave. The queen flinched a little, then stroked him. I'd been about to call him back, but I waited, watching those soot-marked hands move on Pounce's fur. He turned around and coiled himself there, not letting her see his strange eyes. As she petted him, her shoulders and back straightened. Her trembling eased. "I'd thought all the animals had fled, or been . . ." She looked down for a moment, then turned her gaze to Achoo. "A scent hound? Is he yours?"

I looked at the men, but they, great loobies that they were, stood there dumbstruck. Tunstall flapped his hand at me. He wanted *me* to talk to Her Majesty! But one of us had to, and Achoo was staring at me with pleading eyes, her tail wagging. *She* knew the pretty lady wanted to admire her.

"*Pengantar,* Achoo," I said. I turned to Her Majesty, without rising from my knees. From talking to folk who'd been broken by something terrible, I knew I would be more of a comfort to her if I sat below her eye level. Having Achoo come over made it reasonable for me to stay where I was. As the queen offered her hand for Achoo to smell, I explained quietly, "Achoo's a female, Your Majesty. We've been partners three years now."

The queen looked at me, and at the men. "Partners?"

I pointed to Tunstall, then at my uniform. "Achoo, Tunstall, and me, we belong to the Provost's Guards. Senior Guardsman Matthias Tunstall, I should say. I'm Guardswoman Rebakah Cooper. And this is Master—"

The mage bowed. "Farmer Cape."

The queen smiled at the men, but returned her attention to Achoo. She'd not stopped stroking Pounce, either. "How does a scent hound partner a Provost's Guard?" she asked.

I hoped she knew the answer when she was normal. Seemingly she wasn't just now. There was a shaken look in her eyes, as if she'd seen things too terrible to remember. Thinking of the bodies in the garden, I knew the chances were good that our pretty queen had never encountered anything of the like before. "When someone is missing, or something's been stolen, we give Achoo a scent of it," I explained. "Then she goes off and finds it. I go with her to keep her on the scent and to summon help, should she need it."

The queen leaned forward and gripped my arm hard. There was more strength, or desperation, in her fingers than I would have expected. "Is that why you are here? To find my son?"

Acknowledgments

People are always asking where writers get ideas, and they marvel at the odd, curdled expression on the writer's face. It comes from the avalanche of replies to such a complicated question. Short stories, at least, have a simpler answer, and there are people I would like to thank for ideas and shaping. I am particularly tremulous when it comes to short stories (when you see how long some of these are, you'll figure out why), and so my gratitude for any help with them is a rich and gripping thing (for me, anyway).

"Plain Magic"
My thanks to David Fickling and Douglas Hill, who gave me the chance to publish my first (and for a very long time my *only*) fantasy short story, and to Terry Ofner and his daughter Johanna, who loved it and brought it to the United States, where it's had several quiet rebirths.

"Student of Ostriches"
My thanks to the fans who wanted to find out about Liam Ironarm's friend Kylaia al Jmaa and the Shang Unicorn, and to Mallory, who edited it into something less crazy.

"The Dragon's Tale"
To Christina of Undiscovered Treasures, who sold me my first fire opal; to the wicked lady at the gem show next door to New York Sheep and Wool, who sold me the Ethiopian opals that have kept me in thrall ever since; and

to Gardner Dozois and Jack Dann, so patient regarding time and length.

"Lost"
To my mathematicians, particularly Becca, who checked my math, as well as to Lexa, Lisa, and my other math fans who love it when I write outside my comfort zone; to the darkings' fans, particularly their Muse, "Queen Thayet" Raquel, who keep them at the front of my mind, ready for new adventures; and to the former teacher Bruce Coville, who hates people who clip kids' wings as much as I do.

"Elder Brother"
To Bruce again, because he gave me the chance to discover what became of the tree that turned into a man, because as a good editor he let me talk myself into a loony writer's choice; and to the Taliban, which makes me crazy.

"The Hidden Girl"
To the Christians, Jews, and Muslims of the world who actually read all of their holy books, and to the teachers of the world, some of whom risk their careers, if not their very lives, to ensure that we don't grow up to be ignorant.

"Testing"
To the girls of the McAuley Home, whom I still miss. It's because of you that I write for teenagers, and developed survival skills!

"Mimic"
To Claire Smith and Craig Tenney: it may have taken me nearly twenty-five years, and it isn't a children's book, but I finally got it right!

"Huntress"
To Sharyn November, who helped me to get this particular knot out of my craw, to imagine, at least, that justice can be had for the victims of the world.

"Time of Proving"
To David Wyatt, whose art—and in this case, map—still makes me say many enchanted things.

"Nawat"
To Kit, and the mothers who read my private Live Journal, who set me straight on the many ins and outs of breast-feeding—my heartfelt thanks. Had I gone by the advice on-line, I would still be working on the story, or curled up in a closet!

And to Schuyler Hooke, who has been so unendingly patient with a project that was only supposed to be "and three additional short stories"—I owe you so big-time!

THE AUTHOR WHEN FIRST CREATING TORTALL

An avid reader, **TAMORA PIERCE** has written everything from novels to radio plays. Her novels have been translated into eleven languages, and some are available as audiobooks from Listening Library and Full Cast Audio. This is the first time her short fiction has been collected.

She lives in Syracuse, New York, with her husband, Tim, a writer, Web page designer, and Web administrator. They share their home with a myriad of critters, none of whom breathe fire, to their knowledge.